Talk to Me in Cantonese
跟我說廣東話

All MP3 audio files in the book can be downloaded at
https://www.hkupress.hku.hk/+extras/1587audio/.

Talk to Me in Cantonese
跟我説廣東話

Betty Hung
孔碧儀

HKU PRESS
香港大學出版社

Hong Kong University Press
The University of Hong Kong
Pokfulam Road
Hong Kong
https://hkupress.hku.hk

ISBN 978-988-8455-86-7 (*Paperback*)

British Library Cataloguing-in-Publication Data
A catalogue record for this book is available from the British Library.

10 9 8 7 6 5 4 3 2 1

Printed and bound by Hang Tai Printing Co. Ltd., Hong Kong, China

Contents

Chapter 3 Does this bus go to Stanley?   37

Chapter 4 Please repeat   54

Preface

Cantonese is a dialect in China. It is commonly used in the Pearl River Delta region. Being able to speak Cantonese will give you the chance to explore facets of Hong Kong life and will likely bring you closer to the local people.

There are many beginners' textbooks for learning Cantonese as a second language. *A Cantonese Book* is one of them and it has been a popular beginner's textbook since it was published in 1995. However, there is no appropriate intermediate-level Cantonese textbook for learners with basic Cantonese knowledge. *Talk to Me in Cantonese* is for these learners.

In this book, each chapter starts with a real-life situational dialogue and a narrative story, followed by an explanation of useful vocabulary and clear descriptions of grammar structures and drills. At the end of each chapter, there is a wide variety of exercises designed to help enhance learners' ability to express their ideas. The successful features of *A Cantonese Book* have been retained and more communicative-approach practices and integrated skill practices have been added.

Special thanks to Mr. Alan Dowling for advising on the English translation.

How to use this book

Several distinct features of this book are useful and effective for learners.

The book is divided into 10 chapters and covers about 60 grammatical points and over 200 vocabulary items. The contents and examples are designed with reference to authentic situations in Hong Kong, in an attempt to stimulate interest and increase awareness of Cantonese.

The presentation is in romanization, Chinese characters, and English translation. The system chosen, the Yale romanization, is the most intuitive romanization system used in textbooks and references for English-speaking learners. Its visualized tone marks, – / \ , assist learners to read this tonal language. Chinese characters are given for these romanized items. English translation of the entire context is also provided for review after class and self-study.

Each chapter is divided into the following sections:

1. Dialogue: Topics have been carefully chosen and are based on real-life situations. They serve as a summary of the sentence patterns. English translation is provided. There are questions at the beginning to help students understand the contents.

Here are my suggestions on how to study this part:

First, read the questions to get an idea of what you are going to listen to.

Then, listen to the dialogue line by line and repeat.

Read through the script and circle the new words.

Listen again and answer the questions.

Work in pairs and act out the dialogue.

2. Story: The stories are short passages for students to learn to describe an incident or express ideas. This section helps consolidate the grammar points acquired.

Each story is followed by exercises.

The first exercise comprises short or multiple-choice answers to questions that are designed for understanding the contents.

The second exercise is a dialogue practice, which is a variation and extension of the story. There are "completing sentences" and "rearranging dialogue lines" drills.

Here are my suggestions on how to study this part:

Listen to the dialogue and number the lines in the order you hear them.

Listen and complete the dialogue in romanization or Chinese characters.

Work in pairs and act out the dialogue.

3. Vocabulary: About 20 new words are introduced. In the right-hand column, the English equivalents are given. The words are arranged in groups of noun, verb, adjective, adverb, etc.

Learners should listen and repeat the words and then recall in which line of the chapter they have read them.

4. Grammar practice: The book uses a grammar-translation approach. Various forms of grammatical structure are presented. There are example sentences and practice for consolidation.

A detailed explanation is provided to compare the usage of words and grammar patterns that can be confusing. For example, in Chapter 2 the section **Compare the usage of "yùhn 完" and "jó 咗"** explains the differences between the two characters.

Learners will be able to learn grammar and linguistic terms in a gradual manner and enjoy the interesting topics.

Pyramid drills provide a review of key vocabulary and sentence patterns. Their aim is to help learners consolidate the grammar structure introduced.

5. General review: Ample exercises are included to help users attain fluency in Cantonese more efficiently. These exercises focus on integrated skills and include previous knowledge acquired from preceding chapters. There are additional dialogues, vocabulary review, question-and-answer matching exercises, blank-filling practice, and sentence rewriting.

6. Hong Kong culture: This part gives learners a taste of history, culture, and customs of Hong Kong.

The book also includes two supplementary lists in the appendices for learners' further reference.

Appendix 1: Cantonese pronunciation system and practice. This is an introduction to the Yale romanization. Each tone and its pronunciation are indicated. The pronunciation practices are arranged according to finals, that is, endings of a syllable. Each section includes vocabulary practice and listening dictation and comparisons between similar pronunciations. Learners can practise sounds and tones in an authentic way.

Pair-work practice is recommended:

Read aloud all the pronunciation drills.

A reads from the list, then asks B to point it out.

Appendix 2: Vocabulary list is arranged in two ways for easy reference. In the first part, all entries are arranged according to Cantonese phonetic alphabetical order. In the second part, the English translations of these entries are arranged according to the English alphabet. Both parts also list the chapters in which these words are introduced.

1

I've asked Si Si to buy some batteries

Dialogue ◄101.mp3

➤ What are the things that Hong wants?

➤ Did Ga Man remember to buy them?

➤ Can Si Si buy those things?

➤ When will those things be available?

Hōng: Gā Màhn, néih yáuh móuh bōng ngóh máaih yéh a?

康： 嘉 雯 ， 你 有 冇 幫 我 買 嘢 呀 ？

Ga Man, have you bought those things for me?

GM: Há? Máaih māt-yéh a? Ngóh mh gei-dāk wo!

嘉雯： 吓 ？ 買 乜 嘢 呀 ？ 我 唔 記 得 喎 ！

Oh! What is it? I don't remember.

Hōng: Dihn-chìh dahk ga, ngóh giu néih máaih sāam *pack* ma!

康： 電 池 特 價 ， 我 叫 你 買 三 pack 嘛 ！

Batteries are on sale, I've asked you to buy three packs.

GM: A! Ngóh giu jó Sī Sī heui máaih. Néih mahn kéuih lā.

嘉雯： 啊 ！ 我 叫 咗 詩 詩 去 買 。 你 問 佢 啦 。

I've asked Si Si to buy them. Please ask her.

Hōng: Sī Sī, néih yáuh móuh bōng ngóh máaih dihn-chìh a?

康： 詩 詩 ， 你 有 冇 幫 我 買 電 池 呀 ？

Si Si, have you bought me any batteries?

Sī Sī: Ngóh máaih mh dóu a! Kéuih-deih wah móuh fo.

詩詩： 我 買 唔 到 呀 ！ 佢 哋 話 冇 貨 。

I can't buy them. They said they're out of stock.

Hōng: Gám, yáu dāk kéuih lā. Mh-gōi saai. Jī mh jī géi-sìh yáuh fo a?

康： 咁 ， 由 得 佢 啦 。 唔 該 晒 。 知 唔 知 幾 時 有 貨 呀 ？

Never mind, then. Thanks. Do they know when the goods are available?

Sī Sī: Kéuih-deih wah ngóh jī tīng-yaht yáuh la wóh.

詩詩： 佢 哋 話 我 知 聽 日 有 喇 喎 。

They told me they'll be available tomorrow.

Story: I met Gee at the bus stop ◀102.mp3

Gām-jīu ngóh daap bā-sí fāan gūng, hái bā-sí jaahm gin dóu A Jī.

今　朝　我　搭　巴士返　工，喺巴士站　　見　到　阿芝。

I went to work by bus this morning and met Gee at the bus stop.

Ngóh-deih yāt-chàih séuhng chē. Ngóh mahn kéuih heui bīn-douh.

我　哋　一　齊　上　　車。我　問　佢　去　邊　度。

We got on the bus together. I asked her where she was going.

Kéuih wah heui Wāan-Jái. Ngóh gin dóu kéuih yáuh yāt go hóu daaih ge dói,

佢　話　去　灣　仔。我　見　到　佢　有　一個　好大　　嘅袋，

She said she was going to Wan Chai. I saw her carrying a very big bag and

mahn kéuih jouh māt-yéh. Kéuih wah gām-yaht hōi-chí syū-jín,

問　佢　做　乜　嘢。佢　話　今　日　開　始　書展，

asked her what she was going to do. She said the book fair is starting today.

kéuih tùhng pàhng-yáuh yāt-chàih heui máaih syū.

佢　同　朋　友　一　齊　去　買　書。

She and her friends are going to buy books.

Ngóh wah kéuih jī syū-jín yáuh hóu dō mìhng-sīng.

我　話　佢　知書展有　好多明　　星。

I told her there are many celebrities at the book fair.

Ngóh giu kéuih gin-dóu mìhng-sīng, gei-dāk yíng séung, ló chīm méng.

我　　叫佢　見　到　明　星，記　得　影　相、攞簽　名。

I told her if she saw a celebrity, remember to take photos and get an autograph.

Extended dialogue ◀103.mp3

Listen and complete the dialogue with the expressions in the table.

séuhng chē lā 上　車啦	ló chīm méng a 攞簽名呀	gām-yaht hōi-chí 今日開始
néih heui bīn-douh a 你去邊度呀	hóu noih móuh gin la 好耐冇見喇	néih séung jouh māt-yéh 你想做乜嘢
daap nī ga ba-sí ngāam ga la 搭呢架巴士啱喇		gó douh yáuh hóu dō mìhng-sīng 果度有好多明星
yùh-gwó gin-dóu néih jūng-yi 如果見到你鍾意		ngóh tùhng pàhng-yáuh yāt-chàih 我同朋友一齊

J:　Wai! A Wìhng, gam ngāam a!
　　喂！阿榮，咁啱呀！

W:　Haih a.　A Jī, _____.
　　係呀。阿芝，

J:　Chē làih la. _____?
　　車嚟喇。

W:　Ngóh heui Tùhng-Lòh-Wāan, _____.
　　我去銅鑼灣，

J:　_____. Ngóh dōu daap nī ga chē heui Wāan-Jái.
　　　　　　我都搭呢架車去灣仔。

W:　Néih ge dói hóu daaih wo! _____ a?
　　你嘅袋好大喎！　　　　　　　呀？

J:　_____ syū-jín, _____ heui máaih syū.
　　　　　　　　書展，　　　　　去買書。

W:　Ngóh tái dihn-sih wah _____.
　　我睇電視話

　　Néih gei-dāk tùhng kéuih-deih yíng séung, _____!
　　你記得同佢哋影相、

J:　Hóu aak. _____ ge mìhng-sīng,
　　好呃。　　　　　　嘅明星，

　　bōng néih ló chīm méng lā.
　　幫你攞簽名啦。

Vocabulary   ◀104.mp3

1.	bōng	幫	to help; to assist
2.	giu	叫	to ask; to order (someone to do something)
3.	mahn	問	to ask (question)
4.	wah	話	to say; to tell
5.	ló	攞	to take; to fetch
6.	hōi-chí	開始	to start
7.	gei-dāk	記得	to remember
8.	séuhng chē	上車	to get in a car
9.	nī ga chē	呢架車	this car
10.	yíng séung	影相	to take a photo
11.	chīm méng	簽名	to sign one's name; signature
12.	verb + dóu 到		be able to; manage to
13.	dihn-chìh	電池	battery (literally electric pool)
14.	fo	貨	goods; commodity
15.	dói	袋	bag
16.	syū-jín	書展	book fair
17.	mìhng-sīng	明星	celebrity; movie star
18.	gām-jīu	今朝	this morning (literally, today morning)
19.	gam ngāam	咁啱	by coincidence
20.	ngāam	啱	correct; suitable
21.	dahk ga	特價	big sale
22.	yùh-gwó	如果	if
23.	yáu dāk kéuih	由得佢	let it be; never mind
24.	há	吓	what do you mean? what is it?

Grammar practice

I. yáuh móuh 有冇 + verb (Have you . . . ?) ◀105.mp3

e.g., Néih **yáuh móuh** máaih dihn chìh a?

你　有　冇　買　電　池　呀？

Have you bought any batteries?

(Yes) Yáuh 有　　(No) Móuh 冇

* Note: Cantonese does not change the form of a verb to give additional information about when the action takes place. There is nothing equivalent to tenses in English. "Yáuh móuh 有冇" is placed before a verb to ask if a certain action has happened in the past or not.

1. Néih kàhm-yaht **yáuh móuh** fāan gūng a?

   你　琴　日　有　冇　返　工　呀？

2. Néih **yáuh móuh** giu kéuih chīm méng a?

   你　有　冇　叫　佢　簽　名　呀？

3. Kéuih gām jīu **yáuh móuh** jouh *gym* a?

   佢　今　朝　有　冇　做　gym　呀？

4. Néih **yáuh móuh** mahn kéuih séung heui bīn-douh a?

   你　有　冇　問　佢　想　去　邊　度　呀？

✎ **Practice**

a. Use the prompts below to help you.

   i. Ask a question with "yáuh móuh 有冇"

   ii. Answer the question in "i".

b. Ask questions using "yáuh móuh 有冇" and the following phrases. Then answer.

   i. tái dihn-sih

      睇　電　視

   ii. máaih néih jūng-yi ge dói

      買　你　鍾　意　嘅　袋

   iii. gām-jīu sihk jóu-chāan

      今　朝　食　早　餐

II. verb + dóu 到 (to be able to, manage to) ◀106.mp3

Affirmative: verb + dóu 到
                 e.g., Ngóh máaih **dóu** dihn-chìh.
                 我　買　到　電　池。
                 I've managed to buy the batteries.

Negative: verb + mh dóu 唔到
                 e.g., Ngóh máaih **mh dóu** dihn-chìh.
                 我　買　唔　到　電　池。
                 I can't buy the batteries.

Interrogative: verb + mh 唔 + *verb* + dóu 到
                 e.g., Néih máaih **mh** máaih **dóu** dihn-chìh a?
                 你　買　唔　買　到　電　池　呀？
                 Have you managed to buy the batteries?
                 (Yes) máaih dóu 買到   (No) máaih mh dóu 買唔到

1. Ngóh hái deih-tit jaahm **gin dóu** pàhng-yáuh.
   我　喺地鐵站　見到　朋　友。

2. Néih **bōng dóu** kéuih, kéuih hóu hōi-sām.
   你　幫　到　佢，佢　好　開　心。

3. Syū-jín yáuh hóu dō dahk-ga syū, néih **tái mh tái dóu** a?
   書　展有　好　多特　價書，你　睇唔　睇到　呀？

4. Néih **tēng mh tēng dóu** ngóh góng māt-yéh a?
   你　聽　唔　聽　到我　講　乜　嘢　呀？

5. Dī syū, néih **ló mh ló dóu** baat jit a?
   啲　書，你　攞唔　攞到　八　折呀？

6. Ngóh móuh chín, **chéng mh dóu** néih sihk faahn.
   我　冇　錢，請　唔到　你食　飯。

✎ Practice

a. Use the prompts below to help you.
   i.   Make a sentence with "dóu 到".
   ii. Make a sentence with "mh dóu 唔到".

b. Ask questions using "dóu 到" and the following phrases. Then answer.
   i.   séuhng chē
        上　車
   ii. tēng māt-yéh
        聽　乜　嘢
   iii. tīng-yaht luhk dím làih nī-douh
        聽　日　六　點　嚟　呢　度

III. wah 話 (to say)　◀107.mp3

e.g., A Jī **wah** gām-yaht hōi-chí syū-jín.
阿芝 話 今 日 開 始 書 展。
Gee said the book fair started today.

1. Kéuih **wah** nī dī yéh móuh mahn-tàih.
佢　話 呢啲 嘢 冇　問　題。

2. Gā-Màhn **wah** mh heui yám chàh.
嘉 雯　話 唔 去 飲 茶。

IV. wah 話……jī 知 (to tell)　◀108.mp3

e.g., Kéuih-deih **wah** ngóh **jī** tīng-yaht yáuh fo la.
佢　 哋 話 我 知 聽 日 有 貨 喇。
They told me the goods will be available tomorrow.

1. Ngóh **wah** néih **jī**, gó douh ge dím-sām hóu hóu sihk.
我　話 你 知，果度 嘅點 心 好 好 食。

2. Mh-gōi néih **wah** kéuih **jī** Chàhn sāang wán kéuih lā.
唔 該 你 話 佢 知 陳 生　搵 佢　啦。

V. mahn 問 (to ask a question)　◀109.mp3

e.g., Ngóh **mahn** kéuih heui bīn-douh.
我　問　佢 去 邊 度。
I ask him where he was going.

1. Kéuih mahn néih sīng-kèih-luhk yáuh māt-yéh jouh.
佢　問　你 星 期 六 有 乜 嘢 做。

2. Ngóh séung mahn nī go mìhng-sīng ló chīm méng.
我　想　問 呢個 明　星 攞 簽 名。

VI. giu 叫 (to ask or to order someone to do something)　◀110.mp3

e.g., Ngóh **giu** Sī Sī máaih sāam *pack* dihn-chìh.
我　叫 詩詩 買　三　pack 電 池。
I've asked Si Si to buy three packs of batteries.

1. Kéuih-deih **giu** néih hōi-chí. néih tēng mh tēng dóu a?
佢　 哋 叫 你 開 始，你 聽 唔 聽 到 呀？

2. Ngóh **giu** kéuih hah go sīng-kèih yāt hōi wúi.
我　叫 佢 下 個 星　期　一 開 會。

✎ Practice ◀111.mp3

Complete the sentences with the correct words.

giu 叫	mahn 問	wah 話	jī 知

a.

Hōng: "Sī Sī, néih yáuh móuh bōng ngóh máaih dihn-chìh a?"

康：「詩詩，你 有 冇 幫 我 買 電 池 呀？」

☞ Hōng _____ Sī Sī yáuh móuh bōng kéuih máaih dihn-chìh.

康　　　　　詩詩 有 冇 幫 佢 買 電 池。

☞ Hōng _____ Sī Sī bōng kéuih máaih dihn-chìh.

康　　　　　詩詩 幫 佢 買 電 池。

b.

Sī Sī: "Mh-gōi, yáuh móuh nī júng dahk ga dihn-chìh a?"

詩詩：「唔 該，有 冇 呢種 特 價 電 池 呀？」

jīk-yùhn: "Móuh fo a."

職員：「冇 貨呀。」

Sī Sī: "Gám, géi-sìh yáuh fo a?"

詩詩：「咁，幾 時 有 貨呀？」

jīk-yùhn: "Tīng-yaht yáuh fo ga la. Néih tīng-yaht làih máaih lā."

職員：「聽 日 有 貨 㗎喇。你 聽 日 嚟 買 啦。」

☞ Sī Sī _____ jīk yùhn yáuh móuh dahk ga dihn-chìh.

詩詩　　　 職 員 有 冇 特 價 電 池。

☞ Jīk-yùhn _____ Sī Sī _____ móuh fo.

職 員　　　　詩詩　　　 冇 貨。

☞ Sī Sī _____ jīk yùhn géi-sìh yáuh fo.

詩詩　　　 職 員 幾 時 有 貨。

☞ Jīk-yùhn _____ Sī Sī _____ tīng-yaht yáuh fo,

職 員　　　　詩詩　　　 聽 日 有 貨，

_____ kéuih tīng-yaht làih máaih.

　　　 佢 聽 日 嚟 買。

VII. bōng 幫 (to help; to assist) ◀112.mp3

> e.g., Néih **bōng** ngóh ló mìhng-sīng ge chīm méng lā.
>
> 你 幫 我 攞明 星 嘅 簽 名 啦。
>
> *I'll get you your favourite celebrity's autograph.*

1. Mh-gōi néih **bōng** ngóh mahn néih pàhng-yáuh lā.

唔 該 你 幫 我 問 你 朋 友 啦。

2. Néih heui Chāt Sahp-Yāt, gei-dāk **bōng** ngóh máaih yéh.
你 去 七 十 一，記 得 幫 我 買 嘢。

3. Néih jouh mh jouh dóu a? Jouh mh dóu, ngóh **bōng** néih lā.
你 做 唔 做 到 呀？做 唔 到，我 幫 你 啦。

VIII. To modify something with "ge 嘅" ◀113.mp3

> e.g., Kéuih yáuh yāt go hóu daaih **ge** dói
> 佢 有 一 個 好 大 嘅袋。
> *She was carrying a very big bag.*

1. Ngóh kàhm-yaht gin dóu néih jūng-yi **ge** mìhng-sīng.
我 琴 日 見 到 你 鍾 意嘅 明 星。

2. Ngóh-deih daap heui Wāan-Jái **ge** bā-sí.
我 哋 搭 去 灣 仔 嘅巴士。

3. Néih bōng ngóh yíng **ge** séung hóu leng.
你 幫 我 影 嘅相 好 靚。

IX. yáu dāk kéuih 由得佢 (let it be; never mind) ◀114.mp3

> e.g., Máaih mh dóu dihn-chìh, **yáu dāk kéuih** lā.
> 買 唔 到 電 池，由 得 佢 啦。
> *You can't buy batteries, never mind.*

1. Kéuih mh séung jouh, néih **yáu dāk kéuih** lā.
佢 唔 想 做，你 由 得 佢 啦。

2. Yùh-gwó móuh baahk-sīk T sēut, **yáu dāk kéuih**, mh yiu la.
如 果 冇 白 色 T恤，由 得 佢，唔 要 喇。

X. gam ngāam 咁啱 (by coincidence) ◀115.mp3

> e.g., Wai! A Wìhng, **gam ngāam** a! Hóu noih móuh gin la.
> 喂！阿 榮， 咁 啱 呀！好 耐 冇 見 喇。
> *Hi Wing! What a coincidence! Haven't seen you for a long time.*

1. Ngóh séung heui yàuh séui, **gam ngāam** lohk yúh.
我 想 去 游 水，咁 啱 落 雨。

2. Heui máaih yéh yám, hó-lohk **gam ngāam** dahk ga.
去 買 嘢 飲，可 樂 咁 啱 特 價。

3. Heui yám chàh, **gam ngāam** gin dóu pàhng-yáuh.
去 飲 茶，咁 啱 見 到 朋 友。

Pyramid drill   ◄116.mp3

1.

chīm méng

簽　名

mìhng-sīng ge chīm méng

明　星　嘅　簽　名

ló mìhng-sīng ge chīm méng

攞　明　星　嘅　簽　名

bōng ngóh ló mìhng-sīng ge chīm méng

幫　我　攞　明　星　嘅　簽　名

móuh bōng ngóh ló mìhng-sīng ge chīm méng

冇　幫　我　攞　明　星　嘅　簽　名

Néih yáuh móuh bōng ngóh ló mìhng-sīng ge chīm méng a?

你　有　冇　幫　我　攞　明　星　嘅　簽　名　呀？

Did you get the celebrity's autograph for me?

2.

séuhng chē

上　車

giu néih séuhng chē

叫　你　上　車

ngóh giu néih séuhng chē

我　叫　你　上　車

tēng dóu ngóh giu néih séuhng chē

聽　到　我　叫　你　上　車

tēng mh dóu ngóh giu néih séuhng chē

聽　唔　到　我　叫　你　上　車

Néih tēng mh tēng dóu ngóh giu néih séuhng chē a?

你　聽　唔　聽　到　我　叫　你　上　車　呀？

Did you hear me asking you to get into the car?

3.

máaih dihn-chìh

買　電　池

máaih mh dóu dihn-chìh

買　唔　到　電　池

máaih mh dóu dihn-chìh, yáu dāk kéuih

買　唔　到　電　池，由　得　佢

máaih mh dóu dihn-chìh, yáu dāk kéuih wóh

買　唔　到　電　池，由　得　佢　喎

Kéuih wah néih jī máaih mh dóu dihn-chìh, yáu dāk kéuih wóh.

佢　話　你　知　買　唔　到　電　池，由　得　佢　喎。

He told you that if you can't buy the batteries, never mind.

General review

I. Put the words in the correct order to make sentences. ◀117.mp3

1. máaih / mh-gōi / syū / bōng / yāt bún / ngóh
   買 / 唔 該 / 書 / 幫 / 一 本 / 我

2. gó gāan / wah / kéuih / hóu hóu / chāan-tēng / pàhng-yáuh
   果 間 / 話 / 佢 / 好 好 / 餐 廳 / 朋 友

3. Chàhn sāang / béi / néih / nī dī yéh / chīm méng / ló / mh-gōi / lā
   陳   生 / 畀 / 你 / 呢 啲 嘢 / 簽 名 / 攞 / 唔 該 / 啦

4. ba-sí / séuhng dóu / kéuih / ge / séuhng / baat dím / a / mh
   巴士 / 上   到 / 佢 / 嘅 / 上 / 八 點 / 呀 / 唔

II. Listen and complete the following with expressions in the box. ◀118.mp3

bōng 幫	chīm méng 簽 名	giu 叫	tēng mh dóu 聽 唔 到
néih wah ngóh jī 你 話 我 知		yáu dāk kéuih 由 得 佢	

1. Ngóh _____ kéuih góng māt-yéh.
   我   佢 講 乜 嘢。

2. Mh-gōi_____ gāan jáu-dim hái bīn-douh lā.
   唔 該   間 酒 店 喺 邊 度 啦。

3. Néih _____ ngóh hái douh _____ lā.
   你   我 喺 度   啦。

4. Ngóh _____ kéuih tīng-yaht làih.
   我   佢 聽 日 嚟。

5. Gam ngāam móuh fo, gám, _____ lā.
   咁 啱 冇 貨，咁，   啦。

Answers

Story—Extended dialogue

J: Wai! A Wìhng. Gam ngāam a!
喂!阿榮, 咁 啱 呀!
Hi! Wing! What a coincidence!

W: Haih a. A Jī, **hóu noih móuh gin la**.
係呀。阿芝,好 耐 冇 見 喇。
Oh yes, Gee! Haven't seen you for a long time.

J: Chē làih la. **Néih heui bīn-douh a?**
車 嚟喇。你 去 邊 度 呀?
A bus is coming. Where are you going?

W: Ngóh heui Tùhng-Lòh-Wāan, **daap nī ga ba-sí ngāam ga la**.
我 去 銅 鑼 灣, 搭 呢架巴士啱 㗎喇。
I'm going to Causeway Bay. This is my bus.

J: **Séuhng chē lā**. Ngóh dōu daap nī ga chē heui Wāan-Jái.
上 車啦。我 都 搭 呢架車去 灣 仔。
Let's go together. I'm taking this bus to Wan Chai.

W: Néih ge dói hóu daaih wo! **Néih séung jouh māt-yéh a?**
你 嘅袋好 大 㖞!你 想 做 乜 嘢呀?
Your bag is so big. What are you going to do?

J: **Gām-yaht hōi-chí** syū-jín,
今 日 開 始 書展,
Today is the beginning of the book fair.
Ngóh tùhng pàhng-yáuh yāt-chàih heui máaih syū.
我 同 朋 友 一 齊 去 買 書。
I'm going with my friends to buy new books.

W: Ngóh tái dihn-sih wah **gó douh yáuh hóu dō mìhng-sīng**.
我 睇 電 視話 果度 有 好 多 明 星。
I saw it on TV. They said there are many celebrities.
Néih gei-dāk tùhng kéuih-deih yíng séung, **ló chīm méng a!**
你 記得同 佢 哋 影 相、攞簽 名 呀!
Remember to take photos with them and get their autograph.

J: Hóu aak. **Yùh-gwó gin-dóu néih jūng-yi** ge mìhng-sīng,
好 呃。如 果 見 到 你 鍾 意嘅明 星,
That's great! If I see your favourite celebrity,
bōng néih ló chīm méng lā.
幫 你 攞簽 名 啦。
I'll get you her autograph.

Grammar practice translation I

1. Did you go to work yesterday?
2. Did you ask him for an autograph?
3. Did he go to the gym this morning?
4. Did you ask him where he wanted to go?

Practice answer b.

i. Néih yáuh móuh tái dihn-sih a?
你 有 冇 睇電 視呀?
Did you watch TV?

ii. Néih yáuh móuh máaih néih jūng-yi ge dói a?

你　有　冇　買　你　鍾　意　嘅　袋　呀？

Did you buy the bag you like?

iii. Néih gām-jīu yáuh móuh sihk jóu-chāan a?

你　今　朝　有　冇　食　早　餐　呀？

Have you had breakfast this morning?

Grammar practice translation II

1. I met a friend at the MTR Station.
2. You helped him. He's happy.
3. There are many bargain books at the book fair. Can you find them?
4. Did you hear what I said?
5. Can you get a 20% discount for those books?
6. I have no money. I can't buy you lunch.

Practice answer b.

i. Néih séuhng mh séuhng dóu chē a?

你　上　唔　上　到　車　呀？

Can you manage to get on the bus?

(Yes) séuhng dóu 上到　　(No) séuhng mh dóu 上唔到

ii. Néih tēng dóu māt-yéh a?

你　聽　到　乜　嘢　呀？

What did you hear?

(Yes) Ngóh tēng dóu……

　　　我　　聽　　到……

　　　I heard . . .

(No) Ngóh móuh tēng dóu māt-yéh.

　　　我　冇　聽　　到　乜　嘢。

　　　I didn't hear anything.

iii. Néih tīng-yaht luhk dím làih mh làih dóu nī-douh?

你　聽　日　六　點　嚟　唔　嚟　到　呢　度？

Can you come here at 6:00 tomorrow?

(Yes) làih dóu 嚟到　　(No) làih mh dóu 嚟唔到

Grammar practice translation III

1. He said there was no problem with these things.
2. Ga Man said she was not going to have tea.

Grammar practice translation IV

1. I told you the dim sum there was very delicious.
2. Would you please tell him that Mr. Chan was looking for him?

Grammar practice translation V

1. He asked you if you had anything to do on Saturday.
2. I want to get the autograph of this movie star.

Grammar practice translation VI

1. He told you to start. Did you hear that?
2. I asked him to attend a meeting next Monday.

Practice

a.

Hōng: "Sī Sī, néih yáuh móuh bōng ngóh máaih dihn-chìh a?"

康：「詩　詩，你　有　冇　幫　我　買　　電　池　呀？」

Hong: "Si Si, have you bought me any batteries?"

☞ Hōng **mahn** Sī Sī yáuh móuh bōng kéuih máaih dihn-chìh.
康　問　詩詩有　冇　幫　佢　買　電池。
Hong asked Si Si if she had bought him any batteries.

☞ Hōng **giu** Sī Sī bōng kéuih máaih dihn-chìh.
康　叫 詩詩 幫 佢　買　電池。
Hong asked Si Si to buy batteries for him.

b.

Sī Sī: "Mh-gōi, yáuh móuh nī júng dahk ga dihn-chìh a?"
詩詩：「唔該，有　冇　呢種　特　價 電　池呀？」
Si Si: "Excuse me, do you have this type of batteries that is on sale?"

jīk-yùhn: "Móuh fo a. Mh-hóu yi-sī."
職員：「冇　貨呀。唔 好 意思。」
Staff: "They're out of stock. I'm sorry."

Sī Sī: "Gám, géi-sìh yáuh fo a?"
詩詩：「咁，幾 時 有　貨呀？」
Si Si: "Do you know when the goods are available?"

jīk-yùhn: "Tīng-yaht yáuh fo ga la. Néih tīng-yaht làih máaih lā."
職員：「聽　日　有 貨 㗎喇。你 聽 日　嚟買　啦。」
Staff: "They'll be available tomorrow. Please come tomorrow."

☞ Sī Sī **mahn** jīk yùhn yáuh móuh dahk ga dihn-chìh.
詩詩問　職員 有　冇　特　價 電池。
Si Si asked the staff if there were any batteries on sale.

☞ Jīk-yùhn **wah** Sī Sī jī móuh fo.
職員　話 詩詩 知 冇　貨。
The staff told Si Si they were out of stock.

☞ Sī Sī **mahn** jīk yùhn géi-sìh yáuh fo.
詩詩問　職員 幾 時 有　貨。
Si Si asked the staff if he knew when the goods would be available.

☞ Jīk-yùhn **wah** Sī Sī jī tīng-yaht yáuh fo, **giu** kéuih tīng-yaht làih máaih.
職員　話 詩詩 知聽日　有　貨，叫 佢　聽　日　嚟買。
The staff told Si Si that the goods would be available tomorrow and asked her to come then.

Grammar practice translation VII

1. Please do me a favour. Ask your friend about this.
2. When you go to 7-Eleven, remember to buy things for me.
3. Are you able to do it? If you can't, I'll help you.

Grammar practice translation VIII

1. I saw your favourite movie star yesterday.
2. We took the bus that goes to Wan Chai.
3. The pictures you took for me are beautiful.

Grammar practice translation IX

1. He doesn't want to do it. Leave him alone.
2. If you don't have a white T-shirt, it's alright. I don't want it.

Grammar practice translation X

1. I wanted to go swimming, but it happened to rain.
2. I wanted to buy Coke, and it happened to be on sale.
3. I was having tea at the café. I met a friend by coincidence.

General review

I.

1. Mh-gōi bōng ngóh máaih yāt bún syū.
   唔 該 幫 我 買 一 本 書。
   Please buy me a book.

2. Kéuih pàhng-yáuh wah gó gāan chāan-tēng hóu hóu.
   佢 朋 友 話 果 間 餐 廳 好 好。
   His friend said that restaurant was very good.

3. Mh-gōi néih ló nī dī yéh béi Chàhn sāang chīm méng lā.
   唔 該 你 攞 呢 啲 嘢 畀 陳 生 簽 名 啦。
   Please take these things to Mr Chan to sign.

4. Kéuih séuhng mh séuhng dóu baat dím ge bā-sí a?
   佢 上 唔 上 到 八 點 嘅 巴士 呀？
   Is he able to catch the 8:00 bus?

II.

1. Ngóh **tēng mh dóu** kéuih góng māt-yéh.
   我 聽 唔 到 佢 講 乜 嘢。
   I can't hear what he said.

2. Mh-gōi **néih wah ngóh jī** gó gāan jáu-dim hái bīn-douh lā.
   唔 該 你 話 我 知 果 間 酒店 喺 邊 度 啦。
   Would you please tell me where the hotel is?

3. Néih **bōng** ngóh hái douh **chīm méng** lā.
   你 幫 我 喺 度 簽 名 啦。
   Would you please sign here?

4. Ngóh **giu** kéuih tīng-yaht làih.
   我 叫 佢 聽 日 嚟。
   I told him to come tomorrow.

5. Gam ngāam móuh fo, gám, **yáu dāk kéuih** lā.
   咁 啱 冇 貨，咁，由 得 佢 啦。
   It so happens that it is out of stock. Never mind.

Hong Kong culture

Hong Kong Book Fair and Ani-Com and Games Hong Kong

The Hong Kong Book Fair (香港書展) is a very important event held in July and has been running since 1990. It is organized by the Hong Kong Trade and Development Council (TDC) and held at the Hong Kong Convention and Exhibition Centre in Wan Chai. During the book fair, the entire Wan Chai district is filled with people. This event is not only important to publishers and book lovers but also to parents and students, who buy stacks of extracurricular reading material to fill their time in the summer holiday and to study throughout the year. According to the designated theme, each year various writers, scholars, experts, and celebrities are invited to host public forums, book talks, and book signings. Most of the events are related to the history and culture of Hong Kong. The book fair ends with a clearance sale on the last day. Many books are sold at unbelievably low prices!

Following the book fair is the Animation-Comic and Games Hong Kong (ACGHK) event, which is the most popular summer festival for young people. Fans begin to queue up days before the event in order to buy limited-edition comics, character figures, and other collectibles made in Hong Kong and Japan.

The book fair used to be a key market for comics as well, but its fans, assembling in huge numbers, were overly enthusiastic and their erratic behaviour on one occasion resulted in a glass wall entrance being smashed! To meet the market demand for comic books, the Hong Kong Comics Festival has been held since 1999. In recent years, the event also exhibits and sells animation-related and game-related products, such as video games, toys, figures, and models. It also features game and cosplay competitions. Since 2008, the convention has been called ACGHK.

2

Can you lend me an umbrella?

Dialogue ◄201.mp3

➢ Is it raining heavily now?

➢ Do they have an umbrella?

➢ How are they going to leave the office?

➢ When will they leave the office?

Sā Sā: Lohk gán daaih yúh wo! Néih yáuh móuh daai jē a?

莎莎：落 緊 大 雨 喎！你 有 冇 帶 遮呀？

It's raining heavily. Do you have an umbrella?

Lòh: Aìh yah! Ngóh móuh daai jē. Néih yáuh móuh jē je béi ngóh a?

羅： 哎 吔！我 冇 帶 遮。你 有 冇 遮借畀我 呀？

Oh no! I don't have an umbrella. Can you lend me an umbrella?

Sā Sā: Ngóh dāk yāt bá jē.

莎莎：我 得 一 把 遮。

I have only one umbrella.

Lòh: Fong gūng ge sìh-hauh lohk yúh, séung daap dīk-sí jáu dōu hóu nàahn, dím syun a?

羅： 放 工 嘅時候 落 雨，想 搭 的 士 走 都 好 難，點 算 呀？

It started raining just as people finished work, it will be difficult to get a taxi to leave, what can I do?

Sā Sā: Bāt-yùh dáng dī yúh sai síu síu, ngóh jē néih heui déih-tit-jaahm lā.

莎莎：不 如 等 啲 雨 細 少 少，我 遮 你 去 地 鐵 站 啦。

Let's wait until the rain eases a little. I'll walk you to the MTR station with my umbrella.

Lòh: Mh-gōi saai. Gám néih jáu meih a?

羅： 唔 該 晒。咁 你 走 未 呀？

Thank you very much. Are you ready to go?

Sā Sā: Ngóh jouh yùhn nī dī yéh jauh jáu ga la. Néih dáng ngóh sahp fān-jūng lā.

莎莎：我 做 完 呢啲 嘢 就 走 㗎喇。你 等 我 十 分 鐘 啦。

I'll leave after finishing this. It'll be about 10 minutes.

Sahp fān-jūng jī-hauh······
十　分　鐘　之　後
10 minutes later . . .

Lòh:　　Yí? Lohk yùhn yúh la. Mh sái màh-fàahn néih jē ngóh jáu la.
羅：　　咦？落　完　雨　喇。唔 使 麻　煩　　你 遮 我　走　喇。
　　　　Oh! The rain has stopped. I don't have to trouble you.

Story: On a rainy day ◀202.mp3

Gām-yaht fong gūng ge sìh-hauh daht-yìhn lohk daaih yúh.
今 日 放 工 嘅 時 候 突 然 落 大 雨。
It suddenly started raining heavily just as I was finishing work today.

Ngóh móuh daai jē, jān-haih màh-fàahn lak. Hóu-chói ngóh gin-dóu A Lóhng,
我 冇 帶 遮，真 係 麻 煩 嘞。好 彩 我 見 到 阿 朗，
I didn't have an umbrella. It was a big problem. Luckily, I met Long.

kéuih wah kéuih ge chē paak hái gūng-sī làuh-hah,
佢 話 佢 嘅 車 泊 喺 公 司 樓 下，
He said his car was parked downstairs from the office.

kéuih chē ngóh fāan ūk-kéi dōu dāk. Ngóh chóh kéuih ge chē jauh mh sái dáng lohk yùhn yúh.
佢 車 我 返 屋 企 都 得。我 坐 佢 嘅 車 就 唔 使 等 落 完 雨。
He could give me a ride. I went home in his car; then I didn't have to wait for the rain to stop.

Daahn-haih A Lóhng mh haih géi hóu-chói. Kéuih sihk aan ge sìh-hauh lauh jó bá jē hái chāan-tēng,
但 係 阿 朗 唔 係 幾 好 彩。佢 食 晏 嘅 時 候 漏 咗 把 遮 喺 餐 廳，
However, Long was not so lucky. He had left his umbrella in the restaurant at lunchtime.

joi fāan heui chāan-tēng yíh-gīng wán mh dóu la.
再 返 去 餐 廳 已 經 搵 唔 到 喇。
When he returned to the restaurant, it wasn't there.

Questions for the story

I. Choose the correct answer. ◀203.mp3

1. Géi-sìh lohk daaih yúh a?
   幾 時 落 大 雨 呀？
   a. fāan gūng ge sìh-hauh   b. fong gūng ge sìh-hauh
   　 返 工 嘅 時 候 　　　　　　　 放 工 嘅 時 候
   c. sihk aan ge sìh-hauh   d. fāan ūk-kéi ge sìh-hauh
   　 食 晏 嘅 時 候 　　　　　　　 返 屋 企 嘅 時 候

2. Kéuih-deih dím fāan ūk-kéi a?
   佢 哋 點 返 屋 企 呀？
   a. A Lóhng chē ngóh jáu   b. yāt-chàih daap deih-tit
   　 阿 朗 車 我 走 　　　　　　　 一 齊 搭 地 鐵
   c. dáng lohk yùhn yúh   d. A Lóhng jē ngóh jáu
   　 等 落 完 雨 　　　　　　　　 阿 朗 遮 我 走

3. A Lóhng ge chē hái bīn-douh a?
   阿 朗 嘅 車 喺 邊 度 呀？

   a. hái ūk-kéi   b. hái chāan-tēng làuh-hah
      喺 屋 企   喺 餐 廳 樓 下

   c. hái gūng-sī làuh-seuhng   d. hái gūng-sī làuh-hah
      喺 公 司 樓 上   喺 公 司 樓 下

4. A Lóhng ge jē hái bīn-douh a?
   阿 朗 嘅 遮 喺 邊 度 呀？

   a. fāan heui chāan-tēng wán jē   b. mh haih géi hóu-chói
      返 去 餐 廳 搵 遮   唔 係 幾 好 彩

   c. lauh jó hái chāan-tēng   d. kéuih móuh daai jē
      漏 咗 喺 餐 廳   佢 冇 帶 遮

II. Listen and rearrange the dialogue. ◀204.mp3

a. Mh-gōi saai! Néih jān-haih hóu yàhn!
   唔 該 晒！你 真 係 好 人！

   Néih yáuh móuh jē je béi ngóh a?
   你 有 冇 遮 借 畀 我 呀？

b. Fong gūng la. Aai-yah! Lohk daaih yúh a!
   放 工 喇。哎 吔！落 大 雨 呀！

c. Ngóh móuh jē wo. Ngóh sihk aan ge sìh-hauh lauh jó bá jē hái chāan-tēng,
   我 冇 遮 喎。我 食 晏 嘅 時 候 漏 咗 把 遮 喺 餐 廳，

   gei-dāk ge sìh-hauh joi fāan heui wán, yíh-gīng wán mh dóu la.
   記 得 嘅 時 候 再 返 去 搵，已 經 搵 唔 到 喇。

d. Daht-yìhn lohk yúh jān-haih màh-fàahn lak.
   突 然 落 雨，真 係 麻 煩 嘞。

e. Néih jān-haih mh hóu-chói. Móuh jó bá jē, géi màh-fàahn wo.
   你 真 係 唔 好 彩。冇 咗 把 遮，幾 麻 煩 喎。

f. Mh-sái dáng lohk yùhn yúh. Ngóh ge chē paak hái làuh-hah,
   唔 使 等 落 完 雨。我 嘅 車 泊 喺 樓 下，

   bāt-yùh ngóh chē néih fāan ūk-kéi lā.
   不 如 我 車 你 返 屋 企 啦。

g. Ngóh móuh daai jē, géi-sìh lohk yùhn yúh a?
   我 冇 帶 遮，幾 時 落 完 雨 呀？

III. Listen and complete the following with expressions in the table.   ◄205.mp3

gām-yaht sihk aan ge sìh-hauh 今 日　食 晏 嘅 時 候	lauh jó bá jē hái nī-douh 漏　咗把遮喺 呢 度
néih ge jē báai jó hái bīn-douh 你　嘅 遮 擺 咗 喺 邊 度	haih hāak-sīk ge 係 黑　色 嘅
yáuh yàhn ló jó néih ge jē lā 有　人　攞 咗 你 嘅 遮 啦	

Long is going back to the restaurant to find his umbrella.

Lóhng:　　Mh hóu yi-sī, ngóh _____, néih yáuh móuh gin-dóu a?
朗　：　　唔 好 意 思，我　　　　　　你 有　冇　見 到 呀？

gīng-léih: Néih ge jē haih dím-yéung ga?
經　理：你　嘅 遮 係 點 樣　㗎？

Lóhng:　　_____ sūk-gwāt-jē.
朗　：　　　　　　　　　　　　縮 骨 遮。

gīng-léih: Néih géi-sìh lauh hái douh ga?
經　理：你　幾 時 漏　喺 度 㗎？

Lóhng:　　_____.
朗　：

gīng-léih
經　理：_____ a?
　　　　　　　　　　　　　　　　　　呀？

Lóhng:　　Ngóh báai hái mùhn-háu.
朗　：　　我　擺 喺 門　口。

gīng-léih: Ngóh móuh gin-dóu. _____.
經　理：我 冇 見 到。

Vocabulary   ◄206.mp3

1.	yāt bá jē	一把遮	an umbrella
	jē	遮	to cover; to take under an umbrella
2.	chē	車	to take people by car
3.	làuh-hah	樓下	downstairs
4.	chāan-tēng	餐廳	restaurant
5.	màh-fàahn	麻煩	annoying; inconvenient; trouble
6.	hóu-chói	好彩	lucky; fortunately
7.	je	借	to lend; to borrow
8.	daai	帶	to bring along
9.	chóh	坐	to sit; to ride in a car
10.	fong gūng	放工	finish work
11.	fāan heui	返去	to go back
12.	dāk	得	only have
13.	paak	泊	to park (a vehicle)
14.	lauh	漏	miss out
15.	wán	搵	to search, to look for
16.	meih	未	not yet
17.	yùhn	完	to finish
18.	dím-syun	點算	what should I/we do?
19.	jī-hauh	之後	afterwards
20.	yíh-gīng	已經	already
21.	daahn-haih	但係	but; however
22.	bāt-yùh	不如	what about (to suggest)
23.	daht-yìhn	突然	suddenly; all of a sudden
24.	jauh	就	then; soon after
25.	. . . ge sìh-hauh	嘅時候	at the time when . . .
26.	yí	咦	(sentence particle) to express curious

Grammar practice

I. meih 未 (not yet) ◀207.mp3

Negative: meih 未 + verb
              e.g., Ngóh **meih** jáu.
              我　 未　 走。
              I am not leaving yet.

Interrogative: verb + meih a 未呀？
              e.g., Néih jáu **meih** a?
              你　 走　 未　 呀？
              Are you ready to leave now?
              (Yes) jáu la 走 喇   (No) meih jáu 未 走

1. Ngóh meih tēng dóu kéuih wah hōi-chí.
   我　 未　 聽　 到 佢　 話　 開 始。

2. Ngóh meih mahn A Lóhng làih mh làih.
   我　 未　 問　 阿朗　 嚟 唔 嚟。

3. Ngóh meih jī yiu jouh māt-yéh. Néih jī meih a?
   我　 未　 知 要 做 乜　 嘢。你　 知 未　 呀？

4. Kéuih meih fong dóu gūng, mh jī géi-dím fāan ūk-kéi.
   佢　 未　　 放　 到 工，唔 知 幾　 點　 返　 屋 企。

5. Ngóh seuhng go sīng-kèih béi jó chín, dím-gáai meih yáuh fo?
   我　 上　　 個 星　 期　 畀咗 錢，點　 解 未　 有　 貨？

✎ **Practice**

a. Put "meih 未" in the correct places in the sentences.

   i.   A Lóhng jouh yùhn yéh.
        阿 朗　 做　 完　 嘢。

   ii. Ngóh paak hóu chē.
        我　 泊　 好　 車。

   iii. Néih hái nī douh chīm méng.
        你　 喺 呢 度　 簽　 名。

b. Answer the questions using "meih 未".

   i.   Néih dáng jó yih sahp fān jūng, yáuh bā-sí meih a?
        你　 等　 咗 二 十　 分　 鐘，有　 巴 士 未　 呀？

   ii. Sihk jó faahn meih a?
        食　 咗 飯　 未　 呀？

   iii. Kéuih dāk mh dāk-hàahn tùhng ngóh heui syū jín a?
        佢　 得　 唔 得 閒　 同　 我　 去　 書 展 呀？

II. yùhn 完 (finish) ◄208.mp3

Affirmative: verb + yùhn 完

e.g., Ngóh jouh **yùhn** yéh.

我　做　完　嘢。

I've finished work.

Negative: meih 未 + verb + yùhn 完

e.g., Ngóh **meih** jouh **yùhn** yéh.

我　未　做　完　嘢。

I haven't finished work.

Interrogative: verb + yùhn 完 + object + meih a 未呀？

e.g., Néih jouh **yùhn** yéh **meih** a?

你　做　完　嘢　未　呀？

Have you finished work?

(Yes) jouh yùhn 做 完 　　(No) meih jouh yùhn 未 做 完

1. Nī go *talk* sāam dím hōi-chí, sei dím bun **yùhn**.

呢 個 talk 三　點 開 始，四 點 半 完。

2. Máaih **yùhn** yéh jauh heui yám chàh.

買　完　嘢　就　去　飲　茶。

3. Mh hóu sihk **yùhn** faahn jauh fan-gaau.

唔 好 食 完 飯　就　瞓 覺。

4. Lohk **yùhn** yúh **meih** a? Meih a.

落　完　雨　未　呀？未 呀。

5. Hó-lohk jouh **yùhn** dahk ga **meih** a?

可 樂 做 完　特　價 未 呀？

Kàhm-yaht dahk ga **yùhn** la.

琴　日　特　價 完　喇。

✎ Practice

Ask questions using "yùhn 完", and then answer.

a. tái hei

睇 戲

b. sīng-kèih-sāam jouh yéh

星　期　三　做　嘢

c. sihk faahn

食　飯

III. Compare the usage of "yùhn 完" and "jó 咗" ◀209.mp3

> verb + yùhn 完: just finished an action
> verb + jó 咗: accomplished a task

1. Néih tái **yùhn** nī bún syū meih a?
   你 睇 完 呢本 書 未 呀？
   Have you finished reading this book?

   Tái **jó** géi-dō go jūng-tàuh a?
   睇 咗 幾 多 個 鐘 頭 呀？
   How many hours have you spent reading it?

2. Ngóh jouh **yùhn** yéh fong gūng la.
   我 做 完 嘢 放 工 喇。
   I've finished work. I'm ready to leave the office.

   Néih jouh **jó** ge yéh, gei-dāk béi Chàhn sāang chīm méng.
   你 做 咗 嘅嘢，記 得 畀 陳 生 簽 名。
   Remember to ask Mr. Chan to counter-sign what you've done.

3. Néih sihk **yùhn** faahn meih a? Sihk **yùhn** jauh màaih dāan la.
   你 食 完 飯 未 呀？食 完 就 埋 單 喇。
   Have you finished your meal? If you've finished, let's get the bill.

   Néih sihk **jó** faahn meih a? Meih sihk jauh yāt-chàih heui sihk lā.
   你 食 咗飯 未 呀？未 食 就 一 齊 去 食 啦。
   Have you eaten? If you haven't, let's go and eat together.

IV. je 借 (to lend or to borrow) ◀210.mp3

> lend
> Person 1 + je + (counting word) + object + béi + Person 2
> e.g., Ngóh **je** bá jē **béi** néih.
>   我 借 把 遮 畀你。
>   *I'll lend you an umbrella.*
>
> borrow
> *Person 1 + béi + (counting word) + object + Person 2 + purpose*
> e.g., Ngóh **je** jó néih bá jē.
>   我 借 咗 你 把 遮。
>   *I borrowed your umbrella.*

1. Ngóh **je** gāan fóng **béi** pàhng-yáuh jyuh.
   我 借 間 房 畀朋 友 住。
   I'll give my friend a room to stay in.

2. Néih wúih mh wúih **je** chín **béi** kéuih a?
   你 會 唔 會 借 錢 畀佢 呀？
   Will you lend him some money?

3. Néih tái yùhn bún syū meih a? Néih tái yùhn, mh-gōi **je béi** ngóh lā.
   你　睇　完　本　書　未　呀？你　睇　完，　唔　該　借　畀　我　啦。
   Have you finished reading this book?
   Please lend it to me when you've finished reading.

4. Ngóh **je** jó kéuih dī syū.
   我　借咗　佢　啲　書。
   I borrowed his books.

5. Néih haih mh haih **je** jó kéuih ge kāat a?
   你　係　唔　係　借咗　佢　嘅　卡　呀？
   Have you borrowed his card?

✎ Practice

a. Use the prompts below to help you.
   i.　Make a sentence with "je 借" meaning to borrow.
   ii.　Make a sentence with "je 借" meaning to lend.

b. Answer the questions.
   i.　Bīn-go je jó néih ge chē a?
   　　邊　個　借咗　你　嘅　車　呀？
   ii.　Néih je yāt chīn mān béi ngóh dāk mh dāk a?
   　　你　借一　千　蚊　畀　我　得　唔　得　呀？
   iii.　Mh-gōi je jī bāt béi ngóh lā.
   　　唔　該　借支筆　畀　我　啦。

V. jauh 就 (then, soon after)　◀211.mp3

1. Ngóh jouh yùhn nī dī yéh **jauh** jáu ga la.
   我　做　完　呢　啲　嘢　就　走　㗎　喇。

2. Lauh jó go dihn-wá hái chāan-tēng **jauh** móuh jó.
   漏　咗　個　電　話　喺　餐　廳　就　冇　咗。

3. Lohk daaih yúh **jauh** wán mh dóu dīk-sí, hóu màh-fàahn.
   落　大　雨　就　搵　唔　到　的　士，好　麻　煩。

4. Sihk yùhn faahn **jauh** fāan ūk-kéi.
   食　完　飯　就　返　屋　企。

5. Móuh yàhn dāk-hàahn **jauh** mh hóu hōi wúi.
   冇　人　得　閒　就　唔　好　開　會。

✎ Practice

Make sentences using "jauh 就" and the following phrases.

a. móuh jē 冇遮

b. jyun yauh 轉右

c. tái yùhn hei 睇完戲

VI. dāk 得 (only have) ◀212.mp3

1. Ngóh **dāk** yāt bá jē, mh wúih je béi néih.
   我　得　一　把　遮，唔　會　借　畀　你。

2. Ngóh **dāk** sahp mān, mh gau chín sihk faahn.
   我　得　十　蚊，唔　夠　錢　食　飯。

3. Ngóh **dāk** léuhng fān-jūng, jouh mh yùhn dī yéh.
   我　得　兩　分　鐘，做　唔　完　啲　嘢。

VII. bāt-yùh 不如 (to suggest) ◀213.mp3

1. **Bāt-yùh** dáng dī yúh sai síu síu jauh jáu lā.
   不　如　等　啲　雨　細　少　少　就　走　啦。

2. Sei go yàhn, **bāt-yùh** daap dīk-sí lā.
   四　個　人，不　如　搭　的　士　啦。

3. Ngóh **bāt-yùh** béi jó nī bá jē néih la.
   我　不　如　畀　咗　呢　把　遮　你　喇。

VIII. ⋯⋯ge sìh-hauh 嘅時候 (at the time when) ◀214.mp3

1. Fong gūng **ge sìh-hauh** daht-yìhn lohk daaih yúh.
   放　工　嘅　時　候　突　然　落　大　雨。

2. Ngóh sihk aan **ge sìh-hauh** lauh jó bá jē hái chāan-tēng.
   我　食　晏　嘅　時　候　漏　咗　把　遮　喺　餐　廳。

3. Tùhng pàhng-yáuh yāt-chàih **ge sìh-hauh** hóu hōi-sām.
   同　朋　友　一　齊　嘅　時　候　好　開　心。

Pyramid drill   ◄215.mp3

1.

jouh yùhn yéh
做 完 嘢

meih jouh yùhn yéh
未 做 完 嘢

luhk dím meih jouh yùhn yéh
六 點 未 做 完 嘢

Néih luhk dím jouh yùhn yéh meih a?
你 六 點 做 完 嘢 未 呀？

Will you finish work at 6:00?

2.

dī yúh sai síu síu
啲 雨 細 少 少

dáng dī yúh sai síu síu
等 啲 雨 細 少 少

dáng dī yúh sai síu síu ge sìh-hauh
等 啲 雨 細 少 少 嘅 時 候

dáng dī yúh sai síu síu ge sìh-hauh jáu lā
等 啲 雨 細 少 少 嘅 時 候 走 啦

Bāt-yùh dáng dī yúh sai síu síu ge sìh-hauh jáu lā
不 如 等 啲 雨 細 少 少 嘅 時 候 走 啦

Bāt-yùh dáng dī yúh sai síu síu ge sìh-hauh jauh jáu lā.
不 如 等 啲 雨 細 少 少 嘅 時 候 就 走 啦。

Let's wait until the rain eases and then we'll leave.

General review

I. Listen and complete the following with expressions in the table.　◀216.mp3

bāt-yùh 不 如	bōng 幫	daahn-haih 但 係	dahk ga 特 價	làuh-hah 樓 下	yùh-gwó 如 果

dāk bun go jūng-tàuh 得 半 個 鐘 頭	jān-haih hóu-chói 真 係 好 彩
yáuh màh-fàahn ge sìh-hauh 有 麻 煩 嘅 時 候	yíh-gīng hōi-chí 已 經 開 始

1. _____ hó-lohk _____ jauh máaih dō dī.
   　　　　　　　可 樂　　　　　就 買　多 啲。

2. Ngóh heui dou chāan-tēng, kéuih-deih _____ sihk gán yéh.
   我　去　到 餐　廳，佢　哋　　　　　　　食　緊 嘢。

3. Ngóh _____, màh-mā jauh làih _____ ngóh.
   我　　　　　　　媽 媽 就　嚟　　　　　我。

4. A: _____ heui yám ga-fē lā.
   　　　　　　　去　飲　咖啡 啦。

   B: Hóu aak. _____ ngóh _____ dāk-hàahn,
   好　呃。　　　　　我　　　　　得　閒，

   hái _____ *coffee shop* yám, hóu mh hóu a?
   喺　　　　　coffee shop 飲，好　唔　好 呀？

5. Ngóh yáuh hóu dō hóu pàhng-yáuh, _____.
   我　有　好 多 好 朋　友，

II. Match the questions with the appropriate answers.　◀217.mp3

1. Wán gó gāan chāan-tēng, màh mh màh-fàahn a?
   搵　果 間 餐　廳，麻　唔 麻　煩 呀？

2. Néih ge chē paak hái bīn-douh a?
   你　嘅　車 泊　喺 邊　度 呀？

3. Sihk yùhn aan, fāan ūk-kéi meih a?
   食　完　晏，返　屋 企 未　呀？

4. Néih lauh-jó māt-yéh hái jáu-dim a? Wán mh wán dóu a?
   你　漏　咗 乜　嘢 喺 酒 店 呀？搵　唔 搵　到 呀？

5. Kéuih gām-jīu daht-yìhn jáu jó, dím syun a?
   佢　今　朝突　然　走咗，點算　呀？

☐　a. Sihk yùhn aan jauh fāan ūk-kéi la.
　　　食　完　晏　就　返　屋　企　喇。

☐　b. Mh màh-fàahn, ngóh hóu faai wán dóu gó gāan chāan-tēng.
　　　唔　麻　煩　，我　好　快　搵　到果　間　餐　　廳。

☐　c. Ngóh-deih yāt-chàih heui wán kéuih lā.
　　　我　哋　一　齊　去　搵　佢　啦。

☐　d. Ngóh ge chē paak hái gūng-sī làuh-hah.
　　　我　　嘅車　泊　喺公　司樓　下。

☐　e. Ngóh lauh-jó yāt gihn sāam hái jáu-dim, hóu-chói wán dóu.
　　　我　漏　咗一　件　衫　喺酒店，好　彩　搵　到。

Answers

Story

I.

1. b   2. a   3. d   4. c

1. When was it raining heavily?

   a. when I went to work   b. when I finished work   c. when I had lunch   d. when I went home

2. How did they go home?

   a. Long gave me a ride   b. they took MTR together   c. they waited until the rain had stopped

   d. Long took me under his umbrella

3. Where did Long park his car?

   a. at home   b. downstairs from the restaurant   c. upstairs from the office

   d. downstairs from the office

4. Where is Long's umbrella?

   a. he returned to the restaurant to look for his umbrella   b. he was not so lucky

   c. he had left his umbrella in the restaurant   d. he didn't have an umbrella

II.

b. A: Fong gūng la. Aai-yah! Lohk daaih yúh a!

   放　工　喇。哎吔！落　大　雨呀！

   I've finished work. Oh no! It's raining heavily!

d. B: Daht-yìhn lohk yúh jān-haih màh-fàahn lak.

   突　然　落　雨，真　係　麻　煩　嘞。

   It rained suddenly. It's inconvenient.

g. A: Ngóh móuh daai jē, géi-sìh lohk yùhn yúh a?

   我　冇　帶　遮，幾　時　落　完　雨呀？

   I didn't bring an umbrella. When will the rain stop?

f. B: Mh-sái dáng lohk yùhn yúh. Ngóh ge chē paak hái làuh-hah,

   唔　使　等　落　完　雨。我　嘅車　泊　喺　樓　下，

   bāt-yùh ngóh chē néih fāan ūk-kéi lā.

   不　如　我　車　你　返　屋　企　啦。

   You don't have to wait until the rain stops.

   My car is parked downstairs; let me give you a ride home.

a. A: Mh-gōi saai! Néih jān-haih hóu yàhn!

   唔　該　晒！你　真　係　好　人！

   Thank you very much! You're so kind!

   Néih yáuh móuh jē je béi ngóh a?

   你　有　冇　遮借畀我　呀？

   Can you lend me an umbrella?

c. B: Ngóh móuh jē wo.

   我　冇　遮喎。

   I don't have an umbrella.

   Ngóh sihk aan ge sìh-hauh lauh jó bá jē hái chāan-tēng,

   我　食　晏嘅時　候　漏　咗把　遮喺餐　廳，

   I went out to lunch and left my umbrella in the restaurant.

   gei-dāk ge sìh-hauh joi fāan heui wán, yíh-gīng wán mh dóu la.

   記　得嘅時　候　再　返　去　搵，已　經　搵　唔　到　喇。

   When I remembered and returned there, It wasn't there.

e. A: Néih jān-haih mh hóu-chói. Móuh jó bá jē, géi màh-fàahn wo.
   你　真　係　唔　好　彩。冇　咗把　遮，幾麻　煩　　喎。
   You're so unlucky. It's inconvenient without an umbrella.

III.

Lóhng:　Mh hóu yi-sī, ngóh **lauh jó bá jē hái nī-douh,**
朗　：　唔　好　意　思，我　漏　咗把　遮　喺　呢度，
　　　　néih yáuh móuh gin-dóu a?
　　　　你　有　冇　見　到　呀？
　　　　Excuse me; I left my umbrella here. Have you seen it?

gīng-léih:　Néih ge jē haih dím-yéung ga?
經　理：你　嘅遮　係　點樣　　㗎？
　　　　　　What does your umbrella look like?

Lóhng:　**Haih hāak-sīk ge** sūk-gwāt-jē.
朗　：　係　黑　色　嘅縮　骨　遮。
　　　　It's a black collapsible umbrella.

> * Note: "Sūk-gwāt 縮骨" literally means shrink bone.

gīng-léih:　Néih géi-sìh lauh hái douh ga?
經　理：你　幾　時　漏　喺　度　㗎？
　　　　　　When did you leave it here?

Lóhng:　**Gām-yaht sihk aan ge sìh-hauh.**
朗　：　今　日　食　晏　嘅　時　候。
　　　　Today, at lunchtime.

gīng-léih:　**Néih ge jē báai jó hái bīn-douh** a?
經　理：你　嘅遮擺　咗喺　邊　度　呀？
　　　　　　Where did you put your umbrella?

Lóhng:　Ngóh báai hái mùhn-háu.
朗　：　我　擺　喺　門　口。
　　　　I put it at the entrance.

gīng-léih:　Ngóh móuh gin-dóu. **Yáuh yàhn ló jó néih ge jē lā.**
經　理：我　冇　見　到。有　人　攞咗你　嘅遮　啦。
　　　　　　I haven't seen it. Someone has taken your umbrella.

Grammar practice translation I

1. I haven't heard him say it's time to start.
2. I haven't asked Long whether he's coming or not.
3. I don't know what to do yet. Do you know?
4. He was unable to finish his work. I don't know when he'll go home.
5. I paid last week. Why aren't the products available yet?

Practice answers

a.

i. A Lóhng **meih** jouh yùhn yéh.
   阿朗　　未　做　完　嘢。
   Long hasn't finished his work.

ii. Ngóh **meih** paak hóu chē.
   我　未　泊　好　車。
   I haven't parked my car.

iii. Néih **meih** hái nī douh chīm méng.
   你　未　喺呢度　簽　名。
   You haven't signed here.

b.

i. Dáng jó yih sahp fān jūng, meih yáuh bā-sí.

等 咗 二 十 分 鐘，未 有 巴 士。

I've waited for 20 minutes; not one bus has arrived yet.

ii. Ngóh meih sihk faahn.

我 未 食 飯。

I haven't eaten yet.

iii. Kéuih meih dāk-hàahn tùhng ngóh heui syū-jín.

佢 未 得 閒 同 我 去 書 展。

He's not free to accompany me to the book fair yet.

Grammar practice translation II

1. The talk starts at 3:00 and finishes at 4:30.
2. Let's go for tea after shopping.
3. Don't go to bed immediately after dinner.
4. Has the rain stopped? Not yet.
5. Has the promotion for Coke finished? It finished yesterday.

Practice answers

a. Néih tái yùhn hei meih a?

你 睇 完 戲 未 呀？

Have you finished watching the movie?

Answer: Tái yùhn la.

睇 完 喇。

Yes, I've finished watching the movie.

b. Néih sīng-kèih-sāam géi-dím jouh yùhn yéh a?

你 星 期 三 幾 點 做 完 嘢 呀？

What time will you finish work on Wednesday?

Answer: Ngóh sīng-kèih-sāam luhk dím jouh yùhn yéh.

我 星 期 三 六 點 做 完 嘢。

I'll finish work at 6:00 on Wednesday.

c. Ngóh-deih sihk yùhn faahn heui bīn-douh a?

我 哋 食 完 飯 去 邊 度 呀？

Where shall we go after lunch?

Answer: Ngóh-deih sihk yùhn faahn heui Jīm-Sā-Jéui lā.

我 哋 食 完 飯 去 尖 沙 咀 啦。

Let's go to Tsim Sha Tsui after lunch.

Grammar practice translation IV

Practice answers b.

i. Bīn-go je jó néih ge chē a?

邊 個 借咗 你 嘅 車 呀？

Who's borrowed your car?

(Answer) *Peter* je jó ngóh ge chē.

Peter 借咗 我 嘅 車。

Peter has borrowed my car.

ii. Néih je yāt chīn mān béi ngóh dāk mh dāk a?

你 借 一 千 蚊 畀 我 得 唔 得 呀？

Will you lend me $1,000?

(Answer) Dāk, móuh mahn-tàih.

得，冇 問 題。

Yes, okay; no problem.

or

    Mh dāk, ngóh móuh chín.

    唔 得，我 冇 錢。

    No, I don't have any money.

iii. Mh-gōi je jī bāt béi ngóh lā.

唔 該 借 支 筆 畀 我 啦。

May I borrow your pen? / Please lend me a pen.

(Answer) Hóu aak, néih yuhng lā.

    好 呃，你 用 啦。

    Sure.

    or

    Mh hóu yi-sī, ngóh móuh bāt.

    唔 好 意 思，我 冇 筆。

    Sorry; I don't have a pen.

Grammar practice translation V

1. I'll leave after finishing work.
2. I left my phone at the restaurant so now it's lost.
3. When there is heavy rain, we can't find a taxi. It's a problem.
4. Let's go home after dinner.
5. If nobody's free, let's call off the meeting.

Practice answers

a. Néih móuh jē, ngóh jauh je béi néih.

你 冇 遮，我 就 借 畀 你。

If you don't have an umbrella, I'll lend you one.

b. Jyun yauh jauh tìhng chē.

轉 右 就 停 車。

Turn right and then stop the car.

c. Kéuih-deih tái yùhn hei jauh fāan ūk-kéi.

佢 哋 睇 完 戲 就 返 屋 企。

They went home after seeing a movie.

Grammar practice translation VI

1. I've got only an umbrella. I can't lend it to you.
2. I have only $10. It's not enough for a meal.
3. I've got only two minutes. I can't finish the work.

Grammar practice translation VII

1. Let's wait for the rain to ease off a little. Then we'll leave.
2. We have four people. Shall we get a taxi?
3. I'd better lend you an umbrella.

Grammar practice translation VIII

1. It suddenly started raining heavily just as I was finishing work.
2. I left my umbrella at the restaurant at lunchtime.
3. I feel so happy when I'm with my friends.

General review

I.

1. **Yùh-gwó** hó-lohk **dahk ga** jauh máaih dō dī.

如 果 可 樂 特 價 就 買 多 啲。

If there is a promotion, I'll buy more Coke.

2. Ngóh heui dou chāan-tēng, kéuih-deih **yíh-gīng hōi-chí** sihk gán yéh.
   我 去 到 餐 廳，佢 哋 已 經 開 始 食 緊 嘢。
   When I arrived at the restaurant, they had already started to eat.

3. Ngóh **yáuh màh-fàahn ge sìh-hauh**, màh-mā jauh làih **bōng** ngóh.
   我 有 麻 煩 嘅時 候，媽 媽 就 嚟 幫 我。
   When I'm in trouble, my mother will come to help.

4. A: **Bāt-yùh** heui yám ga-fē lā.
      不 如 去 飲 咖 啡 啦。
      Shall we go for a coffee?

   B: Hóu aak. **Daahn-haih** ngóh **dāk bun go jūng-tàuh** dāk-hàahn,
      好 呃。但 係 我 得 半 個 鐘 頭 得 閒，
      Good idea. But I have only half an hour to spare.

      hái **làuh-hah** coffee shop yám, hóu mh hóu a?
      喺 樓 下 coffee shop 飲，好 唔 好 呀？
      Shall we go to the cofee shop downstairs?

5. Ngóh yáuh hóu dō hóu pàhng-yáuh, **jān-haih hóu-chói**.
   我 有 好 多 好 朋 友，真 係 好 彩。
   I'm so lucky to have so many good friends.

II. Question and answer translation

1. Is it a problem to find that restaurant?
   b. There's no trouble; I found that restaurant easily.

2. Where did you park your car?
   d. I parked my car downstairs from my office.

3. Are we going home after lunch?
   a. We'll go home after lunch.

4. What have you left at the hotel? Can you find it?
   e. I left a shirt at the hotel. I'm lucky I found it.

5. He left suddenly this morning. What shall we do?
   c. We'll go and find him together.

Hong Kong culture

Rainstorms and typhoons

Hong Kong has a sub-tropical climate. It rains every month and it rains heavily in summer. Heavy rain can cause flooding, which endangers lives.

The Hong Kong Observatory will alert the public about the occurrence of heavy rain by issuing rainstorm warning signals.

Amber rainstorm warning signal: heavy rain all over Hong Kong, exceeding 30 mm in a one-hour period. There may be flooding in low-lying and poorly drained areas.

Red rainstorm waring signal: heavy rain all over Hong Kong, exceeding 50 mm in a one-hour period. Roads are likely to be severely flooded, causing traffic congestion.

Black rainstorm signal: the highest warning, bringing heavy rain and dark skies all over Hong Kong and exceeding 70 mm in a one-hour period. Low-lying areas are likely to be severely flooded. People should stay indoors or take shelter in a safe place until the heavy rain has passed.

Typhoon season occurs from May to October.

The Hong Kong Observatory will issue typhoon warnings whenever a typhoon is centred within 800 km of Hong Kong.

Signals and precautionary meausures:

No. 1 indicates that a typhoon is centred within 800 km of Hong Kong; the weather begins to be influenced by the typhoon.

No. 3 indicates persistent strong winds; the weather gets very hot and the air becomes increasingly humid.

No. 8 indicates storm-force winds; the typhoon centre is very near Hong Kong.

No. 9 and No. 10 are indicators warning of a direct or near direct hit on Hong Kong from the typhoon. Hurricane-force winds are common.

When typhoon signal number 8 or above is hoisted, people should stay home or find a safe place to shelter; mass transportation stops.

Many Hong Kong people get very excited when they know a typhoon is coming, constantly checking the Hong Kong Observatory's website and news to see if there will be a typhoon signal number 8 and when it might happen. They will be overjoyed when they learn that the typhoon will affect Hong Kong during daytime office hours. They will take it as an extra holiday and start planning indoor activities like playing mahjong or watching movies. They feel especially disappointed when they learn that the typhoon will arrive during the night. At best, this means having a good sleep during the storm but having to go to work as usual the following morning.

Hong Kong is generally not at risk of a major natural disaster due to its location and robust infrastructure. However, a big typhoon might be among a host of other disasters that should be of concern for the city.

3

Does this bus go to Stanley?

Dialogue ◀301.mp3

➢ Where does Yan want to go?

➢ How much is the fare?

➢ What is the problem when Yan is paying the fare?

➢ How did she solve the problem?

➢ Who will tell her when to get off?

Yān:　Mh-gōi, nī ga chē haih maih heui Jūng-Wàahn Máh-Tàuh ga?

欣：　唔 該，呢架車 係 咪 去 中 環 碼 頭 㗎？

Excuse me, does this bus go to the Central Piers?

sī-gēi: Haih a! Hōi chē la. Faai dī séuhng chē lā.

司機：係 呀！開 車 喇。快 啲 上 　 車 啦。

Yes, we're about to go. Get on quickly.

Yān:　Géi chín yāt wái a?

欣：　幾 錢 一 位 呀？

How much is the fare?

sī-gēi: Chāt mān.

司機：七 　 蚊。

$7.00.

Yān:　Aìh yah! Ngóh ge kāat mh gau chín!

欣：　哎 吔！我 　 嘅 卡 唔 夠 　 錢！

Oh no, there is not enough money on my card.

　　　Ngóh dāk luhk mān sáan-jí ja.

　　　我 　 得 六 蚊 散 子咋。

I have only $6 in small change.

sī-gēi: Wán yàhn cheung béi néih lā.

司機：搵 　 人 唱 　 畀 你 啦。

Find someone to give you change.

Yān: Mh-gōi, néih yáuh móuh sahp mān sáan-jí a?
欣：   唔該，你 有 冇 十 蚊 散 子呀？
         Excuse me, do you have change for $10?

Fāi: Móuh mahn-tàih cheung béi néih lā.
輝：   冇 問 題，唱 畀 你 啦。
         No problem. I'll give you change.

Yān: Jān-haih mh-gōi saai.
欣：   真 係 唔 該 晒。
         Thank you so much.

                    *   *   *

Yān: Mh-gōi, dou sei houh máh-tàuh meih a?
欣：   唔 該，到 四 號 碼 頭 未 呀？
         Excuse me, have we arrived at pier No. 4?

sī-gēi: Meih dou, juhng yáuh léuhng go gāai-háu.
司機：   未 到，仲 有 兩 個 街 口。
         We haven't arrived yet; two more blocks to go.

Fāi: Ngóh dōu hái máh-tàuh lohk chē,
輝：   我 都 喺 碼 頭 落 車，

         yāt-jahn néih gān-jyuh ngóh lohk chē lā.
         一 陣 你 跟 住 我 落 車 啦。
         I'm also getting off at the pier; you can follow me.

Yān: Mh-gōi saai. Néih jān-haih hóu-yàhn.
欣：   唔 該 晒。你 真 係 好 人。
         Thank you very much. You're so kind.

Story: Falling asleep on a minibus ◀302.mp3

Kàhm-yaht ngóh daap síu-bā heui Chek-Chyúh wán pàhng yáuh.
琴　日　我　搭　小巴去　赤　柱　搵　朋　友。
Yesterday, I went to Stanley by minibus to see a friend.

Yān-waih sāk chē hóu muhn, ngóh jauh fan jeuhk gaau.
因　為　塞車好　悶，我　就　瞓着　覺。
Because I thought being stuck in a traffic jam was boring, I fell asleep.

Ngóh séng ge sìh-hauh, ga síu-bā yíh-gīng dou jaahm la.
我　醒　嘅時候，架小巴已　經　到　站　喇。
When I woke up, the bus had already reached the final stop.

Ngóh lohk jó chē juhng yiu mahn yàhn dím hàahng heui Chek-Chyúh Gwóng-Chèuhng.
我　落　咗車　仲　要　問　人　點　行　去　赤　柱　廣　場。
After I got off the bus, I had to ask people how to get to Stanley Plaza.

Jeui hauh chìh jó sahp fān-jūng gin pàhng yáuh, jān-haih màh-fàahn!
最　後　遲　咗十　分　鐘　見　朋　友，真係麻　煩！
In the end, I was 10 minutes late meeting my friend. That's really annoying!

Hah chi daap chē, yāt-dihng mh hóu fan jeuhk gaau!
下　次　搭　車，一　定　唔　好　瞓着　覺！
Try not to fall asleep on the bus next time!

Questions for the story

I. Answer the questions. ◀303.mp3

1. Kéuih heui Chek-Chyúh jouh māt-yéh a?
   佢　去　赤　柱　做　乜　嘢呀？

2. Dím-gáai kéuih hái síu-bā fan jeuhk gaau?
   點　解　佢　喺小　巴瞓着　覺？

3. Kéuih séng ge sìh-hauh, síu-bā heui dou bīn-douh a?
   佢　醒　嘅時　候，小　巴去　到　邊　度　呀？

4. Kéuih chìh jó géi-noih gin pàhng-yáuh a?
   佢　遲　咗幾　耐見　朋　友　呀？

II. Listen and complete the dialogue with the expressions in the table.   ◀304.mp3

dou jaahm la 到 站 喇	ngóh chē néih heui lā 我 車 你 去 啦	haih maih heui Chek-Chyúh 係 咪 去 赤 柱
séuhng chē lā 上 車 啦	nī tìuh louh hóu sāk chē 呢 條 路 好 塞 車	hàahng sahp fān-jūng jauh dou 行 十 分 鐘 就 到
Chek-Chyúh Gwóng Chèuhng hái bīn-douh 赤 柱 廣 場 喺 邊 度		

Chàhn: Mh-gōi nī ga chē _____ ga?
陳：　唔 該 呢 架 車 　　　　喫？

sī-gēi: Haih a! _____. Mh-gōi kau ōn-chyùhn dáai.
司機：係 呀！　　　　。唔 該 扣 安 全 帶。

Chàhn: _____. Ga chē sahp fān-jūng móuh hàahng gwo.
陳：　　　　。架 車 十 分 鐘 冇 行 過。

　　　Aai! Bāt-yùh fan yāt jahn sīn lā.
　　　哎！不 如 瞓 一 陣 先 啦。

　　　　　　　* * *

sī-gēi: Wai, _____. Néih heui bīn-douh ga?
司機：喂，　　　　。你 去 邊 度 喫？

Chàhn: _____ a?
陳：　　　　呀？

sī-gēi: Gān-jyuh nī tìuh louh, _____ la.
司機：跟 住 呢 條 路，　　　　喇。

　　　Néih dáng yāt jahn, _____.
　　　你 等 一 陣，　　　　。

Chàhn: Mh-gōi saai.
陳：　唔 該 晒。

Vocabulary   ◄305.mp3

1.	sī-gēi	司機	driver
2.	gāai-háu	街口	crossroads; intersection
3.	nī tiuh louh	呢條路	this road
4.	cheung sáan-jí	唱散子	to get small change
5.	hōi chē	開車	to start a car
6.	lohk chē	落車	to get out of a car; to alight
7.	sāk chē	塞車	traffic jam
8.	dou	到	to arrive
9.	fan jeuhk gaau	瞓着覺	to fall asleep
10.	séng	醒	to wake up; become conscious
11.	gau	夠	enough
12.	muhn	悶	boring
13.	chìh	遲	late
14.	gān-jyuh	跟住	to follow; and then
15.	jeui hauh	最後	at last; in the end
16.	hah chi	下次	next time
17.	yāt-jahn	一陣	a moment
18.	yāt-dihng	一定	certainly; definitely
19.	dím	點	how (to do something)?
20.	juhng	仲	still more
21.	sīn	先	first
22.	ja	咋	(sentence particle) only

Grammar practice

I. juhng 仲 (still more)　◄306.mp3

> e.g., Meih dou máh-tàuh, **juhng** yáuh léuhng go gāai-háu.
> 未　到　碼　頭，仲　有　兩　個　街　口。
> *We haven't arrived at the pier; there are still two more blocks to go.*
>
> Ngóh lohk jó chē, **juhng** yiu mahn yàhn dím hàahng.
> 我　落　咗　車，仲　要　問　人　點　行。
> *I have to ask people how to go there after getting off the bus.*

1. A: Daap nī ga chē, yāt go yàhn béi luhk māan.
   搭　呢架車，一個人　畀　六　蚊。

   B: Ngóh dāk sei māan sáan-jí, **juhng** yiu je néih léuhng māan.
   我　得四蚊散子，仲　要　借你　兩　蚊。

2. A: Yìh-gā géi dím a? **Juhng** yáuh géi-noih lohk tòhng a? Hóu muhn a!
   而　家幾　點呀？仲　有　幾　耐　落　堂　呀？好　悶　呀！

   B: Yìh-gā gáu dím. Ngóh-deih gáu dím bun lohk tòhng.
   而　家九　點。我　哋　九　點　半落　堂。

   Juhng yáuh bun go jūng-tàuh jauh lohk tòhng.
   仲　有　半個鐘　頭就　落　堂。

3. Nī go haih Seuhng-Wàahn jaahm, **juhng** yáuh sāam go jaahm jauh dou Wāan-Jái.
   呢個係上　環　站，仲　有　三　個站　就　到　灣　仔。

✎ Practice

a. A: Juhng yáuh géi-noih haih néih sāang-yaht (*birthday*) a?
   仲　有　幾　耐　係你　生　日　　　呀？

   B: ＿＿＿＿＿＿＿ jauh dou ngóh sāang-yaht.
   　　　　　　　　就　到　我　生　日。

b. Ngóh-deih yáuh sahp go yàhn. Nī douh dāk baat jek chā (*fork*).
   我　哋　有　十　個人。呢度　得　八　隻　叉。

   ＿＿＿＿＿＿＿＿＿ Giu yàhn ló làih lā.
   　　　　　　　　　叫　人　攞　嚟　啦。

c. A: Néih báau meih a?
   你　飽　未　呀？

   B: Chā-mh-dō lā. Ngóh ＿＿＿＿＿ dō dī dím-sām.
   差　唔　多　啦。我　　　　　多　啲　點　心。

II. Specifying an object with a measure word   ◄307.mp3

> e.g., **Ga** síu-bā yíh-gīng dou jaahm la.
> 架　小　巴　已　經　到　站　喇。
> *The bus has arrived at the terminus.*

* Note: We usually say "**nī ga síu-bā** 呢架小巴" (this minibus). Sometimes when the object is understood, the word "**nī** 呢" (this) or "**gó** 果" (that) can be omitted. Thus, to start a phrase with the measure word "**ga** 架" to count a bus functions like "the" in English.

1. **Go** mìhng-sīng hái dī syū chīm méng.
   個　明　星　喺　啲　書　簽　名。

2. Hóu-chói **ga** dīk-sí chóh dóu ngh go yàhn, mh sái wán léuhng ga chē.
   好　彩　架　的　士　坐　到　五　個　人，唔　使　搵　兩　架　車。

3. **Tìuh** louh haih mh haih heui máh-tàuh ga?
   條　路　係　唔　係　去　碼　頭　㗎？

4. **Go** bā-sí sī-gēi hóu hóu yàhn, gei-dāk giu ngóh lohk chē.
   個　巴　士　司　機　好　好　人，記　得　叫　我　落　車。

✎ Practice

Fill in the appropriate measure word.

a. _____ chāan-tēng hóu leng.
   餐　廳　好　靚。

b. _____ jē je jó béi yàhn.
   遮　借　咗　畀　人。

c. _____ syū hóu muhn.
   書　好　悶。

III. gān-jyuh 跟住 (to follow; and then)   ◄308.mp3

> e.g., Néih **gān-jyuh** ngóh hái deih-tit jaahm lohk chē lā.
> 你　跟　住　我　喺　地　鐵　站　落　車　啦。
> *You can follow me to get off at the MTR station.*
>
> Néih séuhng jó chē, **gān-jyuh** béi dihn-wá ngóh.
> 你　上　咗　車，跟　住　畀　電　話　我。
> *You get on the bus and then give me a call.*

1. Kéuih dím-yéung jouh, ngóh jauh **gān-jyuh** kéuih jouh.
   佢　點　樣　做，我　就　跟　住　佢　做。

2. Ngóh **gān-jyuh** dī yàhn hàahng, mh jī hàahng jó heui bīn-douh.
   我　跟　住　啲　人　行，唔　知　行　咗　去　邊　度。

3. Ngóh-deih sihk yùhn faahn, **gān-jyuh** heui tái hei.
我　哋　食　完　飯，　跟　住　去　睇　戲。

4. Néih gin-dóu Chek-Chyúh Gwóng Chèuhng, **gān-jyuh** giu lohk chē jauh ngāam la.
你　見　到　赤　柱　廣　場，　　跟　住　叫　落　車　就　啱　喇。

✎ **Practice**

Describe an activity and the steps to do things, using "gān-jyuh 跟住".

IV. yāt-dihng 一定 (certainly; definitely)　◀309.mp3

> e.g., Hah chi daap chē, **yāt-dihng** mh hóu fan jeuhk gaau!
> 下　次　搭　車，一　定　唔　好　瞓　着　覺！
> *I certainly won't fall asleep on the bus next time.*

1. Néih dáng dahk ga, **yāt-dihng** máaih mh dóu.
你　等　特　價，一　定　買　唔　到。

2. Néih gān-jyuh kéuih jouh **yāt-dihng** ngāam.
你　跟　住　佢　做　一　定　啱。

3. Ngóh heui gāai **yāt-dihng** daai dihn-wá.
我　去　街　一　定　帶　電　話。

V. dím 點 (how)　◀310.mp3

> e.g., Néih **dím** jáu a?
> 你　點　走　呀？
> *How are you going to go?*
>
> Kéuih-deih **dím** fāan ūk-kéi a?
> 佢　哋　點　返　屋　企　呀？
> *How do they go home?*

1. Néih ge dihn-wá **dím** yíng séung ga?
你　嘅　電　話　點　影　相　㗎？

2. Ngóh **dím** gei-dāk géi-sìh je jó kéuih ge dói a?
我　點　記　得　幾　時　借咗佢　嘅　袋　呀？

3. Yùh-gwó néih haih ngóh, néih **dím** jouh nē?
如　果　你　係　我，你　點　做　呢？

4. Néih **dím** a? Néih séung ngóh **dím** bōng néih a?
你　點　呀？你　想　我　點　幫　你　呀？

✎ Practice

Make up questions for these sentences using "dím 點".

a. Ngóh yuhng *Google Map* wán gó gāan chāan-tēng.
   我　用　　Google Map　搵　果　間　餐　　廳。

b. Ngóh pàhng-yáuh bōng ngóh ló dóu kāat.
   我　朋　友　幫　我　攞　到　卡。

c. Ngóh daap deih-tit fāan ūk-kéi.
   我　搭　地　鐵　返　屋　企。

VI. ······ja 咋 (only)   ◀311.mp3

> e.g., Ngóh dāk luhk mān sáan-jí **ja**.
> 我　得　六　蚊　散　子咋。
> *I have only $6 in small change.*

1. Ngóh fong yāt yaht ga **ja**.
   我　放　一　日　假　咋。

2. Ngóh yíng dóu yāt jēung séung **ja**.
   我　影　到　一　張　相　咋。

3. Dāk yāt ga chē heui Wohng-Gok **ja**.
   得　一　架　車　去　旺　　角　咋。

4. Juhng yáuh hóu síu yéh sihk **ja**.
   仲　有　好　少　嘢　食　咋。

Pyramid drill ◀312.mp3

1.

yāt-dihng ngāam

一　定　啱

dī yàhn yāt-dihng ngāam

啲　人　一　定　啱

gān-jyuh dī yàhn yāt-dihng ngāam

跟　住　啲　人　一　定　啱

gān-jyuh dī yàhn hàahng yāt-dihng ngāam

跟　住　啲　人　行　一　定　啱

Néih gān-jyuh dī yàhn hàahng yāt-dihng ngāam.

你　跟　住　啲　人　行　一　定　啱。

You go with these people. That's certainly right.

2.

dou Jūng-Wàahn Máh-Tàuh

到　中　環　碼　頭

yíh-gīng dou Jūng-Wàahn Máh-Tàuh

已　經　到　中　環　碼　頭

yāt go gāai-háu, yíh-gīng dou Jūng-Wàahn Máh-Tàuh

一　個　街　口，已　經　到　中　環　碼　頭

Juhng yáuh yāt go gāai-háu, yíh-gīng dou Jūng-Wàahn Máh-Tàuh la.

仲　有　一　個　街　口，已　經　到　中　環　碼　頭　喇。

One more intersection and you will be at Central Ferry Pier.

General review

I. Put the words in the correct order to make sentences.　◀313.mp3

1. ngóh / séung / lohk chē / hái / Jūng-Wàahn / máh-tàuh / luhk houh
   我 / 想 / 落車 / 喺 / 中 環 / 碼 頭 / 六 號

2. néih / bōng néih / kéuih / kéuih / yāt-dihng / yùh-gwó / wah / dāk / giu
   你 / 幫 你 / 佢 / 佢 / 一 定 / 如 果 / 話 / 得 / 叫

3. ngóh-deih / chāan-tēng / nī tìuh louh / gān-jyuh / jauh / hàahng / dou / sāam fān-jūng
   我 哋 / 餐 廳 / 呢 條 路 / 跟 住 / 就 / 行 / 到 / 三 分 鐘

II. Listen and complete the following with expressions in the table.　◀314.mp3

daht-yìhn 突 然	dím heui 點 去	lauh-jó 漏 咗	mahn 問	wán dóu 搵 到
paak hái gāai-háu 泊 喺 街 口	yáu dāk kéuih 由 得 佢			

1. A: Nī douh móuh deih-tit, _____ heui Gáu-Lùhng-Tòhng?
      呢 度 冇 地 鐵， 去 九 龍 塘？

   B: Ngóh dōu mh jī. Néih _____ Amy lā. Kéuih jyuh Gáu-Lùhng-Tòhng.
      我 都 唔 知。你 Amy 啦。佢 住 九 龍 塘。

2. Ngóh kàhm-yaht _____ go dihn-wá hái dīk-sí,
   我 琴 日 個 電 話 喺 的 士，

   _____ sī-gēi bōng ngóh _____
   司 機 幫 我

3. Ngóh ge chē _____ ge chē-wái.
   我 嘅 車 嘅 車 位。

4. A: Mh hóu yi-sī, ngóh _____ heui mh dóu yám chàh.
      唔 好 意 思，我 去 唔 到 飲 茶。

   B: Mh gán-yiu, _____ lā.
      唔 緊 要， 啦。

III. Choose the correct saying to complete the sentences.　◀315.mp3

1. Syū-jín kàhm-yaht _____ jó.
   書 展 琴 日 咗。

   a. hóu noih móuh gin　　　b. yíh-gīng hōi-chí　　　c. yāt-chàih séuhng chē
      好 耐 冇 見　　　　　　 已 經 開 始　　　　　　 一 齊 上 車

2. _____ máaih jauh yáu dāk kéuih lā, mh gán-yiu ge.
　　　 買　 就 由 得 佢　 啦，唔 緊 要 嘅。

    a. yùh-gwó mh gei-dāk   b. ngóh ge kāat yáuh chín   c. fong gūng ge sìh-hauh
      如 果 唔 記 得   我 嘅 卡 有　 錢   放 工　 嘅 時 候

3. _____ , ngóh jē néih heui déih-tit-jaahm lā.
　　　　 ，我 遮 你 去 地 鐵 站　 啦。

    a. néih daai jó jē   b. néih hóu hóu yàhn   c. ngóh ge jē gau daaih
      你 帶 咗 遮   你 好 好 人   我　 嘅遮 夠 大

4. Ngóh ge chē hái làuh-hah, _____ lā.
　 我　 嘅 車 喺 樓 下，　　　　 啦。

    a. ngóh chē néih jáu   b. jān-haih màh-fàahn   c. néih gān-jyuh lohk chē
      我　 車 你 走   真 係 麻 煩   你 跟 住 落 車

Answers

Story

I.

1. Kéuih heui Chek-Chyúh wán pàhng-yáuh.
   佢 去 赤 柱 搵 朋 友。
2. Yān-waih sāk chē hóu muhn.
   因 為 塞 車 好 悶。
3. Síu-bā yíh-gīng dou jaahm la.
   小 巴 已 經 到 站 喇。
4. Kéuih chìh jó sahp fān-jūng gin pàhng yáuh.
   佢 遲 咗 十 分 鐘 見 朋 友。

II.

Chàhn: Mh-gōi nī ga chē **haih maih heui Chek-Chyúh** ga?
陳： 唔 該 呢 架 車 係 咪 去 赤 柱 㗎？
Excuse me, does this bus go to Stanley?

sī-gēi: Haih a! **Séuhng chē lā**. Mh-gōi kau ōn-chyùhn dáai.
司機： 係 呀！上 車 啦。唔 該 扣 安 全 帶。
Yes. Get on the bus quickly. Please fasten your seatbelt.

Chàhn: **Nī tiùh louh hóu sāk chē**. Ga chē sahp fān-jūng móuh hàahng gwo.
陳： 呢 條 路 好 塞 車。架 車 十 分 鐘 冇 行 過。
The traffic on this road is so heavy. The bus hasn't moved for 10 minutes.

Aai! Bāt-yùh fan yāt jahn sīn lā.
哎！不 如 瞓 一 陣 先 啦。
Let me sleep for a while.

* * *

sī-gēi: Wai, **dou jaahm la**. Néih heui bīn-douh ga?
司機： 喂，到 站 喇。你 去 邊 度 㗎？
We've arrived at the final stop. Where are you going?

Chàhn: **Chek-Chyúh Gwóng Chèuhng hái bīn-douh** a?
陳： 赤 柱 廣 場 喺 邊 度 呀？
Where is Stanley Plaza?

sī-gēi: Gān-jyuh nī tiùh louh, **hàahng sahp fān-jūng jauh dou** la.
司機： 跟 住 呢 條 路，行 十 分 鐘 就 到 喇。
Follow this road. You have to walk 10 minutes.

Néih dáng yāt jahn, **ngóh chē néih heui lā**.
你 等 一 陣，我 車 你 去 啦。
Wait a moment. I'll give you a ride.

Chàhn: Mh-gōi saai.
陳： 唔 該 晒。
Thank you very much.

Grammar practice translation I

1. A: The bus fare is $6.

   B: I have only $4 in small change. I still have to borrow $2 from you.

2. A: What time is it now? How long do we have to wait for the class to finish? It's boring!

   B: It is now 9:00. We finish at 9:30. Half an hour more, the class will be over.

3. This is Sheung Wan station, three more stop, and we will arrive at Wan Chai.

Suggested practice answers

a. A: Juhng yáuh géi-noih haih néih sāang-yaht a?

仲　有　幾　耐　係　你　生　日　呀？

How much longer until your birthday?

B: **Juhng yáuh yāt go yuht** jauh dou ngóh sāang-yaht.

仲　有　一　個　月　就　到　我　生　日。

One more month, it will be my birthday.

b. Ngóh-deih yáuh sahp go yàhn. Nī douh dāk baat jek chā.

我　哋　有　十　個　人。呢　度　得　八　隻　叉。

We have 10 people. There are only 8 forks.

Juhng yiu léuhng jek chā. Giu yàhn ló làih lā.

仲　要　兩　隻　叉。叫　人　攞　嚟　啦。

We need two more forks. Ask someone to bring them.

c. A: Néih báau meih a?

你　飽　未　呀？

Are you full?

B: Chā-mh-dō lā. Ngóh **juhng séung sihk** dō dī dím-sām.

差　唔　多　啦。我　仲　想　食　多　啲　點　心。

I'm almost full. I would like to eat more dim sum.

Grammar practice translation II

1. The celebrity is signing those books.
2. Luckily, this taxi can take five passengers. We don't have to find two taxis.
3. Is this the way to the pier?
4. The bus driver was very kind. He remembered to tell me to get off.

Practice answers

a. **Gāan** chāan-tēng hóu leng.

間　餐　廳　好　靚。

The restaurant is beautiful.

b. **Bá** jē je jó béi yàhn.

把　遮　借　咗　畀　人。

I lent the umbrella to someone.

c. **Bún** syū hóu muhn.

本　書　好　悶。

The book is boring.

Grammar practice translation III

1. I'll follow what he does.
2. I follow the crowd, but don't know where I'm going.
3. After dinner, then we'll go for a movie.
4. When you see Stanley Plaza, then you ask the driver.

Grammar practice translation IV

1. If you wait for the sale, you definitely can't buy it.
2. You can't go wrong if you follow what he does.
3. I definitely bring my phone when I go out.

Grammar practice translation V

1. How do you use your phone to take photos?
2. How can I remember when I borrowed his bag?
3. If you were me, what would you do?
4. How are you? How do you want me to help you?

Practice answers

a. Néih dím wán gó gāan chāan-tēng a?

你　點　搵果間　餐　廳　呀？

How did you find that restaurant?

Ngóh yuhng *Google Map* wán gó gāan chāan-tēng.

我　　用　　Google Map 搵 果 間　餐　廳。

I used Google Maps to find that restaurant.

b. Néih dím ló dóu kāat a?

你　點　攞 到 卡 呀？

How can you get the card?

Ngóh pàhng-yáuh bōng ngóh ló dóu kāat.

我　朋　友　幫　我　攞　到卡。

My friend helped me to get the card.

c. Néih dím fāan ūk-kéi a?

你　點　返　屋 企 呀？

How do you go home?

Ngóh daap deih-tit fāan ūk-kéi.

我　搭　地　鐵 返　屋 企。

I take the MTR home.

Grammar practice translation VI

1. I have only one day holiday.
2. I am only able to take one picture.
3. There is only one bus going to Mong Kok.
4. There is very little food left.

General review

I.

1. Ngóh séung hái Jūng-Wàahn luhk houh máh-tàuh lohk chē.

我　想　喺中　環　六　號　碼 頭 落　車。

I want to get off at Central Pier No. 6.

2. Yùh-gwó néih giu kéuih bōng néih, kéuih yāt-dihng wah dāk.

如　果　你　叫 佢　幫　你，佢　一　定　　話　得。

If you ask him to help, he certainly will say yes.

3. Ngóh-deih gān-jyuh nī tìuh louh hàahng sāam fān-jūng jauh dou chāan-tēng.

我　哋　跟　住　呢 條　路　行　　三　分　鐘　就　到 餐　廳。

We follow this path, walk for 3 minutes, then we will arrive at the restaurant.

II.

1. A: Nī douh móuh deih-tit, **dím heui** Gáu-Lùhng-Tòhng?

呢　度　冇　　地　鐵，點 去　九　龍　　塘？

There is no MTR here. How can I get to Kowloon Tong?

B: Ngóh dōu mh jī. Néih **mahn** *Amy* lā. Kéuih jyuh Gáu-Lùhng-Tòhng.

我　都　唔知。你　問　Amy 啦。佢　住　九　龍　　塘。

I don't know either. You'd better ask Amy. She lives in Kowloon Tong.

2. Ngóh kàhm-yaht **lauh-jó** go dihn-wá hái dīk-sí,

我　琴　日　漏　咗個 電　話 喺 的 士，

I left my phone in the taxi yesterday,

hóu-chói sī-gēi bōng ngóh **wán dóu**.

好　彩 司 機　幫　我　搵　到。

luckily, the driver helped me to look for it.

3. Ngóh ge chē **paak hái gāai-háu** ge chē-wái.
我　嘅車泊　喺街　口　嘅車位。
I parked my car in the parking space at an intersection.

4. A: Mh hóu yi-sī, ngóh **daht-yìhn** heui mh dóu yám chàh.
唔好意思，我　突　然　去　唔到飲　茶。
Sorry, suddenly I realized I couldn't go for tea.

B: Mh gán-yiu, **yáu dāk kéuih** lā.
唔緊要，由得佀　啦。
Never mind, leave it.

III.

1. b Syū-jín kàhm-yaht **yíh-gīng hōi-chí** jó.
書展琴日已經開始咗。
The book fair started yesterday.

2. a **Yùh-gwó mh gei-dāk** máaih jauh yáu dāk kéuih lā, mh gán-yiu ge.
如果唔記得買　就由得佀　啦，唔緊要嘅。
If you forgot to buy then leave it. Never mind.

3. c **Ngóh ge jē gau daaih**, ngóh jē néih heui déih-tit-jaahm lā.
我　嘅遮夠大，　我遮你去地鐵站　啦。
My umbrella is big enough. I can walk to the MTR station under my umbrella.

4. a Ngóh ge chē hái làuh-hah, **ngóh chē néih jáu** lā.
我　嘅車喺樓下，我　車你走啦。
My car is parked downstairs. I'll give you a ride.

Hong Kong culture

How Stanley 赤柱 got its name

Stanley is named after Lord Stanley, the British Secretary of State for the Colonies at the time of the cessation of Hong Kong. In Central, Stanley Street is also named after Lord Stanley. The Chinese name is 士丹利街 Sih Dāan Leih Gāai, a phonetic translation of Stanley, which is very different from the name of the area called 赤柱 Chek Chyúh.

On a map in the nineteenth century, the area is written 赤柱 Chak Ch'u in Hakka.

赤柱 Chak Ch'u means red pillar and refers to the village with tall cotton trees often covered in bright red blossoms. Another explanation of 赤柱 Chak Ch'u is written as a variation of 賊柱 Chaahk Chyu (literally bandit's post), which is related to the legend of the notorious pirate Cheung Po Tsai 張保仔, who was active here.

In Hong Kong, many places have changed their names for a better sound or to avoid bad meanings. Here are a few examples:

樂富 Lok Fu, where a public housing estate of the same name is located, means happy and rich. As there were tigers living in this area, its previous name was 老虎岩 Lóuh Fú Ngàahm or Tiger Rock. But it is believed that tiger sounds too fierce and may cause bad feng shui.

藍田 Lam Tin or blue field was originally 鹹田 Hàahm Tìhn or salt field. The meaning of 鹹 is associated with dirty, as in 鹹濕 hàahm-sāp. It might not be a desirable character to have in the name of a residential area.

欣澳 Yān Ou, or Sunny Bay, means cheerful bay in Chinese. Its original name is 陰澳 Yām Ou, which means shadow bay or dark bay, as it used to be a good place to store cut trees. The place name changed when plans to build the Hong Kong Disneyland Resort on nearby Penny's Bay were decided. The character 欣 Yān, meaning cheerful, is more suitable for the station name of the Disneyland rail link and matches the happy image of Disneyland.

調景嶺 Tìuh Géng Léhng, or Tiu King Ling, literally means harmonize view hill. The earliest name of this place was 照鏡嶺 Jiu Geng Léhng (literally, mirror hill), but later a failed businessman who hanged himself here gave the Chinese name for the place 吊頸嶺 Diu Géng Léhng, meaning hanging neck hill. The name was soon changed to 調景嶺 Tiu King Ling, characters that have similar sounds but with more auspicious meanings. The Hong Kong government once settled a considerable number of former Nationalist soldiers and other Nationalist Party (國民黨) supporters in this place after the Second World War. In 1996, just before the handover, the Nationalist Party residence was completely removed without a trace left for remembrance, as this would be an embarrassing scene for the PRC government.

4
Please repeat

Dialogue ◀401.mp3

➤ Who is she calling?

➤ Why has she made this call?

➤ Is the phone number correct?

➤ Do they know each other?

➤ What does he suggest she do?

Yihp: Wái? Mh-gōi Wòhng sāang hái douh ma?
葉： 喂？唔該王　生　喺度嗎？
Hello, may I speak to Mr. Wong?

Wòhng: Ngóh haih *John Wong.*
王： 我　係　John Wong。
Yes, speaking. I'm John Wong.

Yihp: Wòhng sāang, ngóh méih sāu dóu néih dī chín,
葉： 王　生，我　未　收　到　你　啲錢，
Mr. Wong, I haven't received your money.

néih géi-sìh gwo sou béi ngóh a?
你　幾時過　數畀我　呀？
When will you have the money transferred to my account?

Wòhng: Dáng dáng sīn. Néih joi góng gwo? Néih haih bīn-wái a?
王： 等　等　先。你　再講　過？你　係　邊位呀？
Wait a minute. Please say that again. Who are you?

Yihp: Ngóh haih Yihp Waih Yìuh, ngóh wán Wòhng Jan Wàh, néih haih maih a?
葉： 我　係　葉　惠　瑤，我　搵王　振華，你　係　咪呀？
I am Yip Wai Yiu. I'm calling Wong Chun Wah, is that you?

Wòhng: Ngóh mh haih. Néih dá cho la.
王： 我　唔係。你　打錯喇。
No, it's not. You've called the wong number.

Yihp: Oh! Deui-mh-jyuh. Néih dihn-wá haih maih 9012 6543?

葉：   哦！對　唔　住。你　電　話　係　咪　9012 6543？

Oh! I'm sorry. Is your phone number 9012 6543?

Wòhng: Dihn-wá ngāam, daahn-haih ngóh mh sīk néih ga wo.

王：   電　話　啱，但　係　我　唔　識　你　㗎　喎。

The number is correct, but I don't know you.

Yihp: Haih wo. Néih bá sēng hóu mh tùhng wo.

葉：   係　喎。你　把　聲　好　唔　同　喎。

Oh yes! Something is wrong with your voice.

Séi la! Ngóh béi yàhn āak jó chín!

死　喇！我　畀　人　呃咗　錢！

Oh no! I've been cheated!

Wòhng: Néih faai dī bou gíng lā.

王：   你　快　啲　報　警　啦。

You'd better report it to the police.

Questions for the dialogue

Choose the correct answer.　◀402.mp3

1. Kéuih dá dihn-wá wán bīn-go a?

   佢　打電　話搵　邊　個呀？

   a. Wòhng síu-jé　　　b. Yihp Waih Yìuh

   　王　小　姐　　　　　葉　惠　瑤

   c. Wòhng Jan Wàh　　d. John Wong

   　王　振　華

2. Yihp Waih Yìuh dím-gáai yiu wán Wòhng sāang?

   葉　惠　瑤　點　解　要　搵　王　生？

   a. kéuih meih sāu dóu Wòhng sāang ge chín

   　佢　未　收　到　王　生　嘅　錢

   b. giu Wòhng sāang bōng kéuih bou gíng

   　叫　王　生　幫　佢　報　警

   c. mahn Wòhng sāang dím-yéung gwo sou

   　問　王　生　點　樣　過　數

   d. wán Wòhng sāang je chín

   　搵　王　生　借　錢

3. Yáuh māt-yéh haih ngāam ga?
   有 乜 嘢 係 啱 㗎？

   a. *John Wong* mh séung Yihp Waih Yìuh bou gíng
      John Wong 唔 想 葉 惠 瑤 報 警

   b. Wòhng Jan Wàh gwo jó sou béi Yihp Waih Yìuh
      王 振 華 過 咗 數 畀 葉 惠 瑤

   c. *John Wong* sīk Yihp Waih Yìuh
      John Wong 識 葉 惠 瑤

   d. Wòhng Jan Wàh āak jó Yihp Waih Yìuh
      王 振 華 呃 咗 葉 惠 瑤

Story: Wong Sum Yee calling Ming   ◀403.mp3

Ngóh dá dihn wá béi A Mìhng, kéuih mā-mìh tēng dihn-wá.
我　　打電話畀阿明，佢　　媽咪聽電話。
I called Ming. His mother answered the phone.

Kéuih hóu gán-jēung mahn ngóh haih bīn-go, yáuh māt-yéh sih wán A Mìhng.
佢　好緊張　問　我　係邊　個，有乜　嘢事搵阿明。
She was concerned and asked me who I was and why I was calling Ming.

Ngóh wah kéuih jī ngóh haih Wòhng Sām Yìh, haih A Mìhng ge tùhng-hohk,
我　話佢　知我係王　　心　怡，係阿明　　嘅同　學，
I said my name was Wong Sum Yee, a classmate of Ming.

yān-waih ngóh mh sīk yuhng dihn-nóuh, séung mahn háh kéuih.
因　為我唔識用　　電腦，想　　問　吓佢。
I can't use my computer, so I wanted to ask him to help me.

Gám A Mìhng ge mā-mìh jauh wah ngóh jī kéuih meih fāan ūk-kéi,
咁阿明　　嘅媽咪就　話我知佢　未　返屋企，
So Ming's mother told me that he was not home yet

giu ngóh yāt-jahn joi dá gwo heui.
叫我　一陣再打過　去。
and asked me to call again later.

Yùh-gwó ngóh wah ngóh haih A Mìhng ge néuih pàhng-yáuh,
如果　我　話我係阿明　　嘅女朋　友，
If I had said I was Ming's girlfriend,

kéuih mā-mìh yāt-dihng hóu màh-fàahn.
佢　媽咪一定　好麻煩。
his mother would certainly be very annoyed.

Questions for the story

I. Answer the questions.   ◀404.mp3

1. Wòhng Sām Yìh dá dihn-wá béi A Mìhng jouh māt-yéh a?
   王　　心　怡打電　話畀阿明　　做乜　嘢呀？

2. A Mìhng dím-gáai móuh tēng dihn-wá?
   阿明　點解冇　聽電話？

3. A Mìhng ge mā-mìh giu Wòhng Sām Yìh dím-yéung jouh a?
   阿明　　嘅媽咪叫王　　心　怡點樣　　做呀？

4. Wòhng Sām Yìh haih A Mìhng ge bīn-go a?
   王　　心　怡係阿明　　嘅邊個呀？

II. Listen and rearrange the dialogues when Wong Sum Yee called Ming again.

Dialogue A　◀405.mp3

a. Oh. Néih yāt-jahn joi dá làih lā.

哦。你 一 陣 再 打 嚟 啦。

b. Néih haih bīn-wái a?

你 係 邊 位 呀？

c. Hóu aak, mh-gōi saai.

好 呃，唔 該 晒。

d. *Uncle* àh? Ngóh haih A Mìhng ge tùhng-hohk Wòhng Sām Yìh.

Uncle 牙？我 係 阿 明 嘅 同 學 王 心 怡。

e. Mh haih, dáng dáng sīn. Kéuih fāan làih la. A Mìhng, tēng dihn-wá.

唔 係，等 等 先。佢 返 嚟 喇。阿 明，聽 電 話。

f. Kéuih meih fāan ūk-kéi. Néih mē sih wán kéuih a?

佢 未 返 屋 企。你 咩 事 搵 佢 呀？

g. Wái? Mh-gōi A Mìhng hái douh ma?

喂？唔 該 阿 明 喺 度 嗎？

h. Ngóh ge dihn-nóuh yáuh mahn-tàih, séung kéuih bōng háh ngóh.

我 嘅 電 腦 有 問 題，想 佢 幫 吓 我。

Dialogue B　◀406.mp3

a. Nèih si háh sīk gēi joi hōi gwo lā.

你 試 吓 熄 機 再 開 過 啦。

b. Gám ngóh làih bōng néih *check* háh lā.

咁 我 嚟 幫 你 check 吓 啦。

Néih tīng-yaht géi-dím dāk-hàahn a?

你 聽 日 幾 點 得 閒 呀？

c. Wái? A Mìhng, ngóh ge dihn-nóuh béi sai-lóu yuhng yùhn,

喂？阿 明，我 嘅 電 腦 畀 細 佬 用 完，

yāt séuhng móhng jauh *hang* gēi, dím syun a?

一 上 網 就 hang 機，點 算 呀？

d. Há? Yāt fāan ūk-kéi jauh joi chēut heui?

吓？一 返 屋 企 就 再 出 去？

e. Hóu lā, néih dáng ngóh lā.

好 啦，你 等 我 啦。

f. Si jó la. Mh dāk a. Néih làih tái háh, bōng háh ngóh lā.

試 咗 喇。唔 得 呀。你 嚟 睇 吓，幫 吓 我 啦。

g. Hóu lā, mh-gōi néih lā. Ngóh chéng néih sihk yéh.

好 啦，唔 該 你 啦。我 請 你 食 嘢。

h. Mh hóu dáng tīng-yaht lā. Néih jīk-hāak làih bōng ngóh lā.

唔 好 等 聽 日 啦。你 即 刻 嚟 幫 我 啦。

Vocabulary ◀407.mp3

1.	yāt bá sēng	一把聲	a voice
2.	dihn-nóuh	電腦	computer (literally, electric brain)
3.	sai-lóu	細佬	younger brother
4.	sāu	收	to receive; to collect
5.	āak	呃	to cheat
6.	séi	死	to die
7.	yuhng	用	to use
8.	si	試	to try
9.	chéng	請	to treat; to invite
10.	hōi	開	to turn on (a machine); to open
11.	fāan làih	返嚟	to come back
12.	gwo sou	過數	money transfer
13.	bou gíng	報警	to report to the police
14.	mh-tùhng	唔同	different (literally, not the same)
15.	séuhng móhng	上網	to access to the internet
16.	*hang* gēi	hang 機	computer crash
17.	sīk gēi	熄機	to turn off a machine
18.	gán-jēung	緊張	nervous; excited; concerned
19.	cho	錯	wrong; mistake
20.	yān-waih	因為	because
21.	jīk-hāak	即刻	immediately
22.	verb + háh 吓		indicate casually doing something
23.	yāt 一…… jauh 就……		once . . . then; immediately after
24.	joi 再 + verb + gwo 過		do something again

Grammar practice

I. verb + háh 吓 (to do something casually)   ◄408.mp3

> e.g. Ngóh wán A Mìhng bōng **háh** ngóh.
> 我　　搵　阿明　　幫　吓　我。
> *I asked Ming to help me.*

1. Ngóh séung chēut heui hàahng **háh**.
   我　想　出　去　行　　吓。

2. Ngóh-deih si **háh** hàahng sān ge louh.
   我　　哋　試 吓 行　　新 嘅 路。

3. Séuhng móhng *check* **háh** tīng-yaht ge tīn-hei.
   上　　網　　check 吓　聽　日 嘅 天氣。

4. Yáuh hóu dō mahn-tàih, ngóh yiu tái **háh** dím-gáai.
   有　好 多 問　題，我　要 睇 吓　點　解。

✎ **Practice**

Complete the sentences using "háh 吓".

a. Néih hóu guih wo, _____
   你　好 劫　喎，

b. Néih _____ jūng mh jūng-yi nī gihn sāam.
   你　　　　　　鍾 唔 鍾 意 呢 件　衫。

c. Fong ga bāt-yùh heui Chek-Chyúh _____.
   放　假 不 如 去 赤　柱

d. Ngóh-deih gam ngāam dāk-hàahn, heui _____ lā.
   我　　哋 咁 啱．得　閒，去　　　　啦。

II. joi 再 + verb + gwo 過 (to do something again)   ◄409.mp3

> e.g., *Hang* gēi jauh sīk gēi **joi** hōi **gwo**.
> Hang 機 就　熄機 再 開 過。
> *When the computer crashes, turn it off and start it again.*

1. Dá cho dihn-wá, **joi** dá **gwo**.
   打　錯 電　話，再打 過。

2. Hái chāan-tēng sihk mh báau, fāan ūk-kéi **joi** sihk **gwo**.
   喺 餐　　廳 食 唔 飽，返 屋 企 再 食　過。

3. Yuhng yùhn dihn-chìh yiu **joi** máaih **gwo**.
   用　完　電　池 要 再 買　過。

✎ **Practice**

Make sentences using "joi 再……gwo 過" and the following phrases.
a. chéng 請   b. tái 睇   c. si 試

III. yāt 一……jauh 就 (immediately after; once . . . then)   ◀410.mp3

> e.g., Ngóh ge dihn-nóuh **yāt** séuhng móhng **jauh** hang gēi.
> 我　嘅電腦　一上　　網　　就　　hang 機。
> *My computer crashes whenever I use the internet.*

1. **Yāt** gán-jēung **jauh** mh sīk góng yéh.
   一　緊張　　就　唔識　講　嘢。

2. **Yāt** chīm jó méng **jauh** sāu dóu chín.
   一　簽　咗名　就　　收　到　錢。

3. Kéuih **yāt** jī béi yàhn āak **jauh** bou gíng.
   佢　　一知畀人　呃就　　報　警。

4. **Yāt** wah chéng kéuih sihk yéh **jauh** làih,
   一　話　請　　佢　食　嘢就　嚟，

   giu kéuih jouh yéh jauh hóu noih dōu meih dāk.
   叫　佢　做　嘢就　好　耐　都　未　得。

✎ **Practice**

Complete the sentences.

a. Yāt séuhng chē jauh _____
   一　上　　車　就

b. Yāt tēng dóu hóu pàhng-yáuh bá sēng jauh _____
   一　聽　到　好朋　　友　把聲　就

c. Yāt lohk yúh jauh _____
   一　落　雨　就

IV. béi 畀 (by someone, usually the situation is not good)   ◀411.mp3

> e.g., Ngóh **béi** yàhn āak jó chín.
> 我　畀人　呃咗錢。
> *Someone has cheated me.*
>
> Ngóh ge dihn-nóuh **béi** sai-lóu yuhng yùhn jauh hang gēi.
> 我　嘅電腦　畀細佬用　　完　　就　hang 機。
> *My computer crashed after my younger brother used it.*

1. Kéuih mh séung **béi** yàhn gin dóu.
   佢　唔想　畀人　見　到。

2. Nī go **béi** yàhn yuhng gwo, mh haih sān ge.
   呢個畀人　用　　過，唔係　新　嘅。

3. Dahk-ga fo hóu faai **béi** yàhn máaih jó.
   特　價貨好　快　畀人　買　咗。

Alternative way to describe the same situation without using "béi 畀".

Ngóh **béi** yàhn āak jó chín.
我　畀人　呃咗　錢。

☞ Yáuh yàhn āak jó ngóh ge chín.
有　人　呃咗我　嘅錢。

Ngóh ge dihn-nóuh **béi** sai-lóu yuhng yùhn jauh *hang* gēi.
我　嘅電　腦　畀細佬用　　完　就　hang 機。

☞ Sai-lóu yuhng yùhn ngóh ge dihn-nóuh jauh *hang* gēi.
細佬用　　完　我　嘅電　腦　就　hang 機。

✎ Practice

Rewrite the following sentences using "béi 畀".

a. Kéuih mh séung yàhn bōng kéuih.
   佢　唔想　人　幫　佢。
   ☞

b. Pàhng-yáuh je jó ngóh ge syū.
   朋　友　借咗我　嘅書。
   ☞

c. Mā-mìh yuhng gwo néih ge dihn-nóuh.
   媽咪用　　過你　嘅電　腦。
   ☞

Review: Other usage of "béi 畀" ◄412.mp3

1. give
   Mh-gōi **béi** bá dōu ngóh.
   唔該畀把刀我。
   Please give me a knife.

2. pay (money)
   Ngóh mh gei-dāk **béi** chín.
   我　唔記得畀錢。
   I forgot to pay.

Ngóh **béi** jó yāt baak māan dehng nī bún syū.
我　界咗一百　蚊訂　呢本書。
I paid $100 to reserve this book.

3. (give) to

Ngóh je bá jē **béi** néih lā.
我　借把遮界你　啦。
I'll lend you an umbrella.

Ngóh máaih sāang-yaht láih-maht **béi** pàhng-yáuh.
我　買　生　日　禮　物　界朋　　友。
I'm going to buy a birthday present for my friend.

4. let, allow

Mh hóu **béi** mā-mìh jī.
唔　好　界媽　咪　知。
Don't let Mother know about this.

Mh-gōi **béi** tìuh louh hàahng háh.
唔　該　界條　路　行　吓。
Please give way for people to walk through.

V. cho 錯 (wrong; mistake)　◀413.mp3

> e.g., Néih dá **cho** dihn-wá la.
> 你　打　錯　電　話　喇。
> *You have dialled the wrong number.*

1. Ngóh-deih hàahng **cho** louh. Bīn tìuh louh ngāam a?
我　哋　行　　錯　路。邊　條　路　啱　呀？

2. Móuh **cho**, néih móuh tēng **cho**, haih kéuih góng **cho**.
冇　　錯，你　冇　　聽　錯，係　佢　講　錯。

3. Yáuh móuh gáau **cho**? Kéuih daap **cho** chē heui jó bīn-douh a?
有　冇　搞　　錯？佢　搭　錯　車　去　咗邊　度　呀？

VI. mh-tùhng 唔同 (different)　◀414.mp3

> e.g., Néih bá sēng hóu **mh tùhng**.
> 你　把　聲　好　唔　同。
> *Something is wrong with your voice.*

1. Kéuih ge chīm méng **mh tùhng** jó.
佢　　嘅　簽　名　唔　同　咗。

2. Sai-lóu **mh tùhng** nàahm pàhng-yáuh, mh wúih tēng néih góng.
細　佬　唔　同　　男　　朋　　友，唔　會　聽　néih 講。

3. A: Nī go tùhng gó go yáuh māt-yéh **mh tùhng**?

呢 個 同　果 個 有　乜 嘢 唔 同 ？

B: Móuh **mh tùhng**, daahn-haih mh jī dím-gáai nī go gwai dī.

冇　唔 同 ，　但　係 唔 知 點 解 呢 個 貴　啲 。

VII. jīk-hāak 即刻 (immediately)　◄415.mp3

> e.g., Néih **jīk-hāak** làih bōng ngóh lā.
>
> 你　即 刻　嚟 幫　我　啦 。
>
> *Please come to help me right away.*

1. Hóu faai lohk daaih yúh, ngóh-deih **jīk-hāak** jáu lā.

好 快 落 大　雨 ，我　哋 即 刻　走 啦 。

2. Ngóh lauh-jó daai kāat, séung **jīk-hāak** fāan ūk-kéi ló.

我 漏 咗 帶 卡 ，想　即 刻　返 屋 企 攞 。

3. Ngóh wah móuh sáan-jí, kéuih **jīk-hāak** cheung béi ngóh.

我 話 冇　散　子 ，佢 即 刻　唱　畀 我 。

4. Ngóh **jīk-hāak** giu sī-gēi hái gāai-háu tìhng chē.

我　即 刻　叫 司 機 喺 街　口　停　車 。

Pyramid drill ◀416.mp3

1.

gwo sou béi ngóh

過　數　畀　我

jīk-hāak gwo sou béi ngóh

即　刻　過　數　畀　我

séuhng móhng jīk-hāak gwo sou béi ngóh

上　　網　即　刻　過　數　畀　我

néih si háh séuhng móhng, jīk-hāak gwo sou béi ngóh

你　試　吓　上　　網，即　刻　過　數　畀　我

Bāt-yùh néih si háh séuhng móhng, jīk-hāak gwo sou béi ngóh.

不　如　你　試　吓　上　　網，即　刻　過　數　畀　我。

Can you transfer money to me online right away?

2.

joi hōi gwo

再　開　過

sīk gēi joi hōi gwo

熄　機　再　開　過

dihn-nóuh yiu sīk gēi joi hōi gwo

電　腦　要　熄　機　再　開　過

dihn-nóuh *hang* gēi, yiu sīk gēi joi hōi gwo

電　腦　hang　機，要　熄　機　再　開　過

Yāt hōi dihn-nóuh jauh *hang* gēi, yiu sīk gēi joi hōi gwo.

一　開　電　腦　就　hang　機，要　熄　機　再　開　過。

The computer crashed immediately after being turned on;
I have to shut it down and start again.

General review

I. Match the questions with the answers. ◀417.mp3

1. Yùh-gwó lauh jó jē, néih wúih joi máaih gwo sān ge dihng fāan ūk-kéi ló?
   如 果 漏 咗 遮，你 會 再 買 過 新 嘅 定 返 屋 企 攞？

2. Néih séuhng chē géi-noih jauh fan jeuhk gaau?
   你 上 車 幾 耐 就 瞓 着 覺？

3. Néih béi yàhn āak jó yih baak mān, wúih mh wúih bou gíng a?
   你 畀 人 呃 咗 二 百 蚊，會 唔 會 報 警 呀？

4. Dihn-chìh yuhng yùhn meih a? Sái mh sái sīk gēi a?
   電 池 用 完 未 呀？使 唔 使 熄 機 呀？

5. Ngóh dím-yéung wán dóu jáu-dim a?
   我 點 樣 搵 到 酒 店 呀？

6. Néih kàhm-yaht gwo jó sou béi kéuih meih a?
   你 琴 日 過 咗 數 畀 佢 未 呀？

☐ a. Dihn-chìh hóu faai yuhng yùhn, yiu sīk gēi la.
   電 池 好 快 用 完，要 熄 機 喇。

☐ b. Kàhm-yaht gwo mh dóu sou béi kéuih, gām-yaht joi gwo gwo.
   琴 日 過 唔 到 數 畀 佢，今 日 再 過 過。

☐ c. Ngóh séuhng chē sāam fān-jūng, yíh-gīng fan jeuhk gaau.
   我 上 車 三 分 鐘，已 經 瞓 着 覺。

☐ d. Néih lohk jó chē mahn háh yàhn jauh wán dóu jáu-dim la.
   你 落 咗 車 問 吓 人 就 搵 到 酒 店 喇。

☐ e. Ngóh béi yàhn āak jó chín, yāt-dihng wúih bou gíng.
   我 畀 人 呃 咗 錢，一 定 會 報 警。

☐ f. Ngóh jīk-hāak joi máaih gwo sān ge jē.
   我 即 刻 再 買 過 新 嘅 遮。

II. Write conversations beginning with the following sentences. ◀418.mp3

1. Nī chi hóu màh-fàahn, néih yiu bōng háh ngóh.
   呢 次 好 麻 煩， 你 要 幫 吓 我。

2. Ngóh gām-jīu luhk dím séng jó, gān-jyuh joi fan gwo.
   我 今 朝 六 點 醒 咗，跟 住 再 瞓 過。

III. Listen and complete the following dialogues with expressions in the table. ◀419.mp3

Aìh yah! Ngóh mh gau sáan-jí daap síu-bā. 哎 吔！我 唔 夠 散 子搭 小巴。
Fong gūng ge sìh-hauh hōi-chí lohk yúh, jān-haih màh-fàahn! 放 工 嘅時候 開 始 落 雨，真 係 麻 煩！
Géi chín yāt go yàhn a? 幾 錢 一 個人 呀？
Hóu yéh! Mh gōi saai! Néih jān-haih hóu yàhn! 好 嘢！唔 該 晒！你 真 係 好 人！
Mh-gōi, bīn ga chē heui Chek-Chyúh Gwóng-Chèuhng ga? 唔 該，邊架 車 去 赤 柱 廣 場 㗎？
Móuh mahn-tàih, cheung béi néih lā. 冇 問 題，唱 畀 你 啦。
Ngóh jīk-hāak jáu dōu dāk. Hàahng lā. 我 即 刻 走 都 得。行 啦。

1.
A: _____

B: Néih daap 6X lā.
你 搭 6X 啦。

A: _____

B: Mh jī a. Néih séuhng chē mahn sī-gēi lā.
唔 知呀。你 上 車 問 司機 啦。

2.
A: _____

B: Móuh mahn-tàih.
冇 問 題。

Ngóh ge chē paak hái làuh-hah, bāt-yùh ngóh chē néih jáu lā.
我 嘅車 泊 喺樓 下，不 如 我 車 你 走啦。

A: _____

B: Néih jáu meih a? Yāt-chàih hàahng lā.
你 走 未 呀？一 齊 行 啦。

A: _____

3.
A: _____

Mh-gōi, néih yáuh móuh yih sahp mān sáan-jí a?
唔 該，你 有 冇 二 十 蚊 散 子呀？

B: _____

A: Jān-haih mh-gōi saai.
真 係 唔 該 晒。

Answers

Dialogue

1. c 2. a 3. d

1. Who is she calling?
    a. Miss Wong   b. Yip Wai Yiu   c. Wong Chun Wah   d. John Wong
2. Why does Yip Wai Yiu have to call Mr. Wong?
    a. She hasn't received any money from Mr. Wong.
    b. She asked Mr. Wong to help her call the police.
    c. She asked Mr. Wong how to transfer money to other bank accounts.
    d. She called Mr. Wong to borrow money.
3. Which one is correct?
    a. John Wong doesn't want Yip Wai Yiu to call the police.
    b. Wong Chun Wah has his money transferred to Yip Wai Yiu's account.
    c. John Wong knows Yip Wai Yiu.
    d. Wong Chun Wah cheated Yip Wai Yiu.

Story

I.

1. Wòhng Sām Yìh dá dihn-wá béi A Mìhng jouh māt-yéh a?
    王　心　怡打電話畀阿明　做乜　嘢呀？
    Why did Wong Sum Yee call Ming?

    Wòhng Sām Yìh mh sīk yuhng dihn-nóuh, séung mahn háh A Mìhng.
    王　心　怡唔識用　電腦，想　問　吓阿明。
    Wong Sum Yee can't use her computer, so she wanted to ask Ming.

2. A Mìhng dím-gáai móuh tēng dihn-wá?
    阿明　點解冇聽　電　話？
    Why didn't Ming answer the phone?

    A Mìhng meih fāan ūk-kéi, tēng mh dóu dihn-wá.
    阿明　未　返　屋企，聽　唔到電　話。
    Ming was not at home, so he can't answer the phone.

3. A Mìhng ge mā-mìh giu Wòhng Sām Yìh dím-yéung jouh a?
    阿明　嘅媽咪叫王　心　怡點　樣　做呀？
    What did Ming's mother tell Wong Sum Yee to do?

    A Mìhng ge mā-mìh giu Wòhng Sām Yìh dáng yāt-jahn joi dá gwo heui.
    阿明　嘅媽咪叫王　心　怡等　一　陣再打過　去。
    Ming's mother asked Wong Sum Yee to call again later.

4. Wòhng Sām Yìh haih A Mìhng ge bīn-go a?
    王　心　怡係阿明　嘅邊個呀？
    Who is Wong Sum Yee to Ming?

    Wòhng Sām Yìh haih A Mìhng ge tùhng-hohk tùhng néuih pàhng-yáuh.
    王　心　怡係阿明　嘅同　學同　女朋　友。
    Wong Sum Yee is Ming's classmate and girlfriend.

II.

Dialogue A

g. Yìh: Wái? Mh-gōi A Mìhng hái douh ma?
    怡：喂？唔該阿明　喺度嗎？
    Hello, may I speak to Ming?

b. Bā: Néih haih bīn-wái a?

爸：你 係 邊 位 呀？

May I know who is calling?

d. Yìh: *Uncle* àh? Ngóh haih A Mìhng ge tùhng-hohk Wòhng Sām Yìh.

怡：Uncle 牙？我 係 阿 明 嘅 同 學 王 心 怡。

Hello, uncle. I'm Ming's classmate, Wong Sum Yee.

> * Note: In Chinese, people use "uncle" as a form of address to a friend's father or one's father's friend. "Auntie" as a form of address to a friend's mother or one's mother's friend.

f. Bā: Kéuih meih fāan ūk-kéi. Néih mē sih wán kéuih a?

爸：佢 未 返 屋 企。你 咩 事 搵 佢 呀？

He's not home yet. May I know why you are calling?

h. Yìh: Ngóh ge dihn-nóuh yáuh mahn-tàih, séung kéuih bōng háh ngóh.

怡：我 嘅 電 腦 有 問 題，想 佢 幫 吓 我。

There is a problem with my computer, I need his help.

a. Bā: Oh. Néih yāt-jahn joi dá làih lā.

爸：哦。你 一 陣 再 打 嚟 啦。

Oh! Please call again later.

c. Yìh: Hóu aak, mh-gōi saai.

怡：好 呃，唔 該 晒。

OK. Thank you very much.

e. Bā: Mh haih, dáng dáng sīn. Kéuih fāan làih la. A Mìhng, tēng dihn-wá.

爸：唔 係，等 等 先。佢 返 嚟 喇。阿 明，聽 電 話。

No, wait. He's coming. Ming, the call is for you.

Dialogue B

c. Yìh: Wái? A Mìhng, ngóh ge dihn-nóuh béi sai-lóu yuhng yùhn,

怡：喂？阿 明，我 嘅 電 腦 畀 細 佬 用 完，

Hello? Ming. After my brother used my computer

Yāt séuhng móhng jauh *hang* gēi, dím syun a?

一 上 網 就 hang 機，點 算 呀？

it crashes whenever I access the internet. What can I do?

a. Mìhng: Nèih si háh sīk gēi joi hōi gwo lā.

明：你 試 吓 熄 機 再 開 過 啦。

Try to turn it off and start again.

f. Yìh: Si jó la. Mh dāk a. Néih làih tái háh, bōng háh ngóh lā.

怡：試 咗 喇。唔 得 呀。你 嚟 睇 吓，幫 吓 我 啦。

I've tried. It didn't work. Can you come and have a look?

b. Mìhng: Gám ngóh làih bōng néih *check* háh lā.

明：咁 我 嚟 幫 你 check 吓 啦。

OK. I'll go and check it for you.

Néih tīng-yaht géi-dím dāk-hàahn a?

你 聽 日 幾 點 得 閒 呀？

What time will you be free tomorrow?

h. Yìh: Mh hóu dáng tīng-yaht lā. Néih jīk-hāak làih bōng ngóh lā.

怡：唔 好 等 聽 日 啦。你 即 刻 嚟 幫 我 啦。

I don't want to wait until tomorrow. Is it possible for you to come now?

d. Mìhng: Há? Yāt fāan ūk-kéi jauh joi chēut heui?

明：吓？一 返 屋 企 就 再 出 去？

What? Go out again immediately after home?

g. Yìh: Hóu lā, mh-gōi néih lā. Ngóh chéng néih sihk yéh.
怡 : 好 啦，唔 該 你 啦。我 請 你 食 嘢。
Oh please. I'll give you a treat.

e. Mìhng: Hóu lā, néih dáng ngóh lā.
明 : 好 啦，你 等 我 啦。
Ok. I'll be there soon.

Grammar practice translation I

1. I want to go for a walk.
2. We will try a new route.
3. I'll check the weather tomorrow online.
4. There are lots of problems. I have to take a look at why that happened.

Practice answers

a. Néih hóu guih wo, **fan háh lā**.
你 好 边 喎，瞓 吓 啦。
b. Néih **tái háh** jūng mh jūng-yi nī gihn sāam.
你 睇 吓 鍾 唔 鍾 意 呢 件 衫。
c. Fong ga bāt-yùh heui Chek-Chyúh **wáan háh**.
放 假 不 如 去 赤 柱 玩 吓。
d. Ngóh-deih gam ngāam dāk-hàahn, heui **yám háh chàh** lā.
我 哋 咁 啱 得 閒，去 飲 吓 茶 啦。

Grammar practice translation II

1. It was a wrong number. I'll call again.
2. I didn't eat enough in the restaurant. I'll eat more when I get home.
3. The batteries are used up. I need to buy more.

Practice answers

a. Gām-yaht ngóh chéng néih yám chàh,
今 日 我 請 你 飲 茶，
hah sīng-kèih ngóh joi chéng gwo néih sihk faahn.
下 星 期 我 再 請 過 你 食 飯。
Today I treat you to tea. Next week I'll treat you to dinner.
b. Ngóh mh gei-dāk, yiu joi tái gwo.
我 唔 記 得，要 再 睇 過。
I forgot that. I have to read it again.
c. Yāt chi mh dāk, bāt-yùh joi si gwo.
一 次 唔 得，不 如 再 試 過。
Let's try again, if once is not okay.

Grammar practice translation III

1. When I'm nervous, I don't know what to say.
2. You can receive money immediately after you have signed the paper.
3. He called the police immediately after he found out he had been cheated.
4. When I tell him that I'll treat him to a meal, he will come immediately. When I ask him to do something, it takes a long time and still nothing has been done.

Practice answers

a. Yāt séuhng chē jauh **dá dihn-wá béi néih**.
一 上 車 就 打 電 話 畀 你。
b. Yāt tēng dóu hóu pàhng-yáuh bá sēng jauh **hóu hōi-sām**.
一 聽 到 好 朋 友 把 聲 就 好 開 心。
c. Yāt lohk yúh jauh **faai dī fāan ūk-kéi**.
一 落 雨 就 快 啲 返 屋 企。

Grammar practice translation IV

1. He doesn't want people to see him.
2. Someone has used it; it's not new.
3. People buy bargains quickly.

Practice answers

a. Kéuih mh séung yàhn bōng kéuih.
佢　唔　想　人　幫　佢。
☞ Kéuih mh séung béi yàhn bōng.
佢　唔　想　畀　人　幫。
He doesn't want anyone to help him.

b. Pàhng-yáuh je jó ngóh ge syū.
朋　　友　借咗我　嘅書。
☞ Ngóh ge syū béi pàhng-yáuh je jó.
我　　嘅書畀朋　　友　借咗。
A friend borrowed my book.

c. Mā-mìh yuhng gwo néih ge dihn-nóuh.
媽　咪　用　　過　你　嘅　電　腦。
☞ Néih ge dihn-nóuh béi mā-mìh yuhng gwo.
你　嘅電　腦　畀媽　咪　用　　過。
Your mother has used your computer.

Grammar practice translation V

1. We have gone the wrong way. Which way is right?
2. You're correct. You haven't mistaken what you heard. It is he who said it wrong.
3. How can this be possible? He took the wrong bus. Where has he gone?

Grammar practice translation VI

1. His signature has changed. It's different.
2. A younger brother is different from a boyfriend; he won't listen to you.
3. A: What's the difference between this one and that one?
   B: There is no difference, but I don't know why this one is more expensive.

Grammar practice translation VII

1. It's going to rain heavily soon; we'll leave now.
2. I forgot to bring the card. I want to go home and get it.
3. I said I have no coins and he gave me change.
4. I immediately asked the driver to stop at the intersection.

General review

I.

1. If you forgot your umbrella, will you buy a new one, or will you go home to get it?
   f. I'll buy a new one right away.
2. How long does it take you to fall asleep on the bus?
   c. I'll fall asleep after 3 minutes.
3. If someone cheated you out of $200, would you report it to the police?
   e. If I'm being cheated, I'll certainly report it to the police.
4. Is the battery used up? Do I have to turn off the machine?
   a. The battery will soon be used up; you have to turn off the machine.
5. How can I find the hotel?
   d. Ask people after you get off the bus; then you can find the hotel.
6. Did you transfer the money to his account yesterday?
   b. I couldn't transfer money to his account yesterday. I'll try again today.

II. Suggested conversations

1.

A: Nī chi hóu màh-fàahn, néih yiu bōng háh ngóh.
呢 次 好 麻 煩， 你 要 幫 吓 我。
This time, I am in big trouble. You have to help me.

B: Néih séung ngóh dím-yéung bōng néih a?
你 想 我 點 樣 幫 你 呀？
How do you want me to help you?

A: Ngóh dihn-nóuh *hang jó gēi……*
我 電 腦 hang 咗 機……
My computer crashed.

B: Oh móuh mahn-tàih. Ngóh bōng néih tái háh lā.
哦， 冇 問 題。我 幫 你 睇 吓 啦。
I see. No problem. I'll take a look.

2.

A: Ngóh gām-jīu luhk dím séng jó, gān-jyuh joi fan gwo.
我 今 朝 六 點 醒 咗，跟 住 再 瞓 過。
I woke up at six o'clock this morning, then I went back to sleep.

B: Néih joi séng haih géi dím a?
你 再 醒 係 幾 點 呀？
When you woke up again, what time was it?

A: Ngóh yāt séng jauh gáu dím la.
我 一 醒 就 九 點 喇。
When I woke up, it was already 9:00.

III.

1.

A: **Mh-gōi, bīn ga chē heui Chek-Chyúh Gwóng-Chèuhng ga?**
唔 該，邊 架 車 去 赤 柱 廣 場 㗎？
Excuse me, which bus goes to Stanley Plaza?

B: Néih daap 6X lā.
你 搭 6X 啦。
You can take bus 6X.

A: **Géi chín yāt go yàhn a?**
幾 錢 一 個 人 呀？
What is the fare?

B: Mh jī a. Néih séuhng chē mahn sī-gēi lā.
唔 知 呀。你 上 車 問 司機 啦。
I don't know; ask the driver when you get on.

2.

A: **Fong gūng ge sìh-hauh hōi-chí lohk yúh, jān-haih màh-fàahn!**
放 工 嘅 時候 開 始 落 雨，真 係 麻 煩！
It began to rain when we finished work. That's really annoying!

B: Móuh mahn-tàih.
冇 問 題。
No problem.

Ngóh ge chē paak hái làuh-hah, bāt-yùh ngóh chē néih jáu lā.
我 嘅 車 泊 喺 樓 下，不 如 我 車 你 走 啦。
My car is parked downstairs; I can give you a lift.

A: **Hóu yéh! Mh gōi saai! Néih jān-haih hóu yàhn!**

好 嘢!唔 該 晒!你 真 係 好 人!

That's great! Thank you so much! You're so kind!

B: Néih jáu meih a? Yāt-chàih hàahng lā.

你 走 未 呀?一 齊 行 啦。

Are you ready to leave? Let's go.

A: **Ngóh jīk-hāak jáu dōu dāk. Hàahng lā.**

我 即 刻 走 都 得。行 啦。

I can leave now. Let's go.

3.

A: **Aìh yah! Ngóh mh gau sáan-jí daap síu-bā.**

哎 吔!我 唔 夠 散 子搭 小 巴。

Oh no! I don't have enough small change to take the minibus.

Mh-gōi, néih yáuh móuh yih sahp mān sáan-jí a?

唔 該,你 有 冇 二 十 蚊 散 子呀?

Excuse me; do you have $20 in change?

B: **Móuh mahn-tàih, cheung béi néih lā.**

冇 問 題,唱 畀 你 啦。

No problem. I'll give you change.

A: Jān-haih mh-gōi saai.

真 係 唔 該 晒。

Thank you very much.

Hong Kong culture

Useful facts about phone numbers

The phone numbers in Hong Kong are mostly eight digits.

Mobile phones begin with 5, 6, and 9. Home and office numbers begin with 2 and 3. When the phone system changed from 7 digits to 8 digits, 2 was added before all existing numbers, so phone numbers beginning with 2 are older numbers and therefore are less likely to be bogus numbers used for the purpose of marketing, advertising, or phone scames.

The Hong Kong area code for international calls is 852.

However, beware of phone numbers with +852 displayed. They are likely bogus calls, because +852 is not supposed to be displayed as part of the fixed local numbers. Such calls are made by using prepaid SIM cards bought in convenience stores without requiring user registration; in other words, no personal details of the user can be tracked.

When buying a new mobile phone through a local telecom service provider, customers are given a list from which to choose their new phone number. People prefer to have lucky numbers and avoid unlucky ones.

Numbers such as 1, 2, 6, 8, and 9 are generally considered lucky.

2, yih, sounds like easy. 易 yih.

3, sāam, sounds like alive, lively. 生 sāang.

6, luhk, is associated with endless and continuous. 六六無窮 luhk luhk mòuh kùhng, 陸續 luhk juhk.

8, baat, sounds like get wealthy and be prosperous. 發 faat.

9, gáu, sounds like long lasting and forever. 久 gáu.

Combinations of these numbers are very popular.

28, yih baat, sounds like easy to make money. 易發 yih faat.

118, yāt yāt baat, sounds like to make money and be prosperous every day. 日日發 yaht yaht faat.

138, yāt sāam baat, sounds like make money and be prosperous your whole life. 一生發 yāt sāng faat.

168, yāt luhk baat, sounds like make money and be prosperous wherever you go. 一路發 yāt louh faat.

668, luhk luhk baat, sounds like you can make money and be prosperous wherever you go. 路路發 louh louh faat.

Unlucky numbers are:

4, sei, sounds like death. 死 séi.

5, ngh, sounds like no or not. 唔 mh

Hong Kong people also avoid the following combinations.

58, ngh baat, sounds like not making money and not prosperous. 唔發 mh faat.

528, ngh yih baat, sounds like not easy to make money and not prosperous. 唔易發 mh yih faat.

1358, yāt sāam ngh baat, sounds like a whole life of not making money. 一生唔發 yāt sāng mh faat.

5354, ngh sāam ngh sei, sounds like cannot achieve anything, fit for nothing. 唔三唔四 mh sāam mh sei. Also sounds like neither alive nor dead. 唔生唔死 mh sāang mh séi.

9413, gáu sei yāt sāam, sounds like a narrow escape from death, literally 90% dead, 10% alive. 九死一生 gáu séi yāt sang.

709394, chat lìhng gáu sāam gáu sei, sounds like fooling around. 出嚟搞三搞四 chēut làih gáau sāam gáau sei.

5
Taking sick leave

Dialogue ◄501.mp3

➤ Why is Kei calling Mei Nei?

➤ How does he feel?

➤ Has he seen a doctor?

➤ What must he do today?

➤ Why can't they do it another day?

Gēi: Wái? Méih Nèih, ngóh haih A Gēi.
基： 喂？美　妮，我　係　阿基。

      Mh-gōi néih bōng ngóh chéng ga lā.
      唔 該 你 幫 我 請 假 啦。
      Hello, Mei Nei. This is Kei. I have to take leave; please tell the office manager.

      Ngóh gām-yaht mh syū-fuhk, fāan mh dóu gūng.
      我 今 日 唔 舒 服，返 唔 到 工。
      I'm not feeling well and am unable to go to work today.

M N: Oh. Néih mē sih mh syū-fuhk a?
美妮：哦。你　咩 事 唔 舒 服 呀？
      I see. What's wrong?

Gēi: Ngóh gám-mouh, faat gán sīu, juhng hóu tàuh-tung tīm a!
基： 我　感 冒，發 緊 燒，仲　好 頭 痛 添 呀！
      I have the flu. I have a fever and a bad headache.

M N: Néih tái jó yī-sāng meih a? Yáuh móuh sihk yeuhk a?
美妮：你 睇 咗 醫 生 未 呀？有 冇　食 藥 呀？
      Have you seen a doctor yet? Have you taken any medicine?

Gēi: Kàhm-máahn sihk jó yeuhk, móuh yuhng ge.
基： 琴　晚　食 咗 藥，冇　用　嘅。
      I took some medicine last night; it didn't help.

      Ngóh yāt-jahn heui tái yī-sāng la.
      我　一 陣 去 睇 醫 生　喇。
      I'll go to the doctor later.

M N: Néih yāu-sīk dō-dī lā.
美妮：你　休　息　多　啲　啦。
Take some rest.

Séi la! Néih mh-fāan-gūng, gām-yaht hōi wúi dím a?
死　喇！你　唔　返　工，今　日　開　會　點　呀？
Oh no! You're not coming to work. What will happen at the meeting today?

Ngóh-deih dáng néih tùhng go haak pih-sēn ga wo.
我　哋　等　你　同　個　客　present 㗎喎。
We're depending on you to give a presentation to the client.

Gēi: Gói kèih dāk mh-dāk a? Ngóh behng dou séi-háh séi-háh,
基：　改　期　得　唔　得　呀？我　病　到　死　吓　死　吓，
Can we change the date? I'm so sick, I'm dying,

juhng yiu tùhng go haak pih-sēn?
仲　要　同　個　客　present?
and I still have to give the client a presentation?

M N: Lóuh-sai tùhng go haak dāk gām-yaht dāk-hàahn.
美妮：老　細　同　個　客　得　今　日　得　閒。
The boss and the client are only free today.

Néih tùhng lóuh-sai góng lā.
你　同　老　細　講　啦。
You'd better talk to our boss.

Gēi: Chī-sin ga! Gám ngóh heui tái yùhn yī-sāng fāan làih hōi wúi lā.
基：　黐　線　㗎！咁　我　去　睇　完　醫　生　返　嚟　開　會　啦。
That's crazy! I'd better go back for the meeting after seeing a doctor.

Story: Suffering from a fever ◀502.mp3

Kàhm-yaht ngóh hōi yùhn wúi hóu guih, guih dou tàuh-tung,
琴　日　我　開　完　會　好　劫，劫　到　頭　痛，
I felt so tired after the meeting yesterday that I had a headache,

jauh faai dī fāan ūk-kéi yāu-sīk. Sihk yùhn máahn-faahn, ngóh hōi-chí faat-sīu,
就　快　啲　返　屋　企　休　息。食　完　晚　飯，我　開　始　發　燒，
so I went right home to rest. After dinner, a fever began.

sīu dou yāt baak lìhng yih douh. Ngóh jīk-hāak sihk yeuhk,
燒　到　一　百　零　二　度。我　即　刻　食　藥，
It went up to 102 degrees. I took some medicine

gān-jyuh heui fan-gaau. Daahn-haih sèhng máahn fan mh jeuhk,
跟　住　去　瞓　覺。但　係　成　晚　瞓　唔　着，
and then went to bed. However, I couldn't sleep all night,

mh tìhng làuh beih-séui, hóu sān-fú. Gām jīu ngóh juhng haih behng gán,
唔　停　流　鼻　水，好　辛　苦。今　朝　我　仲　係　病　緊，
I have a very runny nose; it was awful. This morning I was still feeling sick,

jauh chéng ga heui tái yī-sāng.
就　請　假　去　睇　醫　生。
so I took leave and went to see a doctor.

Yī-sāng wah ngóh haih gám-mouh, yāt-dihng yiu yāu-sīk dō dī.
醫生　話　我　係　感　冒，一　定　要　休　息　多　啲。
The doctor said it was a cold. I need to rest more.

Questions for the story

I. Complete the dialogue between a doctor and a patient with expressions in the table.　◀503.mp3

géi-sih hōi-chí faat-sīu 幾　時　開　始　發　燒	yāu-sīk dō dī 休　息　多　啲
tàuh-tung dou hóu sān-fú 頭　痛　到　好　辛　苦	mh tìhng làuh beih-séui 唔　停　流　鼻　水
ngóh gám-mouh, faat sīu 我　感　冒、發　燒	béi néih yāu-sīk léuhng yaht 畀　你　休　息　兩　日
sīu dou yāt baak lìhng yih douh 燒　到　一　百　零　二　度	ngóh yiu tùhng gūng-sī chéng ga 我　要　同　公　司　請　假

D:　Bīn-douh mh-syū-fuhk a?
醫生：邊　度　唔　舒　服　呀？

P:　_____
病人：

D:　　Faat-sīu, sīu dou géi-dō douh a?
醫生：發　燒，燒到　幾　多　度　呀？

P:　　_____
病人：

D:　　_____ ga?
醫生：　　　　　　　喫？

P:　　Kàhm-máahn sihk yùhn faahn hōi-chí.
病人：琴　晚　食　完　飯　開　始。

D:　　Yáuh móuh tàuh-wàhn, tàuh-tung a?
醫生：有　冇　頭　暈、頭　痛　呀？

P:　　_____, juhng yáuh hàuh-lùhng tung.
病人：　　　　　　　，仲　有　喉　嚨　痛。

D:　　Juhng yáuh māt-yéh mh syū-fuhk a?
醫生：仲　有　乜　嘢　唔　舒　服　呀？

P:　　Ngóh sèhng yaht dá hāt-chī,_____.
病人：我　成　日　打　乞　嗤，

D:　　Yám dō dī séui,_____ lā. Dāk ga la. Néih heui ló yeuhk lā
醫生：飲　多　啲　水　　　　　　啦。得　喫喇。你　去　攞藥　啦。

P:　　Yī-sāng,_____.
病人：醫　生，

　　　Mh-gōi sé yī-sāng jí béi ngóh lā.
　　　唔　該　寫　醫　生　紙　畀　我　啦。

D:　　Ngóh sé jí_____ lā.
醫生：我　寫　紙　　　　　　　　　啦。

II. Choose the correct answer.　◀504.mp3

1. Kéuih móuh māt-yéh mh syū-fuhk a?
　　佢　冇　乜　嘢　唔　舒　服　呀？

　　a. faat-sīu　　　b. làuh beih-séui　　c. tàuh-wàhn　　d. hàuh-lùhng tung
　　　發　燒　　　　流　鼻　水　　　　頭　暈　　　　喉　嚨　痛

2. Kéuih géi-sìh hōi-chí faat-sīu?
　　佢　幾　時　開　始　發　燒？

　　a. kàhm máahn　b. gām máahn　　c. gām jīu　　d. hōi yùhn wúi
　　　琴　晚　　　　今　晚　　　　今　朝　　　開　完　會

3. Kéuih dím-gáai fan mh jeuhk a?
   佢　點　解　瞓　唔　着　呀？

   a. làuh hóu dō beih-séui
      流　好　多　鼻　水

   b. tàuh-tung, hàuh-lùhng tung
      頭　痛、喉　嚨　痛

   c. hōi yùhn wúi taai guih
      開　完　會　太　边

   d. sèhng yaht faat-sīu
      成　日　發　燒

4. Kéuih yiu yī-sāng sé yī-sāng jí jouh māt-yéh a?
   佢　要　醫生　寫　醫生　紙　做　乜　嘢呀？

   a. fong ga heui wáan
      放　假　去　玩

   b. chéng ga yāu-sīk
      請　假　休　息

   c. béi lóuh-pòh tái
      畀　老　婆　睇

   d. tùhng gūng-sī sāu chín
      同　公　司　收　錢

Vocabulary ◀505.mp3

1.	chéng ga	請假	to take leave
2.	yāu-sīk	休息	to rest
3.	hōi wúi	開會	to have a meeting
4.	gói kèih	改期	to change the date
5.	behng	病	ill; illness; sick; sickness
6.	gám-mouh	感冒	cold; influenza
7.	faat sīu	發燒	have a fever
8.	tàuh-wàhn	頭暈	dizzy
9.	tàuh-tung	頭痛	headache
10.	hàuh-lùhng tung	喉嚨痛	sore throat
11.	làuh beih-séui	流鼻水	runny nose
12.	douh	度	degree of temperature
13.	yeuhk	藥	medicine
14.	yī-sāng	醫生	doctor; physician
15.	lóuh-sai	老細	boss
16.	haak	客	client; customer
17.	jóu	早	early
18.	syū-fuhk	舒服	comfortable
	mh syū-fuhk	唔舒服	uncomfortable; not feeling well
19.	guih	劫	tired
20.	sān-fú	辛苦	suffering
21.	chī-sin	黐線	crazy (literally, someone has crossed wires)
22.	kàhm máahn	琴晚	last night (literally, yesterday night)
23.	sèhng	成	whole; entire
	sèhng yaht	成日	all day; very often; whole day
24.	juhng	仲	still no change; continue to be
25.	tīm	添	(sentence particle) in addition; and more
26.	verb + gán 緊		indicating action in progress

Grammar practice

I. adjective/verb + dou 到 (to an extent)   ◀506.mp3

> e.g., Ngóh behng **dou** séi-háh séi-háh.
> 我　病　到　死吓　死吓。
> *I'm so sick that I'm dying.*
>
> Ngóh faat-sīu, sīu **dou** yāt baak lìhng yih douh.
> 我　發　燒，燒到　一百　零　二　度。
> *I have a fever, up to 102 degrees.*

1. Ngóh hōi yùhn wúi, guih **dou** tàuh-tung.
   我　開　完　會，攰　到　頭　痛。

2. Gán-jēung **dou** tàuh-wàhn.
   緊　張　到　頭　暈。

3. Syū-fuhk **dou** fan jeuhk gaau.
   舒　服　到　瞓　着　覺。

4. Màh-fàahn **dou** móuh pàhng-yáuh.
   麻　煩　到　冇　朋　友。

✎ **Practice**

Make sentences with "dou 到" and the given words.
a. muhn 悶　　b. faai 快　　c. gwai 貴

II. verb + gán 緊 (action in progress)   ◀507.mp3

> e.g., Ngóh faat **gán** sīu.
> 我　發　緊　燒。
> *I am having a fever.*

1. Lohk **gán** yúh wo. Néih jī mh jī a?
   落　緊　雨　喎。你　知　唔　知呀？

2. Ngóh paak **gán** chē, mh dāk-hàahn góng dihn-wá.
   我　泊　緊　車，唔　得　閒　講　電　話。

3. A: Bìh-bī hái bīn-douh a?
   　　B　B　喺　邊　度　呀？

   B: Bìh-bī fan **gán** gaau.
   　　B　B　瞓　緊　覺。

4. Ngóh dou jó Jūng-Wàahn Máh-Tàuh, dáng **gán** néih làih.
   我　到　咗中　環　碼　頭，等　緊　你　嚟。

5. Ngóh hàahng **gán** heui deih-tit-jaahm.
   我　行　緊　去　地　鐵　站。

✎ Practice

a.　Make a sentence with "**gán** 緊".

b.　Put "gán 緊" in the correct places in the sentences.

　　i.　Ngóh mahn néih 我問你

　　ii.　Kéuih sihk faahn 佢食飯

　　iii.　Ngóh máaih yéh 我買嘢

III. verb + jó 咗……meih 未? (Have you done something yet?)　◀508.mp3

> e.g., Néih tái **jó** yī-sāng **meih** a?
> 　　　你　睇咗醫生　未　呀？
> 　　　*Have you seen the doctor yet?*
> 　　　(Yes) Tái jó 睇咗　　　(No) Meih 未

1.　A: Néih sihk **jó** gám-mouh yeuhk **meih** a?
　　　你　食　咗感　冒　藥　未　呀？

　　B: Meih sihk, yìh-gā jīk-hāak sihk.
　　　未　食，而家即　刻　食。

2.　A: Néih máaih **jó** sān ge dihn-nóuh **meih** a?
　　　你　買　咗新嘅電　腦　未　呀？

　　B: Meih máaih, néih tùhng ngóh heui máaih hóu mh hóu a?
　　　未　買，你　同　我　去　買　好　唔　好呀？

3.　A: Néih lohk **jó** chē **meih** a?
　　　你　落　咗車　未　呀？

　　B: Ngóh gam ngāam hái gāai-háu lohk jó chē la.
　　　我　咁　啱　喺街　口　落　咗車　喇。

4.　A: Néih heui **jó** ngàhn-hòhng cheung chín **meih** a?
　　　你　去　咗銀　行　唱　　錢　未　呀？

　　B: Cheung jó sāam chīn mān, gau mh gau a? Meih gau, ngóh joi heui cheung gwo.
　　　唱　　咗三　千　蚊，夠　唔　夠呀？未　夠，我　再　去　唱　　過。

✎ Practice

Make questions using "jó 咗" and the following phrases, then answer.

a. sihk faahn 食飯　　　b. séng 醒　　　c. gói kèih 改期

Compare the usage of yáuh móuh 有冇 + verb and verb + jó 咗⋯⋯meih 未 ◀509.mp3

> yáuh móuh 有冇 + verb: *Inquire whether an action was completed in the past or not.*
>
> verb + jó 咗⋯⋯ meih 未: *The action is expected to be done sooner or later. Ask whether it has already been done.*

1. A: Néih tái **jó** yī-sāng **meih** a? Meih tái, ngóh tùhng néih heui lā.
   你　睇咗醫生　未　呀？未　睇，我　同　你　去　啦。
   Have you seen the doctor yet? If you haven't, I'll go with you.

   B: Tái jó la.
   睇　咗　喇。

   A: Néih **yáuh móuh** mahn yī-sāng néih māt-yéh behng a?
   你　有　冇　問　醫生　你　乜　嘢　病　呀？
   Did you ask the doctor what illness you are suffering from?

   Yī-sāng dím góng a?
   醫生　點　講　呀？
   What did the doctor say?

   B: Móuh mahn a. Yī-sāng béi jó dī yeuhk ngóh.
   冇　問　呀。醫生界咗啲藥　我。
   I didn't ask. The doctor gave me some medicine.

   Ngóh sihk jó hóu hóu dō la.
   我　食　咗　好　好　多　喇。
   I took some medicine, and I feel much better now.

2. Néih chéng **jó** ga **meih** a?
   你　請　咗假　未　呀？
   Have you asked for leave yet?

   Yáuh móuh wah béi lóuh-sai jī néih mh fāan gūng a?
   有　冇　話界老　細知你　唔　返　工　呀？
   Have you told the boss that you are going to work?

3. A: *Peter* **yáuh móuh** je néih chín a? Kéuih jáu jó wo.
   Peter 有　冇　借你　錢　呀？佢　走　咗　喎。
   Did Peter borrow your money? He has run off.

   B: Haih?! Kéuih je jó ngóh yāt maahn mān a!
   係？！佢　借咗我　一萬　　蚊呀！
   Really?! He borrowed $10,000 from me.

   A: Néih bou **jó** gíng **meih** a?
   你　報　咗警　未　呀？
   Have you reported it to the police?

   B: Meih a. **Yáuh móuh** yuhng a?
   未　呀。有　冇　用　呀？
   Not yet. Does it help?

IV. sèhng 成 + noun (whole; entire)

A. sèhng 成 + counting word + noun (whole, entire)   ◀510.mp3

> e.g., Ngóh **sèhng** máahn fan mh jeuhk.
> 我　成　晚　瞓　唔　着。
> *I couldn't sleep all night.*

1. **Sèhng** gūng-sī yáuh yih sahp go yàhn, kàhm-yaht dāk léuhng go yàhn fāan gūng.
   成　公　司　有　二　十　個　人，琴　日　得　兩　個　人　返　工。

2. **Sèhng** tìuh louh paak jó sahp ga chē.
   成　條　路　泊　咗　十　架　車。

3. Kéuih **sèhng** go dói dōu haih yéh sihk.
   佢　成　個　袋　都　係　嘢　食。

4. Ngóh heui jó Méih-Gwok **sèhng** go sīng-kèih.
   我　去　咗　美　國　成　個　星　期。

✎ Practice

Complete the sentences using "sèhng 成".

1. _____ chē dōu haih fo.
   車　都　係　貨。

2. _____ jáu-dim dāk ngóh-deih jyuh.
   酒　店　得　我　哋　住。

3. Kéuih _____ nìhn dōu fong mh dóu ga.
   佢　　　　年　都　放　唔　到　假。

B. sèhng-yaht 成日 (all day; very often)   ◀511.mp3

> e.g., Ngóh **sèhng-yaht** tàuh-wàhn.
> 我　成　日　頭　暈。
> *I feel dizzy all day long. / I often feel dizzy.*

1. Ngóh **sèhng yaht** hái ūk-kéi.
   我　成　日　喺　屋　企。

2. Ngóh **sèhng-yaht** dōu hóu hōi-sām.
   我　成　日　都　好　開　心。

3. Kéuih sihk yéh ge sìh-hauh, **sèhng-yaht** yiu yíng séung sīn.
   佢　食　嘢　嘅　時　候，成　日　要　影　相　先。

4. Kéuih **sèhng-yaht** behng, **sèhng-yaht** yiu sihk yeuhk.
   佢　成　日　病，成　日　要　食　藥。

V. juhng 仲 (still no change; continue to be)   ◀512.mp3

e.g., Ngóh behng jó, **juhng** yiu tùhng haak hōi wúi?
我　病　咗，仲　要　同　客　開　會？
I'm very ill, and I still need to have a meeting with a client?

Gām jīu **juhng** haih hóu mh-syū-fuhk.
今　朝　仲　係　好　唔　舒　服。
This morning, I was still not feeling well.

1. Néih **juhng** hái douh dáng māt-yéh a? Faai dī séuhng chē lā.
你　仲　喺　度　等　乜　嘢　呀？快　啲　上　車　啦。

2. Mh hóu ló jáu dī yéh, ngóh **juhng** sihk gán.
唔　好　攞　走　啲　嘢，我　仲　食　緊。

3. Dím-gáai sei-yuht **juhng** haih hóu dung?
點　解　四　月　仲　係　好　凍？

4. Kéuih **juhng** hái sā-tāan wáan gán, mh séung fāan ūk-kéi.
佢　仲　喺　沙　灘　玩　緊，唔　想　返　屋　企。

5. Sèhng máahn lohk yúh, fan dou luhk dím séng jó, **juhng** haih lohk gán yúh.
成　晚　落　雨，瞓　到　六　點　醒　咗，仲　係　落　緊　雨。

✎ Practice

Make sentences using "juhng 仲" and the following phrases.

a. jyuh hái Tùhng-Lòh-Wāan 住 喺 銅 鑼 灣

b. dáng bā-sī 等 巴 士

c. sahp-yuht hóu yiht 十 月 好 熱

d. sihk yeuhk 食 藥

e. tái nī bún syū 睇 呢 本 書

VI. ……tīm 添 (in addition; and more)   ◀513.mp3

e.g., Ngóh faat gán sīu, juhng hóu tàuh-tung **tīm** a!
我　發　緊　燒，仲　好　頭　痛　添　呀！
I am suffering from a fever and bad headache.

1. Gām-yaht bē-jáu dahk ga, yáuh máaih yāt sung yāt **tīm**.
今　日　啤　酒　特　價，有　買　一　送　一　添。

2. Ngóh chéng jó ga, tái jó yī-sāng **tīm** la.
我　請　咗　假，睇　咗　醫　生　添　喇。

3. Ngóh tùhng mìhng-sīng yíng yùhn séung, juhng ló dóu kéuih ge chīm méng **tīm**.
我　同　明　星　影　完　相，仲　攞　到　佢　嘅　簽　名　添。

VII. tùhng 同 (towards)   ◀514.mp3

> e.g., Néih **tùhng** lóuh-sai góng néih mh séung jouh lā.
> 你 同 老 細 講 你 唔 想 做 啦。
> *You'd better tell the boss you don't want to do it.*
>
> Ngóh yiu **tùhng** gūng-sī chéng ga.
> 我 要 同 公 司 請 假。
> *I have to take leave from the work.*

1. **Tùhng** ngóh góng gwóng-dūng-wá.
   同 我 講 廣 東 話。

2. Néih **tùhng** kéuih góng wán mh dóu yàhn, móuh mahn-tàih ge.
   你 同 佢 講 搵 唔 到 人，冇 問 題 嘅。

3. Ngóh-deih hōi wúi ge sìh-hauh, néih **tùhng** go haak góng.
   我 哋 開 會 嘅 時 候，你 同 個 客 講。

4. Kéuih **tùhng** néih góng mh hóu yi-sī, kéuih gām-yaht làih mh dóu.
   佢 同 你 講 唔 好 意 思，佢 今 日 嚟 唔 到。

Review: "tùhng 同" meaning "with; and"   ◀515.mp3

> e.g., Lóuh-sai **tùhng** go haak dāk gām-yaht dāk-hàahn.
> 老 細 同 個 客 得 今 日 得 閒。
> *The boss and the client are only free today.*

✎ Practice

Answer questions using "tùhng 同".

a. Néih bīn-douh mh syū-fuhk a?
   你 邊 度 唔 舒 服 呀？

b. Néih tùhng bīn-go sihk faahn a?
   你 同 邊 個 食 飯 呀？

c. Néih sái mh sái heui tái yī-sāng a?
   你 使 唔 使 去 睇 醫 生 呀？

Pyramid drill   ◀516.mp3

1.

séi-háh séi-háh

死 吓 死 吓

behng dou séi-háh séi-háh

病 到 死 吓 死 吓

Ngóh behng dou séi-háh séi-háh

我 病 到 死 吓 死 吓

Ngóh behng dou séi-háh séi-háh, juhng yiu hōi wúi

我 病 到 死 吓 死 吓，仲 要 開 會

Ngóh behng dou séi-háh séi-háh, juhng yiu tùhng haak hōi wúi.

我 病 到 死 吓 死 吓，仲 要 同 客 開 會。

I'm so sick that I'm dying, but I still need to have a meeting with a client.

2.

tái jó yī-sāng

睇 咗 醫 生

tái jó yī-sāng tīm

睇 咗 醫 生 添

juhng tái jó yī-sāng tīm la

仲 睇 咗 醫 生 添 喇

chéng jó ga, juhng tái jó yī-sāng tīm la

請 咗 假，仲 睇 咗 醫 生 添 喇

Ngóh chéng jó ga, juhng tái jó yī-sāng tīm la

我 請 咗 假，仲 睇 咗 醫 生 添 喇

Ngóh tùhng gūng-sī chéng jó ga, juhng tái jó yī-sāng tīm la.

我 同 公 司 請 咗 假，仲 睇 咗 醫 生 添 喇。

I took leave from work and saw a doctor.

General review

I. Match the questions with the answers.   ◀517.mp3

1. Néih dím-gáai bá sēng mh tùhng jó?
   你 點 解 把 聲 唔 同 咗？

2. Néih gin dóu kéuih, kéuih dím a?
   你 見 到 佢， 佢 點 呀？

3. Néih ge tàuh-tung dím a?
   你 嘅 頭 痛 點 呀？

4. Yī-sāng jí dím sé a? Néih yáuh māt-yéh behng a?
   醫 生 紙 點 寫 呀？你 有 乜 嘢 病 呀？

5. Néih lóuh-sai géi-sìh béi néih fong ga?
   你 老 細 幾 時 畀 你 放 假？

☐ a. Ngóh gám-mouh, yī-sāng wah yiu yāu-sīk léuhng yaht.
   我 感 冒， 醫 生 話 要 休 息 兩 日。

☐ b. Dáng lóuh-sai fong ga, ngóh jauh gān-jyuh yāt-chàih fong ga.
   等 老 細 放 假，我 就 跟 住 一 齊 放 假。

☐ c. Ngóh móuh gin kéuih sèhng nìhn, kéuih juhng haih hóu leng.
   我 冇 見 佢 成 年，佢 仲 係 好 靚。

☐ d. Ngóh yān-waih hàuh-lùhng tung, bá sēng mh tùhng jó.
   我 因 為 喉 嚨 痛，把 聲 唔 同 咗。

☐ e. Ngóh tung dou fan mh jeuhk.
   我 痛 到 瞓 唔 着。

II. Listen and complete the dialogue with the expressions in the table.   ◀518.mp3

juhng sihk mh dóu yéh tīm 仲 食 唔 到 嘢 添	mh sái gán-jēung 唔 使 緊 張
ngóh yiu jáu sīn 我 要 走 先	sèhng go yàhn check háh 成 個 人 check 吓
tùhng yī-sāng góng háh 同 醫 生 講 吓	yáuh māt-yéh mh syū-fuhk 有 乜 嘢 唔 舒 服
heui tái yī-sāng 去 睇 醫 生	

A: Deui-mh-jyuh, _____.
   對 唔 住，

B: Néih yiu heui bīn-douh a?
   你 要 去 邊 度 呀？

A: Ngóh mh syū-fuhk, _____ .
　我　唔 舒 服，　　　　　　　　 。

B: Néih _____ a?
　你　　　　　　　　　　 呀 ？

A: Ngóh sèhng yaht tàuh-wàhn, _____ .
　我　成　日　頭　暈，　　　　　　　　　　 。

B: Néih bāt-yùh giu yī-sāng tùhng néih _____ lā.
　你　不 如 叫 醫 生　同　你　　　　　　　 啦 。

A: Ngóh _____ lā. Néih _____, ngóh mh haih daaih behng.
　我　　　　　　啦 。你　　　　　　 ，我 唔 係 大　病 。

III. Match the Cantonese word with the English meaning.

Cantonese word	English meaning
1. tung 痛	a. head
2. tàuh 頭	b. holiday
3. hōi 開	c. car
4. chē 車	d. pain
5. ga 假	e. fall, get down
6. lohk 落	f. start, open

* Note: Cantonese phrases are a combination of words. Each word has its own meaning. When you understand the meaning of a word, it is much easier to remember it. This can help to expand your vocabulary. Find hints from the phrases to complete the exercise.

◀519.mp3

Cantonese phrases	English meaning
hàuh-lùhng tung 喉嚨痛	sore throat
tàuh-tung 頭痛	headache
tàuh-wàhn 頭暈	dizzy
sāk chē 塞車	traffic jam
séuhng chē 上車	get in a car
lohk chē 落車	get off a car
lohk yúh 落雨	to rain
chéng ga 請假	take leave
fong ga 放假	on leave; on holiday

Answers

Story

I.

D: Bīn-douh mh-syū-fuhk a?

醫生：邊 度 唔 舒 服 呀？

What seems to be the problem?

P: **Ngóh gám-mouh, faat sīu.**

病人：我 感 冒、發 燒。

I have the flu and a fever.

D: Faat-sīu, sīu dou géi-dō douh a?

醫生：發 燒，燒 到 幾 多 度 呀？

How high is your fever? What is your temperature?

P: **Sīu dou yāt baak lìhng yih douh.**

病人：燒 到 一 百 零 二 度。

It is 102 degrees.

D: Géi-sìh **hōi-chí faat-sīu** ga?

醫生：幾 時 開 始 發 燒 㗎？

When did the fever begin?

P: Kàhm-máahn sihk yùhn faahn hōi-chí.

病人：琴 晚 食 完 飯 開 始。

It started last night after dinner.

D: Yáuh móuh tàuh-wàhn, tàuh-tung a?

醫生：有 冇 頭 暈、頭 痛 呀？

Do you feel dizzy or have a headache?

P: **Tàuh-tung dou hóu sān-fú**, juhng yáuh hàuh-lùhng tung.

病人：頭 痛 到 好 辛 苦，仲 有 喉 嚨 痛。

I have a bad headache and am suffering from a sore throat.

D: Juhng yáuh māt-yéh mh syū-fuhk a?

醫生：仲 有 乜 嘢 唔 舒 服 呀？

Any other discomfort?

P: Ngóh sèhng yaht dá hāt-chī, **mh tìhng làuh beih-séui.**

病人：我 成 日 打 乞 嚏，唔 停 流 鼻 水。

I sneeze all day. My nose hasn't stopped running.

D: Yám dō dī séui, **yāu-sīk dō dī** lā. Dāk ga la. Néih heui ló yeuhk lā.

醫生：飲 多 啲 水，休 息 多 啲 啦。得 㗎 喇。你 去 攞 藥 啦。

Drink more water, rest well. You will be alright. You can go to get your medicine.

P: Yī-sāng, **ngóh yiu tùhng gūng-sī chéng ga**. Mh-gōi sé yī-sāng jí béi ngóh lā.

病人：醫 生，我 要 同 公 司 請 假。唔 該 寫 醫 生 紙 畀 我 啦。

Doctor, I have to take sick leave. Please write me a note.

D: Ngóh sé jí **béi néih yāu-sīk léuhng yaht** lā.

醫生：我 寫 紙 畀 你 休 息 兩 日 啦。

I'll write you a note to take leave for two days.

II.

1. c   2. a   3. b   4. b

Grammar practice translation I

1. After the meeting, I was so tired that I had a headache.

2. I'm so nervous that I feel dizzy.

3. It was so comfortable that I fell asleep.

4. He is extremely annoying. No one wants to make friends with him.

Practice answers

a. muhn dou séi
閂　到　死
bored to death

b. faai dou tái mh dóu
快　到　睇　唔　到
so fast that I can't see

c. gwai dou chī-sin
貴　到　黐　線
it's so expensive; that's crazy

Grammar practice translation II

1. It is raining now. Did you know that?

2. I am parking my car. I am not free to talk on the phone.

3. A: Where is the baby?

   B: She is sleeping

4. I have arrived at the Central Piers. I'm waiting for you to come.

5. I am walking to the MTR station.

Practice answer b.

i. Ngóh mahn **gán** néih.
我　問　緊　你。
I am asking you.

ii. Kéuih sihk **gán** faahn.
佢　食　緊　飯。
He is having a meal.

iii. Ngóh máaih **gán** yéh.
我　買　緊　嘢。
I am shopping.

Grammar practice translation III

1. A: Have you taken medicine for your cold?

   B: No, I am going to take it now.

2. A: Have you bought a new computer?

   B: No. Will you come to buy with me?

3. A: Have you got off the bus?

   B: I just got off at the intersection.

4. A: Have you gone to the bank to have your money changed?

   B: I have changed $3,000. Is that enough? If this is not enough, I will go the bank to have money changed again.

Practice answers

a. Néih sihk jó faahn meih a? Sihk jó la. / Meih sihk.
你　食　咗　飯　未　呀？食　咗　喇。/未　食。
Have you had lunch yet?

b. Kéuih séng jó meih a? Séng jó la. / Meih séng.
佢　醒　咗　未　呀？醒　咗　喇。/未　醒。
Has he woken up yet?

c. Hōi wúi gói jó kèih meih a? Gói jó la. / Meih gói.
開　會　改　咗　期　未　呀？改　咗　喇。/未　改。
Have you changed the date of the meeting?

Grammar practice translation IV

A.

1. The whole company has 20 staff members, but there were only two people at work yesterday.

2. There are ten cars parked on the road.

3. His bag is all stuffed with food.

4. I went to the US for a whole week.

Practice answers

a. **Sèhng ga** chē dōu haih fo.
　成　　架車都係貨。
The car is filled with goods.

b. **Sèhng gāan** jáu-dim dāk ngóh-deih jyuh.
　成　　間酒店得我　哋住。
We're the only ones in the hotel.

c. Kéuih **sèhng** nìhn dōu fong mh dóu ga.
　佢　成　年都放　唔到假。
He can't be on leave at any time of the year.

B.

1. I spent the whole day home. / I often stay home.
2. I am always happy.
3. When he eats, he often takes photos first.
4. He often gets sick. He has to take medicine every day.

Grammar practice translation V

1. What are you waiting for? Get in the car.
2. Don't take the food away; I am still eating.
3. Why is it still very cold in April?
4. He is still playing on the beach. He doesn't want to go home.
5. It has been raining all night. When I woke up at 6 o'clock, it was still raining.

Practice answers

a. Kéuih juhng jyuh hái Tùhng-Lòh-Wāan.
　佢　仲　住　喺銅　鑼灣。
He still lives in Causeway Bay.

b. Néih juhng dáng gán bā-sī? Néih dáng jó bun go jūng-tàuh la.
　你仲　等　緊巴士？你等　咗半個鐘　頭喇。
Are you still waiting for the bus? You've waited for half an hour.

c. Yíh-gīng sahp-yuht la. Dím-gáai juhng haih hóu yiht?
　已　經　十月喇。點解　仲　係好熱？
It's already October. Why is it still so hot?

d. Ngóh juhng sihk gán yeuhk.
　我　仲　食緊藥。
I still have to take medicine.

e. Néih juhng tái gán nī bún syū?
　你仲　睇緊呢本書？
Are you still reading this book?

Grammar practice translation VI

1. Beer is on promotion today. There is also buy one get one free.
2. I have asked for leave and went to see a doctor.
3. After I took a photo with the celebrity, I also got his autograph.

Grammar practice translation VII

1. Talk to me in Cantonese.
2. Tell him that you can't find anyone (to help him). It is not a problem.
3. When we have the meeting, please talk to the client.
4. He would like to apologize to you. He can't come today.

Practice answers

a. Néih bīn-douh mh syū-fuhk a?

你 邊 度 唔 舒 服 呀？

What seems to be the problem?

Ngóh tàuh-tung tùhng làuh beih-séui.

我 頭 痛 同 流 鼻 水。

I suffer from a headache and a runny nose.

b. Néih tùhng bīn-go sihk faahn a?

你 同 邊 個 食 飯 呀？

Who is going to have dinner with you?

Ngóh tùhng pàhng-yáuh sihk faahn.

我 同 朋 友 食 飯。

I'll have dinner with friends.

c. Néih sái mh sái heui tái yī-sāng a?

你 使 唔 使 去 睇 醫 生 呀？

Do you want to see a doctor?

Mh-gōi néih tùhng ngóh heui tái yī-sāng.

唔 該 你 同 我 去 睇 醫 生。

Please go with me to see a doctor.

General review

I.

1. Why does your voice sound different?

   d. Because I have a sore throat, my voice sounds different.

2. You've met her. How is she?

   c. I haven't seen her for an entire year. She still looks beautiful.

3. How is your headache?

   e. It's so painful that I can't sleep.

4. What did the doctor write in his note? What kind of illness do you have?

   a. I have a cold. The doctor said I have to rest for two days.

5. When will your boss allow you to take leave?

   b. I have to wait for the boss to take leave first, then I can take leave.

II.

A: Deui-mh-jyuh, **ngóh yiu jáu sīn**.

對 唔 住，我 要 走 先。

Sorry, I have to leave now.

B: Néih yiu heui bīn-douh a?

你 要 去 邊 度 呀？

Where are you going?

A: Ngóh mh syū-fuhk, **heui tái yī-sāng**.

我 唔 舒 服，去 睇 醫 生。

I am not feeling well. I am going to see a doctor.

B: Néih **yáuh māt-yéh mh syū-fuhk** a?

你 有 乜 嘢 唔 舒 服 呀？

What seems to be the problem?

A: Ngóh sèhng yaht tàuh-wàhn, **juhng sihk mh dóu yéh tīm**.

我 成 日 頭 暈，仲 食 唔 到 嘢 添。

I have felt dizzy all day, and I can't eat.

B: Néih bāt-yùh giu yī-sāng tùhng néih **sèhng go yàhn** check **háh** lā.
你　不 如 叫 醫 生　同 你　成　個 人　　check 吓　啦。
You'd better ask the doctor to give you a check-up.

A: Ngóh **tùhng yī-sāng góng háh** lā. Néih **mh sái gán-jēung**,
我　　同　　醫 生　講　　吓 啦。你 唔 使 緊　張，
ngóh mh haih daaih behng.
我　唔 係 大　病。
I'll consult the doctor. You don't have to worry; it's not a serious illness.

III.

1. d. tung 痛 = pain
2. a. tàuh 頭 = head
3. f. hōi 開 = start; open
4. c. chē 車 = car; vehicle
5. b. ga 假 = holiday
6. e. lohk 落 = fall; get down

Hong Kong culture

English words used in Cantonese   ◄520.mp3

Native Hong Kongers tend to use a lot of English words when they speak Cantonese and many of these words are not easily recognized by native speakers of English because they have Cantonese-influenced pronunciations and follow the word order of Cantonese.

Here are some examples:

1. Néih ge pān mh wēuk
   你　嘅 plan 唔 work
   Your plan is not going to work.

2. Gēt mh dóu kéuih go pōn
   get 唔 到 佢　個 point
   I can't get his point, can't understand what he meant.

Hong Kong–style English abbreviations

Example

1. **present**, pronounced as pih-sēn, stands for presentation.

   dou néih pih-sēn la.
   到　你 present 喇。
   It's your turn to give a presentation.

2. **con**, stands for contact lens.

   yáuh móuh daai kōn?
   有　冇　戴　con？
   Are you wearing contact lenses?

3. **mon**, stands for monitor, which often refers to the screen of the computer or mobile phone.

   daaih mōn
   大　mon
   a big screen

   yuhng yàhn-jouh-waih-sīng mōn jyuh
   用　人　造　衞　星　mon 住
   to be monitored by satellite

4. **in**, stands for interview.

   Ngóh tīng-yaht īn
   我　聽　日　in
   I have an interview tomorrow.

5. **short**, pronounced sōt, stands for short circuit, which is used not only on machines but also used to describe a crazy person.

   kéuih sōt-jó
   佢　short 咗
   He has gone out of his mind.

ga gēi sōt sōt déi
架 機 short short 哋
The machine is not functioning properly.

6. **tutor**, pronounced as tiuh-tō, stands for tutorial.

Ngóh mh séuhng tiuh-tō.
我　唔　上　　tutor.
I am not going to the tutorial.

7. **secure**, pronounced as saht-kīu, stands for security guard.

kō saht-kīu
call 實 Q
Please call the security guard to get help.

8. O T, abbreviation of overtime, meaning working extra hours.

gām-máahn hōi ōu-tī
今　晚　　開 O T
I have to work extra hours tonight.

6

This is the first time I've been to this mall

Dialogue ◀601.mp3

➤ What is his name?

➤ What makes this staff member so confused about his name?

➤ How many times does he have to say his name?

➤ Why did he receive a gift?

➤ What kind of discount will he receive next time?

Jūng: Mh-gōi, ngóh haih chāam-gā nī go *course* ge.
鍾： 唔 該，我 係 參 加呢個 course 嘅。
Excuse me, I am here to register for this course.

jīk-yùhn: Chéng mahn néih ge méng haih . . . ?
職員： 請 問 你 嘅名 係 ⋯⋯?
May I have your name please?

Jūng: Jūng Dihng Yīng.
鍾： 鍾 定 英。
Chung Ting Ying. (It sounds the same in Chinese and English.)

jīk-yùhn: Néih góng jūng-màhn lā.
職員： 你 講 中 文 啦。
Please say that in Chinese.

Jūng: Jūng Dihng Yīng a—
鍾： 鍾 定 英 呀—
Chung Ting Ying—

jīk-yùhn: Néih jūng-yi māt-yéh dōu dāk. Màh-fàahn néih joi góng gwo lā.
職員： 你 鍾 意 乜 嘢都 得。麻 煩 你 再 講 過 啦。
Whatever you like. Please say that again.

Jūng: Ngóh góng daih sāam chi la. Ngóh giu Jūng Dihng Yīng,
鍾： 我 講 第 三 次 喇。我 叫 鍾 定 英，
This is the third time I've said it. My name is Chung Ting Ying.

yīng-màhn méng haih *Terry Chung*
英　文　名　係　Terry Chung。
My English name is Terry Chung.

jīk-yùhn:　Mh hóu yi-sī, ngóh yíh-wàih néih mahn ngóh séung tēng
職員：　　唔　好　意　思，我　以　為　你　問　我　想　聽
　　　　　I'm sorry. I thought you asked me whether I would like to know

jūng-màhn dihng yīng-màhn.
中　文　定　英　文。
your name in Chinese or English.

Gám chéng mahn néih ge méng dím chyun a?
咁　請　問　你　嘅名　點　串　呀？
How do you spell your name?

Jūng:　　Terry, tī yī ā-lòuh ā-lòuh wāai.
鍾：　　　Terry, T-E-R-R-Y.

jīk-yùhn:　ā-lòuh dihng ē-lòuh a?
職員：　　R　定　L　呀？
　　　　　Is it an R or L?

Jūng:　　ā-lòuh for Romeo, léuhng go ā-lòuh wo!
鍾：　　　R　for Romeo，兩　個　R　喎！
　　　　　R for Romeo. There are two Rs.

jīk-yùhn:　Jūng, haih mh haih sī īk-chyùh U ēn jī a?
職員：　　鍾，係　唔　係　C-H-U-N-G　呀？
　　　　　Chung, is it spelled as C-H-U-N-G?

Jūng:　　Haih a. Móuh cho.
鍾：　　　係　呀。冇　錯。
　　　　　Yes, correct.

jīk-yùhn:　O! Jūng sāang, gūng-héi néih! Néih haih daih yāt baak go yàhn
職員：　　哦！鍾　生，恭　喜　你！你　係　第　一　百　個　人
　　　　　Oh! Mr Chung, congratulations! You are the 100th participant

chāam-gā nī go *course*, ngóh-deih yáuh fahn láih-maht sung béi néih.
參　加呢個 course，我　哋　有　份　禮　物　送　畀你。
in this course. We have a gift for you.

Juhng yáuh hah chi néih chāam-gā ngóh-deih ge *course*, bun ga.
仲　有　下　次你　參　加我　哋　嘅 course、半　價。
And next time you sign up for a course, you can take advantage of our half-price offer.

Jūng:　　O, dō-jeh saai.
鍾：　　　哦，多謝　晒。
　　　　　Oh, thank you very much.

Story: Finding UG22 in a shopping mall   ◀602.mp3

Ngóh yiu hái sēung-chèuhng wán yāt gāan hái UG yah-yih ge pou.
我　要喺商　場　　搵一　間　喺 UG22　　嘅舖。
I want to find shop UG22 in the shopping mall.

Ngóh daih yāt chi heui nī go sēung-chèuhng. Ngóh yíh-wàih UG haih *under ground*,
我　第　一　次　去　呢個商　　場　。　　我　以　為　UG 係 under ground，
This is the first time I've come to this mall. I thought UG was under ground,

só-yíh yāt yahp sēung-chèuhng jauh daap dihn-tāi lohk heui.
所以　一　入　商　場　　就　搭　電　梯落　去。
so I took the escalator down right after I entered the mall.

Lohk dou heui haih *LG*, mh haih *UG*, ngóh gok-dāk hóu gwaai.
落　到　去　係 LG，唔係 UG，我　覺　得　好　怪。
When I reached downstairs, it was LG, not UG. I thought that was strange.

Ngóh mahn jīk-yùhn dím heui *UG22*, kéuih giu ngóh daap līp séuhng heui.
我　問　職　員　點　去 UG22，佢　叫　我　搭　軨　上　　去。
I asked a staff member how to go to UG22. He told me to take the elevator up.

Bīn-go dōu gú mh dóu, yùhn-lòih *UG* haih *upper ground*.
邊　個　都　估　唔到，原　　來　UG 係 upper ground。
Who would have guessed, UG actually means upper ground.

Gám-yéung ge sēung-chèuhng jān-haih màh-fàahn!
咁　樣　　嘅商　場　　真　係　麻　煩！
A shopping mall like this is so annoying!

Questions for the story

Listen and rearrange the dialogue.   ◀603.mp3

a. Chéng mahn UG22 hái bīn-douh a?
　　請　　問　　UG22 喺邊　度　呀？

b. Chéng mahn UG kèih-saht haih māt-yéh yi-sī a?
　　請　　問　　UG 其　實　係　乜　嘢　意思呀？

c. LG haih *Lower Ground*.
　　LG 係　Lower Ground。

d. LG nē? LG haih māt-yéh yi-sī a?
　　LG 呢？LG 係　乜　嘢　意思呀？

e. Mh-gōi saai. Heui sái-sáu-gāan daap līp, nī go sēung-chèuhng jān-haih hóu gwaai.
　　唔　該　晒。去　洗　手　間‵搭　軨，呢個商　　場　　真　係　好　怪。

f. Mh hóu yi-sī, ngóh juhng séung mahn, ga līp hái bīn-douh a?
　　唔　好　意　思，我　仲　想　　問，　架軨喺邊　度　呀？

g. Néih daap līp séuhng heui UG, 22 houh pou hái yauh-mihn daih yih gāan.

你　搭　較上　　去　UG，22 號　舖　喺右　面　　第　二　間。

h. Néih hàahng dou heui sái-sáu-gāan, jauh gin dóu ga līp.

你　行　　到去　洗手　間，　就　見　到　架　較。

i. O, yùhn-lòih haih gám-yéung.

哦，原　來　係　咁　樣。

j. UG haih *upper ground.*

UG 係 upper ground。

Vocabulary   ◄604.mp3

1.	yāt fahn láih-maht	一份禮物	a gift; a present
2.	sēung-chèuhng	商場	shopping mall
3.	yāt gāan pou	一間舖	a shop
4.	bun ga	半價	half-price
5.	jūng-màhn	中文	Chinese
6.	yīng-màhn	英文	English
7.	méng	名	name
8.	chāam-gā	參加	to participate; to join
9.	chéng mahn	請問	may I ask
10.	gūng-héi	恭喜	to congratulate; congratulations
11.	chyun	串	to spell
12.	sung	送	to send; to deliver
13.	gú	估	to guess
14.	daap dihn-tāi	搭電梯	to take the escalator
15.	daap līp	搭軑	to take the elevator
16.	gwaai	怪	strange
17.	gok-dāk	覺得	to think; to feel
18.	kèih-saht	其實	actually
19.	yíh-wàih	以為	think; believed to be
20.	só-yíh	所以	therefore; as a consequence
21.	yùhn-lòih	原來	turn out to be
22.	daih 第 + number		for ordinal numbers
23.	gám-yéung	咁樣	in this way; in such a manner

Grammar practice

I. Question word + dōu 都 (inclusive and exclusive) ◄605.mp3

> e.g., Néih jūng-yi **māt-yéh dōu** dāk.
> 你 鍾 意 乜 嘢 都 得。
> *Whatever you like.*
>
> **Bīn-go dōu** gú mh dóu.
> 邊 個 都 估 唔 到。
> *Who would have guessed.*

1. **Bīn go** deih-tit jaahm **dōu** yáuh ngàhn-hòhng.
   邊 個 地 鐵 站 都 有 銀 行。

2. Ngóh **māt-yéh dōu** mh gei-dāk.
   我 乜 嘢 都 唔 記 得。

3. Gó gāan chāan-tēng **géi-sìh dōu** hóu dō yàhn dáng wái.
   果 間 餐 廳 幾 時 都 好 多 人 等 位。

   Yùh-gwó jān-haih hóu sihk, dáng **géi-noih dōu** móuh mahn-tàih.
   如 果 真 係 好 食，等 幾 耐 都 冇 問 題。

4. Ngóh gám-mouh, **dím** fan **dōu** meih gau.
   我 感 冒，點 瞓 都 未 夠。

✎ Practice

Fill in an appropriate question word to complete the sentences.

a. Kéuih _____ dōu mh séung gin.
   佢 都 唔 想 見。

b. Ngóh _____ dím-sām dōu sihk.
   我 點 心 都 食。

c. Go wúi _____ dōu mh gói kèih.
   個 會 都 唔 改 期。

d. Ngóh _____ dōu mh jī, mh hóu mahn ngóh.
   我 都 唔 知，唔 好 問 我。

e. Heui dou _____ dōu sīk dóu pàhng-yáuh.
   去 到 都 識 到 朋 友。

f. Hóu-chói làuh-hah _____ dōu yáuh dīk-sí.
   好 彩 樓 下 都 有 的 士。

g. _____ dōu yáuh yàhn bōng néih jouh, néih chīm go méng jauh dāk.
   都 有 人 幫 你 做，你 簽 個 名 就 得。

II. daih 第 + number (ordinal number)   ◂606.mp3

e.g., Ngóh **daih yāt chi** heui nī go sēung-chèuhng.
我　第　一　次　去　呢個商　場。
This is the first time I've come to this mall.

Néih haih **daih yāt baak go yàhn** chāam-gā.
你　係　第　一　百　個　人　參　加。
You are the 100th participant.

1. Hóu dō Hēung-Góng yàhn jūng-yi daap dīng-dīng,
好　多香　港　人　鍾　意搭　叮　叮，
yān-waih **daih yāt** pèhng, **daih yih** syū-fuhk.
因　為　第　一　平，　第　二　舒　服。

2. Néih haih **daih yāt chīn go haak**, lóuh-sai wah mh sāu néih chín.
你　係　第　一　千　個　客，老　細　話　唔收你　錢。

3. Ngóh góng **daih sahp chi** la! Néih tēng mh tēng ga?
我　講　第　十　次喇！你　聽　唔聽　㗎？

4. Séuhng mh dóu nī ga bā-sí, ngóh-deih séuhng **daih yih ga** lā.
上　唔到呢架巴士，我　哋上　第　二　架啦。

5. Ngóh yíh-gīng **daih sāam chi** chāam-gā, jīk-yùhn dōu gei-dāk ngóh la.
我　已　經　第　三　次參　加，職員　都記得我　喇。

✎ Practice

a. Make a sentence with "**daih** 第".

b. Answer the questions.
   i. Néih daih géi go dou nī-douh a?
   你　第　幾　個到呢度呀？
   ii. Kéuih daih géi chi chéng ga a?
   佢　第　幾次請　假呀？
   iii. Hái daih géi go gāai-háu lohk chē a?
   喺第　幾個街　口　落　車呀？

III. gok-dāk 覺得 (to think; to feel)   ◂607.mp3

e.g., Ngóh **gok-dāk** hóu gwaai.
我　覺得好怪。
I thought that was strange.

1. Néih **gok-dāk** yiht? Néih haih maih faat-sīu a?
你　覺得熱？你　係咪發　燒呀？

2. Ngóh **gok-dāk** heui bīn-douh wáan dōu chā-mh-dō.
我　覺得去　邊度玩　都差唔多。

3. Ngóh **gok-dāk** wúih chìh, jauh jīk-hāak daap dīk-sí.
   我 覺 得 會 遲，就 即 刻 搭 的 士。

4. Kéuih **gok-dāk** néih mh ngāam.
   佢 覺 得 你 唔 啱。

✎ Practice

Describe how you feel or think.

a. daap dihn-tāi, mh daap līp   b. lohk yùhn yúh
   搭 電 梯，唔 搭 軨   落 完 雨

c. daaih sāk chē   d. tùhng go haak pih-sēn
   大 塞 車   同 個 客 present

IV. yíh-wàih 以為 (think; believed to be)   ◀608.mp3

> e.g., Ngóh **yíh-wàih** néih séung mahn ngóh ge jūng-màhn méng.
> 我 以 為 你 想 問 我 嘅 中 文 名。
> *I thought you wanted to ask my name in Chinese.*
>
> Ngóh **yíh-wàih** UG haih *under ground*.
> 我 以 為 UG 係 under ground。
> *I thought UG was under ground.*

1. Ngóh **yíh-wàih** kéuih mh dāk-hàahn, móuh giu kéuih làih yám chàh.
   我 以 為 佢 唔 得 閒，冇 叫 佢 嚟 飲 茶。

2. Ngóh tái dóu dī yàhn daai jē, **yíh-wàih** lohk gán yúh.
   我 睇 到 啲 人 帶 遮，以 為 落 緊 雨。

3. Ngóh tái dī séung **yíh-wàih** gó douh haih Pòuh-Tòuh-Ngàh, yùhn-lòih haih Ou-Mún.
   我 睇 啲 相 以 為 果 度 係 葡 萄 牙，原 來 係 澳 門。

4. Ngóh **yíh-wàih** wúih hóu gán-jēung, kèih-saht móuh yéh.
   我 以 為 會 好 緊 張，其 實 冇 嘢。

V. só-yíh 所以 (therefore; as a consequence)   ◀609.mp3

> e.g., Ngóh yíh-wàih UG haih *under ground*, **só-yíh** daap dihn-tāi lohk heui.
> 我 以 為 UG 係 under ground，所 以 搭 電 梯 落 去。
> *I thought UG was under ground, so I took the escalator down.*

1. Yān-waih hōi wúi gói jó kèih, **só-yíh** jīk-hāak wah néih jī.
   因 為 開 會 改 咗 期，所 以 即 刻 話 你 知。

2. Ngóh faat sīu, sīu dou yāt baak lìhng yih douh, **só-yíh** heui tái yī-sāng.
   我 發 燒，燒 到 一 百 零 二 度，所 以 去 睇 醫 生。

3. Yān-waih bun ga, **só-yíh** ngóh heui gó gāan chāan-tēng si háh.
因　為　半　價，所以我　去　果　間　餐　廳　試　吓。

4. Kéuih béi yàhn āak jó chín, **só-yíh** bou gíng.
佢　畀人　呃咗錢，所以報　警。

VI. gám yéung 咁樣 (in this way; in such a manner)   ◀610.mp3

e.g., O, yùhn-lòih haih **gám-yéung**.
哦，原　來　係　咁　樣。
Oh, no wonder. That's the way it is.

Gám-yéung ge sēung-chèuhng jān-haih màh-fàahn!
咁　樣　嘅商　場　　真　係　麻　煩！
A shopping mall like this is so annoying!

1. Néih **gám-yéung** chóh mh syū-fuhk.
你　咁　樣　坐　唔　舒　服。

2. Gám, néih gān-jyuh ngóh **gám-yéung** jouh lā.
咁，你　跟　住　我　咁　樣　做　啦。

3. Néih yáuh **gám-yéung** ge lóuh-sai, jān-haih hóu-chói. Gūng-héi néih.
你　有　咁　樣　嘅老　細，真　係　好　彩。恭　喜你。

4. Ngóh mh jūng-yi **gám-yéung**, ngóh wúih chī-sin.
我　唔　鍾　意咁　樣，我　會　黐線。

Pyramid drill ◄611.mp3

1.

māt-yéh

乜　嘢

māt-yéh dōu máaih

乜　嘢　都　買

māt-yéh dōu máaih, móuh chín

乜　嘢　都　買，　冇　錢

māt-yéh dōu máaih, máaih dou móuh chín

乜　嘢　都　買，　買　到　冇　錢

māt-yéh dōu máaih, só-yíh máaih dou móuh chín

乜　嘢　都　買，　所　以　買　到　冇　錢

Kéuih māt-yéh dōu máaih, só-yíh máaih dou móuh chín.

佢　乜　嘢　都　買，　所　以　買　到　冇　錢。

She bought whatever she liked; therefore, she spent all her money.

2.

gám-yéung

咁　樣

Ngóh haih gám-yéung

我　係　咁　樣

Ngóh yíh-wàih haih gám-yéung

我　以　為　係　咁　樣

Ngóh yíh-wàih haih gám-yéung, ngóh mh ngāam

我　以　為　係　咁　樣，　我　唔　啱

Ngóh yíh-wàih haih gám-yéung, yùhn-lòih ngóh mh ngāam.

我　以　為　係　咁　樣，　原　來　我　唔　啱。

I thought it should be like this, but it turned out that I was wrong.

General review

I. Choose the correct word to complete the sentences.   ◀612.mp3

1. Dihn-nóuh sīk gēi _____ mh hóu jīk-hāak joi hōi.
   電　腦　熄　機　　　　唔　好　即　刻　再　開。

   a. yùhn   b. dím   c. jī-hauh   d. bāt-yùh
   　完　　　　　點　　　　之　後　　　　不　如

2. Néih mh sīk jouh jauh _____ yàhn bōng néih lā.
   你　唔　識　做　就　　　　人　幫　你　啦。

   a. wán   b. meih béi   c. giu gán   d. mahn
   　搵　　　　未　畀　　　　叫　緊　　　　問

3. Néih _____ jó chīm méng, chéng néih hái douh chīm lā.
   你　　　　咗　簽　名，　請　你　喺　度　簽　啦。

   a. gám-yéung   b. mh tùhng   c. chyun cho   d. lauh
   　咁　樣　　　　　唔　同　　　　串　錯　　　　漏

4. Ngóh mh jī _____ māt-yéh láih-maht béi pàhng-yáuh, hóu tàuh-tung.
   我　唔　知　　　　乜　嘢　禮　物　畀　朋　友，好　頭　痛。

   a. dāk   b. sung   c. go   d. je
   　得　　　　送　　　　個　　　　借

II. Listen and complete the dialogue with the expressions in the table.   ◀613.mp3

daih yāt chi 第　一　次	gáu dím bun 九　點　半	hóu-chói juhng yáuh 好　彩　仲　有
jīk-hāak hōi-chí jouh 即　刻　開　始　做	chéng néih sihk faahn 請　你　食　飯	jouh yùhn dī yéh meih 做　完　啲　嘢　未
mh gei-dāk jó hōi wúi dī yéh 唔　記　得　咗　開　會　啲　嘢	mh hóu tùhng lóuh-sai góng 唔　好　同　老　細　講	

A: Gām-yaht sahp yih dím hōi wúi. Néih _____ a?
今　日　十　二　點　開　會。你　　　　　　　呀？

B: Séi la! Ngóh _____! Yìh-gā géi dím a?
死　喇！我　　　　　　　！而　家　幾　點　呀？

A: _____ la.
　　　　　　　喇。

B: _____ léuhng go bun jūng-tàuh.
　　　　　　　兩　個　半　鐘　頭。

A: Gám néih _____ lā.
咁　你　　　　　　　啦。

B: Mh-gōi néih _____. Ngóh _____.
唔　該　你　　　　　　。我　　　　　　　。

A: Dāk lā. Néih mh haih _____ mh gei-dāk yéh lā.
得　啦。你唔係　　　　　唔記得嘢啦。

Daaih-tàuh-hā dou séi!
大　頭蝦到死！

Answers

Story

a. A: Chéng mahn UG yah-yih hái bīn-douh a?
請　問　UG22　喺　邊　度　呀？
Excuse me, where is UG22?

g. B: Néih daap līp séuhng heui UG, 22 houh pou hái yauh-mihn daih yih gāan.
你　搭　粒　上　去　UG, 22 號　舖　喺　右　面　第　二　間。
Take the elevator up to UG. Shop 22 is the second on the right.

b. A: Chéng mahn UG kèih-saht haih māt-yéh yi-sī a?
請　問　UG其　實　係　乜　嘢　意思呀？
Actually, what is the meaning of UG?

j. B: UG haih *upper ground*.
UG 係 *upper ground*。
UG is upper ground.

d. A: LG nē? LG haih māt-yéh yi-sī a?
LG 呢？LG 係 乜 嘢　意思呀？
What about LG? What is the meaning of LG?

c. B: LG haih *Lower Ground*.
LG 係 *Lower Ground*。
LG is Lower Ground.

i. A: O, yùhn-lòih haih gám-yéung.
哦，原　來　係　咁　樣。
Oh, no wonder. That's how it is.

f. Mh hóu yi-sī, ngóh juhng séung mahn, ga līp hái bīn-douh a?
唔　好　意　思，我　仲　想　問，架粒喺邊　度　呀？
I'm sorry. I also want to ask where the elevator is.

h. B: Néih hàahng dou heui sái-sáu-gāan, jauh gin dóu ga līp.
你　行　到　去　洗　手　間，就　見　到　架粒。
You walk to the toilet, then you will see the elevator.

e. A: Mh-gōi saai. Heui sái-sáu-gāan daap līp, nī go sēung-chèuhng jān-haih hóu gwaai.
唔　該　晒。去　洗　手　間　搭　粒，呢個　商　場　真　係　好　怪。
Thank you very much. Go to toilet to take elevator. This shopping mall is really strange.

Grammar practice translation I

1. There is a bank in most MTR stations.
2. I don't remember anything.
3. There are many people waiting at that restaurant all the time.
   If the food is really good, it is not a problem no matter how long we have to wait.
4. I have the flu. No matter how much I sleep, it's not enough.

Practice answers

a. Kéuih **bīn-go** dōu mh séung gin.
佢　邊個　都　唔　想　見。
He doesn't want to see anyone.

b. Ngóh **māt-yéh** dím-sām dōu sihk.
我　乜　嘢點　心　都　食。
I eat any kind of dim sum.

c. Go wúi **dím** dōu mh gói kèih.
個　會　點　都　唔　改　期。
The meeting date won't change, no matter what happens.

d. Ngóh **māt-yéh** dōu mh jī, mh hóu mahn ngóh.
我 乜 嘢 都 唔 知，唔 好 問 我。
I don't know anything (about that). Don't ask me.

e. Heui dou **bīn-douh** dōu sīk dóu pàhng-yáuh.
去 到 邊 度 都 識 到 朋 友。
I can make friends wherever I go.

f. Hóu-chói làuh-hah **géi-sìh** dōu yáuh dīk-sí.
好 彩 樓 下 幾 時 都 有 的 士。
It's lucky that there is a taxi downstairs all the time.

g. **Māt-yéh** dōu yáuh yàhn bōng néih jouh, néih chīm go méng jauh dāk.
乜 嘢 都 有 人 幫 你 做，你 簽 個 名 就 得。
Someone will do everything for you; all you need is to sign your name.

Grammar practice translation II

1. Many Hong Kong people like to take the tram because it is cheap and comfortable.

> * Note: "Dīng-dīng 叮叮" is the nickname for street tram; its proper name should be "dihn-chē 電車".

2. You are our 1,000th customer. The boss said he wants to give you free service.
3. I am repeating it for the tenth time. Are you listening?
4. We can't get on this bus; let's get on the next one.
5. I am participating for the third time. The staff all remember me.

Practice b. translation and suggested answers

i. Néih daih géi go dou nī-douh a?
你 第 幾 個 到 呢 度 呀？
You are what number person to arrive?

Ngóh daih yāt go dou nī-douh.
我 第 一 個 到 呢 度。
I'm the first person who arrived here.

ii. Kéuih daih géi chi chéng ga a?
佢 第 幾 次 請 假 呀？
This is what number of times that he took leave?

Kéuih nī go yuht daih luhk chi chéng ga la.
佢 呢 個 月 第 六 次 請 假 喇。
It is the sixth time this month he's taken leave.

iii. Hái daih géi go gāai-háu lohk chē a?
喺 第 幾 個 街 口 落 車 呀？
At which junction should I get off?

Néih hái daih sāam go gāai-háu lohk chē lā.
你 喺 第 三 個 街 口 落 車 啦。
Get off at the third intersection.

Grammar practice translation III

1. You feel hot? Are you suffering from a fever?
2. I think wherever we go for fun, it makes no difference.
3. I think I might be running late, so I'll take a taxi.
4. He thinks that you are wrong.

Suggested practice answers and translation

a. Ngóh gok-dāk daap dihn-tāi faai-dī, mh daap līp la.
我 覺 得 搭 電 梯 快 啲，唔 搭 軨 喇。
I think taking the escalator is faster. I don't want to take the elevator.

b. Ngóh gok-dāk lohk yùhn yúh hóu syū-fuhk.

我　覺　得　落　完　雨　好　舒　服。

I felt more comfortable when the rain stopped.

c. Ngóh gok-dāk daaih sāk chē hóu muhn.

我　覺　得　大　塞　車　好　悶。

I think being stuck in a bad traffic jam is boring.

d. Yiu tùhng go haak pih-sēn, ngóh gok-dāk hóu tàuh-tung.

要　同　個　客　present，我　覺　得　好　頭　痛。

I think it is a headache to present to a client.

Grammar practice translation IV

1. I thought he was not free, so I didn't ask him to come to have tea.
2. I saw people carrying umbrella, so I thought it was raining.
3. When I looked at these photos, I thought it was Portugal. Actually, this is Macau.
4. I thought I would be nervous. Actually, it was nothing.

Grammar practice translation V

1. We have changed the meeting date, so I am so anxious to tell you.
2. I have a fever as high as 102 degrees, so I went to see a doctor.
3. I tried that restaurant because the food was half-price.
4. He was deceived, so he reported it to the police.

Grammar practice translation VI

1. You can't sit like that; it is not comfortable.
2. Well then, follow me and do it this way.
3. You're so lucky to have such a boss. Congratulations!
4. I don't enjoy living my life this way. It drives me crazy.

General review

I. Answers and sentence translation

1. Dihn-nóuh sīk gēi **c. jī-hauh** mh hóu jīk-hāak joi hōi.

電　腦　熄機　之後　唔好　即刻　再開。

Don't turn on the computer immediately after you turn it off.

2. Néih mh sīk jouh jauh **a. wán** yàhn bōng néih lā.

你　唔識做　就　搵　人　幫　你　啦。

If you don't know how to do this, find someone to help you.

> * Note: Other choices and their translation are:
>
> Néih mh sīk jouh jauh **béi** yàhn bōng néih lā.
>
> 你　唔　識　做　就　畀人　幫　你　啦。
>
> *If you don't know how to do this, let people help you.*
>
> Néih mh sīk jouh jauh **giu** yàhn bōng néih lā.
>
> 你　唔　識　做　就　叫　人　幫　你　啦。
>
> *If you don't know how to do this, ask someone to help you.*
>
> Néih mh sīk jouh jauh **mahn** yàhn dím jouh.
>
> 你　唔　識　做　就　問　人　點做。
>
> *If you don't know how to do this, ask someone.*
>
> * Note: When you use mahn 問, you have to ask a question.

3. Néih **d. lauh** jó chīm méng, chéng néih hái douh chīm lā.

你　漏咗簽　名，請　你　喺　度　簽　啦。

Your signature is missing. Please sign here.

4. Ngóh mh jī **b. sung** māt-yéh láih-maht béi pàhng-yáuh, hóu tàuh-tung.

我 唔 知 送 乜 嘢 禮 物 畀 朋 友，好 頭 痛。

I don't know what gift to give to my friend. It's a headache.

II.

A: Gām-yaht sahp yih dím hōi wúi. Néih **jouh yùhn dī yéh meih** a?

今 日 十 二 點 開 會。你 做 完 啲 嘢 未 呀？

There is a meeting at 12:00 today. Have you finished the work?

B: Séi la! Ngóh **mh gei-dāk jó hōi wúi dī yéh**! Yìh-gā géi dím a?

死 喇！我 唔 記 得 咗 開 會 啲 嘢！而 家 幾 點 呀？

Oh no! I have forgotten about the work for the meeting! What time is it now?

A: **Gáu dím bun** la.

九 點 半 喇。

It's now 9:30.

B: **Hóu-chói juhng yáuh** léuhng go bun jūng-tàuh.

好 彩 仲 有 兩 個 半 鐘 頭。

Fortunately, there are still two and a half hours left.

A: Gám néih **jīk-hāak hōi-chí jouh** lā.

咁 你 即 刻 開 始 做 啦。

You'd better start to work immediately.

B: Mh-gōi néih **mh hóu tùhng lóuh-sai góng**. Ngóh **chéng néih sihk faahn**.

唔 該 你 唔 好 同 老 細 講。我 請 你 食 飯。

Please don't tell the boss. I'll treat you to lunch/dinner.

A: Dāk lā. Néih mh haih **daih yāt chi** mh gei-dāk yéh lā.

得 啦。你 唔 係 第 一 次 唔 記 得 嘢 啦。

It's ok. It's not the first time you forgot things.

Daaih-tàuh-hā dou séi!

大 頭 蝦 到 死！

You're so absent-minded!

---

* Note: "Daaih-tàuh-hā 大頭蝦" literally means big head prawn. A prawn with bulging eyes and feelers on a big head looks smart, but when you eat it, there is not much meat. This refers to a person looking good but not being useful. All creatures are considered to be potential food. A very Chinese mindset, right? This saying is now used to laugh at someone being absent-minded, in an affectionate way.

Hong Kong culture

How to read the alphabet with Cantonese pronunciation   ◀614.mp3

ēi	bī	sī	dī	yī	ē-fùh	jī	īk-chyùh	āai
A	B	C	D	E	F	G	H	I
					Air-foo		Egg-choo	

jēi	kēi	ē-lòuh	ēm	ēn	ōu	pī	kīu	ā-lòuh
J	K	L	M	N	O	P	Q	R
		Air-lo						Ah-lo

ē-sìh	tī	U	wī	dāp-bī-U	īk-sìh	wāai	yih-sēt
S	T	U	V	W	X	Y	Z
Air-see			Wee	Dub-Bee-U	Egg-xey		Ee-sad

To spell out a double letter it is easiest to just say the letter twice. Cantonese speakers are not accustomed to hearing "double", but you can say "léuhng go 兩個" letters.

Example of spelling an English word

WOLF   Dub-Bee-U, O, Air-lo, Air-foo
SHERRY   Air-see, Egg-choo, Yee, Ah-lo, Ah-lo, Y

Confusing floor indication in an elevator

When you step into the elevator of a building in Hong Kong, it often drives you crazy. You'll see a panel with various buttons. The buttons have abbreviations, so it is easy to feel confused about which button you should press to go up or down.

To make it more complicated, sometimes a letter goes with a number, such as B1 and B5, or C1 and C5. It might take you a while to figure out which is a lower floor and which is a higher one.

If the buttons are placed side by side, left and right, it is even worse. G or C? C or P? G or FB? You would ask: Why don't they have up ↑ and down ↓ buttons?

The words on the buttons on the elevator panel at MTR stations can be very confusing too. For example, Heng Fa Chuen Station platform is located at "G" and the concourse is located at "U1". There is no U or U2 on the control panel of the elevator.

There are two elevators in the concourse near Exit E at Sheung Wan Station. In the elevator down to the platform for trains to Kennedy Town, the concourse is located at "L1". On the other side of the concourse, there is another elevator down to the platform for trains to Chai Wan. In this elevator, strangely, the concourse is located at "L2"!

Here are some commonly used letters in naming floors: ◂615.mp3

Letter	English	Cantonese
B	basement	deih-fu 地 庫
C	concourse	daaih-tòhng 大 堂
	car park	tìhng-chē-chèuhng 停 車 場
CP	car park	tìhng-chē-chèuhng 停 車 場
F FB	footbridge	tīn-kìuh 天 橋
G	ground	deih-há 地 下
UG	upper ground	seuhng chàhng deih-mín 上 層 地 面
LG	lower ground	hah chàhng deih-mín 下 層 地 面
M	mezzanine	gaap chàhng 夾 層
P	podium	pìhng-tòih 平 台
	parking	tìhng-chē-chèuhng 停 車 場
	platform	yuht-tòih 月 台

7

We had a good time at the party

Dialogue ◀701.mp3

➢ Why can't Shan go to Wah's birthday party?

➢ When did Wah ask Shan to go to the party?

➢ How was the concert?

➢ Did Ko enjoy the party?

➢ What food and drink was served at the party?

Sāan: Néih sīng-kèih-luhk yáuh móuh heui Wàh jē ge sāang-yaht *party* a?
珊 ： 你 星 期 六 有 冇 去 華 姐嘅 生 日 party 呀？
Did you go to Wah's birthday party on Saturday?

Gōu: Yáuh a. Ngóh-deih wáan dāk hóu hōi-sām.
高 ： 有 呀。我 哋 玩 得 好 開 心。
Yes, we had a good time.

Haih lak, A Sāan, néih dím-gáai mh làih a?
係 嘞，阿珊，你 點 解 唔 嚟呀？
Oh, by the way, Shan, why didn't you come?

Sāan: Wàh jē sīng-kèih-sei sīn-ji wán ngóh.
珊 ： 華 姐星 期 四 先至 搵 我。
Wah didn't ask me until Thursday.

Ngóh gam ngāam máaih-jó fēi tái yín-cheung-wúi, só-yíh heui mh dóu.
我 咁 啱 買 咗飛睇演 唱 會，所以 去 唔 到。
It so happens that I had bought tickets to see a concert, so I couldn't go.

Gōu: Gám, gó go yín-cheung-wúi hóu mh hóu-tái a?
高 ： 咁， 果個演 唱 會 好 唔 好 睇呀？
How was the concert? Was it good?

Sāan: *OK* lā. Ngóh tùhng pàhng-yáuh heui tái.
珊 ： OK啦。我 同 朋 友 去 睇。
It was fine. I went with a friend.

Kéuih tái dāk hóu hōi-sām. Ngóh jauh fan jeuhk gaau.
佢 睇 得 好 開 心。我 就 瞓着 覺。
She really enjoyed it. I fell asleep.

Gōu: Aìh-yah! Yùh-gwó néih heui Wàh jē go *party* jauh hóu lā.

高：　哎 吔！如 果 你 去 華 姐 個 party 就 好 啦。

That's too bad. I wish you had come to Wah's party.

Sāan: Haih mē? Ngóh *miss* jó dī māt-yéh a?

珊：　係 咩？我 miss 咗啲 乜 嘢 呀？

Really? What did I miss?

Gōu: Wàh jē hóu sīk jíng yéh sihk. Dī hói-sīn hóu leng,

高：　華 姐 好 識 整 嘢 食。啲 海 鮮 好 靚，

Wah's cooking was great. The seafood was superb.

yáuh yú lā, hā lā, juhng yáuh daai-jí tīm.

有 魚啦、蝦啦，仲 有 帶 子 添。

There was fish, prawns, and scallops too.

Peter daai jó géi jī leng jáu làih.

Peter 帶 咗 幾支 靚 酒 嚟。

Peter brought a few bottles of good wine.

Néih tùhng ngóh-deih yāt-chàih jauh juhng hōi-sām.

你 同 我 哋 一 齊 就 仲 開 心。

If you had come, we'd have been happier.

Sāan: Hah chi yáuh *party* yāt jóu wah ngóh jī.

珊：　下 次 有 party 一 早 話 我 知。

Ngóh māt-yéh yín-cheung-wúi dōu mh heui.

我 乜 嘢演 唱 會 都 唔 去。

Next time there is a party, let me know earlier. I won't go to a concert.

* Note: "Wàh jē 華姐"
Adding the title "jē 姐" after a woman's name is to show respect. For a man, the title "gō 哥" is added after his name; for example, "Wàh gō 華哥".

Story: Preparing for a party　◀702.mp3

Gōu sāang chéng pàhng-yáuh làih ūk-kéi hōi *party*,
高　生　請　朋　友　嚟屋　企　開 party，
Mr. Ko invited friends to his house to have a party,

só-yíh kéuih yāt jóu chēut heui jī-hauh, Gōu táai jauh hóu gán-jēung,
所 以　佢　一　早 出　去 之後，高 太　就　好　緊 張，
so after he left early in the morning, Mrs. Ko was very excited.

hōi-chí jāp yéh, gān-jyuh jíng yéh sihk. Kéuih jéun-beih jó hóu dō sung jáu ge síu-sihk,
開　始　執嘢，跟　住　整　嘢　食。佢　準　備　咗好 多 送　酒嘅 小　食，
She began to tidy the house, and then cooked. She prepared a lot of snacks to go with wine

juhng yáuh hóu leng ge hói-sīn.
仲　有　好　靚　嘅海　鮮。
and very good seafood.

Gōu sāang fāan dou ūk-kéi, gin-dóu taai-táai jeuk dāk hóu leng, ūk-kéi jāp dāk hóu gōn-jehng,
高　生　返　到 屋 企，見 到 太　太　着　得　好　靚，屋 企 執 得 好 乾 淨，
When Mr. Ko returned home, he saw his wife looking beautiful and his house clean.

kéuih hóu hōi-sām. Gōu táai mahn kéuih, "dī yàhn géi dím làih a?"
佢　好　開　心。高 太　問　佢：「啲 人 幾　點　嚟呀？」
He was pleased. Mrs. Ko asked him, "What time will the guests come?"

Gōu sāang wah, "Gām-máahn māt-yéh yàhn làih a? Ngóh-deih sīng-kèih-yaht sīn-ji hōi *party*.
高　生　話：「今　晚　乜 嘢 人　嚟呀？我　哋　星　期　日　先 至 開 party。
Mr. Ko replied, "Who's coming tonight? We're having a party on Sunday.

Néih gáau cho la!"
你　搞　錯　喇！」
You have made a mistake!"

Questions for the story

I. Choose the correct answer. ◀703.mp3

1. Gōu sāang géi-sìh hái ūk-kéi hōi *party* a?
   高　生　幾　時 喺屋 企　開 party 呀？
   a. gām-máahn 今晚　　　　　b. sīng-kèih-yaht 星期日
   c. sīng-kèih-luhk 星期六　　　d. chāt dím 七點

2. Gōu táai hái ūk-kéi jouh māt-yéh a?
   高　太 喺屋 企 做　乜 嘢 呀？

Choose the incorrect statement.

a. jāp gōn-jehng ūk-kéi, jíng hói-sīn tùhng síu-sihk
   執 乾 淨　屋 企、整 海　鮮 同　小　食

b. yāt jóu giu pàhng-yáuh làih jāp yéh, hōi *party*
   一　早 叫 朋　友　嚟執嘢、開 party

c. jeuk dou hóu leng, dáng Gōu sāang fāan ūk-kéi
着 到 好 靚，等 高 生 返 屋 企

d. jíng yéh sihk, jéun-beih gām-yaht ge *party*
整 嘢 食、準 備 今 日 嘅 party

3. Gōu sāang fāan dou ūk-kéi gin-dóu dím-yéung a?
高 生 返 到 屋 企 見 到 點 樣 呀？

Choose the incorrect statement.

a. Gōu táai jeuk dāk hóu leng
高 太 着 得 好 靚

b. ūk-kéi hóu gōn-jehng
屋 企 好 乾 淨

c. Gōu táai jéun-beih tùhng kéuih hōi *party*
高 太 準 備 同 佢 開 party

d. hóu dō pàhng-yáuh, wáan dāk hóu hōi-sām
好 多 朋 友，玩 得 好 開 心

II. Listen and rearrange the dialogue. ◀704.mp3

a. Ngóh jíng jó hóu dō hói-sīn. Yáuh néih jūng-yi sihk ge yú lā, hā lā,
我 整 咗 好 多 海 鮮。有 你 鍾 意 食 嘅 魚 啦、蝦 啦，
juhng yáuh daai-jí tīm.
仲 有 帶 子 添。

b. Lóuh-pòh, néih hóu leng. Gām-yaht heui jó bīn-douh a?
老 婆，你 好 靚。今 日 去 咗 邊 度 呀？

c. Wa! Ngóh-deih dāk léuhng go yàhn, dím sihk dóu gam dō yéh a?
嘩！我 哋 得 兩 個 人，點 食 到 咁 多 嘢 呀？

d. Ngóh bōng néih hōi tói. Ngóh hóu tóuh-ngoh, gām-máahn yáuh māt-yéh sihk a?
我 幫 你 開 枱。我 好 肚 餓，今 晚 有 乜 嘢 食 呀？

e. Hōi *party*? Mh-haih gām-yaht, haih sīng-kèih-yaht wo!
開 party？唔 係 今 日，係 星 期 日 喎！

f. Mē a? Néih wah chéng pàhng-yáuh fāan làih hōi *party* ma.
咩 呀？你 話 請 朋 友 返 嚟 開 party 嘛。
Jéun-beih dō dī, ngāam ga la.
準 備 多 啲，啱 㗎 喇。

g. Gām-yaht mh dāk-hàahn chēut heui, jāp yéh jāp jó yāt yaht.
今 日 唔 得 閒 出 去，執 嘢 執 咗 一 日。
Guih séi ngóh la! Néih a, néih chēut jó heui mh bōng ngóh!
劫 死 我 喇！你 呀，你 出 咗 去 唔 幫 我！

Vocabulary ◄705.mp3

1.	yín-cheung-wúi	演唱會	concert
2.	yāt jēung fēi	一張飛	a ticket
3.	hói-sīn	海鮮	seafood
4.	yú	魚	fish
5.	hā	蝦	prawn; shrimp
6.	daai-jí	帶子	scallop
7.	síu-sihk	小食	snack
8.	yāt jī jáu	一支酒	a bottle of wine
9.	sāang-yaht	生日	birthday
10.	hōi-sām	開心	happy
11.	gōn-jehng	乾淨	clean
12.	tóuh-ngoh	肚餓	hungry
13.	jíng	整	to make; to fix; to cook
14.	jeuk	着	to wear; to dress
15.	chēut heui	出去	to go out
16.	jāp yéh	執嘢	to tidy up; to pack things
17.	gáau cho	搞錯	make a mistake
18.	jéun-beih	準備	to prepare
19.	sīn-ji	先至	until then, emphasize the time is relatively late
20.	yāt jóu	一早	at an early time
21.	gam 咁 + adjective		so; such

Grammar practice

I. verb + dāk 得 + adjective (describe manner of an action)   ◀706.mp3

> e.g., Ngóh-deih wáan **dāk** hóu hōi-sām.
>
> 我　哋　玩　得　好　開　心。
>
> *We had a good time. (literally, played happily)*
>
> Gōu táai jeuk **dāk** hóu leng.
>
> 高　太　着　得　好　靚。
>
> *Mrs. Ko, looking beautiful.*
>
> Ūk-kéi jāp **dāk** hóu gōn-jehng.
>
> 屋　企　執　得　好　乾　淨。
>
> *His house was clean and tidy.*

1. Kéuih-deih hàahng **dāk** hóu faai.

   佢　哋　行　得　好　快。

2. Dī hói-sīn jíng **dāk** hóu hóu sihk.

   啲　海　鮮　整　得　好　好　食。

3. Ngóh wán néih wán **dāk** hóu sān-fú.

   我　搵　你　搵　得　好　辛　苦。

4. Kéuih chéng ga chéng **dāk** taai dō, lóuh-sai mh jūng-yi.

   佢　請　假　請　得　太　多，老　細　唔　鍾　意。

✎ Practice

Complete the following sentences.

a. Kéuih hohk jūng-màhn hohk dāk _____

   佢　學　中　文　學　得

b. Nī ga chē hàahng dāk _____

   呢　架　車　行　得

c. Ngóh yám jáu yám dāk _____

   我　飲　酒　飲　得

II. gam 咁 + adjective (so; such)   ◀707.mp3

> e.g., Ngóh-deih dím sihk dóu **gam** dō yéh a?
>
> 我　哋　點　食　到　咁　多　嘢　呀？
>
> *How can we eat that much?*

1. Néih góng dāk **gam** faai, ngóh tēng mh dóu.

   你　講　得　咁　快，我　聽　唔　到。

2. Hái nī-douh chóh dāk **gam** syū-fuhk, ngóh mh séung jáu.

   喺　呢　度　坐　得　咁　舒　服，我　唔　想　走。

3. Yùh-gwó mh haih yáuh pàhng-yáuh làih, ūk-kéi hóu síu **gam** gōn-jehng.
   如 果　唔 係　有　朋　　友　嚟，屋 企 好 少 咁　乾　淨。

4. Jēung yín-cheung-wúi fēi **gam** gwai, yáuh móuh gáau cho a?
   張　演 唱　　會 飛 咁　貴，有　冇　搞　錯 呀？

5. Wa! Ngóh-deih **gam** hóu-chói, yāt làih dou jauh yáuh wái paak chē.
   嘩！我　　哋 咁　好 彩，一　嚟 到 就 有　位 泊　車。

✎ **Practice**

Make sentences using "gam 咁" and these words.
a. chìh 遲   b. pèhng 平   c. dung 凍

III. Compare the usage of "gam 咁" and "gám-yéung 咁樣"   ◄708.mp3

1. Ngóh **gam** tóuh-ngoh, sihk dī **gám-yéung** ge síu-sihk, dím báau a?
   我　咁　肚　餓，食 啲 咁　樣　嘅 小 食，點 飽 呀？
   I'm so hungry. How can I fill my stomach with these snacks?

2. Kéuih **gam** màh-fàahn, ngóh mh séung bōng **gám-yéung** ge yàhn jouh yéh.
   佢　咁　麻　煩，我 唔 想　幫 咁　樣　嘅 人　做 嘢。
   He is so annoying; I don't want to work for such a person.

3. **Gám-yéung** sāk chē, néih bāt-yùh daap deih-tit lā.
   咁　樣　塞 車，你 不 如 搭　地 鐵 啦。
   In such poor traffic conditions, you'd better take the MTR.

   Deih-tit **gam** faai, sahp fān-jūng jauh heui dou Wāan Jái lā.
   地　鐵 咁 快，十　分 鐘 就 去 到 灣　仔 啦。
   The MTR is so fast, you can get to Wan Chai in 10 minutes.

IV. sīn-ji 先至 (not until, emphasize the time is relatively late)   ◄709.mp3

e.g., Wàh jē sīng-kèih-sei **sīn-ji** wán ngóh.
華　姐 星　期　四 先 至 搵　我。
Wah didn't ask me until Thursday.

Ngóh-deih tīng-yaht **sīn-ji** hōi party, néih gáau cho la!
我　　哋 聽　日　先 至 開 party，你 搞　錯 喇！
We're having a party tomorrow. You made a mistake!

1. Ngóh jāp yùhn yéh **sīn-ji** fan gaau.
   我　執 完　嘢 先 至 瞓　覺。

2. Ngóh máaih jó syū, dáng dāk-hàahn **sīn-ji** tái.
   我　買　咗 書，等　得 閒　先 至 睇。

3. Gáu dím géi **sīn-ji** sihk faahn, hóu tóuh-ngoh.
   九 點 幾 先 至 食 飯， 好 肚 餓。

4. Sahp-yih-yuht **sīn-ji** fong ga, juhng yiu dáng hóu noih.
   十 二 月 先 至 放 假，仲 要 等 好 耐。

✎ **Practice**

Complete the following dialogues.

a. A: Néih fong gūng jī-hauh, sihk faahn sīn dihng fāan ūk-kéi sīn a?
   你 放 工 之 後，食 飯 先 定 返 屋 企 先 呀？

   B: _____

b. Ngóh séung _____ sīn-ji jouh yéh.
   我 想 先 至 做 嘢。

c. _____ sīn-ji gei-dāk yáuh yéh yiu séuhng móhng jouh.
   先 至 記 得 有 嘢 要 上 網 做。

V. yāt jóu 一早 (at an early time) ◂710.mp3

> e.g., Ngóh **yāt-jóu** máaih-jó fēi tái yín-cheung-wúi.
> 我 一 早 買 咗飛 睇 演 唱 會。
> *I had bought tickets to see a concert earlier.*
>
> Gōu sāang **yāt jóu** chēut heui.
> 高 生 一 早 出 去。
> *Mr. Ko went out early in the morning.*

1. Ngóh-deih **yāt jóu** jauh séuhng chē dáng hōi chē.
   我 哋 一 早 就 上 車 等 開 車。

2. Ngóh **yāt jóu** dehng jó tói, dím-gáai juhng yiu dáng tói?
   我 一 早 訂 咗 枱，點 解 仲 要 等 枱？

3. Kéuih **yāt jóu** wah jó ngóh jī mh làih lā.
   佢 一 早 話 咗我 知 唔 嚟 啦。

4. Ngóh kàhm-máahn **yāt jóu** jauh fan gaau.
   我 琴 晚 一 早 就 瞓 覺。

5. **Yāt-jóu** gwo jó néih séung lohk chē gó douh.
   一 早 過 咗你 想 落 車 果 度。

✎ Practice

Answer the questions with "sīn-ji" 先至 or "yāt-jóu" 一早.   ◀711.mp3

a. Néih géi-sìh máaih fēi a?
   你　幾　時　買　　飛呀？

b. Néih géi-sìh hōi-chí jāp ūk?
   你　幾　時　開　始　執屋？

c. Néih *call* jó kéuih meih a?
   你　call 咗佢　未　呀？

d. Néih tīng-yaht géi-dím chēut heui a?
   你　聽　日　幾　點　出　　去呀？

e. Néih yáuh móuh giu kéuih làih *party* a?
   你　有　冇　叫佷　嚟 party 呀？

VI. Time spent   ◀712.mp3

e.g., Ngóh jāp yéh jāp jó **yāt yaht**.
我　　執嘢　執　咗一日。
I spent one day tidying the house.

1. Ngóh dáng ló yeuhk dáng jó **sahp fān-jūng**.
   我　等　攞藥　等　咗十　分　鐘。

2. Kéuih behng jó **yāt go sīng-kèih**.
   佷　病　咗一個星　期。

3. Ngóh tùhng kéuih kīng gái kīng jó **yāt máahn**.
   我　同　佷　傾　偈傾　咗一　晚。

4. Sāk chē sāk jó **sāam go jūng-tàuh**, jān-haih mh hóu-chói.
   塞　車塞咗三　個　鐘　頭，真　係　唔　好　彩。

Pyramid drill ◢713.mp3

1.

fãan jó ūk-kéi

返 咗 屋 企

fãan jó ūk-kéi, móuh heui *party*

返 咗 屋 企，冇　　去 party

fãan jó ūk-kéi, só-yíh móuh heui *party*

返 咗 屋 企，所 以 冇　去 party

yāt-jóu fãan jó ūk-kéi, só-yíh móuh heui *party*

一 早 返 咗 屋 企，所 以 冇　去 party

Ngóh yāt-jóu fãan jó ūk-kéi, só-yíh móuh heui *party*

我 一 早 返 咗 屋 企，所 以 冇 去 party

Ngóh yāt-jóu fãan jó ūk-kéi, só-yíh sīn-ji móuh heui *party*.

我 一 早 返 咗 屋 企，所 以 先 至 冇 去 party。

I had gone home much earlier, so I didn't go to the party.

2.

jāp yéh

執 嘢

jāp yéh jāp jó yāt yaht

執 嘢 執 咗 一 日

Jāp yéh jāp jó yāt yaht, ūk-kéi gōn-jehng

執 嘢 執 咗 一 日，屋 企 乾 淨

Jāp yéh jāp jó yāt yaht, ūk-kéi gam gōn-jehng

執 嘢 執 咗 一 日，屋 企 咁 乾 淨

Jāp yéh jāp jó yāt yaht, ūk-kéi sīn-ji gam gōn-jehng.

執 嘢 執 咗 一 日，屋 企 先 至 咁 乾 淨。

I spent one day tidying the house. Only then was it so clean.

General review

I. Put the words in the correct order to make sentences.   ◄714.mp3

1. hói-sīn / kéuih / sihk / dō / mh syū-fuhk / só-yíh / dāk / taai
   海 鮮 / 佢 / 食 / 多 / 唔 舒 服 / 所 以 / 得 / 太

2. ngóh / yāt bún syū / yāt go yuht / tái syū / tái dāk / tái dóu / hóu maahn / sīn-ji
   我 / 一 本 書 / 一 個 月 / 睇 書 / 睇 得 / 睇 到 / 好 慢 / 先 至

3. mā-mìh / ngóh / dāk hàahn / béi / kīng háh gái / dá dihn wá / yāt / jauh
   媽 咪 / 我 / 得 閒 / 畀 / 傾 吓 偈 / 打 電 話 / 一 / 就

4. ngóh-deih / yín-cheung-wúi / jáu jó / muhn / go / gam / yāt jóu / la
   我 哋 / 演 唱 會 / 走 咗 / 悶 / 個 / 咁 / 一 早 / 喇

5. mìhng-sīng / ngóh / hōi-sām / jūng-yi / yíng séung / fan mh jeuhk gaau /
   明 星 / 我 / 開 心 / 鍾 意 / 影 相 / 瞓 唔 着 覺 /
   ge / hóu / dou / tùhng / jī-hauh
   嘅 / 好 / 到 / 同 / 之 後

II. Circle the odd word out.   ◄715.mp3

1. a. yāt jī jáu   b. yāt ga chē   c. yāt tìuh louh
   一 支 酒   一 架 車   一 條 路

   d. yāt go jūng-tàuh   e. yāt jēung fēi
   一 個 鐘 頭   一 張 飛

2. a. mh syū-fuhk   b. muhn   c. màh-fàahn   d. gán-jēung   e. gáau cho
   唔 舒 服   悶   麻 煩   緊 張   搞 錯

3. a. mìhng-sīng   b. làuh-hah   c. yī-sāng   d. sai-lóu   e. lóuh-sai
   明 星   樓 下   醫 生   細 佬   老 細

4. a. làuh beih-séui   b. tàuh tung   c. tóuh-ngoh   d. gám-mouh   e. faat sīu
   流 鼻 水   頭 痛   肚 餓   感 冒   發 燒

5. a. sī-gēi   b. jāp yéh   c. sāu chín   d. sīk gēi   e. gói kèih
   司 機   執 嘢   收 錢   熄 機   改 期

III. Listen and complete the dialogue with the expressions in the table.   ◀716.mp3

bāt-yùh 不 如	chēut heui 出 去	jī-hauh 之 後	juhng 仲	sāang-yaht 生 日
só-yíh 所以	yāt-jóu 一 早	yāt go yuht 一 個 月	yāt jēung fēi 一 張 飛	yín-cheung-wúi 演 唱 會
gwai dou chī-sin 貴 到 黐 線		jīk-hāak séuhng móhng 即 刻 上 網		yíh-gīng hōi-chí 已 經 開 始

A: _____ néih _____, ngóh-deih _____ sihk faahn,
　　你　　　　，我 哋　　　　食 飯，

　　_____ tái nī go _____ lā.
　　　　　　睇 呢 個　　　啦。

B: Hóu aak. _____ máaih fēi sīn.
　　好 呃。　　　買 飛 先。

A: Ou! _____ maaih fēi maaih jó _____,
　　噢！　　　賣 飛 賣 咗　　　　，

　　_____ hóu wái _____ maaih yùhn la.
　　　　　　好 位　　　賣 完 喇。

　　Chóh daih yih sahp hòhng, _____ yiu gáu baak gáu sahp baat mān,
　　坐 第 二 十 行，　　　　要 九 百 九 十 八 蚊，

　　néih _____ séung mh séung tái a?
　　你　　　　想 唔 想 睇 呀？

B: Wa! Dī fēi _____! Gám ngóh-deih mh hóu heui tái la.
　　嘩！啲 飛　　　！咁 我 哋 唔 好 去 睇 喇。

Answers

Story

I. Answer and translation

1. b   2. b   3. d

1. When will Mr. Ko have a party in his house?

   a. tonight   b. Sunday   c. Saturday   d. 7 o'clock

2. What was Mrs. Ko doing at home?

   a. tidied the house, prepared seafood and snacks

   b. asked friends to come to tidy the house and have a party from the morning

   c. dressed up and waited for Mr. Ko to come home

   d. cooked food and prepared for today's party

3. What did Mr. Ko see when he returned home?

   a. Mrs. Ko was beautiful

   b. his house was clean

   c. Mr. Ko prepared a party for him

   d. many friends were having fun

II.

b. A: Lóuh-pòh, néih hóu leng. Gām-yaht heui jó bīn-douh a?

   老　婆，你　好　靚。今　日　去　咗　邊　度　呀？

   Darling (wife), you're beautiful. Where have you been today?

g. B: Gām-yaht mh dāk-hàahn chēut heui, jāp yéh jāp jó yāt yaht.

   今　日　唔　得　閒　出　去，執　嘢　執　咗　一　日。

   I was not free to go out. I have been tidying the house all day.

   Guih séi ngóh la! Néih a, néih chēut jó heui mh bōng ngóh!

   劫　死　我　喇！你　呀，你　出　咗　去　唔　幫　我！

   I'm dead tired! You were out and didn't help me.

d. A: Ngóh bōng néih hōi tói. Ngóh hóu tóuh-ngoh, gām-máahn yáuh māt-yéh sihk a?

   我　幫　你　開　枱。我　好　肚　餓，今　晚　有　乜　嘢　食　呀？

   I'll help you to set up the table. I'm hungry. What are we going to eat tonight?

a. B: Ngóh jíng jó hóu dō hói-sīn. Yáuh néih jūng-yi sihk ge yú lā, hā lā, juhng yáuh daai-jí tīm.

   我　整　咗　好　多　海鮮。有　你　鍾　意　食　嘅　魚啦、蝦啦，仲　有　帶　子　添。

   I cooked lots of seafood. These are things you like, for example, fish, prawns, and scallops.

c. A: Wa! Ngóh-deih dāk léuhng go yàhn, dím sihk dóu gam dō yéh a?

   嘩！我　哋　得　兩　個　人，點　食　到　咁　多　嘢　呀？

   Wow! There are only two of us. How can we eat that much?

f. B: Mē a? Néih wah chéng pàhng-yáuh fāan làih hōi *party* ma.

   咩呀？你　話　請　朋　友　返　嚟　開 party 嘛。

   What are you saying? You said you've invited some friends home for a party.

   Jéun-beih dō dī, ngāam ga la.

   準　備　多　啲，啱　㗎　喇。

   It's better to prepare more food; this is just right.

e. A: Hōi *party*? Mh-haih gām-yaht, haih sīng-kèih-yaht wo!

   開 party？唔　係　今　日，係　星　期　日　喎！

   Party? It's not today, it's Sunday!

Grammar practice translation I

1. They walked very fast.

2. The seafood is cooked to perfection.

3. I had a hard time finding you.

4. He takes leave too often; his boss does not like him.

Practice

a. Kéuih hohk jūng-màhn hohk dāk hóu hōi-sām.

佢　學　中　文　學　得　好　開　心。

He enjoyed learning Chinese.

b. Nī ga chē hàahng dāk hóu faai.

呢　架　車　行　　得　好　快。

This car goes fast.

c. Ngóh yám jáu yám dāk hóu síu.

我　　飲　酒　飲　得　好　少。

I drink very little.

Grammar practice translation II

1. He speaks so fast; I can't understand him.

2. It is so comfortable sitting here; I don't want to leave.

3. If friends weren't coming to my house, the house wouldn't be so clean.

4. The ticket for the concert is so expensive. How can that be possible?

5. We are so lucky. We found a parking space immediately after we arrived.

Suggested practice answers

Néih **gam chìh** làih, yíh-gīng hōi jó chē la.

你　咁　遲　　嚟，已　經　開　咗　車　喇。

You're so late; the bus has already gone.

Bun ga **gam pèhng**, faai dī máaih dō dī.

半　價　咁　平，　快　啲　買　　多　啲。

It's half-price, so cheap; let's buy a lot of these.

Ngóh gú mh dóu daht-yìhn **gam dung**.

我　估　唔　到　突　然　咁　凍。

I can't believe it has suddenly become so cold.

Grammar practice translation IV

1. I went to bed after tidying up.

2. I've bought some books. I'll wait until I have free time to read them.

3. Having dinner after 9 o'clock means I get hungry.

4. There is no holiday until December. We still have to wait for a long time.

Suggested practice answers

a. A: Néih fong gūng jī-hauh, sihk faahn sīn dihng fāan ūk-kéi sīn a?

你　放　工　之　後，食　飯　先定　　返　屋　企　先呀？

After work, will you have dinner first or go home first?

B: **Ngóh sihk jó faahn sīn-ji fāan ūk kéi.**

我　　食　咗　飯　　先至　返　屋企。

I'll eat before going home.

b. Ngóh séung **sāu jó chín** sīn-ji jouh yéh.

我　　想　　收咗　錢　　先至　做　嘢。

I want to get paid before doing work.

c. **Sīk jó gēi** sīn-ji gei-dāk yáuh yéh yiu séuhng móhng jouh.

熄　咗　機　先至　記　得　有　嘢　要　上　　網　做。

Only after I turned off the machine did I remember I have something to do online.

Grammar practice translation V

1. We have been on the bus a long time, waiting for it to leave.

2. I booked a table for an earlier time. Why do I still have to wait?

3. He told me he was not coming a long time ago.
4. I went to bed very early last night.
5. We have long passed the place you wanted to get off.

Practice question translation and suggested answers

a. Néih géi-sìh máaih fēi a?

你　幾　時　買　飛呀？

When will you buy the tickets?

A: Ngóh tīng-yaht sīn-ji máaih fēi.

我　聽　日　先至買　飛。

I'll buy the tickets tomorrow.

/ Ngóh yāt-jóu máaih jó fēi la.

我　一　早　買　咗飛喇。

I bought the tickets a long time ago.

b. Néih géi-sìh hōi-chí jāp ūk?

你　幾　時　開　始　執　屋？

When will you begin to tidy the house?

A: Ngóh dāk-hàahn sīn-ji jāp ūk lā.

我　得　閒　先至執屋啦。

I'll tidy the house when I am free.

/ Ngóh yāt jóu giu jó A May jāp ūk.

我　一　早　叫　咗阿May執　屋。

I asked May to tidy the house some time ago.

c. Néih *call* jó kéuih meih a?

你　call 咗佢　未　呀？

Have you called him?

A: Ngóh gām-máahn sīn-ji *call* kéuih.

我　今　晚　　先至 call 佢。

I'll call him tonight.

/ Ngóh yāt-jóu *call* jó kéuih la.

我　一　早 call 咗佢　喇。

I called him earlier.

d. Néih tīng-yaht géi-dím chēut heui a?

你　聽　日　幾　點　出　去呀？

What time will you go out tomorrow?

A: Ngóh sāam dím sīn-ji chēut heui.

我　三　點　先至出　去。

I'll go out at 3:00 tomorrow.

Ngóh yāt-jóu jauh chēut heui.

/ 我　一　早　就　出　去。

I'll go out early in the morning.

e. Néih yáuh móuh giu kéuih làih *party* a?

你　有　冇　叫佢　嚟 party 呀？

Did you ask him to come to the party?

A: Ngóh kàhm-máahn sīn-ji giu kéuih làih.

我　琴　晚　先至叫　佢　嚟。

I just asked him to come last night.

/ Ngóh yāt-jóu giu jó kéuih làih.

我　一　早　叫　咗佢　嚟。

I asked him to come much earlier.

Grammar practice translation VI

1. I waited for 10 minutes to get the medicine.
2. He was sick for one week.
3. I talked to him the whole night.
4. I was stuck in traffic for three hours. How unlucky.

General review

I.

1. Kéuih sihk dāk taai dō hói-sīn, só-yíh mh syū-fuhk.
   佢　食 得 太 多 海鮮，所 以 唔 舒 服。
   He ate too much seafood, so he was not feeling well.

2. Ngóh tái syū tái dāk hóu maahn, yāt go yuht sīn-ji tái dóu yāt bún syū.
   我　睇書睇得好慢，　一個月　先至睇到一本　書。
   I read very slowly. It takes me one month to read a book.

3. Ngóh yāt dāk hàahn jauh dá dihn wá béi mā-mìh kīng háh gái.
   我　一 得 閒 就 打 電 話 畀媽咪 傾 吓 偈。
   I call my mother to have a chat whenever I have time.

4. Go yín-cheung-wúi gam muhn, ngóh-deih yāt-jóu jáu jó la.
   個演 唱 會 咁 悶，我 　哋 一早 走 咗 喇。
   The concert was so boring; we left very early.

5. Ngóh tùhng hóu jūng-yi ge mìhng-sīng yíng séung jī-hauh,
   我 同 好 鍾 意嘅明 星 影 相 之後，
   hōi-sām dou fan mh jeuhk gaau.
   開 心 到 瞓 唔 着 覺。
   After I took a photo with my favourite celebrity, I was so happy that I couldn't sleep.

II. Answers and translation

1. d　2. e　3. b　4. c　5. a
1. a. a bottle of wine　b. a vehicle　c. a road　d. an hour　e. a ticket
2. a. uncomfortable　b. boring　c. troublesome　d. nervous　e. make a mistake
3. a. celebrity　b. downstairs　c. doctor　d. younger brother　e. boss
4. a. runny nose　b. headache　c. hungry　d. influenza　e. have a fever
5. a. driver　b. to tidy up　c. to collect money　d. to turn off a machine　e. to change date

III.

A: **Bāt-yùh** néih **sāang-yaht**, ngóh-deih **chēut heui** sihk faahn,
　不 如 你 生 日，我 哋 出 去 食 飯，
　jī-hauh tái nī go **yín-cheung-wúi** lā.
　之後 睇 呢個演 唱　會 啦。
　Shall we go out for dinner and then go to a concert on your birthday?

B: Hóu aak. **Jīk-hāak séuhng móhng** máaih fēi sīn.
　好 呃。即 刻 上　網 買 飛 先。
　Good idea. Let's buy tickets online immediately.

A: Ou! **Yíh-gīng hōi-chí** maaih fēi maaih jó **yāt go yuht**,
　噢！已 經 開 始 賣 飛賣 咗一個月，
　Oh! Tickets went on sale a month ago,
　só-yíh hóu wái **yāt-jóu** maaih yùhn la.
　所 以 好 位 一 早 賣 完 喇。
　so the good seats are all sold out.
　Chóh daih yih sahp hòhng, **yāt jēung fēi** yiu gáu baak gáu sahp baat mān,
　坐 第 二 十 行，一 張 飛要九 百 九 十 八 蚊，
　A ticket costs $998 in row 20.

néih **juhng** séung mh séung tái a?

你 仲 想 唔 想 睇 呀？

Do you still want to go?

B: Wa! Dī fēi **gwai dou chī-sin**!

嘩！啲 飛貴 到 黐 線！

Wow! The tickets are so expensive. That's crazy!

Gám ngóh-deih mh hóu heui tái la.

咁 我 哋 唔 好 去 睇 喇。

In this case, we'd better not go to the concert.

Hong Kong culture

What to do when invited to a Chinese family dinner

Hong Kong people enjoy gathering together to eat. When you are invited to a party, it is mainly about food. If you are invited to a Chinese family dinner, talk to the host and offer to bring fruit, dessert or appetizers. Wine is usually not a good gift; not many Hong Kong Chinese like to drink. If you want to bring flowers, be careful of the flower type and colour choice. White and yellow chrysanthemums should be avoided, as Chinese only bring them to tend graves and dedicate them at the shrine.

What to do when invited to a Chinese wedding banquet

You will need to get a gift cheque when attending a wedding banquet. Nowadays, the amount is expected to be around HK$1,000 per person. It varies with the venue and your relationship with the couple. The idea is to pay for your share of the dinner. Amounts in even numbers are preferred, symbolizing that the married couple are no longer "single". Odd number amounts, in contrast, are given out at funerals, implying that the grieving family would not want another ocassion like that. If you have no time to buy a gift cheque from a bank, you can also put cash or a personal cheque into a red packet. Give the cheque to anyone at the reception desk when you arrive.

Most invitations to a Chinese wedding banquet do not specify the dress code, so casual dress, something similar to workwear, would be fine. Wear something red, pink, purple, yellow or orange as these are considered lucky colours. Avoid wearing grey, white, brown, blue, or green, as these colours are often more appropriate at funerals.

Dinner is normally served from 9 to 11 p.m., and usually only tea will be served before dinner. If you are not used to eating so late, have a little snack before you go to the banquet.

8
Summer is hot and humid

Dialogue ◀801.mp3

➤ How's the weather today?

➤ What's the weather usually like?

➤ Why does Po dislike hot weather?

➤ What does Chu suggest doing this Sunday?

➤ Why would Po like to go to another place?

Jyū: Gām-yaht ge tīn-hei hóu hóu a! Hóu-chíh chāu-tīn hōi-chí la.

朱: 今 日 嘅天氣 好 好呀!好 似 秋 天 開 始 喇。

The weather's so nice today! It's like the beginning of autumn.

Bóu: Haih a! Dī fūng lèuhng-jam-jam, hóu syū-fuhk!

寶: 係 呀!啲風 涼 浸浸,好 舒 服!

Yes! The wind is cool; it's so comfortable.

Jyū: Pìhng-sìh yauh yiht yauh sāp, sān-fú dou séi.

朱: 平 時 又 熱 又 濕,辛 苦 到 死。

Usually it's hot and humid; makes me very uncomfortable.

Bóu: Haih lā, ngóh jeui pa hah-tīn yiht-laaht-laaht.

寶: 係 啦,我 最 怕 夏 天 熱 辣 辣。

That's very true; I hate the burning heat in summer.

Hóu-chói hó-yíh sèhng-yaht heui yàuh-séui.

好 彩 可 以 成 日 去 游 水。

Fortunately, I can often go swimming.

Jyū: Ngóh jūng-yi hàahng sāan dō dī. Bāt-yùh sīng-kèih-yaht ngóh-deih heui Sāi-Gung lā.

朱: 我 鍾 意 行 山 多 啲。不 如 星 期 日 我 哋 去 西 貢 啦。

I love hiking more. Shall we go to Sai Kung this Sunday?

Gó douh hó-yíh hóu hōi-sām wáan yāt yaht, hàahng sāan lā, yàuh séui lā, sihk hói-sīn lā.

果 度 可 以 好 開 心 玩 一 日,行 山 啦、游 水 啦、食 海 鮮 啦。

We can happily spend a day, going hiking, swimming, and eating seafood.

Bóu: Daap chē heui Sāi-Gung géi yúhn, bāt-yùh heui Sehk-Ou lā.
寶： 搭　車去西貢　幾遠，不如去石　澳啦。
It's quite far to go to Sai Kung. Let's go to Shek O.

Ngóh-deih hàahng Lùhng-Jek, jī-hauh heui Sehk-Ou sā-tāan yàuh séui, *B B Q*.
我　哋行　龍　脊，之後去石　澳沙灘游　水、B B Q。
We'll walk on the Dragon's Back, then go swimming and enjoy a barbeque at Shek O beach.

Jyū: Hóu aak. Ngóh jeui jūng-yi B B Q ga la.
朱： 好　呃。我　　最鍾　意 B B Q 㗎喇。
Good. Barbecue is my favourite.

Story: Sunday in Sai Kung   ◄802.mp3

Seuhng go sīng-kèih-yaht tīn-hei gam hóu, jeui ngāam heui Sāi-Gung wáan.
上　個星　期　日　天　氣咁　好，最　啱　去　西　貢　玩。
The weather last Sunday was so nice; it was the best time to go to Sai Kung.

Ngóh tùhng pàhng-yáuh yāt jóu heui Bāk-Tàahm-Chūng hàahng sāan,
我　同　朋　友　一　早　去　北　潭　涌　行　山，
My friends and I went hiking in Pak Tam Chung early in the morning; we

hàahng dou heui Lohng-Ké. Gó-douh haih Hēung-Góng jeui leng ge sā-tāan,
行　　到去　浪　茄。果度　係　香　港　最　靚　嘅沙灘，
walked all the way to Long Ke. It's the most beautiful beach in Hong Kong.

ngóh-deih hóu-chíh hái ngoih-gwok ge *resort*.
我　哋　好似　喺外　國　嘅 resort。
It felt like a resort in a foreign country.

Yàuh yùhn séui, ngóh-deih heui Sāi-Gung Máh-Tàuh sihk hói-sīn.
游　完　水，我　哋去　西　貢　碼　頭　食　海　鮮。
After swimming, we went for seafood at Sai Kung Pier.

Dī hói-sīn yauh hóu-sihk yauh mh gwai.
啲海　鮮　又　好　食　又　唔　貴。
The seafood was delicious and inexpensive.

Tēng-góng Sāi-Gung juhng yáuh hóu dō deih-fōng hóu leng,
聽　講　西　貢　仲　有　好　多　地　方　好　靚，
I heard that there are many more beautiful places in Sai Kung.

ngóh dāk-hàahn yāt-dihng wán pàhng-yáuh heui Sāi-Gung joi wáan gwo.
我　得　閒　一　定　搵　朋　友　去　西　貢　再　玩　過。
When I have time, I'll certainly go to Sai Kung again with friends.

Questions for the story

I. Answer the questions.   ◄803.mp3

1. Kéuih tùhng pàhng-yáuh heui Sāi-Gung bīn-douh wáan a?
   佢　同　朋　友　去　西　貢　邊　度　玩　呀？

2. Lohng-Ké ge sā-tāan hóu-chíh bīn-douh gam leng a?
   浪　　茄嘅沙灘　好　似　邊　度　咁　靚　呀？

3. Kéuih-deih gok-dāk Sāi-Gung ge hói-sīn dím a?
   佢　哋　覺　得西　貢　嘅海　鮮　點　呀？

II. Listen and complete the dialogue with the expressions in the table.   ◀804.mp3

daap dīk-sí yahp heui 搭 的 士 入 去	dím heui 點 去	gam muhn 咁 悶
hàahng gāai 行　街	yāt jóu 一 早	géi yúhn 幾 遠
hàahng sāan 行　山	léuhng go jūng-tàuh 兩 個 鐘 頭	ngóh daai néih heui 我 帶 你 去
sèhng-yaht 成 日	seuhng go sīng-kèih-yaht 上 個 星 期 日	sihk hói-sīn 食 海 鮮
tēng góng 聽 講	tùhng pàhng-yáuh 同 朋 友	yauh dō yàhn 又 多 人
yauh hóu-sihk yauh mh gwai 又 好 食 又 唔 貴	yàuh séui 游 水	

A: Néih _____ heui jó bīn-douh a?
　 你 　　　　　　 去 咗 邊 度 呀？

B: Ngóh _____ heui Sāi-Gung wáan jó _____.
　 我 　　　　　　 去 西 貢 玩 咗 　　　　　。

A: Néih-deih _____ Sāi-Gung a?
　 你 哋 　　　　　　 西 貢 呀？

B: Ngóh-deih hái Hāang-Háu deih-tit jaahm _____.
　 我 哋 喺 坑 口 地 鐵 站 　　　　。

A: Heui Sāi-Gung _____. Gó douh yáuh māt-yéh wáan a?
　 去 西 貢 　　　　。果 度 有 乜 嘢 玩 呀？

B: Ngóh-deih _____ hái Bāk-Tàahm-Chūng _____,
　 我 哋 　　　　　 喺 北 潭 涌 　　　　　，

　 gīng-gwo Deih-Jāt Gūng-Yún,
　 經 過 地 質 公 園，

　 hàahng _____, heui dou Lohng-Ké _____,
　 行 　　　　，去 到 浪 茄 　　　　　，

　 Yeh-máahn hái Sāi-Gung Máh-Tàuh _____.
　 夜 晚 喺 西 貢 碼 頭 　　　　。

A: Ngóh _____ Sāi-Gung ge hói-sīn hóu hóu-sihk.
　 我 　　　　　 西 貢 嘅 海 鮮 好 好 食。

B: Haih a! Dī hói-sīn _____.
　 係 呀！啲 海 鮮 　　　　。

　 Gám, néih sīng-kèih-yaht heui jó bīn-douh a?
　 咁， 你 星 期 日 去 咗 邊 度 呀？

A: Ngóh heui Jīm-Sā-Jéui _____, _____ yauh móuh yéh máaih.
　 我 去 尖 沙 咀 　　　　，　　　　　 又 冇 嘢 買。

B: Hah chi _____ hàahng sāan lā.
　 下 次 　　　　　 行 山 啦。

　 Mh sái sèhng-yaht hàahng gāai, yám chàh _____.
　 唔 使 成 日 行 街、飲 茶 　　　　。

Vocabulary ◂805.mp3

1.	hah-tīn	夏天	summer
2.	chāu-tīn	秋天	autumn
3.	ngoih-gwok	外國	foreign country
4.	deih-fōng	地方	place
5.	sā-tāan	沙灘	beach
6.	fūng	風	wind
7.	sāp	濕	humid; wet
8.	yúhn	遠	far away
9.	yiht-laaht-laaht	熱辣辣	burning hot
10.	lèuhng-jam-jam	涼浸浸	cool
11.	pa	怕	be afraid of; worry about
12.	yàuh séui	游水	swimming
13.	hàahng sāan	行山	hiking (literally, walk on the mountain)
14.	hàahng gāai	行街	shopping (literally, walk on the street)
15.	gīng-gwo	經過	pass by; walk past
16.	pìhng-sìh	平時	usually; normally
17.	yeh-máahn	夜晚	evening; night
18.	géi	幾	quite; rather
19.	jeui	最	most
20.	yauh	又	also; both . . . and
21.	hó-yíh	可以	can; may
22.	hóu chíh	好似	seem like
23.	tēng góng	聽講	hearsay

Grammar practice

I. hó-yíh 可以 (can; may; allow to)   ◂806.mp3

Affirmative: hó-yíh 可以 + verb

e.g., Hóu-chói **hó-yíh** sèhng-yaht heui yàuh-séui.

好 彩 可 以 成 日 去 游 水。

Fortunately, I can go swimming all day.

Gó douh **hó-yíh** hóu hōi-sām wáan yāt yaht.

果 度 可 以 好 開 心 玩 一 日。

We can happily spend a day there.

Negative: mh hó-yíh 唔可以 + verb

e.g., Gām-yaht **mh hó-yíh** yàuh-séui.

今 日 唔 可 以 游 水。

We can't swim today.

Interrogative: hó mh hó-yíh 可唔可以 + verb

e.g., Gāai-háu **hó mh hó-yíh** tìhng chē a?

街 口 可 唔 可 以 停 車 呀?

Can we stop at the intersection?

(Yes) hó-yíh 可以   (No) mh hó-yíh 唔可以

1. Gam sāk chē, ngóh géi-sìh **hó-yíh** lohk chē a?

   咁 塞 車,我 幾 時 可 以 落 車 呀?

2. Hái bā-sí **hó mh hó-yíh** yám yéh, sihk yéh a?

   喺 巴 士 可 唔 可 以 飲 嘢、食 嘢 呀?

3. Hōi wúi ge sìh-hauh **mh hó-yíh** hōi dihn-wá.

   開 會 嘅 時 候 唔 可 以 開 電 話。

4. **Hó mh hó-yíh** bōng ngóh mahn háh pàhng-yáuh a?

   可 唔 可 以 幫 我 問 吓 朋 友 呀?

5. **Hó mh hó-yíh** mh heui gam yúhn máaih yéh a?

   可 唔 可 以 唔 去 咁 遠 買 嘢 呀?

   Hó-yíh hái làuh-hah máaih, gwai dī jauh gwai dī lā.

   可 以 喺 樓 下 買,貴 啲 就 貴 啲 啦。

6. A: Tīn-hei mh hóu, **hó mh hó-yíh** gói kèih a?

   天 氣 唔 好,可 唔 可 以 改 期 呀?

   B: **Mh hó-yíh** gói, yāt gói kèih jauh hóu màh-fàahn.

   唔 可 以 改,一 改 期 就 好 麻 煩。

✎ Practice

a. Use the prompts below to help you.
   i. Make a sentence with "hó-yíh 可以".
   ii. Make a sentence with "mh hó-yíh 唔可以".

b. Ask questions using "hó mh hó-yíh 可唔可以" and the following phrases, and then answer.
   i. hái làuh-hah paak chē
       喺 樓 下 泊 車
   ii. hah go yuht chéng ga
       下 個 月 請 假
   iii. je chín béi ngóh
        借 錢 畀 我

II. Compare the usage of "hó-yíh 可以" and "dóu 到"   ◀807.mp3

> hó-yíh 可以 + verb (can; may; allow to)
> verb + dóu 到 (be able to; manage to)

1. Nī douh **hó-yíh** paak chē, daahn-haih chē wái gam sai, ngóh paak **mh dóu** chē.
   呢 度 可 以 泊 車，但 係 車 位 咁 細，我 泊 唔 到 車。
   It is possible to park here, but the space is so small. I can't park my car.

2. Ngóh **mh hó-yíh** jān-haih fong ga,
   我 唔 可 以 真 係 放 假，

   lóuh-sai yiu sèhng-yaht wán **dóu** ngóh.
   老 細 要 成 日 搵 到 我。
   I can't really be on leave; my boss needs to see me regularly.

III. yauh 又 (and also)   ◀808.mp3

> e.g., Dī hói-sīn **yauh** hóu-sihk **yauh** mh gwai.
> 啲 海 鮮 又 好 食 又 唔 貴。
> *The seafood is delicious and inexpensive.*
>
> Hēung-Góng ge hah-tīn **yauh** yiht **yauh** sāp.
> 香 港 嘅 夏 天 又 熱 又 濕。
> *The summer in Hong Kong is hot and humid.*
>
> Ngóh heui Jīm-Sā-Jéui hàahng gāai, **yauh** dō yàhn **yauh** móuh yéh máaih.
> 我 去 尖 沙 咀 行 街，又 多 人 又 冇 嘢 買。
> *I went shopping in Tsim Sha Tsui. There were many people and I didn't find anything to buy.*

1. Ngóh yìh-gā **yauh** guih **yauh** tóuh-ngoh.
   我 而 家 又 劫 又 肚 餓。

2. Tīn-hei **yauh** sāp **yauh** dung, hóu mh syū-fuhk.
   天 氣 又 濕 又 凍，好 唔 舒 服。

3. Nī gāan chāan-tēng **yauh** pèhng **yauh** hóu sihk **yauh** dō yéh sihk.
呢 間 餐 廳 又 平 又 好 食 又 多 嘢 食。

✎ Practice

Put "yauh 又" in the correct places in the sentences.

a. daap deih-tit hóu faai hóu fōng-bihn
搭 地 鐵 好 快 好 方 便

b. làuh beih-séui tùhng hàuh-lùhng tung
流 鼻 水 同 喉 嚨 痛

c. gāan ūk hóu gōn-jehng hóu syū-fuhk
間 屋 好 乾 淨 好 舒 服

IV. hóu chíh 好似 (seem like; look like; resemble)   ◀809.mp3

e.g., Dī sā-tāan **hóu-chíh** ngoih-gwok ge gam leng.
啲 沙 灘 好 似 外 國 嘅 咁 靚。
The beaches are as beautiful as the ones in foreign countries.

1. **Hóu chíh** séung lohk yúh wo. Néih yáuh móuh daai jē a?
好 似 想 落 雨 喎。你 有 冇 帶 遮 呀？

2. Hóu dō yàhn máaih yéh, **hóu chíh** dī yéh mh sái chín.
好 多 人 買 嘢，好 似 啲 嘢 唔 使 錢。

3. Sihk báau jauh fan, fan báau yauh sihk, **hóu chíh** bìh-bī.
食 飽 就 瞓，瞓 飽 又 食，好 似 BB。

4. Néih sihk dāk gam faai, **hóu-chíh** hóu tóuh-ngoh.
你 食 得 咁 快，好 似 好 肚 餓。

5. A: Néih chíh mh chíh màh-mā a?
你 似 唔 似 媽 媽 呀？

B: Ngóh **hóu chíh** màh-mā, dōu **hóu chíh** bàh-bā.
我 好 似 媽 媽，都 好 似 爸 爸。

✎ Practice

a. Make a sentence with "hóu chíh 好似".

b. Answer these questions with "hóu chíh 好似".

i. Gó douh yáuh móuh yàhn a?
果 度 有 冇 人 呀？

ii. Kéuih yáuh móuh jāp yéh a? Jéun-beih jó meih a?
佢 有 冇 執 嘢 呀？準 備 咗 未 呀？

iii. Nī go yín-cheung-wúi maaih yùhn fēi meih a?
呢 個 演 唱 會 賣 完 飛 未 呀？

V. pa 怕 (be afraid of; worry about; dislike)   ◀810.mp3

> e.g., Ngóh jeui **pa** yiht-laaht-laaht ge tīn-hei.
> 我　最　怕熱辣　辣　嘅天氣。
> *I dislike hot weather the most.*

1. A: Néih **pa mh pa** yāt go yàhn hái ūk-kéi?
   你　怕　唔　怕　一個人　喺屋企？
   B: Ngóh **pa**, só-yíh yāt fāan ūk-kéi jauh hōi dihn-sih.
   我　怕，所以一返屋企就　開　電　視。

2. Ngóh jūng-yi sihk jyū-gū-līk, daahn-haih **pa** fèih.
   我　鍾意食朱古力，但　係怕肥。

3. Ngóh hóu **pa** muhn, só-yíh sèhng-yaht yeuk pàhng-yáuh heui wáan.
   我　好怕悶，所以成　日　約朋　友去　玩。

4. Ngóh mh **pa** màh-fàahn, ngóh jūng-yi bōng yàhn.
   我　唔怕麻　煩，我　鍾意幫　人。

✎ Practice

Make sentences to describe whether you are afraid of the following:

a. dung   b. gin lóuh-sai   c. sihk yeuhk   d. lohk daaih yúh
凍　　　　見老　細　　　食　藥　　　落　大　雨

VI. jeui 最 + adjective (most, superlative)   ◀811.mp3

> e.g., Yìh-gā **jeui** ngāam heui hàahng sāan.
> 而　家最　啱　去行　山。
> *It's the best time of a year to go hiking.*
>
> Ngóh **jeui** jūng-yi BBQ.
> 我　最　鍾　意BBQ。
> *Barbecue is my favourite.*

1. Tùhng pàhng-yáuh yāt-chàih jíng yéh sihk **jeui** hōi-sām.
   同　朋　友　一　齊　整　嘢食最　開　心。

2. Ngóh mh jūng-yi séuhng móhng máaih yéh, ngóh **jeui** pa gáau cho.
   我　唔鍾意上　網　買　嘢，我　最怕搞　錯。

3. Tùhng nī go haak hōi wúi haih **jeui** tàuh-tung ge.
   同　呢個客　開　會係　最　頭痛嘅。

VII. géi 幾 + adjective (quite, rather)   ◂812.mp3

> e.g., Heui Sāi-Gung **géi** yúhn.
> 去　西　貢　幾　遠。
> *Sai Kung is rather far.*

1. Heui sā-tāan yàuh séui **géi** fōng-bihn, daap chē mh haih **géi** yúhn.
   去　沙灘　游　水　幾　方　便，搭　車　唔　係　幾　遠。

2. Kéuih jáu dāk **géi** daht-yìhn, móuh yàhn jī kéuih jáu jó.
   佢　走　得　幾　突　然，冇　人　知　佢　走　咗。

3. Yāt jahn gin go daaih haak, só-yíh ngóh-deih **géi** gán-jēung.
   一　陣　見　個　大　客，所　以　我　哋　幾　緊　張。

Pyramid drill   ◂813.mp3

1.

heui yàuh-séui

去　游　水

sèhng-yaht heui yàuh-séui

成　日　去　游　水

hó-yíh sèhng-yaht heui yàuh-séui

可　以　成　日　去　游　水

ngóh hó-yíh sèhng-yaht heui yàuh-séui

我　可　以　成　日　去　游　水

Hah-tīn ngóh hó-yíh sèhng-yaht heui yàuh-séui

夏　天　我　可　以　成　日　去　游　水

Hah-tīn ngóh jeui hōi-sām hó-yíh sèhng-yaht heui yàuh-séui.

夏　天　我　最　開　心　可　以　成　日　去　游　水。

The happiest thing in summer is that I can often go swimming.

2.

gam leng

咁　靚

dī sā-tāan gam leng

啲　沙　灘　咁　靚

Sāi-Gung dī sā-tāan gam leng

西　貢　啲　沙　灘　咁　靚

Sāi-Gung dī sā-tāan hóu-chíh ngoih-gwok ge *resort* gam leng

西　貢　啲　沙　灘　好　似　外　國　嘅 resort 咁　靚

Tēng-góng Sāi-Gung dī sā-tāan hóu-chíh ngoih-gwok ge *resort* gam leng.

聽　講　西　貢　啲　沙　灘　好　似　外　國　嘅 resort 咁　靚。

I heard that the beaches in Sai Kung are as beautiful as resorts in a foreign country.

General review

I. Listen and rearrange the dialogue. ◀814.mp3

a. Gám hah-tīn néih dím gwo a?
咁 夏 天 你 點 過 呀？

b. Néih dūng-tīn wúih jouh māt-yéh a?
你 冬 天 會 做 乜 嘢 呀？

c. Néih jūng mh jūng-yi Hēung-Góng ge hah-tīn a?
你 鍾 唔 鍾 意 香 港 嘅 夏 天 呀？

d. Ngóh jūng-yi tùhng pàhng-yáuh BBQ, hàahng sāan dōu hóu syū-fuhk,
我 鍾 意 同 朋 友 BBQ，行 山 都 好 舒 服，

dī fūng lèuhng-jam-jam.
啲 風 涼 浸 浸。

e. Gám néih jeui jūng-yi géi-sìh a?
咁 你 最 鍾 意 幾 時 呀？

f. Hah-tīn yiht-laaht-laaht, ngóh jeui pa.
夏 天 熱 辣 辣，我 最 怕。

g. Ngóh sèhng-yaht heui yàuh séui, mh sái gam yiht.
我 成 日 去 游 水，唔 使 咁 熱。

h. Ngóh jeui jūng-yi dūng-tīn, ngóh pa yiht, daahn-haih mh pa dung.
我 最 鍾 意 冬 天，我 怕 熱，但 係 唔 怕 凍。

II. Match the questions with the answers. ◀815.mp3

1. Ngóh-deih hàahng sāan hàahng jó léuhng go jūng-tàuh,
我 哋 行 山 行 咗 兩 個 鐘 頭，

hó mh hó-yíh yāu-sīk háh a?
可 唔 可 以 休 息 吓 呀？

2. Dī yàhn sèhng-yaht heui Tùhng-Lòh-Wāan jouh māt-yéh a?
啲 人 成 日 去 銅 鑼 灣 做 乜 嘢 呀？

3. Hái Yīng-Gwok, chāu-tīn ge tīn-hei dím ga?
喺 英 國， 秋 天 嘅 天 氣 點 㗎？

4. Dī yú hóu-chíh jíng dāk hóu hóu sihk. Ngóh hó mh hó-yíh sihk síu-síu a?
啲 魚 好 似 整 得 好 好 食。我 可 唔 可 以 食 少 少 呀？

5. Néih gám-mouh ge sìh-hauh dím-yéung sān-fú a?
   你 感 冒 嘅時 候 點 樣 辛 苦呀？

☐ a. Néih jūng-yi sihk géi-dō dōu dāk. Giu néih pàhng-yáuh dōu yāt-chàih sihk lā.
      你 鍾 意 食 幾 多 都 得。叫 你 朋 友 都 一 齊 食 啦。

☐ b. Ngóh yauh faat-sīu yauh làuh beih-séui yauh hàuh-lùhng tung, hóu sān-fú.
      我 又 發 燒 又 流 鼻 水 又 喉 嚨 痛，好 辛 苦。

☐ c. Kéuih-deih jeui jūng-yi heui sihk faahn, yám chàh,
      佢 哋 最 鍾 意 去 食 飯、飲 茶，
      juhng yáuh hàahng gāai, máaih yéh.
      仲 有 行 街、買 嘢。

☐ d. Ngóh mh sái yāu-sīk. Néih gok-dāk guih, ngóh-deih jauh yāu-sīk háh lā.
      我 唔 使 休 息。你 覺 得 劾，我 哋 就 休 息 吓 啦。

☐ e. Ngóh meih heui gwo gó douh, tēng-góng chāu-tīn lèuhng-jam-jam,
      我 未 去 過 果 度，聽 講 秋 天 涼 浸 浸，
      hóu syū-fuhk.
      好 舒 服。

Answers

Story

I.

1. Kéuih tùhng pàhng-yáuh heui Sāi-Gung bīn-douh wáan a?

佢 同 朋 友 去 西貢 邊 度 玩 呀？

Where in Sai Kung did he and his friends go?

A: Kéuih-deih heui jó Bāk-Tàahm-Chūng, Lohng-Ké tùhng Sāi-Gung Máh-Tàuh.

佢 哋 去咗北 潭 涌、浪 茄同 西貢 碼頭。

They went to Pak Tam Chung, Long Ke, and Sai Kung Pier.

2. Lohng-Ké ge sā-tāan hóu-chíh bīn-douh gam leng a?

浪 茄嘅沙灘 好 似 邊 度 咁 靚 呀？

Long Ke beach can be compared to which beautiful place?

A: Hóu-chíh ngoih-Gwok ge *resort* gam leng.

好 似 外 國 嘅 resort 咁 靚。

It is as beautiful as a resort in a foreign country.

3. Kéuih-deih gok-dāk Sāi-Gung ge hói-sīn dím a?

佢 哋 覺 得 西貢 嘅海鮮 點 呀？

What do they think about the seafood in Sai Kung?

A: Sāi-Gung dī hói-sīn yauh hóu-sihk yauh mh gwai.

西貢 啲海鮮 又 好 食 又 唔貴。

Seafood in Sai Kung is delicious and inexpensive.

II.

A: Néih **seuhng go sīng-kèih-yaht** heui jó bīn-douh a?

你 上 個星 期 日 去 咗邊 度 呀？

Where were you last Sunday?

B: Ngóh **tùhng pàhng-yáuh** heui Sāi-Gung wáan jó **sèhng-yaht**.

我 同 朋 友 去 西貢 玩 咗成 日。

I went to Sai Kung with friends and spent the whole day there.

A: Néih-deih **dím heui** Sāi-Gung a?

你 哋 點 去 西貢 呀？

How did you go to Sai Kung?

B: Ngóh-deih hái Hāang-Háu deih-tit jaahm **daap dīk-sí yahp heui**.

我 哋 喺坑 口 地鐵站 搭 的 士 入 去。

We took a taxi from Hang Hau MTR station.

A: Heui Sāi-Gung **géi yúhn**. Gó douh yáuh māt-yéh wáan a?

去 西貢 幾遠。果 度 有 乜 嘢 玩 呀？

Sai Kung is quite far. What's fun to do there?

B: Ngóh-deih **yāt jóu** hái Bāk-Tàahm-Chūng **hàahng sāan**, gīng-gwo Deih-Jāt Gūng-Yún,

我 哋 一 早 喺北 潭 涌 行 山，經 過 地質公 園，

We went hiking from Pak Tam Chung early in the morning, past Global Geopark,

hàahng **léuhng go jūng-tàuh**, heui dou Lohng-Ké **yàuh séui**,

行 兩 個鐘 頭，去 到 浪 茄游 水，

walking for two hours, until we reached Long Ke to swim.

yeh-máahn hái Sāi-Gung Máh-Tàuh **sihk hói-sīn**.

夜 晚 喺西貢 碼 頭 食 海鮮。

In the evening, we had seafood at Sai Kung Pier.

A: Ngóh **tēng góng** Sāi-Gung ge hói-sīn hóu hóu-sihk.

我 聽 講 西貢 嘅海鮮 好 好 食。

I heard that the seafood in Sai Kung is delicious.

B: Haih a! Dī hói-sīn **yauh hóu-sihk yauh mh gwai**.

係　呀！啲海鮮又　好　食又　唔貴。

Yes! The seafood is delicious and inexpensive.

Gám, néih sīng-kèih-yaht heui jó bīn-douh a?

咁，你星期日去咗邊度呀？

Well, where were you last Sunday?

A: Ngóh heui Jīm-Sā-Jéui **hàahng gāai**,

我　去尖沙咀行　街，

I went shopping in Tsim Sha Tsui.

yauh dō yàhn yauh móuh yéh máaih.

又　多人又　冇　嘢買。

There were many people and I didn't find anything to buy.

B: Hah chi **ngóh daai néih heui** hàahng sāan lā.

下　次我帶　你去行　山啦。

Next time I'll take you hiking.

Mh sái sèhng-yaht hàahng gāai, yám chàh **gam muhn**.

唔使成　日行　街、飲茶咁悶。

You don't have to go shopping and for yum cha so often. It's boring.

Grammar practice translation I

1. Such a big traffic jam. When can I get off the bus?

2. Are we allowed to eat and drink on the bus?

3. We shouldn't switch on the phone when we are in a meeting.

4. Can you help me to ask your friend?

5. Shall we not go so far to buy things? If we can buy things downstairs, even if it's more expensive, it doesn't matter.

6. A: The weather isn't good. Shall we change the date?

B: We can't change it. If we change the date, there will be a lot of trouble.

Practice b. answers

i. Ngóh hó mh hó-yíh hái làuh-hah paak chē?

我　可唔可以喺樓　下泊　車？

May I park my car downstairs?

(Yes) Néih hó-yíh hái làuh-hah paak chē.

你　可以喺樓　下泊　車。

You can park downstairs.

(No) Néih mh hó-yíh hái làuh-hah paak chē.

你　唔可以喺樓　下泊　車。

You can't park downstairs.

ii. Ngóh hah go yuht hó mh hó-yíh chéng ga?

我　下個月　可唔可以請　假？

May I take leave next month?

(Yes) Móuh mahn-tàih, néih hó-yíh chéng ga.

冇　問　題，你可以請　假。

No problem. you can take leave.

(No) Gūng-sī hóu mòhng, néih mh hó-yíh chéng ga.

公　司好忙，你唔可以請　假。

The company is busy; you can't take leave.

iii. Néih hó mh hó-yíh je dī chín béi ngóh? Je yāt chīn mān dāk mh dāk a?

你　可唔可以借啲錢畀我？借一千　蚊　得唔得呀？

Would you lend me some money, say $1,000?

(Yes) Móuh mahn-tàih, ngóh hó-yíh je yāt chīn mān béi néih.
冇　問　題，我　可　以　借一　千　蚊　畀　你。
No problem. I can lend you $1000.

(No) Mh hó-yíh, ngóh dōu móuh chín.
唔 可 以，我　都　冇　錢。
I can't. I don't have money.

Grammar practice translation III

1. I'm tired and hungry.
2. The weather's damp and cold; it's very uncomfortable.
3. This restaurant is inexpensive and there is a wide selection of tasty food.

Practice answers

a. daap deih-tit yauh faai yauh fōng-bihn
搭　地　鐵 又　快 又　方　便
Taking the MTR is fast and convenient.

b. Ngóh yauh làuh beih-séui yauh hàuh-lùhng tung
我　又　流 鼻 水 又　喉　嚨　痛
My nose is runny and I have a sore throat.

c. gāan uk yauh gōn-jehng yauh syū-fuhk
間　屋 又　乾　淨 又　舒 服
The house is clean and comfortable.

Grammar practice translation IV

1. It seems like it is going to rain. Have you brought an umbrella?
2. Many people are buying things; it seems like it is free.
3. I ate until my stomach was full and then went to bed. I had enough sleep and then ate again. It seemed like I am a baby.
4. You are eating so fast; you look so hungry.
5. A: Do you resemble your mother?
   B: I look like my mother, and I look like my father.

Practice b. answers

i. Gó douh yáuh móuh yàhn a?
果 度 有 冇　人　呀？
Is there anyone?

Gó douh hóu-chíh móuh yàhn.
果 度 好 似 冇　人。
It seems like there is nobody there.

ii. Kéuih yáuh móuh jāp yéh a? Jéun-beih jó meih a?
佢　有　冇　執 嘢 呀？準　備 咗 未 呀？
Has he packed? Is he ready?

Kéuih meih jāp yéh. Kéuih hóu-chíh móuh jéun-beih.
佢　未　執 嘢。佢　好 似 冇　準　備。
He hasn't packed anything. He seems unprepared.

iii. Nī go yín-cheung-wúi maaih yùhn fēi meih a?
呢 個 演 唱　會 賣　完　飛 未 呀？
Have the tickets of this concert been sold out?

Nī go yín-cheung-wúi hóu-chíh maaih yùhn fēi la.
呢 個 演 唱　會 好 似 賣　完　飛 喇。
The tickets for this concert seem to be sold out.

Grammar practice translation V

1. A: Are you afraid of being alone at home?

   B: I am afraid, so I turn on the TV immediately after returning home.

2. I like chocolate, but I'm worried that it will make me fat.

3. I dislike feeling bored, so I often ask friends to go out for fun.

4. I am not afraid of trouble; I like to help others.

Suggested practice answers

a. Ngóh hóu pa dung

   我　好　怕　凍。

   I dislike cold weather.

b. Ngóh mh pa gin lóuh-sai

   我　唔　怕　見　老　細。

   I'm not afraid to meet the boss.

c. Ngóh hóu pa sihk yeuhk.

   我　好　怕　食　藥。

   I hate to take medicine.

d. Ngóh mh pa lohk daaih yúh

   我　唔　怕　落　大　雨。

   I'm not afraid of heavy rain.

Grammar practice translation VI

1. Cooking with friends makes me happy.

2. I don't like to shop online because I am afraid of making mistakes.

3. Having a meeting with this client gives me the biggest headache.

Grammar practice translation VII

1. It's quite convenient to go to the beach to swim. It is not far if you take a bus.

2. He left quite suddenly, so no one knew he had gone.

3. We will meet an important client in a moment, so we are quite nervous.

General review

I.

c. A: Néih jūng mh jūng-yi Hēung-Góng ge hah-tīn a?

   你　鍾　唔　鍾　意香　港　嘅夏　天　呀？

   Do you like the summer in Hong Kong?

f. B: Hah-tīn yiht-laaht-laaht, ngóh jeui pa.

   夏　天　熱辣　辣，我　最　怕。

   Summer is burning hot; I dislike it the most.

e. A: Gám néih jeui jūng-yi géi-sìh a?

   咁　你　最　鍾　意幾　時　呀？

   What is your favourite season?

h. B: Ngóh jeui jūng-yi dūng-tīn, ngóh pa yiht, daahn-haih mh pa dung.

   我　最　鍾　意冬　天，我　怕熱，但　係　唔怕凍。

   I like winter the most. I dislike hot weather, but I am not afraid of the cold.

b. A: Néih dūng-tīn wúih jouh māt-yéh a?

   你　冬　天　會　做　乜　嘢　呀？

   What will you do in winter?

d. B: Ngóh jūng-yi tùhng pàhng-yáuh BBQ, hàahng sāan dōu hóu syū-fuhk,

   我　鍾　意同　朋　友　BBQ，行　山　都　好　舒　服，

   dī fūng lèuhng-jam-jam.

   啲　風　涼　浸　浸。

   I like to have a barbeque with friends. Hiking is also good. The wind is cool.

a. A: Gám hah-tīn néih dím gwo a?

　咁　夏　天　你　點　過　呀？

How do you spend your summer?

g. B: Ngóh sèhng-yaht heui yàuh séui, mh sái gam yiht.

　我　成　日　去　游　水，唔　使　咁　熱。

I often go swimming, so I don't feel so hot.

II. Question and answer translation

1. We have been hiking for two hours. Shall we have a rest?

　d. I don't need to rest. If you feel tired, we can take a rest.

2. What do people often do in Causeway Bay?

　c. They like to eat, enjoy dim sum, and shop.

3. What is the weather like in the UK in the autumn?

　e. I haven't been there. I heard that it is cool in the autumn; it's very comfortable.

4. The fish looks delicious. May I try some?

　a. You can eat as much as you like. Ask your friends to eat with you.

5. How bad do you feel when you have the flu?

　b. I have a fever, a runny nose, and a sore throat. It is terrible.

Hong Kong culture

Enjoying nature in metropolitan Hong Kong

Hong Kong is a metropolitan city, so it is amazing to find that we can reach country parks, hiking trails, and beaches in less than an hour from any part of the busy urban areas. Many popular nature walks can be reached easily by public transport. Here are two trails highly recommended.

Dragon's Back on Hong Kong Island

The starting point is in Shek O Country Park, which can be reached in about half an hour by bus or minibus from Shau Kei Wan MTR station. Hiking along the undulating spinal ridge of Dragon's Back, we can enjoy the stunning coastal scenery of Shek O, Tai Long Wan, Stanley Peninsula, Tai Tam, and the South China Sea. In the distance, we can see the Clear Water Bay Peninsula and the islands in the eastern sea. At the foot of Dragon's Back is Shek O village, with its sandy, wavy beach and alfresco restaurants, making it an excellent way to spend a great half-day outdoors.

Pak Tam Chung to Long Ke in Sai Kung

An excellent section of the 100 km MacLehose trail

Set off from the roundabout next to Pak Tam Chung Holiday Camp, and go via High Island Reservoir East Dam, where you will be enchanted by the panoramic views of the reservoir, rolling peaks, and the peculiar dolosse cofferdam. This is the gateway to Hong Kong's UNESCO Global Geopark. Along this trail you can enjoy many geo-treasures such as sea caves, sea stack Po Pin Chau, and hexagonal and S-shaped rock columns. Finally, after 2.5 hours you will be rewarded when you reach Long Ke Village with its tranquil white sandy beach and emerald green waters. It's around 30 minutes' walk from Long Ke back to East Dam, where you can catch a taxi to return home.

For details, please visit www.discoverhongkong.com.

9
It's getting colder and colder

Dialogue ◂901.mp3

➢ What will the temperature be tonight?

➢ What does Ching suggest Wai do?

➢ How does Wai feel when he is at home?

➢ What made Hong Kong people feel very cold at 10°C?

Wàih: Néih gok mh gok-dāk yuht-làih-yuht dung a?
維： 你 覺 唔 覺 得 越 嚟 越 凍 呀？
Do you feel that it's becoming colder and colder?

Tīn-màhn-tòih wah gām-máahn dāk sahp douh ja!
天 文 台 話 今 晚 得 十 度 咋！
The observatory said the temperature will drop to 10°C tonight.

Jīng: Ngóh mh pa dung ge. Néih dung jauh jeuk dō gihn sāam lā.
晶： 我 唔 怕 凍 嘅。你 凍 就 着 多 件 衫 啦。
I'm not afraid of cold weather. If you feel cold, just put on more clothes.

Wàih: Nī géi yaht ngóh ūk-kéi hóu-chíh syut-gwaih gam dung,
維： 呢 幾 日 我 屋 企 好 似 雪 櫃 咁 凍，
These days, my house is as cold as a fridge.

jeuk géi-dō gihn lāang-sāam dōu mh gau.
着 幾 多 件 冷 衫 都 唔 夠。
No matter how many sweaters I wear, it is still not enough.

Jīng: Kèih-saht hái ngoih-gwok, sahp douh mh syun dung,
晶： 其 實 喺 外 國， 十 度 唔 算 凍，
Actually in foreign countries, 10°C is not considered cold,

daahn-haih Hēung-Góng yàhn jauh wah dung, dung, dung.
但 係 香 港 人 就 話 凍、凍、凍。
but Hong Kong people would say it's very cold.

Néih tái háh néih, sáu dou ngaahng saai gám-yéung.
你 睇 吓 你，手 都 硬 晒 咁 樣。
Look at you; you look as if your hands are stiff.

Wàih: Hēung-Góng dōu mh tùhng ngoih-gwok.

維： 香　港　都　唔　同　外　國。

Hong Kong is very different from foreign countries.

Hēung-Góng hóu dō deih-fōng juhng hōi gán láahng-hei,

香　港　好　多　地　方　仲　開　緊　冷　氣，

Many places in Hong Kong still keep air-conditioning on.

heui bīn-douh dōu dung-bīng-bīng, ngoih-gwok haih mh haih ā?

去　邊　度　都　凍　冰　冰，外　國　係　唔　係吖？

You feel cold wherever you go. Are foreign countries like this?

Story: Air-conditioning ◄902.mp3

Hah-tīn yiht-laaht-laaht sāam sahp géi douh, daahn-haih ngóh gūng-sī ge láahng-hei
夏 天 熱 辣 辣 三 十 幾 度，但 係 我 公 司嘅 冷 氣
Summer is burning hot with temperatures over 30°C, but the air-conditioning in my office is

dung-bīng-bīng, fāan gūng jauh hóu-chíh chóh hái syut-gwaih.
凍 冰 冰，返 工 就 好 似 坐 喺 雪 櫃。
ice cold. When I am at work, I feel like I am sitting in a fridge.

Ngóh dī tùhng-sih sèhng nìhn dōu yiu jeuk lāang-sāam.
我 啲 同 事 成 年 都 要 着 冷 衫。
My colleagues need to wear sweaters all year round.

Ngóh ge wái deui-jyuh láahng-hei háu, dī fūng hóu sāi-leih,
我 嘅 位 對 住 冷 氣 口，啲 風 好 犀 利，
My seat is facing the air-conditioner vent. The airflow is strong.

yáuh-sìh dung dou sáu dōu ngaahng saai, yiu chēut heui hàahng háh.
有 時 凍 到 手 都 硬 晒，要 出 去 行 吓。
Sometimes I feel so cold that my hands are all stiff. I need to go out for a walk.

Hàahng dou heui sēung-chèuhng dōu haih hōi daaih láahng-hei, lèuhng-jam-jam.
行 到 去 商 場 都 係 開 大 冷 氣，涼 浸 浸。
Shopping malls have strong air-conditioning.

Fong gūng daap bā-sí fāan ūk-kéi, ga bā-sí yauh haih yāt go dung-bīng-bīng ge syut-gwaih.
放 工 搭 巴 士 返 屋 企，架 巴 士 又 係 一 個 凍 冰 冰 嘅 雪 櫃。
The bus I take home after work is another fridge.

Ngóh yāt nìhn behng géi chi dōu haih yān-waih yauh yiht yauh dung,
我 一 年 病 幾 次 都 係 因 為 又 熱 又 凍，
Each year I get sick a few times. It is all because of the extreme change in temperature.

néih wah haih maih chī-sin gá?
你 話 係 咪 黐 線 㗎？
Do you think that's crazy?

Extended dialogue

Listen and complete the dialogue with the expressions in the table.   ◀903.mp3

dāk sahp luhk douh 得 十 六 度	yauh jeuk lāang-sāam 又 着 冷 衫	hóu-chíh chóh hái syut-gwaih 好 似 坐 喺 雪 櫃
dung dou sáu dōu ngaahng saai 凍 到 手 都 硬 晒	dī láahng-hei mh sái chín 啲 冷 氣 唔 使 錢	dung dou sèhng-yaht behng 凍 到 成 日 病
juhng yiu béi yī-sāng chín 仲 要 畀 醫 生 錢		

A: Néih hái gūng-sī sái mh sái _____, yauh laahm géng-gān a?
   你 喺 公 司 使 唔 使 _____，又 攬 頸 巾 呀？

B: Nī douh _____.
   呢 度 _____。

   Ngóh ge wái juhng deui-jyuh láahng-hei háu, _____.
   我 嘅 位 仲 對 住 冷 氣 口，_____。

   Ngóh _____, mh sīk jouh yéh la.
   我 _____，唔 識 做 嘢 喇。

A: Gūng-sī haih mh haih chī-sin ga? _____ ge mē?
   公 司 係 唔 係 癡 線 㗎？ _____ 嘅 咩？

B: Haih lā! Dī tùhng-sih _____!
   係 啦！啲 同 事 _____！

   Gūng-sī béi dō dī dihn-fai, _____!
   公 司 畀 多 啲 電 費，_____！

Vocabulary ◀904.mp3

1.	tīn-màhn-tòih	天文台	observatory
2.	syut-gwaih	雪櫃	refrigerator (literally, snow cabinet)
3.	dihn-fai	電費	electricity fee
4.	yāt jek sáu	一隻手	a hand
5.	deui-jyuh	對住	be facing
6.	mh syun	唔算	not considered as
7.	yāt gihn sāam	一件衫	an article of clothing
8.	yāt gihn lāang-sāam	一件冷衫	a sweater
9.	laahm géng-gān	攬頸巾	wrap a scarf around
10.	hōi láahng-hei	開冷氣	turn on the air-conditioner
11.	géi	幾	a few
12.	ngaahng	硬	hard; stiff
13.	sāi-leih	犀利	trenchant; powerful
14.	dōu	都	even (used for emphasis)
15.	verb + saai 晒		all; everything
16.	yuht-làih-yuht	越嚟越	becoming more and more

Grammar practice

I. verb + saai 晒 (all; completely)   ◀905.mp3

Affirmative: verb + saai 晒

e.g., Ngóh ge sáu dōu ngaahng **saai**.

我　嘅手都　硬　　晒。

My hands are all stiff.

Negative: meih 未 + verb + saai 晒

e.g., Ngóh **meih** jouh **saai** dī yéh.

我　未　做　晒　啲嘢。

I have not done everything yet. (to be completed later)

Ngóh jouh **mh saai** dī yéh.

我　做　唔晒　啲嘢。

I am unable to finish all the work.

Interrogative: verb + saai 晒 + object + meih a 未呀？

e.g., Néih jouh **saai** dī yéh **meih a**?

你　做　晒　啲嘢未　呀？

Have you done everything?

(Yes) Jouh saai.   (No) Meih jouh saai. / Jouh mh saai.

做　晒。　　　　未　做　晒。/ 做　唔晒。

1. Dahk ga fo maaih **saai**, hah go yuht sīn-ji yáuh sān fo.
   特　價貨賣　　晒，下　個月　先至　有　新　貨。

2. Ngóh tái **saai** nī dī syū la, séung sung béi yàhn tái.
   我　　睇晒　呢啲　書喇，想　　送　畀人　睇。

3. Kéuih béi yàhn āak **saai** dī chín, ngóh-deih hó-yíh dím bōng kéuih a?
   佢　畀人　呃晒　啲　錢，我　　哋　可以　點幫　佢　呀？

4. A: Néih yám **saai** būi chàh **meih a**?
   你　飲　晒　杯茶　未　呀？

   B: Ngóh **meih** yám **saai**, juhng yáuh yāt bun.
   我　未　飲　晒，仲　有　一　半。

5. Ngóh bá jē taai sai, jē **mh saai** léuhng go yàhn.
   我　把遮太　細，遮唔晒　兩　　個人。

✎ **Practice**

a. Use the prompts below to help you.

   i. Make a sentence with "saai 晒".

   ii. Make a sentence with "mh saai 唔晒".

   iii. Make a sentence with "meih 未……saai 晒".

b. Complete the sentences using "saai 晒".

   i. Yùh-gwó _____ dī síu-sihk jauh daai fāan ūk-kéi lā.

     如 果　　　　啲 小 食 就 帶 返 屋 企 啦。

   ii. Kéuih-deih _____, nī douh dāk ngóh yāt go yàhn.

     佢　哋　　　　　，呢 度 得 我　一 個 人。

   iii. Ngóh _____ dī dihn-chìh, juhng yáuh léuhng lāp néih yuhng lā.

     我　　　　啲 電 池，仲 有 兩　粒，你 用 啦。

> * Note: "Lāp 粒" is the measure word for batteries.

II. yuht-làih-yuht 越嚟越 (becoming more and more)　◀906.mp3

> e.g., Néih gok mh gok-dāk **yuht-làih-yuht** dung a?
> 你 覺 唔 覺 得 越 嚟 越 凍 呀？
> *Do you feel it's getting colder and colder?*

1. Néih hàahng dāk **yuht làih yuht** maahn, néih guih la, yāu-sīk háh lā.
   你 行　得越 嚟越 慢，　你 劫 喇，休 息 吓 啦。

2. Kéuih go haak **yuht làih yuht** màh-fàahn, dím syun a?
   佢　個 客 越 嚟越 麻 煩，點 算 呀？

3. Ngóh faat gán sīu, gok-dāk **yuht làih yuht** yiht.
   我　發 緊 燒，覺 得 越 嚟越　熱。

4. Ga chē **yuht làih yuht** faai, ngóh tìhng mh dóu.
   架 車 越 嚟越 快，我 停　唔 到。

5. Jouh lóuh-sai **yuht làih yuht** sān-fú.
   做 老 細 越 嚟越 辛 苦。

✎ Practice

Complete the sentences with "yuht làih yuht 越嚟越".

a. Hái party wáan dāk _____, ngóh-deih dōu mh séung jáu.
   喺 party 玩 得　　　　　　　，我 哋 都 唔 想　走。

b. Kéuih yān-waih gán-jēung, góng dāk _____
   佢　因 為 緊 張，講 得

c. Dī yúh _____, ngóh yáuh jē dōu móuh yuhng.
   啲 雨　　　　　　　，我 有 遮 都 冇　用。

III. dōu 都 (even, used for emphasis)　◀907.mp3

> e.g., Hēung-Góng **dōu** mh tùhng ngoih-gwok.
> 香　港 都 唔 同 外　國。
> *Hong Kong is very different from foreign countries.*

Ngóh dung dou sáu **dōu** ngaahng saai.
我 凍 到 手 都 硬 晒。
I feel so cold that even my hands are stiff.

1. Sahp-yāt-yuht **dōu** gam yiht, hóu-chíh juhng haih hah-tīn gám-yéung.
   十 一 月 都 咁 熱，好 似 仲 係 夏 天 咁 樣。

2. Gām-yaht haih bīn-go sāang-yaht, néih **dōu** mh gei-dāk?
   今 日 係 邊 個 生 日，你 都 唔 記 得？

3. Ngóh **dōu** meih jéun-beih hóu, néih yíh-gīng yíng jó séung?
   我 都 未 準 備 好，你 已 經 影 咗 相？

4. Ngóh jeui pa dung, ngóh pìhng-sìh **dōu** daai lāang-sāam heui gāai ge.
   我 最 怕 凍，我 平 時 都 帶 冷 衫 去 街 嘅。

5. Mh lohk yúh, ngóh **dōu** sèhng-yaht daai jē.
   唔 落 雨，我 都 成 日 帶 遮。

Review: "dōu 都" meaning "also" or "all" ◄908.mp3

1. Ngóh dī tùhng-sih sèhng nìhn **dōu** yiu jeuk lāang-sāam.
   我 啲 同 事 成 年 都 要 着 冷 衫。
   My colleagues need to wear sweaters all year round.

2. Heui bīn-douh **dōu** dung-bīng-bīng.
   去 邊 度 都 凍 冰 冰。
   I feel cold wherever I go.

3. Yàuh séui, hàahng sāan, ngóh **dōu** jūng-yi.
   游 水、行 山，我 都 鍾 意。
   I like both swimming and hiking.

✎ Practice

a. Make a sentence with "dōu 都".
b. Put "dōu 都" in the correct place. ◄909.mp3
   i. Móuh dahk-ga ___ néih ___ máaih ___ gam dō?
      冇 特 價 你 買 咁 多？
      Gám bun ga ___ néih ___ yiu máaih ___ géi-dō?
      咁 半 價 你 要 買 幾 多？
   ii. Nī go sing-kèih ___ ge tīn-hei ___ hóu hóu.
      呢 個 星 期 嘅 天 氣 好 好。
   iii. Daap līp ___ daap dihn-tāi ___ gam faai.
      搭 較 搭 電 梯 咁 快。
   iv. Ūk-kéi ___ hōi party, jéun-beih ___ yāt baak jī jáu ___ mh gau.
      屋 企 開 party，準 備 一 百 支 酒 唔 夠。

IV. verb + dō 多 (some more)   ◄910.mp3

e.g., Jeuk **dō** gihn lāang-sāam jauh gau lā.
着 多 件 冷 衫 就 夠 啦。
One more sweater will be enough.

1. Jéun-beih **dō** léuhng go *copy* béi lóuh-sai tùhng haak.
   準 備 多 兩 個 copy 畀 老 細 同 客。

2. Nī go sīng-kèih dōu lohk yúh, juhng wúih lohk **dō** sahp yaht.
   呢 個 星 期 都 落 雨，仲 會 落 多 十 日。

3. Ngóh séung ló **dō** yaht ga, daahn-haih tùhng-sih behng saai,
   我 想 攞 多 日 假，但 係 同 事 病 晒，

   ngóh mh hó-yíh chéng ga.
   我 唔 可 以 請 假。

V. mh syun 唔算 (not considered as)   ◄911.mp3

e.g., Sahp douh **mh syun** dung.
十 度 唔 算 凍。
10°C is not considered cold.

1. Chìh sahp fān-jūng **mh syun** chìh.
   遲 十 分 鐘 唔 算 遲。

2. Ngóh ge sáu-gēi séuhng móhng **mh syun** maahn,
   我 嘅 手 機 上 網 唔 算 慢，

   daahn-haih yuhng dihn-nóuh jouh yéh faai dī.
   但 係 用 電 腦 做 嘢 快 啲。

3. A: Hóu dō-jeh néih bōng ngóh, màh-fàahn saai.
   好 多 謝 你 幫 我，麻 煩 晒。

   B: Góng nī dī! Ngóh-deih haih hóu pàhng-yáuh,
   講 呢 啲！我 哋 係 好 朋 友，

   ngóh bōng néih **mh syun** màh-fàahn.
   我 幫 你 唔 算 麻 煩。

4. Heui gēi-chèuhng **mh syun** yúhn, daap dīk-sí heui,
   去 機 場 唔 算 遠，搭 的 士 去，

   yih baak mān **mh syun** gwai.
   二 百 蚊 唔 算 貴。

5. Jūng-màhn **mh syun** nàahn, néih séung hohk, yāt-dihng hohk dóu.
   中 文 唔 算 難，你 想 學，一 定 學 到。

VI. géi 幾 (a few; a general number) ◀912.mp3

> e.g., Nī **géi** yaht ngóh ūk-kéi hóu-chíh syut-gwaih gam dung.
> 呢 幾 日 我 屋 企 好 似 雪 櫃 咁 凍。
> *These last few days, my house is as cold as a fridge.*

1. Hēung-Góng ge hah-tīn yiht-laaht-laaht sāam sahp **géi** douh.
   香 港 嘅 夏 天 熱 辣 辣 三 十 幾 度。

2. Ngóh yāt nìhn behng **géi** chi dōu haih yān-waih yauh yiht yauh dung.
   我 一 年 病 幾 次 都 係 因 為 又 熱 又 凍。

3. Ngóh-deih máaih dō **géi** jī jáu hōi *party* yám lā.
   我 哋 買 多 幾 支 酒 開 party 飲 啦。

4. Léuhng go yàhn tái hei, baak **géi** mān mh syun pèhng.
   兩 個 人 睇 戲，百 幾 蚊 唔 算 平。

5. Daaih sāk chē, tìuh louh yáuh **géi** chīn ga chē.
   大 塞 車，條 路 有 幾 千 架 車。

Review: Usage of "géi 幾" ◀913.mp3

A. quite + adjective

1. Daap chē heui Sāi-Gung **géi** yúhn.
   搭 車 去 西 貢 幾 遠。
   It is quite far to go to Sai Kung.

2. Heui sā-tāan yàuh séui **géi** syū-fuhk.
   去 沙 灘 游 水 幾 舒 服。
   Swimming at the beach is pleasant.

B. how many

1. Néih jeuk jó **géi-dō** gihn lāang-sāam a?
   你 着 咗 幾 多 件 冷 衫 呀？
   How many sweaters are you wearing?

2. Hàahng saai Lùhng-Jek yiu **géi** noih a?
   行 晒 龍 脊 要 幾 耐 呀？
   How long does it take to walk over Dragon's Back?

3. Gām-yaht **géi** yuht **géi** houh?
   今 日 幾 月 幾 號？
   What date is today?

4. Yìh-gā **géi** dím a?
   而 家 幾 點 呀？
   What time is it now?

Pyramid drill ◄914.mp3

1.

yuht làih yuht dung

越 嚟 越 凍

hái ūk-kéi yuht làih yuht dung

喺 屋 企 越 嚟 越 凍

Chóh hái ūk-kéi yuht làih yuht dung

坐 喺 屋 企 越 嚟 越 凍

Chóh hái ūk-kéi yuht làih yuht dung, ngóh ge sáu ngaahng saai

坐 喺 屋 企 越 嚟 越 凍，我 嘅 手 硬 晒

Chóh hái ūk-kéi yuht làih yuht dung, ngóh ge sáu dōu ngaahng saai.

坐 喺 屋 企 越 嚟 越 凍，我 嘅 手 都 硬 晒。

Sitting at home, I feel colder and colder, my hands are stiff.

2.

jeuk lāang-sāam

着 冷 衫

jeuk dō gihn lāang-sāam

着 多 件 冷 衫

jeuk dō gihn lāang-sāam dōu gau

着 多 件 冷 衫 都 夠

sahp douh, jeuk dō gihn lāang-sāam dōu gau

十 度，着 多 件 冷 衫 都 夠

sahp douh mh syun dung, jeuk dō gihn lāang-sāam dōu gau

十 度 唔 算 凍，着 多 件 冷 衫 都 夠

Ngóh gok-dāk sahp douh mh syun dung, jeuk dō gihn lāang-sāam dōu gau.

我 覺 得 十 度 唔 算 凍，着 多 件 冷 衫 都 夠。

I think 10°C is not cold. Putting on one more sweater would be enough.

General review

I. Put the words in the correct order to make sentences.   ◂915.mp3

1. jíng / néih / chāan-tēng / hó-yíh / hōi / hóu-sihk / hōi-sīn / yuht-làih-yuht
   整 / 你 / 餐 廳 / 可以 / 開 / 好 食 / 海 鮮 / 越 嚟 越

2. géng-gān / láahng-hei / néih / néih / dihng / yauh / yauh / hōi / laahm / dung / yiht / a
   頸 巾 / 冷 氣 / 你 / 你 / 定 / 又 / 又 / 開 / 攬 / 凍 / 熱 / 呀

3. ngóh / ngóh / Hēung-Góng / lāang-sāam / sahp géi douh / dung / mh syun /
   我 / 我 / 香 港 / 冷 衫 / 十 幾 度 / 凍 / 唔 算 /

   móuh / yān-waih / yíh-wàih / daai / làih
   冇 / 因 為 / 以 為 / 帶 / 嚟

4. ngóh / dī pàhng-yáuh / sāang-yaht *party* / giu / làih / wáan / hōi-sām / saai / dī / dāk
   我 / 啲 朋 友 / 生 日 party / 叫 / 嚟 / 玩 / 開 心 / 晒 / 啲 / 得

5. daht-yìhn / māt-yéh / dihn-nóuh / gūng-sī / *hang* saai gēi / jouh mh dóu / dōu / ge
   突 然 / 乜 嘢 / 電 腦 / 公 司 / hang 晒 機 / 做 唔 到 / 都 / 嘅

II. Listen and rearrange the dialogue.   ◂916.mp3

a. Chī-sin! Fāan gūng dōu mh sái gam sān-fú lā!
   黐 線！返 工 都 唔 使 咁 辛 苦 啦！

b. Dím sān-fú a?
   點 辛 苦 呀？

c. Haih lak, Máh-Lòih-Sāi-A dī yéh hóu hóu sihk ga wo. Yáuh móuh si háh a?
   係 嘞，馬 來 西 亞 啲 嘢 好 好 食 㗎 喎。有 冇 試 吓 呀？

d. Máh-Lòih-Sāi-A hóu mh hóu wáan a?
   馬 來 西 亞 好 唔 好 玩 呀？

e. Jeui yiht yáuh sāam sahp baat douh,
   最 熱 有 三 十 八 度，

   ngóh-deih yiu hàahng baat go deih-fōng tái yéh, máaih yéh, móuh sìh-gaan sihk faahn,
   我 哋 要 行 八 個 地 方 睇 嘢、買 嘢，冇 時 間 食 飯，

   hóu chìh sīn-ji dou jáu-dim, guih dou séi!
   好 遲 先 至 到 酒 店，劫 到 死！

f. Géi hóu wáan, daahn-haih yiht-laaht-laaht juhng yiu heui hóu dō deih-fōng tái yéh,
   幾 好 玩，但 係 熱 辣 辣 仲 要 去 好 多 地 方 睇 嘢，

   jān-haih hóu sān-fú.
   真 係 好 辛 苦。

g. Sihk jó géi chāan, ūk-kéi yàhn pa laaht, mh jūng-yi sihk.
   食 咗 幾 餐，屋 企 人 怕 辣，唔 鍾 意 食。

h. Néih fong ga heui jó bīn-douh a?
你 放 假 去 咗 邊 度 呀 ?

i. Aai! Ngóh dōu yíh-wàih heui Máh-Lòih-Sāi-A haih deui-jyuh sā-tāan,
哎 ! 我 都 以 為 去 馬 來 西 亞 係 對 住 沙 灘 ,

māt-yéh dōu mh jouh.
乜 嘢 都 唔 做 。

j. Ngóh tùhng ūk-kéi yàhn heui jó Máh-Lòih-Sāi-A wáan.
我 同 屋 企 人 去 咗 馬 來 西 亞 玩 。

III. Choose the appropriate saying to complete the dialogue. ◄917.mp3

A: Néih séung mh séung heui tái yín-cheung-wúi / yī-sāng / syū-jín a?
你 想 唔 想 去 睇 演 唱 會 / 醫 生 / 書 展 呀 ?

Ngóh yáuh hah go sīng-kèih-sāam ge fēi,
我 有 下 個 星 期 三 嘅 飛 ,

yáu dāk kéuih / mh sái chín ge / gok-dāk hóu syū-fuhk.
由 得 佢 / 唔 使 錢 嘅 / 覺 得 好 舒 服 。

B: Wa! Néih yuht-làih-yuht hōi-sām / sèhng yaht gam hóu-chói / gam sāi-leih!
嘩 ! 你 越 嚟 越 開 心 / 成 日 咁 好 彩 / 咁 犀 利 !

Nī go yín-cheung-wúi yāt jóu jauh
呢 個 演 唱 會 一 早 就

maaih gán fēi / maaih saai fēi / joi maaih gwo fēi,
賣 緊 飛 / 賣 晒 飛 / 再 賣 過 飛 ,

séung máaih jauh máaih mh dóu ga. Dō-jeh saai!
想 買 都 買 唔 到 㗎 。 多 謝 晒 !

A: Yān-waih ngóh gūng-sī *sponsor* nī go yín-cheung-wúi,
因 為 我 公 司 sponsor 呢 個 演 唱 會 ,

só-yíh / daahn-haih / gān-jyuh ngóh ló dóu
所 以 / 但 係 / 跟 住 我 攞 到

gám-yéung ge gūng-sī / daih yāt chi / géi jēung fēi,
咁 樣 嘅 公 司 / 第 一 次 / 幾 張 飛 ,

sung béi néih mh syun / tùhng / bōng pàhng-yáuh yāt-chàih heui tái.
送 畀 你 唔 算 / 同 / 幫 朋 友 一 齊 去 睇 。

Answers

Story

A: Néih hái gūng-sī sái mh sái **yauh jeuk lāang-sāam**,
你　喺　公　司　使　唔　使　又　　着　冷　　衫，
yauh laahm géng-gān a?
又　　攬　　頸　　巾　呀？
Why do you have to wear a sweater and a scarf in the office?

B: Nī douh **dāk sahp luhk douh**. Ngóh ge wái juhng deui-jyuh láahng-hei háu,
呢　度　得　十　六　度。我　嘅　位　仲　對　住　冷　氣　口，
It is only 16°C here. My seat is facing the air-conditioning vent.

hóu-chíh chóh hái syut-gwaih.
好　似　坐　喺　雪　櫃。
It feels like I am sitting in a fridge.

Ngóh **dung dou sáu dōu ngaahng saai**, mh sīk jouh yéh la.
我　凍　到　手　都　硬　　晒，唔　識　做　嘢　喇。
It is so cold that my hands are stiff. I can't work.

A: Gūng-sī haih mh haih chī-sin ga? Dī **láahng-hei** mh sái chín ge mē?
公　司　係　唔　係　黐　線　㗎？啲　冷　　氣　唔　使　錢　嘅　咩？
Is the company crazy? Is the air-conditioning free of charge?

B: Haih lā! Dī tùhng-sih **dung dou sèhng-yaht behng**!
係　啦！啲　同　事　凍　到　成　　日　病！
That's very true! It is so cold; many colleagues often get sick.

Gūng-sī béi dō dī dihn-fai, **juhng yiu béi yī-sāng chín**!
公　　司　畀　多　啲　電　費，仲　　要　畀　醫　生　　錢！
The company paid a high electricity bill and paid the doctors!

Grammar practice translation I

1. Discount products are all sold out. New products will be available next month.
2. I have read all these books. I want to give them to other people.
3. He has been cheated out of money. What can we do to help him?
4. A: Have you finished your cup of tea?
   B: I haven't drunk it all. There is still half left.
5. My umbrella is too small. It can't give both of us shelter.

Practice b. suggested answers

i. Yùh-gwó **sihk mh saai** dī síu-sihk jauh daai fāan ūk-kéi lā.
如　果　食　唔　晒　啲　小　食　就　　帶　返　屋　企　啦。
If we can't eat up all the snacks, bring them home.

ii. Kéuih-deih **jáu saai**, nī douh dāk ngóh yāt go yàhn.
佢　　哋　走　晒，呢　度　得　我　　一　個　人。
They have all gone; I am the only one here.

iii. Ngóh **meih yuhng saai** dī dihn-chìh, juhng yáuh léuhng lāp, néih yuhng lā.
我　未　用　　晒　啲　電　池，仲　　有　兩　　粒，你　用　　啦。
I haven't used up all the batteries. There are two left. You can use them.

Grammar practice translation II

1. You are walking slower and slower. Let's have a rest.
2. His client is becoming more and more troublesome. What can he do?
3. I have a fever. I am feeling hotter and hotter.
4. The car is going faster and faster. I can't stop.
5. Being the boss is becoming more and more difficult.

Practice answers

a. Hái party wáan dāk **yuht-làih-yuht hōi-sām**, ngóh-deih dōu mh séung jáu.
喺 party 玩 得 越 嚟 越 開 心，我 哋 都 唔 想 走。
We're having more and more fun at the party. We don't want to leave.

b. Kéuih yān-waih gán-jēung, góng dāk **yuht-làih-yuht faai**.
佢 因 為 緊 張，講 得 越 嚟 越 快。
Because he was nervous, he spoke faster and faster.

c. Dī yúh **yuht-làih-yuht daaih**, ngóh yáuh jē dōu móuh yuhng.
啲 雨 越 嚟 越 大，我 有 遮 都 冇 用。
It is raining harder and harder. Even if I have an umbrella, it's no use.

Grammar practice translation III

1. It is so hot even in November; it seems like it is still summer.
2. You don't even remember whose birthday it is today?
3. I'm not ready yet, but you've taken the photo!
4. I dislike cold weather most. When I go out, I often bring a sweater.
5. Even if I know it is not going to rain, I always bring an umbrella.

Practice b. answers

i. Móuh dahk ga néih dōu máaih gam dō? Gám bun ga néih yiu máaih géi-dō?
冇 特 價 你 都 買 咁 多？咁 半 價 你 要 買 幾 多？
You have bought so many of these even when there is no sale?
How much will you buy if they're half price?

ii. Nī go sing-kèih ge tīn-hei dōu hóu hóu.
呢 個 星 期 嘅 天 氣 都 好 好。
The weather has been very good this whole week.

iii. Daap līp, daap dihn-tāi dōu gam faai.
搭 軨、搭 電 梯 都 咁 快。
Both the elevator and the escalator are fast.

iv. Ūk-kéi hōi party, jéun-beih yāt baak jī jáu dōu mh gau.
屋 企 開 party，準 備 一 百 支 酒 都 唔 夠。
There will be a party at home; even 100 bottles of wine won't be enough.

Grammar practice translation IV

1. Prepare two more copies for the boss and the client.
2. It has been raining this week and it will rain for 10 more days.
3. I wanted to take one more day off, but all my colleagues were sick. I couldn't ask for leave.

Grammar practice translation V

1. Being late for 10 minutes is not considered that late.
2. I access the internet with my mobile phone because it is not slow, but using a computer to do the work is faster.
3. A: Thank you so much for helping me.
   B: Don't mention it! We are good friends. It is no trouble at all.
4. Going to the airport does not take that long if you go by taxi. I don't consider $200 expensive.
5. Learning Chinese isn't considered difficult. If you want to learn, you can.

Grammar practice translation VI

1. Summer in Hong Kong is burning hot with temperatures over 30 degrees.
2. Every year I get sick a few times, all because of the extreme change in temperature.
3. Let's buy a few more bottles to drink at the party.
4. It costs over $100 for two people to go to a movie. It is not cheap.
5. There is a bad traffic jam. There are a few thousand cars on the road.

General review

I. Answers and translations

1. Néih jíng hōi-sīn yuht-làih-yuht hóu-sihk, hó-yíh hōi chāan-tēng.
   你 整 海鮮 越 嚟 越 好 食,可以 開 餐 廳。
   You're getting better at cooking seafood. You can open your own restaurant.

2. Néih yauh hōi láahng-hei yauh laahm géng-gān, néih yiht dihng dung a?
   你 又 開 冷 氣 又 攬 頸 巾,你 熱 定 凍 呀?
   You turned on the air-conditioning and wear a scarf. Do you feel hot or cold?

3. Ngóh móuh daai lāang-sāam làih Hēung-Góng,
   我 冇 帶 冷 衫 嚟 香 港,
   I didn't bring a sweater to Hong Kong,
   yān-waih ngóh yíh-wàih sahp géi douh mh syun dung.
   因 為 我 以 為 十 幾 度 唔 算 凍。
   because I think 13–19°C is not considered that cold.

4. Ngóh giu saai dī pàhng-yáuh làih sāang-yaht *party*, wáan dāk hōi-sām dī.
   我 叫 晒 啲 朋 友 嚟 生 日 party,玩 得 開 心 啲。
   I have asked all my friends to come to the birthday party. We can have more fun.

5. Gūng-sī ge dihn-nóuh daht-yìhn *hang* saai gēi, māt-yéh dōu jouh mh dóu.
   公 司 嘅 電 腦 突 然 hang 晒 機,乜 嘢 都 做 唔 到。
   All the computers in the office crashed suddenly. Nothing can be done.

II.

h. A: Néih fong ga heui jó bīn-douh a?
   你 放 假 去 咗 邊 度 呀?
   Where did you go on holiday?

j. B: Ngóh tùhng ūk-kéi yàhn heui jó Máh-Lòih-Sāi-A wáan.
   我 同 屋 企 人 去 咗 馬 來 西 亞 玩。
   I travelled to Malaysia with my family.

d. A: Máh-Lòih-Sāi-A hóu mh hóu wáan a?
   馬 來 西 亞 好 唔 好 玩 呀?
   Was it fun to visit Malaysia?

f. B: Géi hóu wáan, daahn-haih yiht-laaht-laaht juhng yiu heui hóu dō deih-fōng tái yéh,
   幾 好 玩,但 係 熱 辣 辣 仲 要 去 好 多 地 方 睇 嘢,
   jān-haih hóu sān-fú.
   真 係 好 辛 苦。
   It's quite fun. However, we had to go sightseeing to many places in hot weather. It was uncomfortable.

b. A: Dím sān-fú a?
   點 辛 苦 呀?
   How uncomfortable was it?

e. B: Jeui yiht yáuh sāam sahp baat douh,
   最 熱 有 三 十 八 度,
   ngóh-deih yiu hàahng baat go deih-fōng tái yéh, máaih yéh, móuh sìh-gaan sihk faahn,
   我 哋 要 行 八 個 地 方 睇 嘢、買 嘢,冇 時 間 食 飯,
   hóu chìh sīn-ji dou jáu-dim, guih dou séi!
   好 遲 先 至 到 酒 店,攰 到 死!
   The hottest day was 38°C. We had to go sightseeing in eight places followed by shopping, no time to eat, and we arrived at the hotel very late. We were dead tired!

a. A: Chī-sin! Fāan gūng dōu mh sái gam sān-fú lā!
   黐 線!返 工 都 唔 使 咁 辛 苦 啦!
   That's crazy! Even tougher than working!

i. B: Aai! Ngóh dōu yíh-wàih heui Máh-Lòih-Sāi-A haih deui-jyuh sā-tāan, māt-yéh dōu mh jouh.
哎！我　都　以　為　去　馬　來　西　亞　係　對　住　沙　灘，乜　嘢　都　唔　做。
Yeah! I thought travelling to Malaysia meant beaches and relaxation.

c. A: Haih lak, Máh-Lòih-Sāi-A dī yéh hóu hóu sihk ga wo. Yáuh móuh si háh a?
係　嘞，馬　來　西　亞啲嘢　好　好　食　㗎喎。有　冇　試吓呀？
By the way, Malaysian food is delicious. Have you tried it?

g. B: Sihk jó géi chāan, ūk-kéi yàhn pa laaht, mh jūng-yi sihk.
食　咗　幾　餐，　屋　企　人　怕辣，唔　鍾　意食。
We had a few meals. My family dislikes eating hot and spicy food.

III.

A: Néih séung mh séung heui tái **yín-cheung-wúi** a?
你　想　唔　想　去　睇演　唱　　會呀？
Ngóh yáuh hah go sīng-kèih-sāam ge fēi, **mh sái chín ge**.
我　有　下個星　期　三　　嘅飛，唔使錢　嘅。
Do you want to go to a concert? I have tickets for next Wednesday. They're free.

B: Wa! Néih **gam sāi-leih**! Nī go yín-cheung-wúi yāt jóu jauh **maaih saai fēi**,
嘩！你　咁　犀利！呢個演唱　　會一早就　賣　　晒飛，
séung máaih **dou** máaih mh dóu ga. Dō-jeh saai!
想　買　都　買　唔　到㗎。多　謝晒！
Wow! You're marvellous! Tickets for this concert were sold out a long time ago.
Even if I want to buy one, it's not possible to get tickets. Thank you very much!

A: Yān-waih ngóh gūng-sī *sponsor* nī go yín-cheung-wúi,
因　為　我　公　司　sponsor　呢個演唱　　會，
só-yíh ngóh ló dóu **géi jēung fēi**, sung béi néih **tùhng** pàhng-yáuh yāt-chàih heui tái.
所　以　我　攞到　幾　張　　飛，送畀你　同　朋　友　一　齊　去　睇。
My company sponsored this concert, so I can get a few tickets to give you and your friends.

Hong Kong culture

Cold and very hot weather warnings

Hong Kong is a place of mild weather with an average temperature of 16–29°C.

The Hong Kong Observatory issues the "very hot" weather warning when the temperature is over 33°C. Under a very hot weather warning the public is advised to be alert for the risk of heat stroke and sunburn. But those who are very enthusiastic about hiking may still hit the trails no matter what the weather condition.

The Hong Kong Observatory issues the "cold" weather warning when the temperature drops below 15°C. This is considered cool, not cold, to most people, but every year when temperature drops below 10°C within one day, people can die due to the sudden weather change. People have a risk of heart attack and those who have respiratory disease should be careful in cold weather.

On 25 January 2016, the coldest temperature recorded in the last 59 years was 3°C in urban areas. Kindergarten and primary school classes were suspended. Huge crowds rushed to the peak of Tai Mo Shan (the highest mountain in Hong Kong, at 957 m) to experience the freezing cold (–6°C) and to feel the frost and ice. More than 200 people called for emergency assistance. About 20 participants of a cross-country run were sent to hospital after experiencing symptoms related to hypothermia. Many others found the roads frosty; they were too slippery for them to go downhill.

These weather warnings also alert the relevant government departments, such as the Home Affairs Department, to open temporary shelters. Efficient and effective health care from the government enables Hong Kong citizens to enjoy one of the longest life expectancies in the world. That is an average age of 87.3 years for women and 81.2 years for men.

10
The buffet is great value!

Dialogue ◂1001.mp3

➢ Why is the buffet popular?

➢ Why is Ho so hungry?

➢ What does Kei want to start with?

➢ Why doesn't Ho want any sushi?

➢ Why does Kei think the barbecued food was no good?

➢ Why does Ho like to start with dessert?

Kèih: Nī gāan chāan-tēng hóu chēut-méng, yiu jóu géi go sīng-kèih *book* ga.

琪： 呢 間 餐 廳 好 出 名，要 早 幾 個 星 期 book 㗎。

This is a famous restaurant. We have to book a few weeks in advance.

Nī-douh ge jih-joh-chāan jeui dái, māt-yéh dōu yáuh.

呢 度 嘅自助餐 最 抵，乜 嘢 都 有。

The buffet here is the best value. You can get everything you want.

Hòuh: Ngóh sèhng-yaht meih sihk yéh, hóu tóuh-ngoh!

豪： 我 成 日 未 食 嘢，好 肚 餓！

I haven't eaten all day. I'm so hungry!

Faai dī chēut hēui tái háh lā. Néih séung sihk māt-yéh sīn a?

快 啲 出 去 睇 吓 啦。你 想 食 乜 嘢 先 呀？

Let's go up and have a look. What do you want to eat first?

Kèih: Ngóh sihk sā-léut sīn.

琪： 我 食 沙 律 先。

I'll start with salad.

Hòuh: Yàhn yàhn dōu sihk sā-léut sīn, néih máih gān-jyuh yàhn lā.

豪： 人 人 都 食 沙 律 先，你 咪 跟 住 人 啦。

Everyone starts with salad. Don't follow the crowd.

Yí? Nī dī haih māt-yéh a? Hóu-chíh géi hóu sihk wo.

咦？呢 啲 係 乜 嘢 呀？好 似 幾 好 食 喎。

Oh well. What are these? They look quite nice.

Kèih: Mh jī a, ló dī si háh lā. Sauh-sī dōu mh cho gám-yéung wo.

琪: 唔知呀，攞啲試 吓 啦。壽 司 都 唔 錯 咁 樣 喎。

I don't know. Let's try some. The sushi looks quite good too.

Hòuh: Dāk géi júng yú gam muhn. Ngóh sihk sīu hōi-sīn, néih ngāam mh ngāam a?

豪: 得 幾 種 魚 咁 悶。我 食 燒海 鮮，你 啱 唔 啱 呀？

There are only a few types of fish, so boring.
I'll have barbecued seafood. Does that suit you?

Kèih: Néih máih sihk gam dō sīu yéh a! Síu-sām yauh hàuh-lùhng tung.

琪: 你 咪 食 咁 多 燒嘢呀！小 心 又 喉 嚨 痛。

Don't eat too much barbecued food. Be careful not to get a sore throat again.

* Note: Chinese believe that if a person eats too much barbecued food, he or she will have a sore throat.

Hòuh: Wai, tìhm-bán mh sái pàaih-déui, bāt-yùh heui ló jó sīn.

豪: 喂， 甜 品 唔 使 排 隊，不 如 去 攞 咗 先。

There is no need to queue for dessert. Shall we get some first?

Kèih: Bīn-douh yáuh yàhn yāt hōi-chí jauh sihk tìhm-bán ga?

琪: 邊 度 有 人 一 開 始 就 食 甜 品 㗎？

Who starts a meal with dessert?

Néih jih-géi heui ló lā. Ngóh joi tái háh sīn.

你 自 己 去 攞啦。我 再 睇 吓 先。

You go yourself. I'll have a further look around.

Story: Buffets ◄1002.mp3

Yāt bāan pàhng-yáuh yāt-bihn kīng-gái, yāt-bihn sihk hóu yéh,
一 班 朋 友 一 便 傾 偈，一 便 食 好 嘢，
A group of friends, enjoying good food while chatting,

dahk-biht hōi-sām. Yùh-gwó yàhn yàhn jūng-yi sihk ge yéh mh tùhng,
特 別 開 心。如 果 人 人 鍾 意 食 嘅 嘢 唔 同，
this is particularly pleasant. If everyone wants to have different food,

jeui hóu jauh sihk jih-joh-chāan. Jih-joh-chāan hóu dái,
最 好 就 食 自 助 餐。自 助 餐 好 抵，
Then it would be best to have a buffet. Buffets are good value for money.

séung sihk māt-yéh dōu yáuh: sā-léut, sauh-sī, hói-sīn, tìhm-bán . . .
想 食 乜 嘢 都 有：沙 律、壽 司、海 鮮、甜 品……，
There is everything you want to eat: salad, sushi, seafood, dessert . . .

jūng-yi géi-dō ló géi-dō. Daahn-haih hóu dō yàhn gin-dóu gam dō yéh sihk,
鍾 意 幾 多 攞 幾 多。但 係 好 多 人 見 到 咁 多 嘢 食，
you can get as much as you like. However, when people see so much food,

dōu séung si-háh nī dī, si-háh gó-dī, sihk dou taai báau, sān-fú jih-géi.
都 想 試 吓 呢 啲、試 吓 果 啲，食 到 太 飽，辛 苦 自 己。
they can't help trying everything, and they become too full, which can make them feel uncomfortable.

Juhng yáuh-sìh ló dāk taai dō, sihk mh saai, hóu sāai.
仲 有 時 攞 得 太 多，食 唔 晒，好 嘥。
Sometimes they take too much food but can't finish it; it's wasteful.

Questions for the story

I. Choose the correct answer. ◄1003.mp3

1. Dím-gáai yāt bāan yàhn sihk yéh, jeui ngāam sihk jih-joh-chāan?
   點 解 一 班 人 食 嘢，最 啱 食 自 助 餐？
   a. sihk yùhn jih-joh-chāan dahk-biht hōi-sām.
      食 完 自 助 餐 特 別 開 心。
   b. jih-joh-chāan māt-yéh dōu yáuh, yàhn yàhn jūng-yi sihk mh tùhng ge yéh dōu dāk.
      自 助 餐 乜 嘢 都 有，人 人 鍾 意 食 唔 同 嘅 嘢 都 得。
   c. yāt bāan yàhn sihk jih-joh-chāan jeui dái.
      一 班 人 食 自 助 餐 最 抵。
   d. yāt bāan yàhn yiu yāt-bihn kīng gái, yāt-bihn sihk hóu yéh.
      一 班 人 要 一 便 傾 偈，一 便 食 好 嘢。

2. Dím-gáai yáuh yàhn sihk jih-joh-chāan sihk dou hóu sān-fú?
   點 解 有 人 食 自 助 餐 食 到 好 辛 苦？
   a. sā-léut, sauh-sī, hói-sīn, tìhm-bán dōu mh hóu sihk.
      沙 律、壽 司、海 鮮、甜 品 都 唔 好 食。

b. gin-dóu gam dō yéh sihk, daahn-haih sihk-mh-saai, hóu sāai.
　　見 到 咁 多 嘢 食，但 係 食 唔 晒，好 嘥。

c. māt-yéh dōu séung si, sihk dou taai báau.
　　乜 嘢 都 想 試，食 到 太 飽。

d. yáuh yàhn séung ló hóu dō yéh béi yàhn sihk.
　　有 人 想 攞 好 多 嘢 畀人 食。

II. Extended dialogue

Listen and complete the dialogue with the expressions in the table.　◀1004.mp3

dī 啲	dou 到	gam ngāam 咁 啱	gok-dāk 覺 得	gwo 過	jeui 最	joi 再	juhng 仲
kèih-saht 其 實	máih 咪	meih 未	saai 晒	taai 太	tīm 添	yíh-gīng 已 經	

A: Néih _____ māt-yéh jeui hóu sihk?
　　你 　　　乜 嘢 最 好 食？

B: _____ māt-yéh dōu hóu sihk.
　　　　　乜 嘢 都 好 食。

　　Ngóh _____ jūng-yi cheese cake, hóu-sihk _____ tìhng mh dóu háu.
　　我 　　　鍾 意 cheese cake，好 食 　　　停 唔 到 口。

A: Néih _____ séung sihk māt-yéh _____ a?
　　你 　　　想 食 乜 嘢 　　　呀？

B: Ngóh yáuh hóu dō júng tìhm-bán _____ si, yiu chēut heui joi ló _____.
　　我 有 好 多 種 甜 品 　　　試，要 出 去 再 攞 　　　。

A: Néih _____ ló dāk taai dō, sihk mh _____ jauh sāai.
　　你 　　　攞 得 太 多，食 唔 　　　就 嘥。

B: Yí? _____ yauh yáuh cheese cake la. Faai _____ heui ló lā.
　　咦？ 　　　又 有 cheese cake 喇。快 　　　去 攞 啦。

A: Ngóh _____ sihk dāk _____ báau, _____ sihk jauh sān-fú jih-géi.
　　我 　　　食 得 　　　飽，　　　食 就 辛 苦 自 己。

Vocabulary   ◀1005.mp3

1.	jih-joh-chāan	自助餐	buffet
2.	sauh-sī	壽司	sushi
3.	tìhm-bán	甜品	dessert
4.	júng	種	type; kind; variety
5.	báau	飽	full stomach
6.	dái	抵	good value; deserve
7.	sāai	嘥	wasteful
8.	chēut-méng	出名	famous
9.	síu-sām	小心	be careful; take care
10.	dahk-biht	特別	special; particularly; especially
11.	sīu	燒	to barbecue; to roast
12.	pàaih-déui	排隊	to queue
13.	kīng gái	傾偈	to chat; to talk
14.	nī bihn	呢便	this side
15.	yàhn yàhn	人人	everyone
16.	jih-géi	自己	by oneself
17.	taai 太 + adjective		excessively; too; over
18.	máih 咪 + verb		don't (do something)
19.	yāt bihn	一便	doing two actions at the same time; simultaneously

Grammar practice

I. yāt-bihn 一便……yāt-bihn 一便…… (simultaneously)   ◀1006.mp3

> e.g., Yāt bāan pàhng-yáuh **yāt-bihn** kīng-gái, **yāt-bihn** sihk hóu yéh.
> 一 班 朋 友 一 便 傾 偈，一 便 食 好 嘢。
> *A group of friends chatting while eating good food.*

1. Hēung-Góng yàhn jūng-yi **yāt-bihn** hàahng gāai, **yāt bihn** tái sáu-gēi.
   香 港 人 鍾 意 一 便 行 街，一 便 睇 手 機。

2. Néih **yāt-bihn** jíng yéh sihk, ngóh **yāt-bihn** jāp yéh.
   你 一 便 整 嘢 食，我 一 便 執 嘢。

3. Dī yàhn **yāt-bihn** tái yín-cheung-wúi, **yāt-bihn** yíng séung.
   啲 人 一 便 睇 演 唱 會，一 便 影 相。

✎ **Practice**

Complete the sentences.

a. Ngóh yāt bihn yám jáu _____
   我 一 便 飲 酒

b. Kéuih yāt-bihn hōi wúi _____
   佢 一 便 開 會

c. Ngóh-deih yāt bihn hàahng sāan _____
   我 哋 一 便 行 山

II. bīn-douh 邊度……? (How can it be possible?)   ◀1007.mp3

> e.g., **Bīn-douh** yáuh yàhn yāt hōi-chí jauh sihk tìhm-bán ga?
> 邊 度 有 人 一 開 始 就 食 甜 品 㗎？
> *Who starts a meal with dessert?*

1. Nī dī yéh **bīn-douh** yáuh yàhn yiu ga?
   呢 啲 嘢 邊 度 有 人 要 㗎？

2. Néih mh góng dō dī, **bīn-douh** hó-yíh hohk-dóu yīng-màhn?
   你 唔 講 多 啲，邊 度 可 以 學 到 英 文？

3. Néih mh daai chín, **bīn-douh** máaih-dóu yéh a?
   你 唔 帶 錢，邊 度 買 到 嘢 呀？

4. Kéuih bá sēng gam sai, ngóh **bīn-douh** tēng dóu a?
   佢 把 聲 咁 細，我 邊 度 聽 到 呀？

✎ Practice

Complete the sentences.

a. Kéuih ge méng gam gwaai, _____?

   佢　嘅名　咁　怪，

b. Ngóh móuh kéuih dihn-wá, _____?

   我　冇　佢　電　話，

c. Néih mh jouh yéh, _____?

   你　唔　做　嘢，

III. Use question words like "whatever", "wherever", "whoever"   ◀1008.mp3

> e.g., Jūng-yi **géi-dō** ló **géi-dō**.
>
> 　　　鍾　意幾　多攞幾　多。
>
> *You can get as much as you like.*

1. Fong ga ge sìh-hauh, séung **géi-dím** séng jauh **géi-dím** séng.

   放　假嘅時　候，想　　幾　點醒　就　幾　點　醒。

2. Séung sihk **māt-yéh** jauh giu **māt-yéh**.

   想　　食乜　嘢就　叫乜　嘢。

3. Néih séung heui **bīn-douh**, ngóh chē néih heui **bīn-douh**.

   你　想　去　邊　度，我　車　你　去　邊　度。

4. Hó-yíh chóh **géi-noih** jauh **géi-noih**, mh sái gam faai jáu.

   可　以　坐　幾　耐　就　幾　耐，唔　使　咁　快　走。

✎ Practice

Fill in the appropriate question word from the list.   ◀1009.mp3

māt-yéh	bīn-go	dím	géi-dō chín	géi-sìh
乜　嘢	邊　個	點	幾　多錢	幾　時

a. _____ sā-tāan leng jauh heui _____ sā-tāan yàuh séui.

   　　沙　灘　靚　就　去　　　　沙　灘　游　水。

b. Lóuh-sai wah _____ hōi wúi jauh _____, fong ga dōu yiu fāan gūng-sī.

   老　細話　　　　開　會就　　　　，放　假都　要　返　公　司。

c. Néih béi jó _____ jauh sāu _____, máih sāu dō.

   你　畀咗　　　就　收　　　，咪　收　多。

d. Néih _____ behng jauh sihk _____ yeuhk, yiu tēng yī-sāng góng.

   你　　　　病就　食　　　　藥，要　聽　醫　生　講。

e. Kéuih jūng-yi _____ jouh, ngóh-deih jauh gān-jyuh _____ jouh.

   佢　鍾　意　　　　做，我　哋　就　跟　住　　　　做。

IV. máih 咪 + verb (please don't)   ◀1010.mp3

e.g., Néih **máih** sihk gam dō a!

你　咪　食　咁　多呀！

Don't eat too much!

* Note: "Máih 咪" can be replaced by "mh hóu 唔好" (not good to).

e.g., Néih **mh hóu** sihk taai dō.

你　唔好　食　太　多。

Please don't eat too much.

1. Ngóh góng gwóng-dūng-wá góng dāk mh ngāam, néih **máih** siu.

我　講　廣　東　話　講　得　唔　啱 ， 你　咪　笑。

2. Giu kéuih **máih** jáu, kéuih meih màaih dāan.

叫　佢　咪　走 ，佢　未　埋　單。

3. Kéuih mh haih hóu yàhn, néih **máih** je chín béi kéuih.

佢　唔　係　好　人 ，你　咪　借　錢　畀佢。

4. Néih **máih** sīk gēi, ngóh juhng séung yuhng dihn-nóuh.

你　咪　熄　機 ，我　仲　想　用　電　腦。

5. Nī go haih "yàhn" jih, yāt go yàhn ge yàhn,

呢　個　係　「人」字 ，一　個　人　嘅　人 ，

nī go haih "yahp" jih, yahp heui ge yahp, néih **máih** gáau cho.

呢　個　係　「入」字 ，入　去　嘅　入 ，你　咪　搞　錯。

✎ Practice

Put "máih 咪" in the correct place.   ◀1011.mp3

a. Kéuih chī-sin, néih tēng kéuih góng.

佢　癲線 ，你　聽　佢　講。

b. Néih bou gíng, mh sái gam gán-jēung, dáng háh sīn lā.

你　報　警 ，唔　使　咁　緊　張 ，等　吓　先　啦。

c. Jūng-Wàahn sāk gán chē, néih daap dīk-sí làih.

中　環　塞　緊　車 ，你　搭　的　士　嚟。

d. Néih giu ngóh bōng kéuih jouh yéh.

你　叫　我　幫　佢　做　嘢。

V. taai 太 + adjective (excessively; too)　◀1012.mp3

> e.g., Ngóh sihk dou **taai** báau.
> 我　食　到 太 飽。
> *I ate too much; my stomach was too full.*

1. Ngóh pa ló dāk **taai** dō yéh sihk, sihk mh saai.
　我　怕 攞得太 多 嘢 食，食 唔 晒。

2. Yiht-laaht-laaht heui hàahng sāan, **taai** sān-fú la.
　熱　辣　辣 去 行　　山，太 辛 苦 喇。

3. Hōi láahng-hei lèuhng-jam-jam, **taai** syū-fuhk la.
　開 冷　氣 涼　浸 浸，太 舒 服 喇。

　Ngóh jīk-hāak fan jeuhk gaau.
　我　即 刻 瞓 着　覺。

4. Néih ge jē **taai** sāp, máih ló yahp ūk-kéi.
　你　嘅 遮 太 濕，咪　攞 入 屋 企。

✎ Practice

Complete the sentences.　◀1013.mp3

a. Mh sái pàaih déui dōu máaih dóu daih yāt hòhng fēi, néih _____
　唔 使 排　隊 都 買 到 第 一 行　飛，你

b. Hàahng heui gāai-háu daap bā-sí _____
　行　　去 街 口 搭 巴 士

c. Jíng tìhm-bán _____, yauh mh haih sihk dāk hóu dō.
　整 甜 品 _____，又 唔 係 食 得 好 多。

VI. dái 抵 (good value)　◀1014.mp3

> e.g., Nī-douh ge jih-joh-chāan jeui **dái** sihk.
> 呢度　嘅自助餐　最 抵 食。
> *The buffet here is great value.*

1. Nī go dói hóu **dái** máaih, ngóh máaih jó sahp go sung béi pàhng-yáuh.
　呢 個 袋 好 抵 買，我 買 咗 十 個 送　畀朋　友。

2. Sahp mān yáuh sahp gihn sauh-sī, taai **dái** la.
　十　蚊 有　十 件 壽 司，太 抵 喇。

3. Néih yuhng mh dóu gam dō, sāai jó jauh mh **dái**.
　你 用　唔 到 咁 多，嘥 咗 就 唔 抵。

4. Pàaih déui dáng jó gam noih sīn-ji wah ngóh jī maaih saai, jān-haih mh **dái**.
　排　隊 等 咗 咁 耐 先 至 話 我 知 賣　晒，真 係 唔 抵。

Pyramid drill   ◀1015.mp3

1.

sihk géi-dō jauh géi-dō

食　幾　多　就　幾　多

jūng-yi sihk géi-dō jauh géi-dō

鍾　意　食　幾　多　就　幾　多

Jih-joh-chāan jūng-yi sihk géi-dō jauh géi-dō

自　助　餐　鍾　意　食　幾　多　就　幾　多

Jih-joh-chāan dái sihk, jūng-yi sihk géi-dō jauh géi-dō

自　助　餐　抵　食，鍾　意　食　幾　多　就　幾　多

Jih-joh-chāan jeui dái sihk, jūng-yi sihk géi-dō jauh géi-dō.

自　助　餐　最　抵　食，鍾　意　食　幾　多　就　幾　多。

Buffets are the best value for money; you can eat as much as you like.

2.

yāt-bihn wáan, yāt-bihn sihk yéh

一　便　玩，一　便　食　嘢

yāt-bihn wáan, yāt-bihn sihk yéh, sāai yéh sihk

一　便　玩，一　便　食　嘢，嘥　嘢　食

Néih máih yāt-bihn wáan, yāt-bihn sihk yéh, sāai yéh sihk

你　咪　一　便　玩，一　便　食　嘢，嘥　嘢　食

Néih máih yāt-bihn wáan, yāt-bihn sihk yéh, sāai saai dī yéh sihk.

你　咪　一　便　玩，一　便　食　嘢，嘥　晒　啲　嘢　食。

Don't play while you eat; you're wasting the food.

3.

taai dō

太　多

Sihk tìhm-bán taai dō

食　甜　品　太　多

Sihk géi júng tìhm-bán taai dō

食　幾　種　甜　品　太　多

Sihk géi júng tìhm-bán bīn-douh taai dō

食　幾　種　甜　品　邊　度　太　多

Sihk géi júng tìhm-bán, bīn-douh syun taai dō a?

食　幾　種　甜　品，邊　度　算　太　多　呀？

I'm just eating a few desserts. Why would you consider that too much?

General review

I. Match the questions with the answers.   ◄1016.mp3

1. Joi heui gwo Nàahm-Ā-Dóu ge chāan-tēng sihk hói-sīn, hóu mh hóu a?
   再 去 過 南　丫 島 嘅 餐　廳　食 海 鮮，好 唔 好 呀？

2. Néih mh jíng yéh sihk, bīn-douh yáuh yéh sihk a?
   你 唔 整 嘢 食，邊 度 有 嘢 食 呀？

3. Néih dím-gáai sèhng-yaht tàuh-tung a?
   你 點 解 成 日 頭 痛 呀？

4. Fong ga séung mh séung daap fēi-gēi heui bīn-douh wáan léuhng yaht a?
   放 假 想 唔 想 搭 飛 機 去 邊 度 玩 兩　日 呀？

5. Wohng-Gok máaih yéh gam dái, néih bāt-yùh heui tái háh lā.
   旺　角 買　嘢 咁 抵，你 不 如 去 睇 吓 啦。

☐ a. Syut-gwaih juhng yáuh hóu dō yéh sihk. Ngóh sihk síu-síu yéh jauh báau.
   雪 櫃 仲 有 好 多 嘢 食。我　食 少 少 嘢 就　飽。

☐ b. Ngóh mh séung heui. Ngóh jeui pa dō yàhn, máih sān-fú jih-géi.
   我 唔 想　去。我　最 怕 多 人，咪 辛 苦 自 己。

☐ c. Máih joi làih nī douh, dī hói-sīn dōu mh dái sihk.
   咪　再 去 果 度，啲 海 鮮 都 唔 抵 食。

☐ d. Ngóh hái gūng-sī sèhng-yaht deui-jyuh láahng-hei háu, taai daaih fūng, só-yíh tàuh-tung.
   我 喺 公 司 成 日 對 住 冷　氣 口，太 大　風，所 以 頭　痛。

☐ e. Daap fēi-gēi heui bīn-douh wáan léuhng yaht dōu taai guih yauh taai yúhn.
   搭　飛 機 去 邊 度 玩 兩　日 都 太 劫 又 太 遠。

II. Listen and rearrange the dialogue.   ◄1017.mp3

At a Chinese restaurant

a. Dāk, ngóh jīk-hāak heui ló go choi-páai béi néih tái.
   得，我 即 刻 去 攞 個 菜 牌 畀 你 睇。

b. Gām-yaht ge yàuh séui lùhng-hā tùhng daai-jí dōu hóu leng.
   今 日 嘅 游 水 龍　蝦 同　帶 子 都 好 靚。

   Mh haih sèhng-yaht yáuh ga.
   唔 係 成 日 有 㗎。

c. Gám-yéung jauh yiu saai sahp jek, syun-yùhng jīng daai-jí lā.
   咁　樣　就 要 晒 十 隻，蒜 蓉　蒸 帶 子 啦。

d. O, yāt wùh hēung-pin, yāt wùh séui lā.
   哦，一 壺 香　片，一 壺 水 啦。

e. Géi-dō wái a? Yám māt-yéh chàh a?
幾 多 位 呀？飲 乜 嘢 茶 呀？

f. Hói-sīn jauh gau la, ngóh séung giu dī choi tīm.
海 鮮 就 夠 喇，我 想 叫 啲 菜 添。

g. Hóu. Dī daai-jí dím maaih a?
好。啲 帶 子 點 賣 呀？

h. Juhng yiu māt-yéh tīm a?
仲 要 乜 嘢 添 呀？

i. Lùhng-hā dím jíng hóu-sihk a?
龍 蝦 點 整 好 食 呀？

j. Mh hóu yi-sī, ngóh-deih móuh luhk chàh wo.
唔 好 意 思，我 哋 冇 綠 茶 喎。

k. Māt-yéh hói-sīn leng a?
乜 嘢 海 鮮 靚 呀？

l. Sahp go yàhn. Yáuh móuh luhk chàh a?
十 個 人。有 冇 綠 茶 呀？

m. Séung sihk māt-yéh a?
想 食 乜 嘢 呀？

n. Seuhng tōng guhk lùhng-hā lā.
上 湯 焗 龍 蝦 啦。

o. Yih sahp mān yāt jek, hóu dái sihk.
二 十 蚊 一 隻，好 抵 食。

Dāk sahp jek ja, bāt-yùh néih yiu saai lā.
得 十 隻 咋，不 如 你 要 晒 啦。

Answers

Story

I. Answers and translation

1. b   2. c

1. Why is buffet most suitable for a group of people to dine out?

    a. People feel very happy after having buffet.

    b. There's everything at the buffet; people can have different food.

    c. Buffet is best value for money to a group of people.

    d. A group of friends can enjoy good food while chatting.

2. Why do some people feel uncomfortable having buffet?

    a. Salad, sushi, seafood, and dessert are not tasty.

    b. People see so much food, but they can't have them all.

    c. They can't help trying everything, and they become too full.

    d. Some people want to take lots of food for others to eat.

II.

A: Néih **gok-dāk** māt-yéh **jeui** hóu sihk?

你 覺 得 乜 嘢 最 好 食？

What is most delicious?

B: **Kèih-saht** māt-yéh dōu hóu sihk.

其 實 乜 嘢 都 好 食。

Actually, everything is delicious.

Ngóh **jeui** jūng-yi cheese cake, hóu-sihk **dou** tìhng mh dóu háu.

我 最 鍾 意 cheese cake，好 食 到 停 唔 到 口。

I like cheesecake the most. It is so delicious that I can't stop eating it.

A: Néih **juhng** séung sihk māt-yéh **tīm** a?

你 仲 想 食 乜 嘢 添 呀？

Is there anything else you want to eat?

B: Ngóh yáuh hóu dō júng tìhm-bán **meih** si, yiu chēut heui joi ló **gwo**.

我 有 好 多 種 甜 品 未 試，要 出 去 再 攞 過。

There are many kinds of dessert I haven't tried. I must go up again to get more.

A: Néih **máih** ló dāk taai dō, sihk mh **saai** jauh sāai.

你 咪 攞 得 太 多，食 唔 晒 就 嘥。

Don't get too much. If you can't finish, it's wasteful.

B: Yí? **Gam ngāam** yauh yáuh cheese cake la. Faai dī heui ló lā.

咦？咁 啱 又 有 cheese cake 喇。快 啲 去 攞 啦。

Oh well. It so happens that they're serving cheesecake again. I'll go up and get some.

A: Ngóh **yíh-gīng** sihk dāk **taai** báau, **joi** sihk jauh sān-fú jih-géi.

我 已 經 食 得 太 飽，再 食 就 辛 苦 自 己。

I'm already too full. If I keep eating, I might be sick.

Grammar practice translation I

1. Hong Kong people like to go shopping and look at their mobile phones at the same time.

2. While you cook, I tidy things up.

3. People take photos while at the concert.

Practice answers

a. Ngóh yāt bihn yám jáu, yāt-bihn sihk síu-sihk.

我 一 便 飲 酒，一 便 食 小 食。

I'll have some snack while I drink.

b. Kéuih yāt-bihn hōi wúi, yāt-bihn séuhng móhng.

佢 一 便 開 會，一 便 上 網。

He accessed to the internet during the meeting.

c. Ngóh-deih yāt bihn hàahng sāan, yāt-bihn kīng gái.

我 哋 一 便 行 山，一 便 傾 偈。

We chatted while hiking.

Grammar practice translation II

1. Who wants something like this?

2. If you don't speak more often, how can you learn English?

3. If you don't bring any money, how can you buy anything?

4. His voice is so soft. How can I hear him?

Practice answers

a Kéuih ge méng gam gwaai, bīn-douh gei-dāk a?

佢 嘅 名 咁 怪，邊 度 記 得 呀？

His name is so weird. How will I remember it?

b. Ngóh móuh kéuih dihn-wá, bīn-douh wán dóu kéuih a?

我 冇 佢 電 話，邊 度 搵 到 佢 呀？

I haven't got his phone number. How can I contact him?

c. Néih mh jouh yéh, bīn-douh yáuh chín a?

你 唔 做 嘢，邊 度 有 錢 呀？

If you don't work, how can you have money?

Grammar practice translation III

1. When I am on vacation, I can get up any time I want.

2. Order anything you like to eat.

3. I'll give you a ride anywhere you want to go.

4. You can sit as long as you like. There's no need to leave in a hurry.

Practice answers

a. **Bīn-go** sā-tāan leng jauh heui **bīn-go** sā-tāan yàuh séui.

邊 個 沙 灘 靚 就 去 邊 個 沙 灘 游 水。

We go swimming at beautiful beaches.

b. Lóuh-sai wah **géi-sìh** hōi wúi jauh **géi-sìh**, fong ga dōu yiu fāan gūng-sī.

老 細 話 幾 時 開 會 就 幾 時，放 假 都 要 返 公 司。

We'll have meetings anytime the boss decides. We have to go to the office even during holidays.

c. Néih béi jó **géi-dō chín** jauh sāu **géi-dō chín**, máih sāu dō.

你 畀 咗 幾 多 錢 就 收 幾 多 錢，咪 收 多。

You can take what you paid for. Don't take more.

d. Néih **māt-yéh** behng jauh sihk **māt-yéh** yeuhk, yiu tēng yī-sāng góng.

你 乜 嘢 病 就 食 乜 嘢 藥，要 聽 醫 生 講。

You have to listen to the doctor and take whatever medicine is prescribed.

e. Kéuih jūng-yi **dím** jouh, ngóh-deih jauh gān-jyuh **dím** jouh.

佢 鍾 意 點 做，我 哋 就 跟 住 點 做。

We'll follow the way he likes to do things.

Grammar practice translation IV

1. If I speak Cantonese incorrectly, please don't laugh.

2. Ask him not to leave. He hasn't settled the bill.

3. He is not an honest person. Don't lend him money.

4. Don't turn off the computer. I still want to use it.

5. This character is "人 yàhn", a person. This character is "入 yahp", enter from, go in. Please don't mix them up.

Practice answers

a. Kéuih chī-sin, néih **máih** tēng kéuih góng.

佢 黐線，你 咪 聽 佢 講。

He's crazy. Don't listen to him.

b. Néih **máih** bou gíng, mh sái gam gán-jēung, dáng háh sīn lā.

你 咪 報 警，唔 使 咁 緊 張， 等 吓 先 啦。

Don't call the police, and don't be nervous. Wait a little while.

c. Jūng-Wàahn sāk gán chē, néih **máih** daap dīk-sí làih.

中 環 塞緊車，你 咪 搭 的 士 嚟。

There is a traffic jam in Central. Don't come here by taxi.

d. Néih **máih** giu ngóh bōng kéuih jouh yéh.

你 咪 叫我 幫 佢 做 嘢。

Don't ask me to help him with anything.

Grammar practice translation V

1. I worried that I'd get too much food. I can't eat it all.

2. Hiking in such hot weather is very uncomfortable.

3. I felt cool after turning on the air-conditioning. It was really comfortable. I fell asleep immediately.

4. Your umbrella is too wet. Don't bring it into the house.

Suggested practice answers

a. Mh sái pàaih déui dōu máaih dóu daih yāt hòhng fēi, néih **taai hóu-chói la!**

唔 使 排 隊 都 買 到 第 一 行 飛，你 太 好 彩 喇！

You don't have to queue to get front-row tickets. You're so lucky!

b. Hàahng heui gāai-háu daap bā-sí **taai yúhn**

行 去 街 口 搭 巴 士 太 遠。

It's too far to walk to the intersection to take a bus.

c. Jíng tìhm-bán **taai màh-fàahn**, yauh mh haih sihk dāk hóu dō.

整 甜 品 太 麻 煩， 又 唔 係 食 得 好 多。

Making dessert is a lot of trouble, and you can't eat a lot.

Grammar practice translation VI

1. This bag is good value. I bought ten for my friends.

2. Ten dollars for ten pieces of sushi is excellent value.

3. If you can't eat that much and waste it, that's too bad.

4. I queued for a long time before someone told me it was sold out. What a waste of time!

General review

I. Question and answer translation

1. Shall we go again to the restaurant on Lamma Island to have seafood?

   c. Don't go there again. The seafood isn't worth it.

2. If you don't cook, what do you eat?

   a. There is plenty of food in the fridge. A little will be enough.

3. Why do you often get headaches?

   d. When I'm in the office, I am facing the air-conditioning vent all day. The airflow is too strong, so I get a headache.

4. Do you want to go somewhere for two days of holiday?

   e. Flying somewhere to spend two days is too tiring and too far.

5. Mong Kok is good for shopping. Let's go and take a look.

    b. I don't want to go. I really dislike the crowds. I don't want to feel annoyed.

II.

e. A: Géi-dō wái a? Yám māt-yéh chàh a?

    幾 多 位 呀？飲 乜 嘢 茶 呀？

    How many people? What kind of tea do you want?

l. B: Sahp go yàhn. Yáuh móuh luhk chàh a?

    十 個 人。有 冇 綠 茶 呀？

    There are ten of us. Do you have green tea?

j. A: Mh hóu yi-sī, ngóh-deih móuh luhk chàh wo.

    唔 好 意 思，我 哋 冇 綠 茶 喎。

    Sorry, we don't serve green tea.

d. B: O, yāt wùh hēung-pin, yāt wùh séui lā.

    哦，一 壺 香 片，一 壺 水 啦。

    Oh I see. Then a pot of Jasmine tea, and a pot of water please.

m. A: Séung sihk māt-yéh a?

    想 食 乜 嘢 呀？

    What would you like to eat?

k. B: Māt-yéh hói-sīn leng a?

    乜 嘢 海 鮮 靚 呀？

    Any nice seafood?

b. A: Gām-yaht ge yàuh séui lùhng-hā tùhng daai-jí dōu hóu leng.

    今 日 嘅 游 水 龍 蝦 同 帶 子 都 好 靚。

    Live lobster and scallops are good today.

    Mh haih sèhng-yaht yáuh ga.

    唔 係 成 日 有 㗎。

    We don't often have them.

i. B: Lùhng-hā dím jíng hóu-sihk a?

    龍 蝦 點 整 好 食 呀？

    How do you cook the lobster?

n. A: Seuhng tōng guhk lùhng-hā lā.

    上 湯 焗 龍 蝦 啦。

    How about cooking it in broth?

g. B: Hóu. Dī daai-jí dím maaih a?

    好。啲 帶 子 點 賣 呀？

    Good. How much are the scallops?

o. A: Yih sahp mān yāt jek, hóu dái sihk.

    二 十 蚊 一 隻，好 抵 食。

    Dāk sahp jek ja, bāt-yùh néih yiu saai lā.

    得 十 隻 咋，不 如 你 要 晒 啦。

    $20 a piece. That's good value.

    There are only ten. Take them all.

c. B: Gám-yéung jauh yiu saai sahp jek, syun-yùhng jīng daai-jí lā.

    咁 樣 就 要 晒 十 隻，蒜 蓉 蒸 帶 子 啦。

    Then I'll take all 10 pieces, steamed with garlic paste please.

h. A: Juhng yiu māt-yéh tīm a?

仲　要　乜　嘢　添呀？

Do you want anything else?

f. B: Hói-sīn jauh gau la, ngóh séung giu dī choi tīm.

海　鮮　就　夠　喇，我　想　　叫啲菜　添。

There is enough seafood. I want to have some other dishes/vegetables.

a. A: Dāk, ngóh jīk-hāak heui ló go choi-páai béi néih tái.

得，我　即　刻　去　攞個菜　牌　畀你　睇。

Okay, I'll get you the menu.

Hong Kong culture

Local Hong Kong fast-food menus   ◀1018.mp3

In a local fast-food restaurant (茶餐廳 chàh-chān-tēng), reading the menu is a lot of fun.

You will find different ways to serve instant noodles on a proper menu: in soup, stir-fried, marinated with satay sauce, to name a few. Many restaurants charge extra when you specify the Nissin brand of instant noodles (出前一丁 chēut chìhn yāt dīng); it is the soul food of Hong Kong people.

Almost nothing on the menu is named after Hong Kong or the UK. You will find very "international" dishes, but they are all Hong Kong–style food, and often, only Hong Kong people understand how those dishes are cooked.

For Japanese-style food, the most common dish is fried udon with seafood (日式海鮮炒烏冬 Yaht sīk hói-sīn cháau wū-dūng). This is fried thick noodles in teriyaki sauce. The seafood includes fake crab sticks, frozen clams, squid, and shrimp. Another popular dish is fried rice with eel (日式鰻魚炒飯 Yaht sīk maahn-yùh cháau faahn), which has chopped teriyaki grilled eel stirred into egg-fried rice.

Thai style means spicy dishes.

Thai-style fried noodles (泰式炒河 Taai sīk cháau hó), which are very different from Pad Thai, are fried flat rice noodles with curry powder. Another popular Thai dish is noodles in Tom Yum soup (冬蔭公湯河 dūng-yām-gūng tōng hó) and is often served as a variation of instant noodles or noodles in wonton soup. These dishes are quite different from what you can find in an authentic Thai restaurant.

Vietnamese style means using sliced Vietnamese sausage and adding fish sauce in addition to soy sauce for seasoning. Vietnamese-style noodles in soup (越式湯河 Yuht sīk tōng hó) are noodles in soup with sliced Vietnamese sausage. Local Hong Kong restaurants never serve raw sliced beef with noodles in soup, which is the popular dish Pho Bo found in most authentic Vietnamese restaurants.

Italian style means tomato sauce. Italian-style baked seafood with rice (意大利焗海鮮飯 Yi-Daaih-Leih guhk hói-sīn faahn) is fried rice topped with prawn and fish in tomato sauce.

When you think of Italian food, probably spaghetti comes to your mind. Hong Kong chefs' invention of stir-fried spaghetti with sliced beef, black pepper, and soy sauce (乾炒黑椒牛肉意粉 gōn cháau hāak-jīu ngàuh-yuhk yi-fán) is a superb and "must-try" fusion dish.

Spanish style is very similar to Italian style; sliced black olives are often added to the tomato sauce.

Spanish omelette (西班牙奄列 Sāi-Bāan-Ngàh ām-liht), served at set breakfast, is omelette with ham, sausage, and green pepper. No potato is found in this omelette.

The most common Portuguese-style dish is stewed chicken with rice (葡國雞飯 Pòuh-Gwok gāi faahn). This is a Macau invention, a kind of non-spicy curry with coconut milk sauce.

Hawaiian ham steak (夏威夷火腿扒 Hah-Wāi-Yìh fó-téui pá) means there is a ring of canned pineapple on a ham steak. This dish is usually served with steamed rice or plain boiled vegetables.

Don't expect Mexican-style meat sauce (墨西哥肉醬 Mahk-Sāi-Gō yuhk jeung) to be a spicy dish with Mexican chilli. Instead, it is usually Bolognese sauce with kidney beans. Why are kidney beans associated with Mexico? I guess no Hong Kong person can answer that question.

In local bakeries, there is a sweet bun called Mexican bun (墨西哥包 Mahk-Sāi-Gō bāau), which originated from Spanish concha and is very similar to pineapple bun (菠蘿包 bō-lòh bāau), another kind of sweet bun popular in Hong Kong. Mexico is a Spanish-speaking country; a Hong Kong businessman discovered this bun in Mexico and introduced it as a Mexican bun.

Russian Borscht (羅宋湯 lòh sung tōng) is found on almost all local fast-food menus, but it's not nearly as good as the original style. The ingredients of this soup include tomato, potato, carrot, and cabbage. Local restaurants do not use beetroot.

Beef Stroganoff, Russian-style shredded beef stew (俄國牛柳絲 Ngòh-Gwok Ngàuh-láuh-sī), is a common dish, but it is not very popular in Hong Kong.

Two other popular dishes believed to be foreign food are actually Hong Kong inventions.

Singaporean fried rice noodles (星州炒米 Sīng Jāu cháau máih) are fried thin rice noodles with curry powder, shrimp, and onion. When you try this dish in Singapore, you will find Singaporeans call it "Hong Kong fried noodles".

Swiss chicken wings (瑞士雞翼 Seuih-Sih gāi-yihk) are stewed chicken wings with sweet soy sauce. The older-generation Hong Kong chefs who did not speak English mispronounced "sweet" as "Swiss" and called the dish "Swiss-style". Many Hong Kong people do not know this, however. They are very eager to try the authentic Swiss chicken wings when they visit Switzerland.

Appendix 1
Cantonese pronunciation system and practice

The Hong Kong government does not use a proper romanization system. Street signs and personal names are romanized in a random way. This kind of romanization cannot be used for systematic teaching and learning. Here are some examples:

Chinese Characters	Hong Kong Road Sign/Surname	Yale Romanization
灣仔	Wan Chai	Wāan Jái
柴灣	Chai Wan	Chàaih Wāan
薄扶林	Pok Fu Lam	Bok Fuh Làhm
藍田	Lam Tin	Làahm Tìhn
尖沙咀	Tsim Sha Tsui	Jīm Sā Jéui
深水埗	Sham Shui Po	Sām Séui Bóu
長洲	Cheung Chau	Chèuhng Jāu
徐	Chui / Tsui	Chèuih
周	Chau / Chow / Chou	Jāu
林	Lam / Lim / Lum	Làhm

This book uses Yale romanization, a popular system for English speakers developed by Yale University.

Each Cantonese syllable consists of three elements:

1. Initial: the sound of the consonant at the beginning of the syllable. There are 19 initials in all.
2. Final: the sound of the vowel or consonant at the end of the syllable. There are 51 finals in all.
3. Tone: the relative pitch or variation of pitch of a syllable. There are 6 tones in all.

Examples of a syllable:

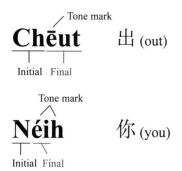

Initials

		as in English	*example*			*as in English*	*example*
1.	b	boy	bā 巴	11.	l	law	lā 啦
2.	ch	similar to "ts"	chā 叉	12.	m	mother	mā 媽
3.	d	dig	dá 打	13.	n	no	náh 那
4.	f	far	fā 花	14.	ng	singer	ngàh 牙
5.	g	game	gā 家	15.	p	park	pa 怕
6.	gw	guava	gwā 瓜	16.	s	sand	sā 沙
7.	h	home	hā 蝦	17.	t	till	tā 他
8.	j	similar to "z"	jā 渣	18.	w	water	wā 娃
9.	k	kill	kā 卡	19.	y	yes	yáh 也
10.	kw	quite	kwā 誇				

Finals

		as in English	*example*			*as in English*	*example*
	long a				**short a**		
1.	a	far	gā 加				
2.	aai	aisle	taai 太	10.	ai	lye	sai 細
3.	aau	how	bāau 包	11.	au	out ("t" silent)	sau 瘦
4.	aam	arm	sāam 三	12.	am	sum	sām 心
5.	aan	aunt	sāan 山	13.	an	sun	sān 新
6.	aang	no equivalent	sāang 生	14.	ang	dung	gāng 羹
7.	aap	harp ("p" silent)	daap 答	15.	ap	up ("p" silent)	sāp 濕
8.	aat	art ("t" silent)	baat 八	16.	at	gut ("t" silent)	bāt 筆
9.	aak	ark ("k" silent)	baak 百	17.	ak	duck ("k" silent)	dāk 得
	long e				**short e**		
18.	e	yes	sé 寫	21.	ei	day	fēi 飛
19.	eng	length	tēng 聽				
20.	ek	echo	sek 錫				
	long eu				**short eu**		
22.	eu	her	hēu 靴	25.	eui	deuil (French)	heui 去
23.	eung	learning	hēung 香	26.	eun	nation	seun 信
24.	euk	turk ("k" silent)	geuk 腳	27.	eut	no equivalent	chēut 出

	as in English	*example*		*as in English*	*example*
long i			**short i**		
28.	i	bee	si 試	34.	ing	single	sīng 星
29.	iu	yew	siu 笑	35.	ik	sick ("k" silent)	sīk 識
30.	im	seem	dim 店				
31.	in	seen	sīn 先				
32.	ip	jeep ("p" silent)	tip 貼				
33.	it	seat ("t" silent)	tit 鐵				
long o			**short o**		
36.	o	sore	dō 多	42.	ou	toe	gōu 高
37.	oi	boy	hōi 開				
38.	on	on	gōn 乾				
39.	ong	song	tōng 湯				
40.	ot	ought ("t" silent)	hot 渴				
41.	ok	cock ("k" silent)	gwok 國				
long u			**short u**		
43.	u	fruit	fu 褲	47.	ung	Achtung (German)	sung 送
44.	ui	"oo" + "ee"	būi 杯	48.	uk	hook ("k" silent)	ūk 屋
45.	un	soon	bun 半				
46.	ut	boot ("t" silent)	fut 闊				
long yu					
49.	yu	Dessus (French)	yú 魚			
50.	yun	Une (French)	yúhn 遠			
51.	yut	chute (French)	yuht 月			

* Notes:

1. "m" and "ng" can also be treated as finals.
2. "m" and a long "m" are said without opening the mouth.
3. "ng" is similar to the "ng" in singing, but is said further back in the mouth.

Tones

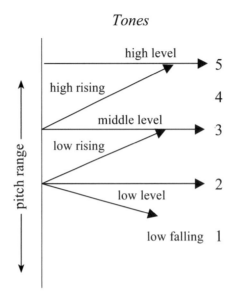

Tones		Tone Mark	Example	
1	high level	with " - " on top of the first vowel	sī	poem 詩
2	high rising	with " / " on top of the first vowel	sí	history 史
3	middle level	none	si	try 試
4	low falling	with " \ " on top, an "h" after the vowel(s)	sìh	time 時
5	low rising	with " / " on top, an "h" after the vowel(s)	síh	market 市
6	low level	with an "h" after the vowel(s)	sih	matter 事

Six tones practice

high level	middle level	low level	low falling	high rising	low rising
mā 媽 (mother)	ma 嗎 (what)	mah 罵 (scold)	màh 麻 (linen)	má 痳 (measles)	máh 馬 (horse)
sē 些 (some)	se 舍 (house)	seh 射 (shoot)	sèh 蛇 (snake)	sé 寫 (write)	séh 社 (society)
yī 衣 (clothes)	yi 意 (meaning)	yih 二 (two)	yìh 怡 (delightful)	yí 椅 (chair)	yíh 已 (already)
chō 初 (beginning)	cho 錯 (wrong)	choh	chòh 鋤 (dig)	chó 楚 (clear)	chóh 坐 (sit)
fū 夫 (husband)	fu 富 (rich)	fuh 父 (father)	fùh 扶 (hold on)	fú 苦 (bitter)	fúh 婦 (woman)
sāam 3	sei 4	yih 2	lìhng 0	gáu 9	ńgh 5
bīn 邊 (Who is coming in?)	go 個	yahp 入	làih 嚟		

Middle level

Fong ga yiu fan gaau fan dou gau
放　假要瞓覺　瞓到　夠。
I want to have as much sleep as I need on holiday.

Low level

Sahp yih yuht yih sahp luhk houh
十　二　月　二　十　六　號
26th December

High rising

Hóu séung tái dóu
好　想　　睇到
I really want to see (a scene)

Low rising

Néih yáuh móuh séuhng móhng máaih yéh?
你　有　冇　上　　網　　買　　嘢？
Did you shop online?

Initials with vowels a, e, i, o, u

ba 巴	be 啤（酒）	bi B	bo 波	
cha 叉	che 車	chi 次	cho 坐	
da 打	de 爹	di 啲	do 多	
fa 化	fe 啡	fi	fo 火	fu 夫
ga 加	ge 嘅	gi	go 個	gu 古
gwa 瓜	gwe		gwo 果	
ha 下	he	hi	ho 可	
ja 炸	je 姐	ji 支	jo 左	
ka 卡	ke 茄			ku 箍
kwa 誇				
la 啦	le	li	lo 羅	lu
ma 媽	me 咩	mi 咪	mo 摩	
na 拿	ne 呢	ni 呢（個）	no 糯	
nga 牙			ngo 我	
pa 怕	pe	pi	po 婆	
sa 沙	se 些	si 市	so 梳	
ta 他		ti T	to 拖	tu
wa 蛙	we	wi	wo 窩	wu 胡
ya 也	ye 爺	yi 衣	yo	

Vocabulary practice

bā sí 巴士	*bus*
dō jeh 多謝	*thank you*
sòh gwā 傻瓜	*idiot*
só sìh 鎖匙	*key*
dá gú 打鼓	*play a drum*
chā mh dō 差唔多	*almost; more or less the same*
chē dá jī sí 車打芝士	*cheddar cheese*
hī hī hā hā 嘻嘻哈哈	*sound of laughter*
lìh lī làh làh 呢呢拿拿	*hurry up; hurriedly*
mī mī mō mō 咪咪摩摩	*do things slowly*
bàh bā màh mā 爸爸媽媽	*father and mother*
gòh gō jèh jē 哥哥姐姐	*elder brother; elder sister*

Exercise   ◄1101.mp3

Part I. Listen to the pronunciation and fill in the appropriate initials.

1. ___o ___a   2. ___o ___i   3. ___o ___o

Part II. Listen to the pronunciation and fill in the appropriate finals.

1. m___ g___   2. y___ g___   3. d___ s___

Part III. Listen and choose the correct romanization.

1. a. ka fe   b. ga fe   c. ga he   d. ka fa
2. a. chi so   b. ji su   c. ju so   d. chi su
3. a. a ye   b. nga pi   c. nga yi   d. a wi
4. a. sa ce   b. je chi   c. nga fe   d. ja che
5. a. ke ji   b. ge se   c. ku si   d. ga je

Finals: aai, aam, aan, aau

aai

aai 嗌	baai 拜	chaai 猜	daai 大	faai 快
gaai 街	gwaai 怪	haai 鞋	jaai 債	kaai 楷
laai 拉	maai 買	naai 奶	ngaai 捱	paai 派
saai 晒	taai 太	waai 壞		

aam

chaam 參	daam 淡	gaam 監	haam 喊	jaam 站
laam 藍	naam 男	ngaam 癌	saam 三	taam 貪

aan

aan 晏	baan 班	chaan 餐	daan 蛋	faan 反
gaan 揀	gwaan 慣	haan 閒	jaan 賺	laan 懶
maan 晚	naan 難	ngaan 顏	paan 盼	saan 山
taan 攤	waan 環			

aau

aau 拗	baau 包	chaau 抄	gaau 交	haau 考
jaau 找	kaau 靠	laau 撈	maau 貓	naau 鬧
ngaau 咬	paau 跑	saau 稍		

Vocabulary practice

faai chāan 快餐	*fast food*
cháau faahn 炒飯	*fried rice*
gaam láam 橄欖	*olive*
jáam ngáahn 眨眼	*to blink*
gáan dāan 簡單	*simple*
gaam gaai 尷尬	*embarrassed; awkward*
aai gāau 嗌交	*to quarrel*
Taai Sāan 泰山	*Tarzan; Tai Shan*
daaih gáam ga 大減價	*a big sale*
yáai dāan chē 踩單車	*to ride a bicycle*

Exercise   ◀1102.mp3

Part I. Listen to the pronunciation and fill in the appropriate initials.

1. ___aam ___aai   2. ___aan ___aau   3. ___aan ___aan

Part II. Listen to the pronunciation and fill in the appropriate finals.

1. w_____ d_____   2. h_____ p_____   3. h_____ b_____

Part III. Listen and choose the correct romanization.

1. a. taai taam	b. taai taan	c. daai daam	d. daai daan
2. a. maai daan	b. ngaai daam	c. paai taan	d. naai taan
3. a. laam saam	b. laan saan	c. naan chaan	d. ngaan saan
4. a. ngaau kaau	b. naau gaau	c. laau kaau	d. laau gaau
5. a. maan laan	b. waan naan	c. waai naam	d. waai naan

Compare similar pronunciations.

aam and aan

cháam 慘	cháan 產	dāam 擔	dāan 單
hàahm 鹹	hàahn 閒	jaahm 站	jaahn 賺
sāam 三	sāan 山	gāam fáan 監犯 *prisoner*	

Finals: aang, aak, aap, aat

aang

aang 罌	chaang 橙	gaang 耕	haang 坑	jaang 爭
kwaang 框	laang 冷	maang 猛	ngaang 硬	paang 棚
saang 生	waang 橫			

aak

aak 呃	baak 白	chaak 拆	gaak 格	gwaak 摑
haak 客	jaak 窄	maak 擘	ngaak 額	paak 拍
saak 索	waak 或			

aap

chaap 插	daap 答	gaap 夾	haap 呷	jaap 集
laap 立	naap 納	ngaap 鴨	saap 圾	taap 塔

aat

aat 壓	baat 八	chaat 察	daat 達	faat 發
gwaat 刮	jaat 札	kaat 卡	laat 辣	maat 抹
naat 捺	saat 殺	taat 撻	waat 挖	

Vocabulary practice

hàahng gāai 行街	*go shopping*
faak dáan 發蛋	*beat the egg*
paak maaih 拍賣	*auction*
lāang sāam 冷衫	*sweater*
baahn faat 辦法	*method*
hāak baahk 黑白	*black and white*
chàahng ngáahn 撐眼	*dazzling; too bright for the eyes*
gāam chaat 監察	*supervise and control*
ngaahng bāang bāang 硬板板	*stiff; inflexible*

Exercise   ◀1103.mp3

Part I. Listen to the pronunciation and fill in the appropriate initials.

1. ___aap   2. ___aak   3. ___aang   4. ___aat   5. ___aang

Part II. Listen to the pronunciation and fill in the appropriate finals.

1. d_____ h_____   2. f_____ d_____   3. ch_____ p_____

Part III. Listen and choose the correct romanization.

1. a. chaat waat   b. chaap waak   c. chaak waat   d. chaak waak
2. a. laak taak   b. ngaat data   c. laat taat   d. naat daang
3. a. naap jaap   b. laap saap   c. laap chaap   d. naam saat
4. a. chaang maan   b. saak maan   c. saang maang   d. saan maang
5. a. chaap kaat   b. chaat kaak   c. saap gaat   d. jaat gaak

Compare similar pronunciations.

aan and aang
sāang dáan 生蛋 *laid eggs*
sāan 山   sāang 生
maahn 慢   maahng 孟

aak and aat
baat baak 八百 *800*
chaak laahn 拆爛 *tear down*   chaat ngàh 刷牙 *brush one's teeth*
maak hōi 擘開 *open wide*   maat tói 抹枱 *wipe the table*
waahk wá 畫畫 *draw a picture*   waaht báan 滑板 *skateboard*

aam and aap
chāam gā 參加 *participate*   chaap wá 插畫 *illustration*
dāam jē 擔遮 *hold an umbrella*   daap chē 搭車 *ride in a car*
hàahm choi 鹹菜 *pickles*   haap chou 呷醋 *jealous*
gaam láam 橄欖 *olive*   laahp ngaap 臘鴨 *cured duck*
bā sí jaahm jaahp hahp 巴士站集合 *assemble at the bus stop*

aang and aak
wàahng waahk 橫畫 *a horizontal stroke*
hàahng yàhn 行人 *pedestrian*   haak yàhn 客人 *guest; customer*
cháang yuhk 橙肉 *orange with skin removed*   chaak yuhk 拆肉 *remove meat from crab or fish*

aan and aat
chaat yāt chaan 擦一餐 *have a good big meal*
maahn máan maat 慢慢抹 *wipe slowly*
daahn tāat 蛋撻 *egg tart*   faahn faat 犯法 *break the law*
laahn jí 爛紙 *torn paper*   laaht jīu 椒 *chilli*
jaan-sìhng 贊成 *agree with; approve of*
jaat sìhng yāt jaat 扎成一紮 *tie into a bundle*

aap, aat, and aak
yāt baak baat sahp 一百八十 *180*
yāt go cháap 一個插 *an ice pick*
yāt go cháat 一個刷 *a scrubber*
yāt go cháak 一個賊 *a thief; a robber*
jaahp jyuh 閘住 *close off*   jaat jyuh 扎住 *tie together*
jyuh jaahk 住宅 *residence*
gaap béng 夾餅 *waffle*   gaak jái béng 格仔餅 *Belgian waffle*

Finals: ai, am, an, au

ai

ai 矮	bai 幣	chai 妻	dai 低	fai 肺
gai 計	gwai 貴	hai 系	jai 制	kai 啟
kwai 規	lai 黎	mai 米	nai 泥	ngai 危
pai 批	sai 西	tai 提	wai 位	yai 曳

am

am 暗	bam 泵	cham 侵	gam 今	ham 含
jam 針	kam 琴	lam 林	sam 心	tam 氹
yam 飲				

an

an 夭	ban 笨	chan 陳	dan 燉	fan 分
gan 根	gwan 均	han 恨	jan 真	kan 近
kwan 裙	man 文	ngan 銀	pan 貧	san 身
tan 吞	wan 溫	yan 人		

au

au 勾	chau 臭	dau 豆	fau 否	gau 九
hau 口	jau 走	kau 扣	lau 留	mau 某
ngau 牛	sau 手	tau 頭	yau 右	

Vocabulary Practice

jān haih 真係	*really; truly*
tàuh wàhn 頭暈	*dizzy*
māu dāi 踎低	*squat*
sái sáu 洗手	*wash one's hands*
jáu làuh 酒樓	*Chinese restaurant*
yàhn háu 人口	*population*
máih fán 米粉	*vermicelli*
Aū Jāu 歐洲	*Europe*
jān gwai 珍貴	*precious*
sāi kàhn 西芹	*celery*
sān tái 身體	*body*
yauh sáu 右手	*right hand*
sān màhn 新聞	*news*
jām gau 針灸	*acupuncture*

Exercise   ◀1104.mp3

Part I. Listen to the pronunciation and fill in the appropriate initials.

1. ___an ___ai   2. ___au ___ au   3. ___au ___au

Part II. Listen to the pronunciation and fill in the appropriate finals.

1. j_____ t_____   2. s_____ y_____   3. y_____ w_____

Part III. Listen and choose the correct romanization.

1. a. wun taan   b. wan tan   c. won taan   d. wam tan
2. a. wai hau   b. mai kaau   c. waai kau   d. gwai hou
3. a. chan san   b. jan sum   c. chan saam   d. jan sam
4. a. ngau waai   b. au wai   c. yau wai   d. yaau wai
5. a. sam maai   b. cham mai   c. chaam mai   d. cham nai

Compare similar pronunciations.
aai and ai
fai chàaih 廢柴 *loser*
jaai jái 債仔 *debtor*
waaih waih 壞胃 *bad for the stomach*
daaih go 大個 *grown up*   daih go 第個 *another one*
fān paai 分派 *allocate; assign a task*   fān pāi 分批 *divide into batches*
taai táai tái tái 太太睇睇 *Madam, please take a look.*
gwāai jái máaih gwāi jái 乖仔買龜仔 *My dear son bought a tortoise.*

aam and am
dāam sām 擔心 *worry*
làhm sìh chē jaahm 臨時車站 *temporary station*
gáam síu 減少 *reduce*   gam síu 咁少 *so few; such a small amount*
jám tàuh 枕頭 *pillow*   làahm kàuh 籃球 *basketball*

aan and an
dāan sān 單身 *single; bachelor*
fáan fan 反瞓 *toss and turn during sleep*
gáan gán 揀緊 *selecting*
sāan sàhn 山神 *mountain god*
wàahn wàhn 還魂 *resurrection*
yāt maahn mān 一萬蚊 *ten thousand dollars*

am and an
chàhm chān 尋親 *looking for one's family member*
sān sām 身心 *body and soul*
gām-yaht 今日 *today*   gahn yaht 近日 *recently*
yám jáu 飲酒 *drink alcohol*   yán sauh 忍受 *endure; bear*
kàhn-lihk lihn kàhm 勤力練琴 *practise playing the piano intensely*

aau and au
māau gáu 貓狗 *cat and dog*
síu cháau 小炒 *stir-fried dishes*   síu-cháu 小丑 *clown*
háau-si 考試 *examination*   háu si 口試 *oral examination*

Finals: ang, ak, ap, at

ang

ang 鶯	bang 崩	chang 層	dang 登	gang 梗
gwang 轟	hang 杏	jang 贈	kang 啃	mang 盟
nang 能	pang 朋	sang 生	tang 藤	wang 宏

ap

ap 噏	chap 輯	gap 急	hap 合	jap 汁
kap 及	lap 立	nap 凹	sap 十	yap 入

at

bat 不	chat 七	dat 凸	fat 佛	gat 吉
gwat 骨	hat 乞	jat 質	kat 咳	lat 甩
mat 物	pat 匹	sat 失	wat 屈	yat 一

ak

bak 北	dak 得	hak 克	jak 則	lak 肋
mak 麥	sak 塞			

Vocabulary practice

yahp háu 入口	*entrance; import*
hahng yàhn 杏仁	*almond*
kwāi jāk 規則	*rule; regulation*
yàuh chāt 油漆	*paint*
waht daht 核突	*ugly; disgusting*
maht sāt 密室	*secret chamber*
chāt sahp yāt 七十一	*71; 7-Eleven*
dáng yāt jahn 等陣	*wait a moment*
háu lahp sāp 口立濕	*junk food*
lāk lāk kāk kāk 勒勒卡卡	*stuttering*
sāp sāp lahp lahp 濕濕立立	*wet and sticky*
Hàhng Sāng Ngàhn Hòhng 恒生銀行	*Hang Seng Bank*

Exercise   ◀1105.mp3

Part I. Listen to the pronunciation and fill in the appropriate initials.

1. ___at   2. ___ak   3. ___ang   4. ___ap   5. ___ak

Part II. Listen to the pronunciation and fill in the appropriate finals.

1. n_____ d_____   2. l_____ gw_____   3. b_____ h_____

Part III. Listen and choose the correct romanization.

1. a. gang haai   b. kang aai   c. geng hat   d. gang hai
2. a. sak jak   b. sat jat   c. sat jak   d. sat chat
3. a. kap saau   b. kap sap   c. kap sau   d. kat sam
4. a. hap faat   b. ham fat   c. haap fak   d. hup fat
5. a. sum gap   b. sem gaak   c. sam gap   d. saam gat

Compare similar pronunciations.

aang, ang and an

bāng 崩	bān 賓	
dahng 鄧	dahn 燉	
sāang-yi 生意 *business*	yī-sāng 醫生 *doctor*	sān yi 新意 *new idea*
chaang 撐	chàhng 層	chàhn 陳
gāang 耕	gāng 羹	gān 根
hàahng 行	hàhng 恆	hàhn 痕
jāang 踭	jāng 箏	jān 真
màahng 盲	màhng 萌	màhn 文
pàahng 棚	pàhng 朋	pàhn 貧

aak and ak

baak 百	bāk 北
jaak 窄	jāk 則
maak 擘	mahk 麥

aap and ap

saahp sahp jek dáan 焓十隻蛋 *boil ten eggs*
gaap sām 夾心 *sandwich* ; *cream biscuit*   sām-gāp 心急 *anxious*
jaahp gwó jāp 雜果汁 *mixed fruit juice*

aat and at

gaht jáat 甲由 *cockroach*
kāt jó jēung kāat *cut* 咗張咭 *cancel a credit card / member's card*
waaht 滑   waht 核

ap, at, and ak

sahp yāt 十一 *11*	
sāt chē 失車 *lost car*	sāk chē 塞車 *traffic jam*
hāk sīk 黑色 *black*	hāt sihk 乞食 *be a beggar*
kāp gōn 吸乾 *soak up*	gōn kāt 乾咳 *dry cough*
chēut yahp 出入 *go in and out*	chāt yaht 七日 *7 days*

daht-yìhn gei-dāk yiu dahp yan
突 然 記 得 要 揼 印
suddenly remember I need to stamp the ticket

Finals: eng, ek, ei, ing, ik

eng

beng 餅	cheng 青	deng 釘	geng 頸	heng 輕
jeng 正	leng 靚	meng 命	peng 平	seng 腥
teng 廳	yeng 贏			

ek

chek 尺	dek 笛	hek 吃	jek 隻	kek 劇
lek 叻	pek 劈	sek 石	tek 踢	

ei

bei 比	dei 地	fei 飛	gei 記	hei 起
kei 企	lei 里	mei 未	nei 你	pei 皮
sei 四	wei 喂			

ing

bing 冰	ching 清	ding 丁	ging 京	hing 兄
jing 靜	king 傾	ling 零	ming 名	ning 寧
ping 平	sing 姓	ting 聽	wing 永	ying 英

ik

bik 逼	chik 戚	dik 的	gik 激	jik 直
kik 棘	kwik 隙	lik 力	mik 覓	pik 僻
sik 色	tik 剔	wik 域	yik 益	

Vocabulary practice

néih deih 你哋	*you (plural)*
bēi péi 卑鄙	*despicable*
fēi gēi 飛機	*airplane*
tek bō 踢波	*play football; kick a ball*
jek gwāt 脊骨	*spine*
sing gīng 聖經	*bible*
mihng lihng 命令	*order*
pìhng jihng 平靜	*calm*
gihng dihk 勁敵	*a rival; formidable opponent*
jīk gihk 積極	*be positive; play an active role*
gwai bān teng 貴賓廳	*VIP room*
chéng behng ga 請病假	*take sick leave*
pèhng leng jeng 平靚正	*inexpensive and good quality*
sīng kèih sei 星期四	*Thursday*
dīk sí sī gēi 的士司機	*taxi driver*

Exercise   ◀1106.mp3

Part I. Listen to the pronunciation and fill in the appropriate finals.

1. y_____ ch_____   2. b_____ k_____   3. d_____ f_____

4. j_____ l_____   5. ch_____ s_____   6. g_____ l_____

Part II. Listen and choose the correct romanization.

1. a. sei ying   b. seng ying   c. sik yik   d. si jing

2. a. jing sing   b. jeng sing   c. jing sik   d. jeng sek

3. a. se sik   b. sik se   c. sik si   d. sek si

4. a. sing kei   b. seng ki   c. seng gei   d. sing king

5. a. jing yik   b. ching ying   c. ching yeng   d. jing yin

Compare similar pronunciations.

e and ei

bē léi 啤梨 *pear*

ngóh-deih dē-dìh 我哋爹哋 *our daddy*

néih ge fēi-gēi 你嘅飛機 *your airplane*

séi sèh 死蛇 *dead snake*

sé sei chi 寫四次 *write four times*

kèh lèh 騎呢 *weird; awkward*   kéih léih 企理 *tidy*

aai, ai, and ei

máaih Méih Gwok máih 買美國米 *buy US rice*

sei gihn sai sāai sí sāam 四件細晒士衫 *four small-size shirts*

daih yih daaih cháan deih 第二大產地 *second-largest producing area*

ang and eng

hahng yàhn béng 杏仁餅 *almond cookies*

bāng dáai 繃帶 *bandage*   behng yàhn 病人 *patient*

Dahng sāang 鄧生 *Mr. Tang*   dehng dāan 訂單 *order form*

chéng séuhng seuhng chàhng 請上上層 *please go upstairs*

hehng hēng hāng làih tēng háh 輕輕哼嚟聽吓 *softly hum me the tune*

eng and ing

deui jeng 對正 *exactly facing*   jing-mihn 正面 *front*

tēng chīng-chó 聽清楚 *listen carefully*

taai pèhng 太平 *too cheap*   taai pìhng 太平 *peaceful*

chēng sīk 青色 *green*   chīng-sīk 清晰 *clear*

sāam léhng 衫領 *collar*   sām líhng 心領 *thankful*

dehng wái 訂位 *reserve the seats*   dihng wái 定位 *locate one's position*

chīm méng 簽名 *signature*   Chīng Míng 清明 *Ching Ming Festival*

ek and ik

daaih sehk 大石 *big stone*   daaih sihk 大食 *big appetite*

tek jáu 踢走 *kick away*   tīk jáu 剔走 *eliminate; remove*

Finals: im, in, iu, ip, it

im

yim 厭	chim 簽	dim 店	gim 檢	him 欠
jim 尖	kim 箝	lim 簾	nim 念	sim 閃
tim 甜				

in

yin 現	bin 便	chin 千	din 電	gin 見
hin 蜆	jin 煎	kin 虔	lin 連	min 面
nin 年	pin 片	sin 先	tin 天	

iu

yiu 要	biu 表	chiu 超	diu 吊	giu 叫
hiu 囂	jiu 招	kiu 橋	liu 了	miu 妙
niu 尿	piu 票	siu 小	tiu 條	

ip

yip 頁	chip 妾	dip 碟	gip 劫	hip 協
jip 接	lip 獵	nip 聶	sip 涉	tip 貼

it

yit 熱	bit 必	chit 切	dit 跌	git 結
hit 歇	jit 折	kit 揭	lit 裂	mit 滅
pit 撇	sit 泄	tit 鐵		

Vocabulary practice

chìh sihn 慈善	*charity*
gím yihm 檢驗	*to inspect; to examine*
sīn tīn 先天	*inborn; congenital*
chìhn mihn 前面	*front*
tīn yiht 天熱	*summer*
sip sehk 攝石	*magnet*
chīu sìh 超時	*overtime*
jīu jí 招紙	*carton label*
yìuh yìhn 謠言	*rumour*
dím sām 點心	*dim sum*
tìhm bán 甜品	*dessert*
wùh díp 蝴蝶	*butterfly*

Exercise   ◀1107.mp3

Part I. Listen to the pronunciation and fill in the appropriate finals.

1. s_____ y_____   2. b_____ y_____   3. h_____ t_____
4. s_____ d_____   5. g_____ y_____

Part II. Listen and choose the correct romanization.

1. a. chiu chin   b. jiu ching   c. kiu jin   d. chau chin

2. a. bik yiu   b. pit yau   c. bip yeu   d. bit yiu

3. a. kin chik   b. gin chit   c. king jit   d. ging chip

4. a. bit nin   b. piu jin   c. biu yin   d. piu ying

5. a. jin bing   b. jing bin   c. chim bing   d. jim bin

Compare similar pronunciations.

in and ing

nìhn lìhng 年齡 *age*   lìhng gín 零件 *spare parts*
dín yìhng 典型 *typical case; model*   mìhng hín 明顯 *obvious*
sīng sīn 升仙 *become a god*   tīng-yaht ge tīn-hei 聽日嘅天氣 *weather tomorrow*
jīn yú 煎魚 *pan-fried fish*   jīng yú 蒸魚 *steamed fish*
chìhn choi 前菜 *appetizer*   jīng-chói 精彩 *wonderful*
lín saht 揀實 *squeeze tight*   líng saht 拎實 *screw tight*
gīn hóu siu 堅好笑 *really funny*   gihng hóu-siu 勁好笑 *super funny*

im and in

jihm bin 漸變 *gradual change*
lāai lím 拉簾 *draw curtain*   lāai lín 拉鍊 *fastner*
gīm-jīk 兼職 *part-time job*   gīn-chìh 堅持 *persist*
sím dihn 閃電 *lightning*   sīn tìhm 鮮甜 *delicious (seafood)*
chìhm séui 潛水 *diving*   chín séui 淺水 *shallow water*
dím sām 點心 *dim sum; savoury*   dihn-sām 電芯 *battery*

im and ip

yihp jīm 葉尖 *tip of a leaf*
dím yahp heui 點入去 *click into*   sip yahp heui 攝入去 *insert*

in and it

tīn-yiht 天熱 *hot weather; summer*   jit yín 折現 *cash rebate*

ik and ing

jihk jihng 寂靜 *silent*   tìhng jīk 停職 *suspension of an employee*
yihng-sīk 認識 *know*

ip, it, and ik

gīk liht 激烈 *fierce*
chān-chīk 親戚 *relative*   chān-chit 親切 *kind*
tīp-sí 貼士 *tips*   tit-sín 鐵線 *wire*
jihk jip 直接 *direct*   yiht-lihk 熱力 *heat*
dá gip 打劫 *robbery*   dá kīk 打棘 *knotted*   dá lit 打咧 *tie a knot*

Finals: oi, on, ong, ok, ot, ou

oi

oi 愛	choi 菜	doi 代	goi 改	hoi 開
joi 再	koi 鈣	loi 來	noi 內	ngoi 外
soi 腮	toi 台			

on

on 安	gon 乾	hon 汗	ngon 岸

ong

bong 磅	chong 床	dong 當	fong 房	gong 港
gwong 廣	hong 行	jong 裝	kong 抗	kwong 礦
long 浪	mong 芒	nong 囊	ngong 昂	pong 旁
song 爽	tong 湯	wong 王		

ok

ok 惡	bok 博	chok	dok 踱	fok 霍
gok 各	gwok 國	hok 學	jok 作	kok 確
kwok 擴	lok 落	mok 莫	nok 諾	ngok 岳
pok 樸	sok 索	tok 托	wok 獲	

ot

got 割	hot 渴

ou

ou 澳	bou 保	chou 草	dou 到	gou 高
hou 好	jou 早	lou 老	mou 毛	nou 腦
ngou 傲	pou 鋪	sou 掃	tou 肚	

Vocabulary practice

hói dóu 海島	*island*
hóu chói 好彩	*lucky*
bōng mòhng 幫忙	*help; assist*
gong lohk 降落	*to land; to descend*
gok douh 角度	*angle*
tóuh-ngoh 肚餓	*hungry*
bou gou 報告	*report*
chōu lóuh 粗魯	*rough; rude*
lóuh-tóu 老土	*old-fashioned*
pòuh tòuh tòhng 葡萄糖	*glucose*
mōng gwó bou dīn 芒果布甸	*mango pudding*

Exercise   ◀1108.mp3

Part I. Listen and choose the correct romanization.

1. a. hoi po   b. hoi pou   c. hot pot   d. oi pou
2. a. gon jeng   b. kon jing   c. gong jeng   d. gon jing
3. a. fou jong   b. fe chong   c. fo chong   d. fok chon
4. a. saau gok   b. sei go   c. sau got   d. sau gon
5. a. tin tong   b. tim tong   c. tim ton   d. ting ton

Part II. Listen and write the pronunciations.

1. _____ 2. _____ 3. _____
4. _____ 5. _____ 6. _____

Compare similar pronunciations.

o and ou

bóu fo 補課 *to make up a lesson*   ló louh 裸露 *nude; naked; exposed*
tóuh ngoh 肚餓 *hungry*   jóu jó 早咗 *earlier than usual*
hó-yíh 可以 *can; possible*   hóu yih 好易 *very easy*
ngóh móuh mó néih 我冇摸你 *I didn't touch you.*
a sóu sòh jó 阿嫂傻咗 *My sister-in-law has gone crazy.*
dóu dō jó 倒多咗 *pour in too much*

o and ok

bohk hòh 薄荷 *mint*
gwóng bo 廣播 *broadcast*   gwóng bok 廣博 *broad*
mó hāak 摸黑 *move in darkness*   hāak mohk 黑幕 *shady; inside story*

ot and ok

háu hot 口渴 *thirsty*   séui hok 水壳 *water ladle*

on and ong

hòhn 寒   hòhng 航
gón sìh-gaan 趕時間 *run out of time*   góng faai dī 講快啲 *speak faster*

Initials n and ng

nàahm 南   ngàahm 岩   nàahn 難   ngáahn 眼
naauh 鬧   ngáauh 咬   nàih 泥   ngàih 危
náu 扭   ngáuh 偶   noh 糯   ngoh 餓
nok 諾   ngohk 岳   nòhng 囊   ngòhng 昂
nouh 怒   ngouh 傲   noih ngoih 內外 *inside and outside*

Finals: ui, un, ut, ung, uk

ui

wui 會	bui 貝	pui 配	gui 劾	kui 潰
fui 灰	mui 每			

un

wun 換	bun 半	fun 款	gun 管	mun 門
pun 判				

ut

wut 活	but 勃	fut 闊	kut 括	mut 末
put 潑				

ung

chung 聰	dung 冬	fung 風	gung 工	hung 紅
jung 中	kung 窮	lung 龍	mung 夢	nung 濃
pung 碰	sung 送	tung 同	yung 用	

uk

uk 屋	buk 卜	chuk 束	duk 毒	fuk 福
guk 谷	huk 哭	juk 祝	kuk 曲	luk 六
muk 木	puk 仆	suk 叔	tuk 禿	yuk 肉

Vocabulary practice

būn ūk 搬屋	*move to a new flat*
gūng fū 功夫	*Kung Fu; martial art*
gūk gūng 鞠躬	*to bow*
muhk luhk 目錄	*table of contents; catalogue*
kut wùh 括弧	*brackets*
jung duhk 中毒	*being poisoned*
chùhng fūk 重複	*repeat*
chūng duhng 衝動	*be impetuous*
hùhng dāng 紅燈	*red light*
tái yuhk gún 體育館	*sports stadium; gymnasium*

Exercise   ◀1109.mp3

Part I. Listen and choose the correct romanization.

1. a. yaau gut   b. yau guk   c. yau kuk   d. yaau gun
2. a. fun waan   b. faan wun   c. fan wut   d. faan wung
3. a. buk hoi   b. buk koi   c. bu hot   d. but hoi
4. a. sei mui   b. sui moi   c. sai mui   d. saai moi
5. a. tung yung   b. tun yung   c. tuk yui   d. tong yun

Part II. Listen and write the pronunciations.

1. _____ 2. _____ 3. _____
4. _____ 5. _____ 6. _____

Compare similar pronunciations.

un and ung

wùhn-chūng 緩衝 *buffer*
gún-léih gūng-sī 管理公司 *management company*
fūn fū 歡呼 *cheer; acclaim*   fūng fu 豐富 *rich; abundant*
daaih mùhn 大門 *main gate*   daaih múng 大懵 *muddle-headed*
hōi pún ga 開盤價 *opening price*   hōi pùhng chē 開篷車 *a convertible car*

ong and ung

jōng juhng 莊重 *solemn*
hōng-jōng 康莊 *broad and free*   hùhng-júng 紅腫 *red and swollen*
chong-jok 創作 *creation*   chūng-jūk 充足 *abundant*
sōng láih 喪禮 *funeral*   sung láih 送禮 *give a present*

ok and uk

gwok-jai guhk-sai 國際局勢 *international situation*
gai-juhk gūng-jok 繼續工作 *continue to work*
lūk lohk sāan 碌落山 *roll downhill*
jit-muhk 節目 *programme*   jeh mohk 謝幕 *respond to a curtain call*
jing-guhk 政局 *political situation*   jing-kok 正確 *correct*
jeung būk būk 漲卜卜 *swell up*   bohk yīt yīt 薄衣衣 *very thin*

u and ut

kut wùh 括弧 *brackets*
lóuh fú 老虎 *tiger*   fut lóu 闊佬 *generous rich man*

ut and uk

buht hōi 撥開 *push away*   būk tói 卜枱 *reserve a table*
fut douh 闊度 *width*   fūk douh 幅度 *range; scope*
muht-léi-fā 茉莉花 *jasmine*   fā-lèih-muhk 花梨木 *rosewood*

waai, wai, and ui

wàaih fā 槐花 *sophora flower*   mùih gwai fā 玫瑰花 *rose*
hóu gwaai 好怪 *strange*   hóu gwai 好貴 *expensive*
hóu guih 好劫 *tired*   guih dou gwaih dāi 劫到跪低 *so tired that I knelt*

aan, an, and un

sān báan bún 新版本 *new version*
ló gwaan gun gwān 攞慣冠軍 *always be a champion*
pìhng gwān yāt gun sahp mān 平均一罐十蚊 *average price is $10 a can*

Finals: yu, yun, yut

yu

yu 雨	chyu 柱	jyu 住	syu 書

yun

yun 軟	chyun 村	dyun 短	gyun 卷	hyun 圈
jyun 專	kyun 拳	lyun 聯	nyun 暖	syun 孫
tyun 斷				

yut

yut 月	chyut 掇	dyut 奪	hyut 血	jyut 絕
kyut 決	lyut 劣	syut 雪	tyut 脫	

Vocabulary practice

yúh jyū 乳豬	suckling pig
jyūn jyu 專注	focus on; concentrate
syùhn jyun 旋轉	to swirl
chyúh chyùhn 儲存	to store up
gyūn hyut 捐血	donate blood
pun kyut 判決	judgment (by a court of law)
jyú kyùhn 主權	sovereign rights
hói-tyùhn 海豚	dolphin
tōng yún 湯丸	sweet dumpling
tyùhn yùhn 團圓	family reunion
syut mìhng syū 說明書	user menu

Exercise ◀1110.mp3

Part I. Listen and choose the correct romanization.

1. a. sum yu   b. sam yun   c. sem yun   d. sam yut
2. a. dyu fu   b. dyut fo   c. dyun fu   d. dyun fo
3. a. syu go   b. sut gyu   c. syut go   d. syut gou
4. a. tyu lai   b. dyut le   c. tyut nei   d. tyut lei
5. a. lyun lok   b. lyun luk   c. lyu lot   d. lyut long

Part II. Listen and write the pronunciations.

1. _____ 2. _____ 3. _____
4. _____ 5. _____

Compare similar pronunciations.

u and yu

fu-yuh 富裕 *rich*
wū-táu yú 烏頭魚 *flathead mullet*
fuh-fún-chyu 付款處 *cashier*

un, ung, and yun

buhn lyuhn 叛亂 *riot* gyūn fún 捐款 *donation*
jyūn-mùhn 專門 *specialized* lyuhn lùhng 亂籠 *disorder*
hùhng hyūn 紅圈 *red circle* yuhng yùhn 用完 *used up*
lyùhn tùhng 聯同 *joined together* jūng dyuhn 中斷 *discontinue*

ut and yut

put séui 潑水 *splash water* syut séui 雪水 *ice water*
kut daaht 豁達 *open-minded* kyut dāk 缺德 *wicked*
fut-lohk 闊落 *spacious* tyut-lohk 脫落 *fall off*

Finals: eui, eun, eut

eui

cheui 吹	deui 隊	geu i 句	heui 去	jeui 最
keui 區	leui 淚	neui 女	seui 水	teui 退
yeui 銳				

eun

cheun 春	deun 敦	jeun 津	leun 輪	seun 信
teun 盾	yeun 潤			

eut

cheut 出	jeut 卒	leut 律	seut 恤

Vocabulary practice

jéun héui 准許	*allow to; permit to*
chēui séui 吹水	*boast; chit-chat*
chēun tīn 春天	*spring*
sēui teui 衰退	*decline*
leuht sī seun 律師信	*letter from a lawyer*
yeuhn sèuhn gōu 潤唇膏	*lip balm*
jeui sēui kéuih 最衰佢	*it's all his fault*
mh jéun chēut heui 唔准出去	*not allowed to go out*
heui Lèuhn-Dēun máaih T sēut	
去 倫 敦 買 T 恤	
go to London to buy a T-shirt	

Exercise ◄1111.mp3

Part I. Listen and choose the correct romanization.

1. a. ching cheun   b. cheng chun   c. jing cheun   d. chin cheui
2. a. faak leut   b. fa leui   c. fat leun   d. faat leut
3. a. jeui seu   b. cheui siu   c. cheui seu   d. jeun siu
4. a. leung cheun   b. leui jeung   c. leun jeun   d. lun jeun
5. a. fok teu   b. fo teui   c. fot teut   d. fo deui

Part II. Listen and write the pronunciations.

1. _____   2. _____   3. _____

4. _____   5. _____

Compare similar pronunciations.

eui and oi

deui doih 對待 *treat*

séui yú 水魚 *turtle*

géui kèih 舉旗 *raise a flag*

lèuih dihn 雷電 *thunder and lightning*

kéuih joi 拒載 *(taxi driver) refuse to take a passsenger*

heui hói bīn 去海邊 *go to the seaside*

chéui chòih 取材 *to collect material*

yùh sōi 魚鰓 *gill*

gói kèih 改期 *change the date*

dihn tòih 電台 *radio station*

eun and yun

yùhn yeuhn 圓潤 *rounded*

bō lēi jēun 玻璃樽 *glass bottle*

seun mehng 信命 *believe in fate*

lèuhn láu 輪流 *take turn*

chēun gyún 春卷 *spring roll*

bō lēi jyūn 玻璃磚 *glass brick*

syun mehng 算命 *fortune-telling*

nyúhn làuh 暖流 *warm current*

Finals: eu, eung, euk

eu

geu 鋸	heu 靴

eung

cheung 長	geung 姜	heung 向	jeung 張	keung 強
leung 兩	neung 娘	seung 想	yeung 羊	

euk

cheuk 卓	deuk 剁	geuk 腳	jeuk 雀	keuk 卻
leuk 略	seuk 削	yeuk 約		

Vocabulary practice

yeuhk séui 藥水	*medicinal syrup*
yèuhng chūng 洋葱	*onion*
hēung chéung 香腸	*sausage*
séung jeuhng 想像	*imagine*
sēung lèuhng 商量	*consult; discuss*
yeuk léuk 約略	*approximate*
jeuk yeuk 雀躍	*jump for joy*
kèuhng yeuhk 強弱	*strong and weak*
cheuk sēung 灼傷	*burn; scorch*
léuhng seui 兩歲	*two years old*

Yáuh Hēung Góng geuk mh hóu jeuk hēu
有　香　港　腳　唔　好　着　靴
If you have athlete's foot, don't wear boots.

Exercise　◀1112.mp3

Part I. Listen and choose the correct romanization.

1. a. hong jeung　　b. kung cheuk　　c. hung jeuk　　d. kong cheung
2. a. hyun seu　　b. heung seui　　c. heuk seui　　d. heu seu
3. a. lai geuk　　b. leu geui　　c. laai geuk　　d. laai geu
4. a. seun cheung　　b. seung cheung　　c. seung cheuk　　d. song cheung
5. a. taai yeung　　b. teu yong　　c. teui yeun　　d. tai yeuk

Part II. Listen and write the pronunciations.

1. _____　　2. _____　　3. _____

4. _____　　5. _____

Compare similar pronunciations.

eu and eui

geu muhk 鋸木 *to saw*
hēu sēng 噓聲 *make catcalls*

géui muhk 櫸木 *beech*
séuhng heui 上去 *go up*

eun and eung

yāt jēun XO jeung 一樽XO醬 *a bottle of XO sauce*
sēung deui leuhn 相對論 *theory of relativity*
jī yeuhn 滋潤 *nourishing*
seun sēung 信箱 *letterbox*

jih yéuhng 飼養 *feeding (animal)*

eung, ong, and ung

lèuhng sóng 涼爽 *cool and fresh*
chīng cheung 清唱 *a cappella*
chúhng ching 重秤 *heavy in weight*
hōng lohk 康樂 *recreation*
gēung fa 僵化 *rigid*
jung fā 種花 *gardening*
kwòhng yàhn 狂人 *mad man*

léuhng sung 兩餸 *two side dishes*
chīng chōng 清倉 *clearance (sale)*
héung lohk 享樂 *enjoyment*
lohk hūng 落空 *come to nothing*
fa jōng 化妝 *make-up*
kèuhng yàhn 強人 *strong man*
kùhng yàhn 窮人 *poor man*

euk and eut

chīu cheuk 超卓 *excellent*
jeuk jái 雀仔 *bird*
fāt leuhk 忽略 *ignore*

chīu chēut 超出 *exceed*
jēut jái 卒仔 *sacrificial pawn*
faat leuht 法律 *law*

euk, uk, and ok

chīu-cheuk 超卓 *excellent*
chīu chok 超 chok *looking so cool*
guhk geuk 焗腳 *(rubber shoes) impermeable*
jeuk sūk 雀粟 *bird feed*
jok gā 作家 *writer*
luhk yuht 六月 *June*

chīu chūk 超速 *(car) speeding*
geuk gá 腳架 *tripod*
ga lēi gok 咖喱角 *samosa; curry puff*
gā juhk 家族 *family*
yeuhk yún 藥丸 *pills*
lohk yúh 落雨 *rain*

e, eng, ek, ei, eui, eun, eut, eu, eung, and euk

séi 死	sé 寫	séng 醒	sehk 石		
seui 歲	seun 信	seuht 術	sèuh sir	sēung 傷	seuk 削
deih 地	dē 爹	dēng 釘	dehk 笛		
deui 對	deun 頓	déu 朵	deuk 啄		
chē 車	chéng 請	chek 尺	chēui 吹	chēun 春	chēut 出
chēung 昌	cheuk 卓				
he hea	hēng 輕	hek 吃	heui 去	hēu 靴	heung 向

Romanization practice answers

Initials with vowels a, e, i, o, u

I.
1. s, f: sō fá 梳化 *sofa*
2. h, y: hó yíh 可以 *can*
3. b, l: bō lòh 菠蘿 *pineapple*

III.
1. b. ga fē 咖啡 *coffee*
2. a. chi só 廁所 *toilet*
3. c. ngàh yī 牙醫 *dentist*
4. d. jā chē 揸車 *to drive a car*
5. a. ké jí 茄子 *aubergine*

II.
1. o, u: mòh gū 磨菇 *mushroom*
2. i, a: yìh gā 而家 *now*
3. o, i: dō sí 多士 *toast*

Finals: aai, aam, aan, aau

I.
1. t, n: táahm náaih 淡奶 *condensed milk*
2. m, p: maahn páau 慢跑 *jogging*
3. f, d: fáan daahn 反彈 *bounce back*

III.
1. c. daaih dáam 大膽 *daring; bold*
2. a. màaih dāan 埋單 *to settle the bill*
3. b. láahn sáan 懶散 *be lazy*
4. d. láau gaauh 撈攪 *messy*
5. b. waahn naahn 患難 *adversity*

II.
1. aai, aan; waaih dáan 壞蛋 *bad guy; bad egg*
2. aau, aai; háau pàaih 考牌 *to pass a test to obtain a licence*
3. aam, aau; haam bāau 喊包 *a child who cries easily*

Finals: aang, aak, aap, aat

I.
1. t: taap 塔
2. gw: gwaak 摑
3. w: wàahng 橫
4. s: saat 殺
5. j: jāang 爭

III.
1. d. chaak waahk 策劃 *to plan; to plot*
2. c. laaht taat 辣撻 *dirty*
3. b. laahp saap 垃圾 *rubbish; garbage*
4. c. sāang máahng 生猛 *alive; energetic*
5. a. chaap kāat 插卡 *insert a card*

II.
1. aap, aak: daap haak 搭客 *passenger*
2. aat, aat: faat daaht 發達 *prosperous*
3. aak, aang: chaak pàahng 拆棚 *remove the scaffolding*

Finals: ai, am, an, au

I.
1. m, t: mahn tàih 問題 *problem; question*
2. s, k: sáu kau 手扣 *handcuffs*
3. ng, l: ngàuh láuh 牛柳 *beef tenderloin*

II.
1. am, au—jám tàuh 枕頭 *pillow*
2. ai, au—sāi yáu 西柚 *grapefruit*
3. an, ai—yān waih 因為 *because*

III.

1. b. wàhn tān 雲吞 *wonton dumpling*
2. a. waih háu 胃口 *appetite*
3. d. jān sām 真心 *true heart*
4. c. yāu waih 優惠 *favourable*; *preferential price*
5. b. chàhm màih 沉迷 *indulge*

Finals: ang, ak, ap, at

I.

1. m: maht 物
2. b: bāk 北
3. p: pàhng 憑
4. ch: chāp 輯
5. d: dahk 特

II.

1. ap, at—nāp daht 凹凸 *concave and convex*
2. ak, at—lahk gwāt 肋骨 *rib*; *rib cage*
3. at, ang—bāt hahng 不幸 *unfortunate*

III.

1. d. gáng haih 梗係 *of course*
2. b. saht jāt 實質 *substance*
3. c. kāp sāu 吸收 *absorb*
4. a. hahp faat 合法 *legal*; *lawful*
5. c. sām gāp 心急 *feeling anxious*

Finals: eng, ek, ei, ing, ik

I.

1. ing, ek: yīng chek 英呎 *English foot*
2. ei, ek: bēi kehk 悲劇 *tragedy*
3. eng, ei: dehng fēi 訂飛 *to reserve a ticket*
4. ing, ik: jīng lihk 精力 *energy*
5. eng, ik: chēng sīk 青色 *green*
6. ing, ei: gīng léih 經理 *manager*

II.

1. a. séi yìhng 死刑 *death penalty*
2. c. jing sīk 正式 *formal*; *official*
3. d. sehk sih 碩士 *master's degree*
4. a. sīng kèih 升旗 *raise a flag*
5. b. chìhng yìhng 情形 *condition*; *situation*

Finals: im, in, iu, ip, it

I.

1. iu, im: sīu yìhm 消炎 *anti-inflammatory*
2. it, in: bīt yìhn 必然 *inevitable*
3. ip, iu: hip tìuh 協調 *to coordinate*; *to harmonize*
4. im, in: sím dihn 閃電 *lightning*
5. it, ip: git yihp 結業 *shut down a business*

II.

1. a. chīu chìhn 超前 *ahead of time*
2. d. bīt yiu 必要 *essential*; *necessary*
3. b. gin chit 建設 *to contruct*
4. c. bíu yín 表演 *performance*; *to perform*
5. d. jihm bin 漸變 *gradual change*

Finals: oi, on, ong, ok, ot, ou

I.

1. b. hōi pou 開舖 *a shop open for business*
2. a. gōn jehng 乾淨 *clean*
3. c. fo chōng 貨倉 *warehouse*
4. c. sāu got 收割 *harvest*
5. a. tīn tòhng 天堂 *paradise*

II.

1. got hōi 割開 *cut open*
2. sóng lóhng 爽朗 *frank and open*
3. gōn chou 乾燥 *dry*
4. lohk tòhng 落堂 *finish a class*
5. Hòhn Gwok 韓國 *Korea*
6. bō choi 菠菜 *spinach*

Finals: ui, un, ut, ung, uk

I.
1. b. yàuh gúk 郵局 *post office*
2. b. faahn wún 飯碗 *rice bowl*
3. d. buht hōi 撥開 *push aside*
4. c. sai múi 細妹 *younger sister*
5. a. tūng yuhng 通用 *in common use*; *interchangeable*

II.
1. luhk púih 六倍 *sixfold*; *six times*
2. bui buhn 背叛 *betray*
3. gūn jung 觀眾 *audience*; *spectator*
4. fūi fuhk 恢復 *resume*
5. wuht put 活潑 *lively*; *vivacious*
6. múhn jūk 滿足 *satisfy*

Finals: yu, yun, yut

I.
1. b. sām yúhn 心軟 *soft-hearted*; *irresolute*
2. c. dyún fu 短褲 *shorts*
3. d. syut gōu 雪糕 *ice-cream*
4. d. tyut lèih 脫離 *break away from*
5. a. lyùhn lok 聯絡 *to contact*

II.
1. yuh syun 預算 *budget*
2. kyut dyuhn 決斷 *be decisive*
3. syūn chyùhn 宣傳 *to promote*; *to propagate*
4. jyun hyūn 轉圈 *turn around*
5. yuht yúh 粵語 *Cantonese*

Finals: eui, eun, eut

I.
1. a. chīng chēun 青春 *youth*
2. d. faat leuht 法律 *law*
3. b. chéui sīu 取消 *to cancel*
4. c. leuhn jeuhn 論盡 *clumsy*
5. b. fó téui 火腿 *ham*

II.
1. séui jéun 水準 *standard*
2. teui chēut 退出 *withdraw*
3. deih kēui 地區 *area*; *region*
4. tóu leuhn 討論 *discussion*
5. sēut sāam 恤衫 *shirt*

Finals: eu, eung, euk

I.
1. c. húng jéuk 孔雀 *peacock*
2. b. hēung séui 香水 *perfume*
3. d. lāai geu 拉鋸 *seesaw battle*
4. b. sēung chèuhng 商場 *shopping mall*
5. a. taai yèuhng 太陽 *the sun*

II.
1. deuih jéung 隊長 *team captain*
2. chèuhng hēu 長靴 *knee-high boots*
3. fōng heung 方向 *direction*
4. yúhn yeuhk 軟弱 *weak*
5. jeuhn leuhng 盡量 *try one's best*

Appendix 2
Vocabulary list

Part 1

Cantonese	English meaning	Chapter
āak 呃	to cheat	4
báau 飽	full stomach	10
Bāk-Tàahm-Chūng 北潭涌	Pak Tam Chung	8
bāt-yùh 不如	what about (to suggest)	2
behng 病	ill; illness; sick; sickness	5
behng-yàhn 病人	patient	5
bōng 幫	to help; to assist	1
bou gíng 報警	to report to the police	4
bun ga 半價	half-price	6
chāam-gā 參加	to participate; to join	6
chāan-tēng 餐廳	restaurant	2
chāu-tīn 秋天	autumn	8
chē 車	to take people by car	2
(yāt ga) chē （一架）車	a vehicle	1
chéng 請	to treat; to invite	4
chéng ga 請假	to take leave	5
chéng mahn 請問	may I ask	6
cheung sáan-jí 唱散子	to get small change	3
chēut heui 出去	to go out	7
chēut-méng 出名	famous	10
chìh 遲	late	3
chī-sin 黐線	crazy (literally, someone has crossed wires)	5
chīm méng 簽名	to sign a name; signature	1
cho 錯	wrong; mistake	4
chóh 坐	to sit; to ride in a car	2

Cantonese	English meaning	Chapter
chyun 串	to spell	6
daai 帶	to bring along	2
daai-jí 帶子	scallop	7
daaih-tàuh-hā 大頭蝦	absent-minded person (literally, big head prawn)	6
daahn-haih 但係	but; however	2
daap dihn-tāi 搭電梯	to take the escalator	6
daap līp 搭軨	to take the elevator	6
dái 抵	good value; deserve	10
daih 第 + number	for ordinal numbers	6
dāk 得	only have	2
dahk-biht 特別	special; particularly; especially	10
dahk ga 特價	special price; bargain sale	1
daht-yìhn 突然	suddenly; all of a sudden	2
deih-fōng 地方	place	8
deui-jyuh 對住	be facing	9
dím 點	how (to do something)?	3
dím-syun 點算	what should I/we do?	2
dihn-chìh 電池	battery (literally, electric pool)	1
dihn-fai 電費	electricity fee	9
dihn-nóuh 電腦	computer (literally, electric brain)	4
dói 袋	bag	1
dōu 都	even (used for emphasis)	9
verb + dóu 到	be able to; manage to	1
dou 到	to arrive	3
douh 度	degree of temperature	5
fāan heui 返去	to go back	2
fāan làih 返嚟	to come back	4
faat sīu 發燒	have a fever	5
fan jeuhk gaau 瞓着覺	to fall asleep	3
fo 貨	goods; commodity	1
fong gūng 放工	finish work	2
fūng 風	wind	8
gāai-háu 街口	crossroads; intersection	3
gáau cho 搞錯	make a mistake	7
…… ge sìh-hauh 嘅時候	at the time when . . .	2
gei-dāk 記得	to remember	1

Cantonese	English meaning	Chapter
gam 咁 + adjective	so; such	6
gām-jīu 今朝	this morning (literally, today morning)	1
gám-mouh 感冒	cold; influenza	5
gam ngāam 咁啱	by coincidence	1
gám-yéung 咁樣	in this way; in such a manner	6
verb + gán 緊	indicating action in progress	5
gán-jēung 緊張	nervous; excited; concerned	4
gān-jyuh 跟住	to follow; and then	3
gau 夠	enough	3
géi 幾	quite; rather	8
géi 幾	a few	9
gīng-gwo 經過	pass by; walk past	8
giu 叫	to ask; to order (someone to do something)	1
gói kèih 改期	to change the date	5
gok-dāk 覺得	to think; to feel	6
gōn-jehng 乾淨	clean	7
gú 估	to guess	6
guih 攰	tired	5
gūng-héi 恭喜	to congratulate; congratulations	6
gwaai 怪	strange	6
gwo sou 過數	money transfer	4
hā 蝦	prawn; shrimp	7
há 吓 ?	What do you mean? What is it?	1
verb + háh 吓	indicate casually doing something	4
hah chi 下次	next time	3
hah-tīn 夏天	summer	8
haak 客	client; customer	5
hàahng gāai 行街	shopping (literally, walk on the street)	8
Hāang-Háu 坑口	Hang Hau	8
hàahng sāan 行山	hiking (literally, walk on the mountain)	8
hang gēi hang 機	computer crash	4
hàuh-lùhng tung 喉嚨痛	sore throat	5
hó-yíh 可以	can; may	8
hōi 開	to turn on (a machine); to open	4
hōi chē 開車	to start a car	3
hōi-chí 開始	to start	1

Cantonese	English meaning	Chapter
hōi láahng-hei 開冷氣	turn on air-conditioning	9
hōi-sām 開心	happy	7
hói-sīn 海鮮	seafood	7
hōi wúi 開會	to have a meeting	5
hóu chíh 好似	seem like	8
hóu-chói 好彩	lucky; fortunately	2
ja 咋	(sentence particle) only	3
jāp yéh 執嘢	to tidy up; to pack things	7
jauh 就	then; soon after	2
jē 遮	an umbrella; to cover; to take under an umbrella	2
je 借	to lend; to borrow	2
jeui 最	most	8
jeui hauh 最後	at last, in the end	3
jeuk 着	to wear; to dress	7
jéun-beih 準備	to prepare	7
jī-hauh 之後	afterwards	2
jih-géi 自己	by oneself	10
jih-joh-chāan 自助餐	buffet	10
jīk-hāak 即刻	immediately	4
jíng 整	to make; to fix; to cook	7
joi 再 + verb + gwo 過	do something again	4
jóu 早	early	5
júng 種	type; kind; variety	10
juhng 仲	still more	3
juhng 仲	still no change; continue to be	5
jūng-màhn 中文	Chinese (language)	6
kàhm máahn 琴晚	last night (literally, yesterday night)	5
kèih-saht 其實	actually	6
kīng gái 傾偈	to chat; to talk	10
laahm géng-gān 攬頸巾	wrap a scarf around	9
lauh 漏	miss out	2
làuh beih-séui 流鼻水	runny nose	5
làuh-hah 樓下	downstairs	2
lèuhng-jam-jam 涼浸浸	cool	8
ló 攞	to take; to fetch	1
lohk chē 落車	to get out of a car; to alight	3

Cantonese	English meaning	Chapter
Lohng-Ké 浪茄	Long Ke	8
lóuh-sai 老細	boss	5
Lùhng-Jek 龍脊	Dragon's Back	8
mh syū-fuhk 唔舒服	uncomfortable; not feeling well	5
mh syun 唔算	not considered as	9
mh-tùhng 唔同	different (literally, not the same)	4
màh-fàahn 麻煩	annoying; inconvenient; trouble	2
máih 咪 + verb	don't (do something)	10
mahn 問	to ask (question)	1
meih 未	not yet	2
méng 名	name	6
mìhng-sīng 明星	celebrity; movie star	1
muhn 悶	boring	3
ngāam 啱	correct; suitable	1
ngaahng 硬	hard; stiff	9
ngoih-gwok 外國	foreign country	8
nī bihn 呢便	this side	10
nī ga chē 呢架車	this vehicle	1
nī tìuh louh 呢條路	this road	3
pa 怕	be afraid of; worry about	8
pàaih-déui 排隊	to queue	10
paak 泊	to park (a vehicle)	2
pìhng-sìh 平時	usually; normally	8
sā-tāan 沙灘	beach	8
sāai 嘥	wasteful	10
verb + saai 晒	all; everything	9
sáan-jí 散子	small change	3
sāang-yaht 生日	birthday	7
Sāi-Gung 西貢	Sai Kung	8
sāi-leih 犀利	trenchant; powerful	9
sai-lóu 細佬	younger brother	4
sāk chē 塞車	traffic jam	3
sān-fú 辛苦	suffering	5
sāp 濕	humid; wet	8
sāu 收	to receive; to collect	4
sauh-sī 壽司	sushi	10

Cantonese	English meaning	Chapter
séi 死	to die	4
Sehk-Ou 石澳	Shek O	8
séng 醒	to wake up; become conscious	3
sèhng 成	whole; entire	5
sèhng yaht 成日	all day, very often; whole day	5
séuhng chē 上車	to get in a car	1
sēung-chèuhng 商場	shopping mall	6
séuhng móhng 上網	to access the internet	4
si 試	to try	4
sī-gēi 司機	driver	3
sīk gēi 熄機	to turn off a machine	4
sīn 先	first	3
sīn-ji 先至	until then (emphasize the time is relatively late)	7
sīu 燒	to barbeque; to roast	10
síu-sām 小心	be careful; take care	10
síu-sihk 小食	snack	7
só-yíh 所以	therefore; as a consequence	6
sūk-gwāt-jē 縮骨遮	collapsible umbrella	2
sung 送	to send; to deliver	6
syū-fuhk 舒服	comfortable	5
syū-jín 書展	book fair	1
syut-gwaih 雪櫃	refrigerator (literally, snow cabinet)	9
taai 太 + adjective	excessively; too; over	10
tàuh-tung 頭痛	headache	5
tàuh-wàhn 頭暈	dizzy	5
tēng góng 聽講	hearsay	8
tīm 添	(sentence particle) in addition; and more	5
tìhm-bán 甜品	dessert	10
tīn-màhn-tòih 天文台	observatory	9
tóuh-ngoh 肚餓	hungry	7
wah 話	to say; to tell	1
wán 搵	to search; to look for	2
yān-waih 因為	because	4
yàhn yàhn 人人	everyone	10
yāt bá jē 一把遮	an umbrella	2
yāt bá sēng 一把聲	a voice	4

Cantonese	English meaning	Chapter
yāt bihn 一便	doing two actions at the same time; simultaneously	10
yāt-dihng 一定	certainly; definitely	3
yāt fahn láih-maht 一份禮物	a gift; a present	6
yāt ga chē 一架車	a vehicle	1
yāt gāan pou 一間舖	a shop	6
yāt gihn sāam 一件衫	an article of clothing	9
yāt gihn lāang-sāam 一件冷衫	a sweater	9
yāt-jahn 一陣	a moment	3
yāt 一⋯⋯ jauh 就⋯⋯	once . . . then; immediately after	4
yāt jek sáu 一隻手	a hand	9
yāt jēung fēi 一張飛	a ticket	7
yāt jī jáu 一支酒	a bottle of wine	7
yāt jóu 一早	at an early time	7
yāt tìuh louh 一條路	a road	3
yauh 又	and also; both . . . and	8
yáu dāk kéuih 由得佢	let it be; never mind	1
yàuh séui 游水	swimming	8
yāu-sīk 休息	to rest	5
yeh-máahn 夜晚	evening; night	8
yeuhk 藥	medicine	5
yí 咦	(sentence particle) to express curiosity	2
yíh-gīng 已經	already	2
yī-sāng 醫生	doctor; physician	5
yíh-wàih 以為	think; believed to be	6
yín-cheung-wúi 演唱會	concert	7
yīng-màhn 英文	English	6
yíng séung 影相	to take a photo	1
yiht-laaht-laaht 熱辣辣	burning hot	8
yú 魚	fish	6
yùh-gwó 如果	if	1
yùhn 完	to finish	2
yúhn 遠	far away	8
yùhn-lòih 原來	turn out to be	5
yuhng 用	to use	4
yuht-làih-yuht 越嚟越	becoming more and more	9

Part 2

English meaning	Cantonese	Chapter
be able to	verb + dóu 到	1
absent-minded person	daaih-tàuh-hā 大頭蝦	6
to access the internet	séuhng móhng 上網	4
actually	kèih-saht 其實	6
be afraid of	pa 怕	8
afterwards	jī-hauh 之後	2
all; everything	verb + saai 晒	9
all day	sèhng yaht 成日	5
all of a sudden	daht-yìhn 突然	2
already	yíh-gīng 已經	2
and also	yauh 又	8
and then	gān-jyuh 跟住	3
to arrive	dou 到	3
to ask	giu 叫	1
to ask (question)	mahn 問	1
to assist	bōng 幫	1
at the time when . . .	……ge sìh-hauh 嘅時候	2
at last	jeui hauh 最後	3
autumn	chāu-tīn 秋天	8
bag	dói 袋	1
to barbeque; to roast	sīu 燒	10
big sale	dahk ga 特價	1
battery	dihn-chìh 電池	1
beach	sā-tāan 沙灘	8
because	yān-waih 因為	4
become conscious	séng 醒	3
becoming more and more	yuht-làih-yuht 越嚟越	9
believed to be	yíh-wàih 以為	6
be careful; take care	síu-sām 小心	10
birthday	sāang-yaht 生日	7
boring	muhn 悶	3
to borrow	je 借	2
boss	lóuh-sai 老細	5
both . . . and	yauh 又	8

English meaning	Cantonese	Chapter
to bring along	daai 帶	2
buffet	jih-joh-chāan 自助餐	10
burning hot	yiht-laaht-laaht 熱辣辣	8
but; however	daahn-haih 但係	2
can; may	hó-yíh 可以	8
celebrity	mìhng-sīng 明星	1
certainly; definitely	yāt-dihng 一定	3
to change the date	gói kèih 改期	5
to chat	kīng gái 傾偈	10
to cheat	āak 呃	4
Chinese (language)	jūng-màhn 中文	6
clean	gōn-jehng 乾淨	7
client; customer	haak 客	5
(an article of) clothing	yāt gihn sāam 一件衫	9
by coincidence	gam ngāam 咁啱	1
cold; influenza	gám-mouh 感冒	5
to collect	sāu 收	4
to come back	fāan làih 返嚟	4
comfortable	syū-fuhk 舒服	5
commodity	fo 貨	1
computer	dihn-nóuh 電腦	4
computer crash	hang gēi hang 機	4
concerned	gán-jēung 緊張	4
to congratulate; congratulations	gūng-héi 恭喜	6
to cook	jíng 整	7
cool	lèuhng-jam-jam 涼浸浸	8
correct	ngāam 啱	1
to cover	jē 遮	2
crazy	chī-sin 黐線	5
definitely	yāt-dihng 一定	3
degree of temperature	douh 度	5
to deliver	sung 送	6
dessert	tìhm-bán 甜品	10
to die	séi 死	4
different	mh-tùhng 唔同	4
dizzy	tàuh-wàhn 頭暈	5

English meaning	Cantonese	Chapter
do something again	joi 再 + verb + gwo 過	4
doctor; physician	yī-sāng 醫生	5
don't (do something)	máih 咪 + verb	10
downstairs	làuh-hah 樓下	2
driver	sī-gēi 司機	3
early	jóu 早	5
at an early time	yāt jóu 一早	7
electricity fee	dihn-fai 電費	9
English	yīng-màhn 英文	6
enough	gau 夠	3
entire; whole	sèhng 成	5
especially	dahk-biht 特別	10
even (used as emphasis)	dōu 都	9
evening; night	yeh-máahn 夜晚	8
everyone	yàhn yàhn 人人	10
excessively; too; over	taai 太 + adjective	10
excited	gán-jēung 緊張	4
be facing	deui-jyuh 對住	9
to fall asleep	fan jeuhk gaau 瞓着覺	3
famous	chēut-méng 出名	10
far away	yúhn 遠	8
to feel	gok-dāk 覺得	6
to fetch	ló 攞	1
a few	géi 幾	9
to finish	yùhn 完	2
finish work	fong gūng 放工	2
first	sīn 先	3
fish	yú 魚	6
to fix	jíng 整	7
to follow	gān-jyuh 跟住	3
for ordinal numbers	daih 第 + number	6
foreign country	ngoih-gwok 外國	8
fortunately	hóu-chói 好彩	2
full stomach	báau 飽	10
to get out of a car	lohk chē 落車	3
to get in a car	séuhng chē 上車	1

English meaning	Cantonese	Chapter
a gift	yāt fahn láih-maht 一份禮物	6
to go back	fāan heui 返去	2
to go out	chēut heui 出去	7
good value	dái 抵	10
goods	fo 貨	1
to guess	gú 估	6
half-price	bun ga 半價	6
a hand	yāt jek sáu 一隻手	9
happy	hōi-sām 開心	7
hard	ngaahng 硬	9
have a fever	faat sīu 發燒	5
to have a meeting	hōi wúi 開會	5
headache	tàuh-tung 頭痛	5
hearsay	tēng góng 聽講	8
to help	bōng 幫	1
hiking	hàahng sāan 行山	8
how (to do something)?	dím 點	3
humid; wet	sāp 濕	8
hungry	tóuh-ngoh 肚餓	7
if	yùh-gwó 如果	1
ill; illness	behng 病	5
immediately	jīk-hāak 即刻	4
immediately after	yāt 一……jauh 就……	4
in the end	jeui hauh 最後	3
in this way; in such a manner	gám-yéung 咁樣	6
influenza	gám-mouh 感冒	5
to invite	chéng 請	4
to join	chāam-gā 參加	6
last night	kàhm máahn 琴晚	5
late	chìh 遲	3
to lend	je 借	2
let it be; leave it	yáu dāk kéuih 由得佢	1
to look for	wán 搵	2
lucky	hóu-chói 好彩	2
to make	jíng 整	7
make a mistake	gáau cho 搞錯	7

English meaning	Cantonese	Chapter
manage to	verb + dóu 到	1
may	hó-yíh 可以	8
may I ask	chéng mahn 請問	6
medicine	yeuhk 藥	5
miss out	lauh 漏	2
mistake	cho 錯	4
a moment	yāt-jahn 一陣	3
money transfer	gwo sou 過數	4
most	jeui 最	8
movie star	mìhng-sīng 明星	1
name	méng 名	6
nervous	gán-jēung 緊張	4
next time	hah chi 下次	3
night; evening	yeh-máahn 夜晚	8
not considered as	mh syun 唔算	9
not feeling well	mh syū-fuhk 唔舒服	5
not yet	meih 未	2
observatory	tīn-màhn-tòih 天文台	9
once . . . then	yāt 一……jauh 就……	4
by oneself	jih-géi 自己	10
only	ja 咋	3
only have	dāk 得	2
to open	hōi 開	4
to order (someone to do something)	giu 叫	1
to pack things	jāp yéh 執嘢	7
to park (a vehicle)	paak 泊	2
to participate	chāam-gā 參加	6
particularly	dahk-biht 特別	10
pass by; walk past	gīng-gwo 經過	8
patient	behng-yàhn 病人	5
place	deih-fōng 地方	8
powerful	sāi-leih 犀利	9
prawn	hā 蝦	7
to prepare	jéun-beih 準備	7
a present	yāt fahn láih-maht 一份禮物	6
to queue	pàaih-déui 排隊	10

English meaning	Cantonese	Chapter
quite; rather	géi 幾	8
to receive	sāu 收	4
refrigerator	syut-gwaih 雪櫃	9
to remember	gei-dāk 記得	1
to report to the police	bou gíng 報警	4
to rest	yāu-sīk 休息	5
restaurant	chāan-tēng 餐廳	2
a road	yāt tìuh louh 一條路	3
to roast	sīu 燒	10
runny nose	làuh beih-séui 流鼻水	5
to say; to tell	wah 話	1
scallop	daai-jí 帶子	7
seafood	hói-sīn 海鮮	7
to search	wán 搵	2
seem like	hóu chíh 好似	8
to send, to deliver	sung 送	6
a shop	yāt gāan pou 一間舖	6
shopping	hàahng gāai 行街	8
shopping mall	sēung-chèuhng 商場	6
shrimp	hā 蝦	7
to turn off a machine	sīk gēi 熄機	4
sick; sickness	behng 病	5
to sign your name; signature	chīm méng 簽名	1
simultaneously	yāt bihn 一便	10
concert	yín-cheung-wúi 演唱會	7
to sit	chóh 坐	2
small change	sáan-jí 散子	3
snack	síu-sihk 小食	7
so; such	gam 咁 + adjective	6
soon after	jauh 就	2
sore throat	hàuh-lùhng tung 喉嚨痛	5
special	dahk-biht 特別	10
to spell	chyun 串	6
to start	hōi-chí 開始	1
to start a car	hōi chē 開車	3
stiff	ngaahng 硬	9

English meaning	Cantonese	Chapter
still more	juhng 仲	3
still no change; continue to be	juhng 仲	5
strange	gwaai 怪	6
street junction	gāai-háu 街口	3
suddenly	daht-yìhn 突然	2
suffering	sān-fú 辛苦	5
suitable	ngāam 啱	1
summer	hah-tīn 夏天	8
sushi	sauh-sī 壽司	10
a sweater	yāt gihn lāang-sāam 一件冷衫	9
swimming	yàuh séui 游水	8
to take; to fetch	ló 攞	1
take care	síu-sām 小心	10
to take an elevator	daap līp 搭軨	6
to take escalator	daap dihn-tāi 搭電梯	6
to take a photo	yíng séung 影相	1
to take leave	chéng ga 請假	5
to talk	kīng gái 傾偈	10
to tell; to say	wah 話	1
then	jauh 就	2
therefore; as a consequence	só-yíh 所以	6
think; believed to be	yíh-wàih 以為	6
to think	gok-dāk 覺得	6
this morning	gām-jīu 今朝	1
this road	nī tìuh louh 呢條路	3
this side	nī bihn 呢便	10
this car	nī ga chē 呢架車	1
a ticket	yāt jēung fēi 一張飛	7
to tidy up	jāp yéh 執嘢	7
tired	guih 劮	5
too; excessively	taai 太 + adjective	10
traffic jam	sāk chē 塞車	3
to treat	chéng 請	4
trenchant; powerful	sāi-leih 犀利	9
troublesome; trouble	màh-fàahn 麻煩	2
to try	si 試	4

English meaning	Cantonese	Chapter
to turn on (a machine)	hōi 開	4
turn on air-conditioning	hōi láahng-hei 開冷氣	9
turn out to be	yùhn-lòih 原來	5
type; kind; variety	júng 種	10
an umbrella	yāt bá jē 一把遮	2
uncomfortable; not feeling well	mh syū-fuhk 唔舒服	5
until then (emphasize the time is relatively late)	sīn-ji 先至	7
to use	yuhng 用	4
usually; normally	pìhng-sìh 平時	8
very often	sèhng yaht 成日	5
a voice	yāt bá sēng 一把聲	4
to wake up	séng 醒	3
walk past	gīng-gwo 經過	8
wasteful	sāai 嘥	10
to wear	jeuk 着	9
wet	sāp 濕	8
what about (to suggest)	bāt-yùh 不如	2
What do you mean?	há 吓？	1
What should I/we do?	dím-syun 點算	2
whole; entire	sèhng 成	5
whole day	sèhng yaht 成日	5
wind	fūng 風	8
a bottle of wine	yāt jī jáu 一支酒	7
worry about	pa 怕	8
wrap a scarf around	laahm géng-gān 攬頸巾	9
wrong; mistake	cho 錯	4
younger brother	sai-lóu 細佬	4